The Promise of a Single Kiss . . .

Margaret Esterly is desperate—and desperation can lead to shocking behavior! Beautiful and gently-bred, she was the essence of prim, proper English womanhood—until fate widowed her and thrust her into poverty overnight. Now she finds herself at a dazzling masked ball, determined to sell a volume of scandalous memoirs to the gala's noble host. But amid the heated fantasy of the evening, Margaret boldly, impetuously, shares a moment of passion with a darkly handsome gentleman . . . and then flees into the night.

Who was this exquisite creature who swept into Michael Hawthorne's arms and then vanished? The startled, yet pleasingly stimulated Earl of Montraine is not about to forget the intoxicating woman of mystery so easily—especially since Michael's heart soon tells him that he has at last found his perfect bride. But once he locates her again, will he be able to convince the reticent lady that their moment of ecstasy was no mere accident . . . and that just one kiss can lead to paradise?

Other Avon Romantic Treasures by
Karen Ranney

If You've Enjoyed This Book,
Be Sure to Read These Other
AVON ROMANTIC TREASURES

KAREN RANNEY

After the Kiss

An Avon Romantic Treasure

AVON BOOKS
An Imprint of HarperCollinsPublishers

This is a work of fiction. Names, characters, places, and incidents are products of the author's imagination or are used fictitiously and are not to be construed as real. Any resemblance to actual events, locales, organizations, or persons, living or dead, is entirely coincidental.

AVON BOOKS
An Imprint of HarperCollins*Publishers*
10 East 53rd Street
New York, New York 10022-5299

Copyright © 2000 by Karen Ranney
ISBN: 0-380-81298-3
www.avonromance.com

First Avon Books paperback printing: October 2000

Avon Trademark Reg. U.S. Pat. Off. and in Other Countries, Marca Registrada, Hecho en U.S.A.
HarperCollins® is a trademark of HarperCollins Publishers Inc.

Printed in the U.S.A.

WCD 10 9 8 7 6 5 4 3 2 1

*A friend is someone who knows you well
and likes you anyway.
To Ginger Cole
Thanks for being my friend.*

Prologue

London
1820

In London it was never truly quiet. The clatter of carriage wheels across the cobbles plucked a sleeper from the faraway world of dreams. The shouts of young rowdies, the calls of the barrow girls, a baby's cry, they all acted as sentinel to the coming of a new day.

London was crowded of late. People had poured into the city from the countryside in order to board one of the innumerable ships that awaited them in the harbor. England, it seemed, was migrating. Even as she clung to the edge of wakefulness, Margaret Esterly envied the travelers their new beginnings.

Their bedchamber above the bookshop was small, the air close on this autumn dawn. Her hand stretched out, touched Jerome's pillow. Where was her husband?

No doubt downstairs, seated at his desk, studying the ledgers by the light of the candle again. There was a look in his eyes lately, one that was not able to mask the concern there.

She rolled over on her back, threw her arm over her eyes.

There was nothing she could do. The bookshop was not doing well. For some reason their trade had fallen off in the past few months. Days would pass and the bell over the downstairs door would remain stubbornly silent.

Jerome had become more and more withdrawn, barely speaking to her. Nor were any of her suggestions met with any enthusiasm. He simply did not wish to discuss their problems or their uncertain future. Going to him now would only embarrass him. She had done so once before and he'd closed the ledgers and extinguished the candle and refused to speak of it.

She brushed her hand over her face. It trembled in the air, clutching at the smothering blackness. Nightmares loomed and she turned, restless, as if to avoid them.

She began to cough, the effort of it pulling her into full wakefulness. Opening her eyes, she looked about her and felt a surge of fear. The cloud was not a dream, but smoke.

Jerome. Where was Jerome?

She stood, intent on reaching the door. It was only a few feet to her left, but it seemed much farther in the blinding smoke. Grabbing the latch, she pulled the door ajar. Flames spread upward from the staircase, pooled across the floor. The fire obliterated the hallway as she watched, panicked.

"Jerome!" From somewhere below came the sound of a window shattering. "Jerome!" The floor shuddered as if the building itself cringed. But there was no answering voice in the fire's fury.

Margaret pushed the door shut as the flames licked up the wall. There was no escape down the staircase. Dropping to her knees in order to breathe through the billowing clouds of inky smoke she crawled on hands and knees to the tiny room adjoining the bedchamber.

Once there, she lay still for a moment, her face pressed against the warm floor. Her eyes smarted, her lungs felt as if they were coated with grime.

The maid slept in this tiny anteroom. She called out, but Penelope didn't answer. She reached the cot and shook the girl's shoulder. No response. She shook her harder, her fingers moving to Penelope's face, her palms slapping the young girl's cheeks.

The fire had a voice of its own. One that roared and deafened the air even as it colored it black. She screamed in Penelope's ear, her shouts in tandem with a silent and fervent prayer.

Please let Jerome be safe. Please.

Penelope began to cough. One reassurance, at least.

A moment later the two women crawled to the lone window, a wide gray square mounted high in the wall and blessedly still visible in the smoke. Together they pushed the candlestand directly below it. Margaret moved back and helped Penelope mount the small table. The maid could, by reaching up only about a foot, grasp the sill and pull herself to safety.

Margaret had stopped coughing in the last few moments. Only now it felt as if a band were being pulled tightly around her throat.

Penelope disappeared through the window.

The air was so thick it felt as if it were a solid thing. The boards beneath her feet felt as if they were on fire, as if the flames sought her out even in the darkness.

Someone called out to Penelope, and Margaret heard the girl's shout in response. A blessing, then, that she was safe. Perhaps Jerome, too, had been able to escape from the burning building and waited for her below.

In mounting the candlestand, she stubbed her toe upon the small chest that served as their strongbox. She picked it up and pushed it through the window, just before following. On the other side of the window she fell a few feet, even as her hands scrabbled against the side of the building for a handhold. The fire flared up at her from a downstairs window, singeing her feet. Eager hands reached out and pulled her to safety. Someone shouted, then slapped at the burning hem of her nightrail, lowering her to safety.

Once on the ground, she lay there for a moment, pressing the heels of her hands against her eyes. Small aches were beginning to make themselves known, the abrasions on her hands, the scrape on her elbow, her feet smarted: she was surprised to see how red and blistered they appeared when she blinked open her eyes.

As she watched in horror, the upper floor of the bookshop crumbled into the center of the building. Moments. They had been only moments from death.

"Jerome?" She stood and looked around her. A cape was laid across her shoulders.

She pushed through the crowd. "Jerome? Have you seen him? My husband? Jerome?" She pulled on sleeves, grabbed arms, but no one answered her. One by one, the men who fought the fire lowered their eyes. Her neighbors looked away, or down at the ground. All except her friends, the Plodgetts. Maude was crying, while Samuel slowly shook his head from side to side, his expression revealing both his sadness and the truth.

Jerome did not emerge from the crowd. He didn't stretch out his hands to grip hers nor reassure her with a smile. People began to move back, as if to give her room to grieve. Margaret turned and stood looking at the burning building in shock.

The fire had a voracious appetite, devouring all of Jerome's precious books, the rare editions, the treasured volumes. The buckets of water thrown at the blaze succeeded only in containing it, not in lessening its destruction. As she stared, the back of the building fell, sending soot and cinders into the air. A last wall of books caught fire, a monument to Jerome's love of antiquity, of Roman poets and Greek philosophers.

"Come away, Miss Margaret," Penelope was saying. The maid placed her arm around Margaret's shoulders.

She glanced at Penelope dully. The girl's cheeks were bright red, her brown hair askew. Beneath her borrowed wrapper her nightrail was coated with soot.

Margaret shook herself free, remained staring at the pyre.

A fiery grave.

Behind her people whispered. She could hear the drone of speech. *Tragedy* and *horror* were uttered side by side with the words *blessing* and *fortunate*. She stood in her nightrail, and a borrowed cape waiting for Jerome to appear, but knowing with a sickening sense of disbelief that he never would. He had died in the fire. How could that be a blessing? How could she possibly be considered fortunate?

Words had been stripped from her. There were only the smoldering timbers and the stench of paper and leather and gilt reduced to embers. A sense of unreality overtook her, as if this moment were not quite true. Soon she would awaken from this odd and unsettling dream.

But it wasn't a dream. Pink clouds as delicate as feathers streaked across a blue sky. Dawn had come to London.

The fire flared, a final greedy lick of fiery lips in appreciation for the banquet it had consumed. A triumphant, glittery smile to mock her sudden and unexpected widowhood.

Jerome.

She began to cry, the tears soundless and painful.

"It is done, Your Grace."

Alan Stilton, Duke of Tarrant, studied the man standing in front of him.

His library was a room designed to display his treasures, magnificent paintings by Rubens, a fresco in the style of Giorgione, cabinets of mahogany and glass filled with those books that interested him.

Peter defiled the room with his presence. An ugly man, he'd been rendered even more unacceptable by the addition of a long red gouge down one cheek.

So, Jerome had fought back.

Peter, a former boxer, was employed ostensibly as his coachman. In actuality, he served in many guises. His giant size and misshapen face led him to be viewed with some caution by the other staff.

He'd hired the man nearly a decade ago after witnessing Peter fight an opponent nearly to the death. The zeal he'd displayed even when obviously losing had impressed him. The desperation it had revealed had intrigued Tarrant even more. He'd hired him and never regretted the decision. Peter possessed one underestimated value—he was fanatically loyal.

"He is dead?" Tarrant asked, gazing at the surface of his desk. He moved a gold inkwell to the left, smoothed his hand over the letter from his factor. Inconsequential acts to mask the degree of his interest in Peter's answer.

"Yes, Your Grace," Peter said respectfully.

"And the books?" Tarrant glanced up at him.

"They could not be found," the servant said, ducking his head as if ashamed. A curious act, one of a penitent. Or a man who knew his place in life.

Tarrant nodded, thinking that he should no doubt consider himself one of the damned this day. A demon. He had ordered the murder of his brother and stood listening to the proof of his deed. How odd that he did not feel a shred of remorse for it.

He stood, walked to window, intent on the view in front of him. It would not do for Peter to know how much the loss of the *Journals* bothered him. They were the only proof, a legacy to be hoarded and guarded through the coming decades.

"And the bookshop?"

"It is nothing but cinders, Your Grace."

An option if the books could not be found.

"And the woman? Margaret?" His stomach clenched as he spoke her name. An irritant, his bastard brother's wife.

"She survived the fire, Your Grace. I waited and watched."

A pity, that.

He raised his hand, wiggled his fingers, an effortless dismissal. Peter did not need the words. In moments, Tarrant heard the door shut quietly behind him.

The view from this room was of a quiet square. A nest of green flanked by townhouses. A prestigious address, a street occupied by earls and a duke or two. He preferred Wickhampton to London, but this house served him well enough.

At the moment, he didn't see the row of trees and the iron gate, or the crushed stone walk that led artfully through the small park. Instead, he was fifteen years old again, and being told of his father's indiscretion.

"You have a brother, Alan."

"Sir?"

His father's face with its hawk-nosed and jutting chin had simply stared like a marble bust back at him. "Do you question my words or the existence of the boy?"

"Neither, sir," he said, cautious as he had always been by his father's anger.

"He is but a few months younger than you, Alan," his father had announced. As if pleased by the sign of his masculine prowess. To breed two sons within months of each other seemed to him to be a great feat. It had merely been distasteful to Alan. "I have made provisions for him in my will, and wish you to administer his funds."

He had smiled, Alan remembered. Some faint agreement. An expression that quite adequately had hidden his true thoughts.

His father had wanted him to welcome a halfbrother and pretend that the by-blow was at least the equal of him. He had done so, for twelve years. The moment his father had died he had taken on the mantle of responsibility, forcing down the rage he'd felt along with the disgust. For twelve years he had been exactly what his father would have wished, a steward to the bastard, born because of a relationship between a maid and a duke.

Until today.

He studied the leaden gray sky and wondered why the sun was not shining brightly. It was a brilliant day. He was, finally, free. Not only from Jerome's eternally affable and grating nature, but his father's shade, whispering in his ear the indefinable truth. The old man had always felt more fondness for his bastard than for his rightful heir.

Alan was, suddenly, almost rapturously happy. The *Journals* had been destroyed, but all was not completely lost. He would never again be bothered with Jerome. Or his wife, Margaret.

The Duke of Tarrant smiled.

Chapter 1

*A great courtesan possesses both
curiosity and courage.*

The Journals of Augustin X

*Wiltshire Downs, England
Early spring, 1822*

Naked, he sat cross legged upon a brilliantly
hued carpet, a voluptuous woman on his lap.
Her bare legs were on either side of his hips, her feet
crossed at his back. One masculine hand rested on her
thigh, fingers splayed, while the other curved around
her waist. Her head was arched back, throat exposed,
eyes closed, the look on her face one of sublime pleasure. His head bent, the edge of his smile carnal and
anticipatory, captured forever in the act of his tongue
gently touching an elongated nipple.

The artist had drawn the man in a state of arousal,
a condition surely accentuated out of all proportion.

No man, Margaret Esterly thought, could be quite *that* large.

Her gaze returned to the painting time and again, even as a flush crept up her neck. A scene of sensuality and abandon. Almost shocking. But beautiful in a strange and unsettling way. That was the only reason, Margaret told herself, that she studied it with such avid curiosity.

The caption that accompanied the drawing was both confusing and evocative: *The face, the ears, the breasts are rich with sensation. But close attention must be made to speak softly, murmuring words of tenderness in anticipation of the pleasure to come.*

"You're too fascinated with those books, Miss Margaret."

She blinked, glanced up, her face warming.

On the other side of the table, Penelope sat chopping onions and frowning at her. The two years since they'd left London had brought a few changes to their lives, chief among them the friendship they shared. A not surprising development, considering that they were both London born and raised.

Margaret wanted almost desperately to be quit of London and its memories. To her surprise, Penelope was more than willing to join her in the country.

With Jerome's death, she had no family. Her parents had died of influenza when she was only a child. Her grandmother, a former governess, had raised her, but she had passed on a year after her marriage to Jerome.

The small cottage Margaret had rented from Squire Tippett two years ago wasn't a prepossessing place. The only furniture was a bureau, two small cots, two chairs and a small wooden table she despaired of ever making stand straight. Finally, she had shimmied a piece of wood beneath one leg, but it still wobbled from side to side. A fireplace took up one whole wall, a welcome warmth during the winters on the Downs.

"It's a good thing you hide them above the rafters when the girls come. I can just imagine what their mothers in the village would say if they knew you read such things," Penelope scolded.

Silbury Village, their new home, was situated in a river valley with a commanding view of the chalk uplands and the stark white form cut into the hillside. Majestically sized, not unlike the White Horse at Westbury, it was difficult to discern the shape of the carving except in spring when the villagers trimmed and re-cut the turf. Then, it was all too evident that the angles and curves formed the image of a crown. As if some ancient royal presence had marked this place forever his.

Almost completely encircling the village was the Bristol River, its waters churning through two grist mills. Perched above Silbury on a nearby hill were the skeletal remains of a priory. The town itself was full of twisting paths and unexpected steps, and houses constructed from the stones of the ruins, giving the buildings an aged, almost pallid appearance.

It was, as Samuel had told her, an inward looking place. The villagers were content enough to build the clocks for which they were famed and ignore the world. It was because of her friend that she was here at all. Samuel had been born in the village and knew the squire from which she rented her small cottage.

Penelope stood, emptied the contents of the bowl into the stew over the fire. Their main meal of the day had not contained meat for weeks, but they were never short of onions. Margaret was beginning to detest the smell and taste of them.

"I have never read the third volume," Margaret said in her own defense. "He writes most compellingly about the Orient, Penelope."

Penelope turned and looked at her, one eyebrow rising. A perfect chastisement, Margaret thought. She could not have done better with her students.

Another change in her life. She had begun teaching a few girls from the village over the last year. Doing so had given her an opportunity to use those lessons her Gran had taught her.

She would never have children of her own; that fact had been proven during her five-year marriage to Jerome. But three mornings a week, seven little girls ranging from five to ten years of age came to her cottage. For those hours, she thought not about her precarious financial situation, nor of her loneliness, but of each girl's talents and needs. Annie's enthusiasm for learning was delightful, as was the way Dorothy was advancing in her reading. She answered their questions and smiled at their laughter.

In turn, she learned from her students. On their walks she'd been shown how to listen for the grouse, or watch a new moon in order to predict the growing season. Margaret had stood in a meadow as she'd been instructed by seven excited voices, concentrating upon the clouds and feeling small and insignificant beneath the bowl of sky. Had she'd ever truly seen the sky in London?

It was, after all, a satisfactory life. One that would be remarkably content but for two things—her loneliness and the fact that she was nearly desperate for money.

She glanced down at the book on the table again. The painter had been an artist of some talent. Her fingers trailed across the illustration of muscled shoulders, down a tapering back and over the length and breadth of one thigh. This man appeared in numerous small illustrations sprinkled throughout the *Journals of Augustin X*. In each of them he had been proudly naked, involved in some sensual and surely forbidden act. His shoulders were broad, his back tapering to his waist. His buttocks were perfectly formed as if to coax a palm to curve around both of them. A stranger, possibly a figment of the artist's imagination. Yet she knew him more intimately than she had known her husband.

But even more shocking than the paintings was her own unfettered imagination. Too many times she'd envisioned herself as the woman in his arms. Surfeited with pleasure, languid with the memory of it. Her eyes holding secrets and promising lessons, her smile curved in pure, unalloyed joy.

A few days after the fire she'd found the three books tucked into the bottom of the strongbox. For months, the *Journals of Augustin X* had remained in the small chest, untouched. But during their first winter here, bored and lonely, Margaret had extracted the first volume and begun to read it.

Augustin had evidently been a well traveled man of leisure and some wealth. He had written, in exquisite detail, about the scenery of the lands he'd visited. Her fingers trailed over a passage.

My journey through China began in Qinghai on the Tibetan Plateau at the Huang He River. At the place the Wei River enters the Huang He in central Shaanxi province we were treated to great hospitality. It was there I met Ming Wu and spent one of my most memorable nights in the land of the Manchu.

The true nature of the *Journals of Augustin X*, however, was not a travelogue. Instead, it was a graphic account of Augustin's erotic journey throughout the world. Each of his *Journals* was tantamount to a book of instructions on how to engage in the sensuality he portrayed in such exquisite detail. He seemed especially entranced with the courtesans he'd met, many of whom educated him on the higher delights of sensuality. He had even fancied himself in love with one, and his tender farewell to her had brought tears to Margaret's eyes.

That first winter she told herself it was better to destroy the books. But they were the only link to the bookshop and her life with Jerome. Besides, reading them occasionally gave her something to do other than to worry about their perilous financial condition.

Her conscience chuckled in the silence. Very well, perhaps she *was* too fascinated with these books. The *Journals* revealed a world she'd never before known, one of amorous encounters and erotic acts she'd never thought to witness.

"They're evil things, Miss Margaret," Penelope said, glancing over her shoulder at the book on the table. "Cursed."

"They aren't cursed. They are simply books," Margaret said patiently. "Only a collection of words."

"And pictures," Penelope said. "Any man who ever touched me that way would get the back of my hand, Miss Margaret,"

Penelope's cheeks, round and rosy on most days, were now fiery with color. Her pointed chin jutted out at Margaret. Even her straight brown hair seemed to curl with indignation. Her dark eyes met Margaret's gaze and in them was the righteousness of the never tempted.

Margaret admitted that she was not as pure in thought. Some nights she lay in her cot and wished her life had been different. At the same time, she recognized that the past years had taught her well. Turmoil had come to her in the guise of the fire and the death of her husband. It was wiser to wish for consistency than for chaos. Excitement was for other people.

If there were moments, like this afternoon, when she wondered what her life might have been like if she had never married Jerome, then it was to be expected. She simply pushed those errant thoughts away.

Margaret closed the tooled cover of the book, ensuring that the tissue was in place over each of the page sized paintings. One overlay did not fit correctly and she opened the book to straighten it. But it wasn't one of the protective pages at all. She frowned as she pulled the paper free.

It was a list of ten names, all with notations beside them in Jerome's cramped scrawl.

Penelope bent over her shoulder. "What is it, Miss Margaret?"

"Some kind of list," she said. Together they read Jerome's writing.

Jeremy Pendergrast—detests French literature. Only as a last resort.

Horace Blodgett—haggles too much. Not a candidate for a quick sale.

Ned Smith—Father controls his purse. A possible sale, if he's not spent the remainder of his quarterly allowance.

John Blaketon—very likely. In competition with Babidge.

Charles Townsende—unlimited funds, very likely quick sale.

Jerome's notes continued with another five names, all with varying commentaries beside them.

"What do you think it is, Miss Margaret?"

Margaret turned it over, then studied it again. "I think Jerome meant to sell the *Journals*," she said finally.

"Sell them? Why would he do such a thing?"

Because he'd been as desperate as they were for money, she thought—a comment she did not voice to Penelope.

"I've seen books the like of the *Journals* in the shop before, Penelope. I've no doubt that they brought a tidy profit."

Penelope looked surprised. "It doesn't sound right that Mr. Esterly would dabble in such cursed things."

"They are not cursed," Margaret said patiently. "Or do you blame them for all our misfortunes?"

"No," Penelope said slowly. "But it does seem as if something has brought us to this pass. If only it hadn't been so hot," she sighed.

"Or if the chickens hadn't died," Margaret contributed.

"Or the roof had not collapsed."

"Or the chimney hadn't become blocked, or the cows hadn't sickened, or we hadn't had to sell the pigs too soon," Margaret said, attempting to smile. A myriad of disasters had befallen them over the past two years.

"Or the garden hadn't wilted. And do not forget

the west wall," Penelope added. "It was a right pretty disaster."

"Yes," Margaret said, standing, "but we learned well enough to be masons on our own."

"It's been a difficult time," Penelope admitted. The truth hung in the air between them. "Perhaps we should have stayed in London."

"At the time, any place but London was preferable as I remember," Margaret said, opening the strongbox and tucking the third *Journal* below the nearly empty money tray. "Besides, there are some compensations for our country life." She smiled at the younger woman. "Or have you forgotten Tom?"

Penelope's cheeks blossomed with color. The young groom worked at Squire Tippett's and had courted Penelope over the last two years. They were so much in love that it was unexpectedly painful to witness them together. Margaret's marriage to Jerome had been one of gentle affection. An agreeable union, but one that somehow lacked the longing looks and gentle laughter Penelope and Tom shared.

"I wonder what the books would fetch?"

Penelope stared at her in surprise. "You can't be thinking of selling them, Miss Margaret?"

Margaret picked up the list and studied the names again. "There are at least three viable prospects here, Penelope. Men, I believe, who would purchase the books without hesitation. If we do not do something, we will have to return to the City and find occupations to support us."

Penelope looked as stricken as Margaret felt. Returning to London would mean that Penelope would have to leave Tom and she would have to leave her girls' school. They would either have to go into service, or take a job in one of the shops.

Unfortunately, she made no income from teaching the girls. The residents of Silbury Village had been as hard hit as she and Penelope by the drought. She would not have felt proper about asking money from people who could ill afford it.

"Couldn't you go to the duke, Miss Margaret?"

She glanced at Penelope. "No," Margaret said quickly. "Not the duke." Whatever happened, she would never seek assistance from Tarrant.

She remembered only too well their last meeting, the day after Jerome had perished in the fire.

"I have come only to tell you what happened," she'd said. Her hands were clenched so tightly in her lap that the knuckles shone white and bony.

She'd not learned of Jerome's tie to the duke until after their marriage. It had shamed him to be bastard born, the half-brother to the tenth Duke of Tarrant.

"You might have conveyed the fact of his death in a letter, madam. Or do you have another, less obvious reason for your presence here?" The Duke of Tarrant's eyes were great black holes in his narrow and austere face. His long fingers drummed impatiently against the desktop like claws.

A giant bird of prey, the Duke.

However much she told herself not to be cowed by him, she was. She thought great thoughts and had wonderful retorts to each of his barbed remarks and criticisms. But always later . . . never at the occasion of their meeting.

He had made her wait to see him, a deliberate act of rudeness she'd come to expect from him. For an hour she'd stood in the foyer, uncomplaining. Only then had she been directed to this cavernous room of swooping shadows. Books lined the walls, but their spines of gilt appeared fresh and untouched. There was not one comfortable chair to encourage a reader to sit and peruse a volume, no candles perched upon well-arranged tables. A person would not wish to linger here, but it was a chamber that oddly suited the Duke of Tarrant.

"I thought it my duty to come," she said.

"So that we might mourn Jerome together?" he asked contemptuously.

"Jerome held you in great affection," she said, willing her voice not to tremble.

He glanced at her as if she were an insect, something beneath his regard.

"Did he?" he asked, his fingers tapping against the desktop. "No doubt because I dispensed enough funds to him to ensure he lived well. You no doubt believe that because you are his widow you are entitled to as much consideration. But that relationship is ended, here and now. Do not presume to expect anything from me."

"I do not," she said, stung. She stood facing him, her hands fisted in the material of her skirt. "Is that why you've disliked me all these years? Because I had the presumption to marry into your family?"

He smiled thinly. "My father indulged himself with Jerome's mother. A mistake. Our line had never before been sullied by bastardy. Jerome was an obligation, never family."

"What was I?" She detested confrontation, but this moment had been coming for years. Her heart was beating so hard that she thought it might leap from her chest. Tarrant, however, looked remarkably relaxed, absorbed in the actions of his fingers toying with the end of a quill.

"An irritant who never knew her place." He looked

up at her, his smile vanishing. "You dared to address me by my Christian name once, as I recall."

"And kissed you on your cheek when we parted," she said, willing her smile to remain fixed in place.

An expression of displeasure flitted over his face.

"So," Margaret said, "because I did not heed your consequence, you have always disliked me?"

"You are common," he said, standing. "Your only claim to propriety is the fact that your grandmother was a governess. Your father was a soldier and your mother took in washing."

"I see," she said, nodding. "Honest employment, but not quite the equal of a duke."

He didn't answer. There was, after all, nothing he needed to say. His half-hooded eyes gleamed with contempt.

He picked up a small bell on the corner of his desk. One faint ring, that was all it took before a liveried footman opened the door and stepped aside. Beyond him stood the majordomo—somber, dignified, as regal as any member of the nobility.

Her lips trembled, but she held them tight as she walked from the room.

"No, not the duke," Margaret said now. "He would be pleased to see me beg."

She studied the list once more. Here was the very answer to their dilemma. If she sold only one book, she could keep the other two as a bit of security for her future.

"I think, Penelope," she said, "that we should consider the *Journals* our salvation."

The other woman shook her head slowly, but Margaret only smiled.

She would take the precaution of signing Jerome's name. Not only because some men refused to do business with a woman, but to protect her reputation. Also, she'd send a quick note to Samuel and Maude, asking if she could use the draper's address. That way, no one in the village would ever know that she was in possession of such shocking literature.

Life in Silbury village was simple and elemental. Those who obeyed the strictures of propriety were praised and applauded. Those who did not were ostracized. There were two women in the village whose opinion counted greatly—Sarah Harrington and Anne Coving.

Sarah's influence as arbiter of morality was not to be underestimated. In the hierarchy of the village she reigned supreme, her opinion solicited and generally followed by most of the other matrons. Sarah had been among the first to send her daughter to Margaret's school.

Her sister, Anne, was a teller of tales. If there was news to hear in Silbury, Anne was not only privy to it but ensured that it was spread far and wide.

What would Sarah say if she even knew of the existence of these shocking *Journals*? Or if she discovered that Margaret was planning to sell the volume of carnal literature? Or, even worse, that she had read not only this volume, but another as well?

There was no doubt as to the other woman's reaction. No longer would Margaret be considered a proper widow, someone held up as an example of decorum and proper behavior. Instead, she would be made a pariah. Sarah would not allow her daughter to attend her small school, and Anne would ensure the tale was told throughout the village. Her school would be unattended.

Everything she had come to value in her life was in jeopardy by this one action. A thought that made

Margaret consider her decision carefully. In the end, it was not as if she had any choice. If she didn't sell the *Journal* she couldn't remain in Silbury.

Margaret picked up her stationery box, then sat at the table again and began to write.

Chapter 2

A man's impatience is a woman's triumph.

The Journals of Augustin X

Michael Hawthorne, Earl of Montraine, nodded to his host across the room. The Earl of Babidge—Babby, to his friends—was currently engaged in his most favorite occupation, gossip. He held court over a small group, all of whom looked entranced at his words. Michael smothered a smile and turned aside.

Babby had spared no expense for this occasion. His cavernous second-floor ballroom was lit by hundreds of beeswax candles, all constantly being replaced by ubiquitous footmen. The accompanying yellow light rendered the room as bright as a sunlit day and warmed it substantially. The tall doors to the terrace had been thrown open to the night to counteract the heat.

Babby was a great believer in gilt. What could not be festooned in gold was trimmed in it. There were three large mirrors in ornate gilded frames mounted on the south wall. What walls were not mirrored or hung with crimson were painted. Set within the gilded moldings were scenes etched in delft of Babby's country estate, or life in the City. The artist had followed Babby around for a month with sketch-book in hand.

Tonight Babby had decided upon a masked ball to enliven the season. Consequently, the room was filled with people attempting, for at least a few hours, to be who they were not. There was a plethora of Greek goddesses and men dressed oddly—and chillingly, for this spring night—in togas. More than one stout peer was crowned with laurel leaves.

As for himself, he dressed simply in formal attire. That was not, however, the reason for the surprised looks sent his way. He rarely attended these events unless required to escort his sisters and mother. When he did so, he disappeared into a quiet chamber, or sought sanctuary with friends in the smoking or gaming rooms. Tonight, however, he was attempting to be affable. Almost sociable.

Three matrons roosting upon the settee against the wall nodded at him in approval. He returned the gesture, smiling slightly. They subjected each guest to a sweeping inspection, one that encompassed costume and demeanor, hairstyle to footwear. A judgment was rendered by either a slight smile or a forbidding frown. By their sudden shocked looks he knew that the most recent arrival had ventured far beyond the bounds of propriety.

The lady standing in the doorway was not un-known to him. A beautiful woman married to an ag-ing peer, a combination that encouraged daring. She did not disappoint. Her costume revealed more than it concealed, leaving no doubt as to the shape of lovely legs, or the enticing curve of hips. She sent him a provocative look, one designed to entice, he had no doubt. Perhaps another time.

This night was for more serious matters. He had come to Babby's party to find a wife.

It was time he married, a fact that had exploded into his consciousness by one small and almost overlooked fact. All three of his sisters were being presented this season. Proof enough that the years had flown by. If he did not want his lineage continued by a nephew, he must concentrate upon matrimony.

In addition, there was the small matter of dwindling capital. The war with Napoleon had been ruinous, and their fortunes over the last decade had suffered like so many others. Add to that the drought that had decimated their harvests in addition to the foolish investments his father had made, and the resultant disaster was one of monumental and extravagant proportions.

They needed an almost desperate infusion of cash, else he would be forced to sell those properties not entailed.

It seemed that it was a more lengthy process to catch the eye of a wealthy noble than it was a rich heiress. A title or a respectable heritage wasn't the least important in his case, while his mother had her heart set on, at the very least, earls for her daughters. Therefore, Michael was the sacrificial lamb destined to be hauled up to the altar and roasted. He was not, however, going to the flames without a few bleats of his own.

His requirements for a bride were sensible. Logical. A woman who would not expect love, but with whom he could deal agreeably. Someone engaged in her own interests. A woman who would give him sons but not difficulties. Above all, he didn't want a woman of a violent temperament.

The conversation swirled around him like the drone of bees as he walked around the edge of the dance floor. Once it pierced his concentration, caught him off guard. It was a disconcerting experience to find himself the topic of whispers.

"It's a pity Montraine is so handsome," one young miss said. "He truly has the most fearsome glower. And he is much too somber. He rarely smiles."

"Indeed," the other woman said behind her fan. "Charlotte says he's most inflexible and terribly stern, and acts twice his age. She is quite afraid of him."

"Her own brother?" The fan was in rapid motion.

"Well, I for one would never countenance his suit. Could you imagine being constantly frowned at in that forbidding way of his?"

"It is said that he is involved in something secret with the government. Some master, or something."

He was tempted to lean over their shoulders and tell them that his sister Charlotte was not to be considered a source of information since she was, more often than not, irritated at him. The name Code Master was an embarrassing sobriquet Babby had announced to one and all after his success at breaking the French code during the war.

As a member of the Black Chamber of England's Foreign Office, he was only one of many men who labored independently and alone for a dual purpose— to solve ciphers and protect the empire. It was occasionally tedious, always mind absorbing work that he loved.

But the French cipher that had led them to discover Napoleon's plans to march on the east had been such a monumental undertaking and happy accident that word of it had slipped out. It irritated him to no end, since most of the people who now knew the name presumed that his occupation made him exciting, dangerous, and romantic.

Michael continued his progression around the perimeter of the dance floor, his attention focused on the dancers. Not unlike, he thought with some degree of humor, a wolf seeking its mate.

It seemed to him that his requirements for a wife were not onerous.

His life ran on a strict schedule. Monday, Wednesday, and Friday he boxed in the morning. Tuesday and Thursday he rode. He worked from nine in the morning until well after seven at night, with two hours in the afternoon set aside for lunch and personal correspondence. Family obligations occupied two nights a week. Other than that, his time was his own to do with what he wished. Most of the time, however, he found himself either involved with his newly designed mathematical engine or engrossed in a cipher. He did not wish to be pulled from a fascinating code because a woman expected him to pay her homage, take her shopping, or approve a frock.

In addition, she must not be too young, because incessant giggling would drive him mad. She should possess some sense and be level-headed and dispassionate.

He asserted the same authority over his own emotions.

His childhood had been marked by his parents passionate arguments, each occurrence ending with his mother throwing something and his father responding by breaking something equally expensive or shooting out a window. On the nights when their rages woke his sisters up, they found their way to his room. On such occasions he would reassure them that all was right in their world, a necessary lie and one they came, eventually, to see as such.

Finally, he'd rebelled, seeking sanctuary from the cacophony of his own home at his friend Robert's house whenever the confrontations escalated. It was an irony that his wish for privacy had led to his love of ciphers. He'd not wanted his family to be able to read his notes to Robert and had devised several codes that they used to communicate.

Give him a code any time. Ciphers did not cry and run from the room. A logical progression did not scream at the top of its lungs and then shoot a hole through the library window.

Or put a bullet through his head because his mistress had left him for another man. A gruesome discovery for a boy of fourteen. But even then, he'd been the only calm one in a house filled with tears and screams. He had been the one to pull the note from beneath his father's limp arm and read those last words. A confession of obsessive love and despair. *I cannot live without her.* A warning and a caution to the boyish Michael to refrain from such excess.

He was determined to do so.

The females in his family, however, preferred not to see the world logically and dispassionately. His sisters were princesses of drama and his mother the queen of histrionics. Only one more reason to find a wife with some degree of sense about her. She might be someone with whom he could talk. Perhaps she might even become a confidante. As it was, he would never confide in his family for fear that his secrets would be fodder for London gossip the next day.

Michael presented himself in front of Miss Gloria

Ronson, bowing slightly. She was the daughter of a knight, but he was not concerned with her antecedents as much as the fact that she was also rumored to be an heiress. True, she was shy, but she also seemed like someone who might suit him.

"I believe this is our dance," he said. He smiled, wondering why his companion looked startled.

He bent his arm and she placed her gloved hand atop it. The musicians began the opening bars and the first movement began. He turned to his side, held his hand out for her. Her gloved fingers touched his, but she said nothing further, simply stared at the oak boards of the floor.

Her reticence was delightfully charming. As if she heard his thoughts, she looked over at him. He smiled at her and once more she appeared startled, looking away for a moment and then shyly smiling in return.

The evening was looking suddenly more favorable.

Chapter 3

*An experienced courtesan prefers a lover
with long fingers, a sign of impressive
masculine attributes.*

The Journals of Augustin X

Margaret stepped down from the carriage, smiled at the driver, and ignored the loudly voiced complaints of her fellow passengers. The wisest course was to take a hired hack to Maude and Samuel's house on Stanton Street. But she hadn't the funds to take a hack to Stanton Street and then back to the Earl of Babidge's house in the morning. Nor was it close enough to walk, as the earl's home was situated far from the draper's shop.

The only alternative was to travel on to the earl's home and hope that he would agree to see her despite the lateness of the hour.

She hoped that the Earl of Babridge would prove as agreeable in person as he had in his letter. His had been the first response to the three letters she'd sent.

His letter was tucked inside her reticule, but she didn't need to read it again to recall his words. His eagerness had brought her a sense of welcome relief. *I would be very interested in perusing the* Journal *with the idea of purchasing it.*

She whispered a prayer and a few minutes later gave the earl's address to the driver of the hack. At their destination, she dismounted from the hack, pressed a coin into the driver's hand, and promised him the other if he waited for her. At his agreement, she turned and looked up at the house.

The structure was three stories tall, painted a white that gleamed in the light of the gas lamps. She walked slowly up the steps, gripping the *Journal* tightly. Mounted high on the ebony surface of the door was a polished brass knocker in the shape of a lion's head. A fanlight above the door glowed with reflected light.

Margaret straightened her spencer, surreptitiously pulling it down in the back with one hand. It was difficult to look entirely proper when one's clothes barely fit. The spencer and the dress beneath it had been bought second hand. But they were clean and well mended. If the color was a washed-out blue and did nothing to flatter her complexion or compliment her eyes, it was just as well. Vanity was foolishness. She had greater concerns at the moment.

But she didn't want to seem desperate to the earl. It was one of those lessons she'd learned from Jerome. People rarely wished to buy from someone who looked as if they needed the sale.

She had to knock three times to be heard over the sound of music and laughter coming from behind the door. A solemn-faced majordomo opened the door only slightly, peering out through the space, his eyes portraying that disinterested gaze Margaret had noted in only the very best servants.

"I realize that I have missed my appointment," Margaret explained, retrieving the letter from her reticule and showing it to him. "But could the earl spare a moment to see me?"

"His lordship is entertaining," he said stonily.

"Nor do I wish to intrude," Margaret said, "but would it not be possible to see him?" Her smile was a bit too bright, but the butler looked unimpressed at her efforts to charm him.

"Please," she said finally. "I've been traveling all day."

After a long moment in which he studied her intently, he admitted her.

She sat where he indicated, on a hard upholstered bench against the wall. Music spilled down the stairs, a melody so cheerful that it was almost capable of banishing her fears. But they returned in full measure as the moments lengthened. What if the earl didn't buy the *Journal*? She would have made the journey to London for nothing, and spent the last of her money doing so.

A few minutes later the butler returned.

"His lordship will be with you directly," he said, bowing to her, a gesture so small that it was merely perfunctory. "If you will follow me."

The room he led her to was a library, one in which a blazing fire was lit even though no one was in the chamber. A bit of profligacy she appreciated at the moment. Two comfortable chairs, a desk and tall mahogany bookshelves lined with books made the chamber a warm and cozy place. A patterned rug beneath her feet seemed almost foreign in design, its colors muted and aged.

A few moments later a man entered the room. "I am sorry to keep you waiting," he said. He checked his entrance at her appearance, then glanced around the library. "You are not the person I expected to see," he said hesitantly.

She stood at his entrance, the manners of a lifetime coming to the fore. Not that of subservience, but of service. She was, after all, the widow of a tradesman and had been trained in the art of selling. Respect, either feigned or real, was an integral part of success.

"Is it your wish not to deal with a woman, my lord?" She prayed that the sudden panic she felt would not be mirrored in either her voice or her expression.

"Not at all," he said, coming further into the room. "It was simply that it was unexpected." He poured himself a glass of brandy from the sideboard, his back to her. He cleared his throat, glanced over his shoulder at her, then turned, his attention on the floor rather than her face. His fingers tapped against the glass in a staccato pattern. His right foot ground into the carpet.

The Earl of Babidge reminded her, oddly enough, of a hedgehog. Short and rotund, his round face and narrowed eyes looked the human counterpart of that timid creature.

She untied the *Journal*, removed the wrapping, and placed the book in the center of his desk. She said nothing as he glanced quickly at her, then at the book.

He walked slowly to the desk, sat behind it. From beneath her lashes, she saw him place his glass down, then use both hands to open the *Journal*'s cover. His face, round and solemn, began to pinken as he slowly turned one page after another.

She returned to her intense study of her hands, willing herself not to feel an embarrassment akin to the earl's. But it was difficult not to remember the man in the paintings.

She looked away, studied the closed curtains. A burgundy velvet, to match the color of the chairs arranged before the fire.

The earl reverently stroked the leather binding, trailed his fingers across the embossed gilt of the title. "I have never seen the like. Is it just the one?"

"There are three, my lord," she said, "but I've no wish to sell the others at the present time."

"I would be willing to buy all of them," the earl said, "although your price for this one volume seems somewhat excessive." He placed the book on the top of his desk, as if he had no interest in it. His gaze sharpened, became almost cunning as he waited for her response.

"I am sorry, my lord. But it is the price I gave you to understand in my letter," Margaret said, hiding her smile. If there was anything she had learned in the past two years it was how to bargain.

She moved to pick up the book, but he pulled it back out of reach. His smile was rueful as he fumbled with a drawer in his desk, then drew out a small metal box. Inserting a key into the lock, he folded back the top and withdrew a sum of money.

He stood and handed her the amount she had listed in her correspondence. "I believe you will find this correct."

She tucked the money away in her reticule, and thanked him.

"Do not forget, if you wish to sell the other books, I am to have first choice."

She smiled, agreed, and in moments had taken her leave of him.

Her arms felt oddly empty now that she no longer had the *Journal* clasped in them. Instead of feeling regret she should be relieved. In her reticule she had the proceeds from the sale of the book. She had a home to return to, even if it was a tiny cottage on the Downs. She was healthy, blessed with Penelope's friendship and an occupation that gave her pleasure.

If she was lonely, it would pass soon enough.

In the street the hack was waiting. But music still flowed from the house behind her in the wall. A gate stood open, its curving trellis canopy almost an invitation.

It was an enticement almost as alluring as the paintings in Augustin's *Journals*.

She descended the steps, but instead of walking on to the hack, she turned and entered the gate. A precipitous action. One that would change her life.

Michael left the ballroom to escape, if only for a moment, the clashing scent of the women's perfume, the drone of conversation, and the heat of the room. He stepped out into the terrace, looked up at the stars, and wished himself home.

Robert had delivered an intriguing cipher to him just before he left the house tonight. At first Michael thought the code was a Caesar cipher, a deceptively easy puzzle, one that he had mastered as a schoolboy. However, the more he studied it, the more difficult it proved. Another complication was that it utilized the Cyrillic alphabet, in which he lacked knowledge. But he would learn it, even if it meant solving the code.

He had danced twice with Miss Ronson. More than that would sully her reputation. The second dance had been more revealing than the first, in that she had, of her own accord, spoken an entire sentence to him.

"I have been trying to get your attention all night, Michael," Elizabeth said. He turned and watched his youngest sister follow him from the ballroom. She was dressed as a princess, pearls sewn to the bodice of her diaphanous pink gown. He couldn't help wonder how much it had cost.

"Have you been ignoring me?"

"Not at all," he said, smiling. "I've simply had other things on my mind."

She removed her mask and smiled up at him. "You were too busy looking at the young ladies as if they're sheep, Michael. Ready to be shorn."

"On the contrary," he said. "*I'm* feeling like the sacrificial lamb."

"Are you absolutely certain you must wed an heiress?"

"The simple answer is yes. The more involved one would entail the economic situation in England, our investments, and our mother's determination to outspend any woman in London," he said dryly.

"But why have you been addressing so much attention to Miss Ronson?"

"She has an agreeable nature," he said. "In addition, she's an heiress."

"She doesn't have a penny, Michael. Her uncle brought her to London to find her a rich husband."

Bloody hell.

"I should have known," he said, disgusted. "She was one of the few women I've met tonight I thought I might like. She didn't giggle once."

She smiled. "I know very well why you feel that way. But Charlotte cannot help being silly, and Ada will surely not be so intense about her causes in time."

"I don't agree with you, Elizabeth. Neither of our sisters has shown the least evidence of behaving in a rational manner since the day they were born."

She sighed. "They can be difficult," she conceded.

"Perhaps it's what's to be expected, given our parentage."

She was silent, then. He knew there was nothing she could say. She had been only six when their father had died, but had been as devastated as he. Nor was it easy for her, living with their mother and sisters. Of all his relatives, Elizabeth was the only one he genuinely liked. The others he tolerated because of his duty.

He bent down and kissed her on the cheek. "Go away, imp," he said. "Go seek your own spouse and allow me to select mine."

She left him then, entered the ballroom. She looked back only once, shaking her head.

If Miss Ronson was as desperate as he, then he must turn his sights elsewhere, and do so tonight.

There were three other candidates. Perfectly acceptable women whose fortunes were not in doubt. One was a friend of his sister Charlotte; another Babby's third cousin. A third was the niece of a duke.

He blew out a breath and wished he had a measure of brandy. But indulging in drink at this particular moment smacked of cowardice. Instead, he faced the ballroom again.

He would return in a moment. But for now he needed a brief respite before he went about the business of saving his family.

Chapter 4

A woman's smile is an aphrodisiac.

The Journals of Augustin X

The garden ended abruptly at a set of wide brick steps. Margaret hesitated at the bottom, looked up. The terrace was half shrouded in darkness, but the sound of the music was louder, almost beckoning. She slowly mounted the steps, keeping to the shadows.

In a moment she had forgotten that she was trespassing. A masked ball. She had heard of the like, but had never before glimpsed a scene such as this.

She had never envied the nobility and she didn't now. Her path had been preordained from the moment of her birth. A commonplace existence, not one of privilege and wealth. But she had hoped to have a little more laughter in her life.

She stared, wide-eyed, at the spectacle before her.

Headdresses towered above the powdered hair of some of the women, feathers and jewels adorned others. There were costumes that were shocking in their brevity and others that were so cumbersome she wondered at their weight. One man, in particular, summoned her smile. His attire was that of a bear, complete with a massive head that he carried beneath his arm. The rest of the ensemble looked hairy and hot, evidenced by the scarlet hue of his cheeks.

There were silks so translucent that the shape of an arm or the long line of leg could be seen. Satin in resplendent jeweled tones of indigo and azure and emerald seemed to capture the light of the hundreds of candles mounted in sconces upon the walls. Diamonds sparkled, pearls gleamed, and tiny masks adorned with trailing feathers appeared designed less to hide a wearer's identity than to attract the eye toward an inviting smile.

She moved to the side of the terrace, where the shadows were greatest. Only then did she see him. An onlooker, just as she was. A tall man with broad shoulders who stood in the corner of the terrace opposite her.

As she watched, he strode toward the ballroom. She took a step backward, until she felt the wall at her back. He turned suddenly and stared into the darkness.

"Who's there?" he asked, his deep voice holding an edge of irritation.

He came closer. The faint candlelight from the windows illuminated his face. She stared, startled.

The man in the *Journals of Augustin X.*

No, of course it couldn't be. She'd never truly seen his face. But this man's hair was black and his square jaw mimicked the painted profile. Did Augustin's subject have such an aquiline nose? Or lines bracketing full lips, as if framing his mouth for a kiss? It was too dark to see the color of his eyes, but his brows were bold slashes against his face. A monochrome of shadow and moonlight. Masculine perfection adorned with a frown.

"Who are you?" he demanded.

How did she answer that question? The full truth seemed too harsh for the moment. A purveyor of amorous literature. A woman fighting back poverty. One whose thoughts were certainly forbidden. Any or all of the descriptions might be true.

"Well?"

Evidently, silence was not an acceptable alternative.

"Does it matter who I am?" she asked softly.

"That answer gives you away if nothing else," he said.

The remark surprised her. "Does it?"

"I shall not tell," he said. "Your secret is safe with me," he said, his voice clipped.

He looked back at the ballroom, then again toward where she stood.

"That's very polite of you," she said, confused.

"My own sisters used to skulk in the shadows, too," he offered. "Gazing at the dancers with a look of longing."

He thought her a young miss, hiding in the darkness and dreaming until she herself attended a ball.

"Would you believe me if I told you that I am not a schoolgirl?"

"Is that a rhetorical question, or are you telling me?"

"A question from a man who evidently does not trust a simple statement," she said, stung.

"An answer from a woman who has learned the art of prevarication."

"I have never been called a liar before," she said, affronted.

"I did not call you one," he said, moving still closer. "I simply indicated that you had learned the art of it."

"So there is a difference," she asked, only slightly mollified, "between the lie and the liar?"

"Is there?"

"I am truly not a young girl escaped from the schoolroom." There, a clear enough statement.

"Then you should not be here," he said. "Have you no duties that await you?"

"I am not a servant, either. Do you always come to conclusions so quickly?"

"Yes." The frankness of his answer made her smile. He moved even closer. Now she could almost hear him breathe, he stood so near.

"Then you are a guest of Babby's?" he asked.

"Perhaps I am only a figment of your imagination."

"I have often believed that imagination is perilous," he said surprisingly. She had the most absurd desire to laugh. "It is, after all, the antithesis of rational thought."

He sounded utterly sincere.

"Do you consider that valuable?"

"Invaluable," he said shortly.

"I take it, then, that you have never lain on your back in a meadow, and tried to see the shapes of things in clouds?" Nor had she, until under the influence of seven giggling girls.

He seemed to study her. She had the distinct impression that he could see through the darkness. "No."

"Or envisioned something happening that might never occur?"

"What is the point?"

"Enjoyment."

"Why not simply do it? Why just imagine it?"

He would, wouldn't he? It was there in the tone of his voice, in his stance. An almost implacable will that declared itself. He would not see obstacles as a barrier, merely a gate like the one at the end of the garden.

"Have you never wished to be someone other than yourself?" As she did? Sometimes she lay awake at night and prayed to be removed from the life she lived, if only in her dreams. She had learned soon enough that it was dangerous to wish for such things. Her dreams had become heated things, leaving her wishing for more than her future promised.

"No," he said bluntly. "Have you?"

"Yes," she said, surprising herself with the truth.

There was silence between them, as if he were as startled as she by her response.

"Why are you out here on the terrace alone? Have you no concern that your reputation will suffer?"

"Are you someone I should fear?" She felt oddly safe with him. A paradox, because she sensed his power. An authority of rank, she suspected, and character.

"Are you waiting for someone?"

She didn't belong here. Is that what he wished to determine? Why, in order to send her from here with a chastisement for daring to glimpse the nobility at play?

"An assignation? You do come to the strangest conclusions."

The darkness gave her freedom she'd never before experienced. She felt almost heady with it. Yesterday she would not have imagined that tonight she would stand in the darkness, trading barbs with a man with the demeanor of a prince. A man who reminded her of scenes she should not have witnessed, for all that they were drawn with brush and paint.

"What judgment would you have me reach?" he asked, relentless.

"Is it necessary that you come to one at all?" she asked.

Suddenly, he stretched out his hand. "Show yourself," he demanded.

It would be boldness to step out of the shadows. She should leave. Flee from this place. Instead, she stretched out her hand and noted in wonder that it trembled.

They each wore gloves. His were blazing white in the shadows, hers tinged gray by numerous washings. Yet that simple touch of cotton against silk seemed to open the door inside her. A great and hollow place.

A gentle tug and she was being bathed by the faint shimmer of light from the ballroom windows.

What did he see when he looked at her? A woman with auburn hair whose eyes were muddy green? Her smile was tentative, almost faint. Moored onto her face by a measure of fear as he surveyed her intently.

"A country princess," he said softly.

"Is that what you think?" She should tell him, of course, that it was not a costume she wore, but one of her two dresses. But to do so would mark her a trespasser to this night, not a guest. Honesty would banish her from the terrace, and she found, suddenly, that she did not wish to leave.

It was early spring, the night chilled by a faint breeze. A whisper of winter still lingered in the wind. She had only a shawl, but she wasn't chilled. The moment itself, or this one spot upon the terrace, felt warm. Rare and special and imbued with a poignant and almost ceremonial silence.

He held her hand gently, his fingers laced with hers. His gloved thumb brushed against the inside of her bare wrist, a curiously seductive touch.

Come to me. A whisper of longing only in her mind. She could almost feel the words, they were so strong. A thought passing from him to her? Or her own loneliness speaking? He was a stranger to her, yet she felt as if she knew him. Or his counterpart, painted on paper with such detail she could almost feel the muscles beneath her stroking finger.

He slowly pulled his hand away. The smile slipped from her face as he removed his glove, then reached out and did the same with hers, tucking it in his pocket.

She should have spoken then. Refuted his actions, demanded an explanation. But she said nothing even as he touched her. His palm was warm, large, square, and callused.

Her breath felt tight; her heart beat even faster as if in anticipation. It had been so long since she had been touched, even in friendship. Could she hunger for touch as she did food?

She would return to Silbury Village and become Widow Esterly again. Not Margaret of the wicked thoughts. She would teach her students, take tea with Sarah Harrington, listen to Anne Coving's tales. In time she would return to herself.

But for now she stood silent and unprotesting of a man's intrusive touch. She was not bound to this moment, only trapped in her own curiosity. And longing, perhaps.

The music seemed louder, a waterfall of sound. Encapsulating them not in silence, but in a melody so perfect and so joyous that it ridiculed her more decorous thoughts.

"I did not see you inside," he said. Another invitation to truth.

"No," she answered simply.

He took one step back and she followed it, not realizing that she did so until she heard the sound of her slippers. His hand slowly lifted until it stretched to his side, hers captured with his in the linkage of their fingers. She stood directly in front of him, a partner in a silent dance.

Before she could object, before she could announce to him that she did not know the steps, she was following them, and him, in an intricate pattern. An enchanted quadrille on a London terrace in the shadowed light from a hundred flickering candles. And in the brilliance of his eyes that sparkled at her almost wickedly as she began to smile again. She was as complicit in this deed as he. Adept at it, as the moments passed and they moved to the music of violins and cellos.

For all that she counseled herself against foolishness, it felt as if she trembled inside. As if something light and golden were being given life. She continued to smile, unable to hide a surprising joy.

The music slowed, then stopped, the moment silent.

She had never before understood the meaning of yearning. Not until this moment when she stared at a man etched in moonlight. She was Margaret Esterly, widow. A commonplace person, rooted in practicality. Not a gypsy of the senses.

His thumbs reached up beneath her chin, tilted her head back so that he might inspect her, discern who she was through her appearance. She wondered what he saw. He stretched out his hand and touched the edge of her jaw. A stroke against the smooth, soft flesh of her cheek. An improvident gesture. A prohibited one.

He released her finally, and they stared at each other, smiles forgotten.

She stood on tiptoe, her hands braced against his shoulders for support, and leaned toward him. Her mouth was only inches from his, her heart racing so fast it felt as if it was going to leap from her chest.

"Montraine? Montraine, by God, is that you?"

A couple emerged from the ballroom. The man strode forward, his smile one of greeting.

Margaret turned and ran.

Michael endured the greeting of an acquaintance, fighting against the urge to bolt from the terrace in pursuit of her.

She had, surprisingly, been about to kiss him. He could feel her breath on his lips even now.

Her skin was creamy, pale almost. Her cheeks bloomed with the color of strawberries. A woman who should have been draped in satin and velvet and silk, but who wore her costume of cotton with an almost regal air.

They had spoken as if they had been old friends. And, with the same familiarity, she had gently ridiculed his logic.

Did he know her? Who was she? A question he had asked her and one which she had managed to avoid answering each time.

Her mouth was made for kissing.

An idiotic thought. He was here for only one reason, to find a wife. Not to stand staring out in the darkness after a woman who'd fled from him as if she were terrified. He walked to the head of the steps, fingered her glove in his pocket. She'd almost kissed him.

There was a cipher at home, one that fascinated him. It would be wiser to return to his library than to marvel at the purity of the moon kissed face of a woman he did not know.

He was not a creature of his impulses. Even so, he felt a surprising amount of regret as he turned and walked away.

Chapter 5

*A courtesan who has learned to delay
her pleasure only increases it.*

The Journals of Augustin X

"**Y**ou're certain you've never heard of a woman of that description?"

Michael sat in Babby's library, staring at the pattern of smoke from his cheroot.

Babby glanced over at him, his eyes twinkling. "You must be excessively smitten, Montraine. It's the fourth time in a week you've asked me."

"Not smitten, Babby. Simply curious." Enough to hold onto a glove. A small faded glove with a bit of lace around the wrist.

"I've seen you more in the past week, Montraine, than I have this whole last year."

Babby was an amiable friend. His brown eyes were almost constantly amused, as if he saw life as a grand adventure. His round face and portly body looked to belong to a man much older. Michael doubted, however, that Babby would ever reach his advanced years. Babby had three failings. He never missed the hunting season although he was a lamentable shot, his left foot bearing only four toes as proof of his ineptitude. He drank brandy to excess. And, the most dangerous of all, he tended to run afoul of husbands when he openly ogled their wives.

"You are rarely so intent about a female, Montraine."

"I only wished to know more about her," Michael said. Ever since that night he told himself that she was an interlude in his life. A small wave in the ocean of it. Nothing more. But he couldn't get her out of his mind. Like a wave she had effortlessly disappeared. Vanished.

He'd begun to casually ask about her. No one, however, could remember a woman wearing a plain cotton dress and jacket to the ball. Or could link a woman with auburn hair and pale ivory skin to a woman they knew. None of his solicitations ever resulted in a smile, a nod, a fond remembrance. Not one person told him—"Of course, I know her." No one did.

Perhaps he had not been descriptive enough. He should have told them that her lips were perfectly formed, the upper as full as the lower, and they curved into a delightful smile. Or that her hand was slender with unexpected calluses on the tips of her fingers, as if she were an avid horsewoman or labored at her needlework too long.

"Tell me the truth? Is it *tres* hush hush? One of those government things?" Babby grinned at him. "I'm as silent as a stone."

An overstatement. Babby divulged anything to anyone, given the slightest encouragement.

He should forget her and concentrate upon finding a wife.

He had not yet broached the subject of marriage and matrimony with any of the male relatives or the women on his list. He had a curious reluctance to do so. An oddity for him, not at all in keeping with his nature. He was a man who, once he'd decided upon a course, acted upon it with little hesitation.

"I wish I could assist you," Babby said now. "What does this mystery woman of yours look like again?"

"Of medium height," Michael said. "With dark hair. I think it an auburn shade. She has a mole high up on one cheek. Her eyes . . ." He didn't know. It had been too dark to see.

Babby frowned, put his cigar down in a footed porcelain dish etched in gold, then stood and walked to his glass-encased bookshelf, extracted his watch fob, and used the key hanging there to unlock the case.

"A magnificent figure," Babby said, turning. "One that tempts you to lift her skirts to see if what her dress hints at is real." He finished Michael's musings so perfectly that it was a moment until he realized what Babby was saying.

He felt a surge of irritation at Babby's effortless lechery.

"You know her, then," Michael said, willing his voice to appear as dispassionate as possible. The anticipation he felt was out of keeping. He should have been merely relieved at finding her. Not impatiently waiting until Babby finally got to the point.

"I saw her but a week ago. If she's the woman you mean. It was the beauty spot that did it. You never mentioned that before." He grinned at Michael. "Is it real, do you think?"

He withdrew a volume from the case. Holding it

gently between his hands, Babby carried it over and placed it carefully on the surface of his desk.

The cover of the book was brown leather, the shade of a venerable oak. Inscribed within a gilt shield on the front were two initials, *A* and *X*. Below that, the title *His Tales of Adventure Through Places of Antiquity and Delight* had been embossed in the leather.

"She sold me this book. The first volume of *The Journals of Augustin X*." He slid the book across to Michael.

Michael opened the book to the frontispiece. There, penned in a swooping hand, were the words *Jerome Esterly, Bookseller* and an address in London.

He glanced up at Babby.

"His wife," Babby said, as if the question in his mind had been given voice.

His wife. Michael frowned. He had spent the week wondering about another man's wife. No wonder she ran from him.

He opened the book and scanned it, his fingers turning the pages quickly. As a child, he had been interested by few things outside of mathematics. Consequently, Michael found that the easiest way to return to his true interest was to conquer a boring subject as quickly as possible. He'd taught himself to read quickly, often so fast that his tutors had doubts he had read the material at all. Only his ability to repeat his lessons in full had saved him from being dismissed as a liar and punished with a cane.

His mind registered the tiny scribbled notations in the margins at each chapter heading before his attention was captured by the passages.

Michael glanced over at his friend. "I had no idea you collected such things, Babby." He closed the book and placed it on the desk between them, willing his expression to remain affable, almost disinterested.

"There is nothing like these books, Montraine." Babby stretched out his hand and picked up the volume, stroked the leather cover with reverence. "I have since learned a great deal about them. It is said that they were last owned by a general close to Napoleon. How they came to be in England, I don't know. Probably spoils of war, or something like that."

"The bookshop is one you frequent?" A visit would not be an oddity. Once there, he could rediscover the elusive Mrs. Esterly, inform her that he did not dally with other men's wives.

"It was until it burned to the ground," Babby said regretfully. He sighed. "Esterly must have found a new place of business."

"How did you communicate with her?"

Babby's toothy grin was startling. "I see," he said. "You want her address. You are indeed clever, Montraine. There's not a hope of it, though. I've sacked that incompetent secretary of mine and hired a new man. If he finds her letter in that rat's nest of my correspondence, I'll send it along to you."

"Let me know, will you?" Michael stood, buried his disappointment in a smile. A great many pleasantries later, Michael was blessedly quit of the room and left to ponder the mystery before him. Not that of the Cyrillic cipher, nor even of a woman he didn't know at all. But why he should care.

It would be better simply to forget the entire episode. Rein in his curiosity and expend his energies on his work and his search for an acceptable wife.

Not on a woman who danced in the moonlight.

Margaret leaned against the door frame of the cottage door and watched as Penelope walked down the hill from Squire Tippett's house. Her bonnet swung by one hand and her step was light, almost skipping.

A smile curved Margaret's lips. A week ago Tom had come to see her, delaying his visit until Penelope had gone to the village. His solemn expression and the fact that he had gripped his hat nervously between both hands was a foreshadowing of his words.

"I've a bit of money saved, and a willingness to work hard. I know you're not her family and all," he'd said. "But you're the closest thing she's got."

The stories of Penelope's youth had not been pleasant ones. Margaret could not help but wonder what untold experiences had marked her life. The relatives she had left behind in London were never mentioned, nor had Margaret ever broached Penelope's privacy by asking.

She nodded, hands folded atop the table. His face was red with embarrassment, his brown hair neatly combed. Even his clothes looked to have been brushed, and his boots shined. His brown eyes looked everywhere but at her, however.

"She's my friend," Margaret said, attempting to ease him in his task.

"She's told me that," he said. "And she thinks highly of you."

"That is nice to hear," she said.

"I've got steady work at Squire Tippett's," he said. "I care for the horses there. I'm learning from the head groom and I've a future if I stay and work hard."

In a burst of enthusiasm and courage he continued. "I'd like to marry Penelope, Miss Margaret. I think I'd do her proper." He was so intent upon impressing her and so very much in love that it almost hurt to look at him.

"I think she is very fortunate to have someone like

you, Tom. How could I not approve of you? I hope you and Penelope are very happy."

"Would you not tell her that I've spoken with you, then, Miss Margaret? I have it in my mind that it should be something of a surprise," he said, his face almost radiant with joy.

He had beamed at her when she had agreed, ducked his head, and left the cottage. She had walked to the window and watched him. Halfway up the lane he threw his hat into the air and danced a circle beneath it.

Now Penelope echoed that same delight. Her face was alight with a smile as she reached the cottage, her news expected. "Tom's asked me to marry him, Miss Margaret," Penelope announced, her eyes shining.

"I am so very pleased for you," Margaret said, hugging her friend. "Tom is a wonderful young man."

"But I've no wish to leave you alone here," Penelope said, pulling back.

Margaret smiled, the expression surprisingly difficult. "It's not me we should be thinking of, but you, dear Penelope. Have you decided when?"

"I can't wait another year, Miss Margaret," she said. "Tom's got the squire's blessings for a few weeks from now. We'll have to live with his mother for a time, until we can afford our own place, but we can make do."

It would be unwise to wish for a different future. Or remember the man who sometimes colored her dreams. She had almost kissed him. Montraine. Margaret turned away, closed the cottage door, and stepped inside.

The boundaries of her world were small indeed. The walls were too close, the roof too low. Sometimes she had to escape, to walk upon the Downs and seek out the highest place she could find.

She had done the same with her thoughts, perhaps, in trying to escape the truth of her future. It loomed before her, black and gray, tinted by the color of her widowhood.

It would do no good to wish for what she could not have.

The Countess of Montraine announced herself to Smytheton, sailing over the threshold of Michael's library like a queenly ship followed by three dinghies.

His butler knew that he was never to be disturbed unless he was expecting a visitor. The only exception to that rule was his family. Besides, Michael wasn't at all sure if even Smytheton could keep them out if they were determined to see him.

He leaned back in his chair, set aside his paperwork, and waited.

He did not, like so many of his contemporaries, employ a secretary. It was not only that the nature of his work made such an intrusion unwise, but mostly because he was an intensely private man. He did not want another person rifling through his letters and reading copies of his notes. He understood the necessity of servants even as he made little use of them. His valet, Harrison, was likely to go for days without seeing him, a fact the man reminded him of often.

His mother looked determined and his sisters had varying expressions on their faces. Elizabeth looked amused, Ada bored, and Charlotte worried. An indication, then, that this was to be a confrontation of sorts. Michael wondered if they knew how tentative a hold he had on his temper right at this moment.

He had just reviewed the quarterly accounts. Despite the fact that she knew quite well their financial situation was perilous, the knowledge did not stop his mother from charging an entire wardrobe on a whim. "My dear boy," she would say each time he spoke to her, "you cannot expect us to look like paupers, especially when we are attempting to launch your sisters. It's important that they look their very best."

He leaned back in his chair, frowned at them. Elizabeth only smiled. Ada, his oldest sister, looked away. Charlotte, the middle one, feigned an interest in the study of her fingers.

His sister Charlotte had his mother's blond hair and deep brown eyes. But her expression, more often than not, was pinched and unhappy. As if she envied everyone and everything she saw.

Ada, on the other hand, seemed to do everything in her ability to minimize her good looks. The oldest and the tallest of the three sisters, she tended to hunch over until she looked almost spinsterish. He did not doubt that he would have to support Ada for the rest of her life, what with her disgust for marriage and her fine-tuned ability to scare away every suitor from here to Cornwall.

Elizabeth was a muted version of their father, with her soft brown hair and light blue eyes. She even had his charm, as if the paternal influence had been stamped firmly upon both her features and her nature.

The Countess of Montraine, however, eclipsed all her daughters in demeanor and force of character. She was always dressed exquisitely, today in an outfit of green silk—something new and ruinously expensive, no doubt. Her pale blond hair was arranged in ringlets beneath her fashionable bonnet. The picture of a wealthy, titled woman pleased with her life. Except, of course, that the coffer was empty and her expression was nowhere close to being amenable. Her eyes, an angry brown, were riveted on him, her mouth pursed in a moue of disapproval. He wondered what he had done now to earn that fierce look.

"You simply cannot constrain us to four hundred guests, Michael," she said angrily, thereby declaring war with her first words.

"I cannot?" he asked. He leaned his head back and studied the ceiling. The corners of the room were adorned with four intricately carved plaster cherubs who held ribbons leading to the center of the ceiling. There, a painting depicted white clouds limned pink and indigo against a pale blue sky. Dawn in heaven. The Italianate composition never failed to make him smile. Except in moments like now.

"It will not do, my dear boy. This ball is one of the premier events of the season."

"If we could only entertain at Setton. It is so much larger than *their* country house," Charlotte said.

"Whose house?" he asked, frowning.

"The Kittridges, Michael," Elizabeth supplied. She smiled at him and then looked away when their mother frowned at her.

The animosity that existed between his mother and Helen Kittridge dated from their first season. The other woman had been a reigning beauty at the same time his mother had been presented. The two had considered each other rivals from the first. Nor had the antipathy eased over the years. Sally Kittridge, Helen's daughter, was the same age as Charlotte, a case of history repeating itself. Perhaps that was the reason his mother was desperate to get them all married advantageously—to outdo Helen Kittridge in this one matter.

"The Kittridges have entertained twice as often as we have, Michael. Your sisters are so much more attractive than that Sally girl."

"Their house is much larger than ours, Mother," he said patiently. "Is it your plan to buy another?"

"Could we?" She looked hopeful.

He restrained his comment by a hair's breadth and merely shook his head.

His mother had already hosted two large events this season, and he had paid for both of them without a comment. Plus, his sisters had spent enough to outfit the whole of England, and he'd not said a word. But this last extravagance seemed excessive. Especially in view of their last quarter's expenditure. His temper was nudged up a notch.

"Instead of increasing the guest list, would it not be better to shorten it?" A sensible notion, one his mother did not seem to understand.

"Do not be boorish, Michael. It is doubtful all who are invited will attend. Even if they did so, people ebb and flow through these events all the time. One guest leaves, another arrives."

"So you would have us provide food and refreshments for how many?" The ball in question was taking on the look and feel of a military campaign.

"I would stop below a thousand, surely," she said.

"How much before a thousand?"

"Eight hundred," she said, and frowned down at him.

"Make it three hundred," he said, irritated, "and I will not cavil on the cost. More than that, and the money must come from somewhere. Either from your annual allowances, or by avoiding next season altogether."

Ada gasped. "You would not think to oppress us by keeping us at Setton, Michael."

"The choice is yours to make, Ada," he said with equanimity.

"I doubt that Sally Kittridge's brother is as mean as you!" This from Charlotte. He simply sent her a look that stifled any further complaints.

"Very well," his mother said, evidently recognizing just how far he could be pushed. "Three hundred."

She narrowed her eyes at him. "But I do hope, Michael, that these economies will not continue for long. You are taking steps to ensure that fact?"

"In due course," he said, realizing that time was against him.

As annoying as they were, they were his family. He was bound by his honor and his duty to protect them, even if it meant sacrificing himself upon a matrimonial altar.

The irrefutable fact was that he was going to have to marry an heiress. And soon.

Chapter 6

<hr/>

*Beauty means little when it is
all on the surface.*

The Journals of Augustin X

Penelope occasionally remained in the cottage during the girls' lessons. They had come to look upon her as another teacher. While her experience in the classroom might be lacking, she made up for it with uncommon common sense. Today, however, she was intent upon attacking the lean-to in the back of the cottage, clearing it of debris and making room for the chickens that Margaret planned to purchase soon.

Margaret collected the slates from Dorothy, smiled her thanks for the help, and stored them in the bottom drawer of the cupboard.

A moment later, she stood at the door of the cottage and said farewell to the girls.

"I want you to practice your m's and n's, Hortense," she admonished. "There are two hills in an m."

The girl nodded and smiled shyly.

"And Dorothy, you're not to read more than an hour with only one candle. The strain will hurt your eyes."

There were no books in their small, improvised school, but Margaret had devised a system to address that problem. Each girl must pen one story per week, but instead of Margaret grading it, she was to hand it to her reading partner to judge. That way, not only was a spirit of cooperation developed among the girls, but reading, writing, and composition practice were encouraged.

"Yes, Miss Margaret."

She smiled at the title. They had adopted it quite easily after having heard Penelope address her as such.

The smallest of her charges, little Mary, smiled a gap-toothed grin at her. "Can we go to the Standing Stones tomorrow, Miss Margaret?"

The Stones were huge gray monoliths so old that they appeared to be part of the earth itself. The circle of stones had obviously been made by man, however. The granite blocks had been chiseled into rectangular shapes and erected on the hill behind the cottage. Sometimes Margaret and the girls climbed there in order to view the scenery below, or for a change of locale in which to have their lessons.

"I will be away tomorrow, I'm afraid, Mary," she said, cupping her hand gently around the little girl's face. "I must go to London again."

Five faces stared up at her in disappointment.

"When you return, then?" Nan asked.

"If everyone does well on their sums, yes."

"Barbara cheats. I've seen her. She writes the answers on her sleeve." Margaret glanced at the speaker.

Of course. Abigail. The girl stared narrow-eyed at Barbara, who only stared back at her open mouthed.

"She's telling a fib, Miss Margaret," Barbara protested, turning away from Abigail.

"Am not," Abigail sneered.

"You are. I'm not a cheat," Barbara said fiercely.

Margaret stepped between them before Abigail could reach out and pull the other girl's hair. She patted Barbara on the shoulder, frowned at Abigail, and sent them both on their way.

Once the rest of the girls were gone, Margaret moved the table to a spot below the rafters, and standing atop it, touched the edge of the strongbox and pulled it to her inch by inch. Slowly she lowered it, then set it on the table before jumping down.

The money from the sale of the first *Journal* would be enough to last her for some time if she was careful, but there was not, regrettably, enough for luxuries.

Penelope had left London without hesitation, accompanying her to Silbury Village even though her future was uncertain. The past two years had been difficult ones, but through it all they'd shared their friendship. She could not let the occasion of Penelope's marriage pass without marking it with a gift. There was, however, only one way she could afford it—to sell the second book earlier than she'd originally planned.

A week ago she had written to the Earl of Babidge again and asked if he would be interested in buying the second volume. His enthusiastic assent had been forwarded to her from Samuel a few days ago.

Margaret wrapped the book and set it on the cupboard.

The anticipation she felt was unwarranted. Of course the Earl of Babidge knew the man called Montraine. He had been a guest at his ball, while she had been an interloper. But there was no reason for her to ask about him or ever see him again. They had shared an enchanted moment upon a dark terrace, but it was never to be repeated.

She should not think of that night. It had been an improvident act, one of recklessness. Margaret admonished herself even as honesty surfaced. She wished they had kissed.

The gear slipped, but failed to engage. Michael softly swore and adjusted it again. This time it slipped into the grooves properly. The softly whirring sound as he turned the crank was proof that it was properly aligned.

Michael stood over the table in his library, his mathematical engine in pieces before him.

He considered himself fortunate to have been of service in his life. Not only to his family, but to his country. He was proud of his accomplishments and especially of the machine he had devised. The engine was an invention intrinsically his. The creation of it had started with a thought, a theory. Could the more mundane duties of code breaking be performed by rote?

He had begun by duplicating a clock's mechanism, using the interconnecting gears as both a means of movement, and with a metal key, a method of propulsion. At first, the engine was little more than a rudimentary abacus. He'd punched out the numbers one through ten on a series of individual cards of heavy vellum. When two of these cards were inserted into a slot, small slate blocks on which numbers had been incised were turned over until the proper sum was displayed.

His plans for developing the engine further changed the day he began adjusting the alignment of the inner and outer gears. He'd taken the engine apart, held the gears in his hands, rotating them slowly while an idea occurred to him. The teeth of the smaller gear was half the size of the larger, which meant that it would have to turn twice as fast. What if he numbered the smaller gear and added letters to the outer? A certain series of rotations would have to occur before each number and letter would be used again. That number of rotations could serve as a cipher key. The result was not a code solving machine, nor an abacus, but an engine that wrote ciphers.

He'd tested the codes by asking his other Black Chamber associates, through Robert, to attempt to solve them. So far they had not been able to do so.

The knock on the door of Michael's library was followed almost instantly by the sight, not of Smytheton's somber face, but the rather agreeable one of his closest friend.

"If you're working, I will return at another time," Robert Adams said.

Michael smiled invitingly. "I've put that blasted code of yours away for the moment," he said.

"Instead, you're working on something much less abstract," Robert said, coming to his side.

Their friendship had begun as boys. Setton was not far from Robert's boyhood home. They'd cut across fields and woods to meet each other, played Knight and Saracen, Roundhead and Cavalier on the old ramparts of Robert's home, raced through the labyrinth of Setton's corridors and hallways.

They had known each other too long and too well to be impressed with each other's consequence, even if Michael was now earl and his friend a force to be reckoned with in the government. The fact that Robert was unknown for the most part did not dilute his power. It might, in fact, have enhanced it. His title was innocuous and subservient, Junior Secretary of Foreign Affairs—designed, Michael suspected, to mask the degree of influence Robert actually wielded. One of his duties was acting as head of the Black Chamber.

Another knock interrupted them. Smytheton appeared carrying a silver salver. "There's word for you, sir. This came by messenger."

From the disdain in Smytheton's voice, Michael could well imagine the messenger's appearance. No doubt one of the small boys often pressed into service. Not clean but quick.

Michael took the envelope from the tray.

"I vow that man could peel the paint off a wall with his frown," Robert said, grinning when the door shut behind Smytheton.

"Smytheton doesn't suffer fools gladly. I think I'm the only person he likes, and even that is conditional."

"At least he's younger than Peterson. Does the old man still work for your mother, or have you pensioned him off?"

"He's determined not to retire until Smytheton does," Michael said.

Peterson had his nose out of joint because Smytheton hadn't acquired his post in the same fashion he had, coming up through the ranks. Smytheton was not disposed to like many people at all and simply ignored Peterson's petulance, which only made the antipathy worse.

Michael had long since decided that it was a blessing his house was not designed to house many servants. The constant bickering as to position and duties was enough to give a saint a headache. As it was, his valet appeared every two days to ensure himself of the state of Michael's wardrobe, then complained the entire time that there was not sufficient storage space for the clothing he'd sent for, or for a room for himself.

"I've offered to pension Peterson off," Michael said. "But he has his pride. Besides, his father did not retire until he was eighty, and I think Peterson believes he would be a failure if he didn't equal that achievement."

"How old is he?"

"Seventy-two," Michael said, smiling. He tore open the envelope Smytheton had handed him.

I have agreed to purchase another of the Journals, *Montraine. Mrs. Esterly will be at my home on the 14th.*

His breath caught. Odd, to feel that much anticipation to see a stranger again.

"That look could only be caused by a woman," Robert said. "A bridal candidate?" Robert smiled, an amused expression that indicated he saw too much.

"Nothing," Michael admitted, "so honorable as that."

He returned to his desk, sat behind it. Robert occupied the chair opposite him. "I have the most damnable curiosity about a woman. I met her once and yet she's been constantly in my thoughts of late."

"It's lust," Robert offered, sitting back. "It alone binds men and women together. Women would have it otherwise, I think. Did you realize that it's one of the seven deadly sins?"

"Are you going to quiz me on them?" Michael asked, smiling.

"There are those who say you never forget anything once you've read it. Let's just say I'm testing a theory," Robert said, a twinkle in his eye.

Michael laughed and closed his eyes for a moment, saw the image of the page in his mind. One of his tutors had held secret thoughts of becoming a Jesuit. Michael's religious training, therefore, had been thorough. In fact, his entire education had been both diverse and uncommon. His father had dismissed a string of tutors, not because any had failed in his duty, but because he'd wished Michael continually challenged.

"Pride, covetousness, lust, anger, gluttony, envy, sloth," Michael recited, then opened his eyes.

"I'm impressed," Robert said. He stood and investigated the cabinet against the wall with some familiarity. A few moments later he dropped into the chair, a glass of brandy in his hand. He pushed the one he'd poured for Michael across the desk.

"Who is she?"

"I'm not entirely sure," Michael said. He didn't have to close his eyes to remember her. There was a tiny mole high up on her left cheek as if to call attention to her eyes, wide and brimming with some emotion he had not been able to discern. Her face was oval, the shape of cameos and rare beauties. Her mouth, tinted pink, was curved in a tremulous smile.

A lovely woman, but then, there were women of great beauty in London. Not only English women, but from any country in the known world. London seemed to be the hub of the universe at times, and the women glittering stars that occupied the heavens.

Then what was the fascination he felt for this

woman? In his top desk drawer was a faded glove. How many times had he removed it from its place of honor, studied the shape of it? A bit of nonsense unlike him.

It was not at all rational.

Why this one woman of all those created? He did not understand why he could not be as fascinated with one of his bridal candidates.

He had enjoyed his relationships with women, considered them pleasurable. But they had never been counted as necessary to his well-being as was air or food. Lust was a secondary emotion, one that he had aligned, in his mind, next to the need for companionship. Desirable, but not wholly required in order to live.

Lust—that was all this feeling was. Or curiosity. But the intensity of it surprised him.

"She is selling a collection of books," he said. "A rather arcane set of volumes entitled the *Journals of Augustin X.*"

Robert remained silent for a moment, considered the brandy in his glass. "I've heard of those before. I wonder where?" He shook his head as if to jar loose a memory, then smiled ruefully. "It has slipped from me, I'm afraid."

"No doubt crowded out by all those other secrets of yours."

"I am but a Junior Secretary," he said, grinning. "I exist only to serve."

Michael eyed him dubiously. "And I suppose it's a rumor that you employ all those shadowy creatures of yours?"

"Are you any closer to solving the Cyrillic cipher?" Robert asked with a smile. Evidently, the question had been too pointed.

"No," Michael said, making no effort to hide his irritation. "But I will."

Robert sighed. "I'd hoped you, at least, would have come to some conclusion. No one else has had any success, either."

The more difficult and important the cipher, the more individuals in the Black Chamber were assigned to it. Michael no more knew their names than they did his. Only that the Cyrillic cipher must be important indeed to warrant the attention it was receiving.

But Michael had vowed to solve it first. He thrived on competition and suspected that was the very reason Robert had told him the cipher was being shared.

Robert's machinations made Michael smile. His old friend was not unlike a snake, so entwined in his own schemes that one day he would find himself feasting on his own tail.

But for now, something even more fascinating than Robert's stratagems intrigued him. Another type of mystery. That of the unforgettable Mrs. Esterly.

When she came to Babby's house to sell the *Journal*, he was also going to be present. Perhaps when he saw her again, the riddle would be solved, the attraction dissipated. It would be over once he saw her in the sunlight. She would be another attractive woman. Nothing more.

He smiled, and toasted Robert with his brandy. His old friend gazed at him quizzically, but raised his own glass in salute.

Chapter 7

*A wise courtesan will never allow passion
to overwhelm her other senses.*

The Journals of Augustin X

Because Silbury Village was of some repute due
to the skill of its craftsmen, it was not entirely
isolated; the London coach stopped here twice a
week. A convenience, since it meant that she didn't
have to walk to the nearest crossroads.

The journey from her cottage had been short
enough, the walk easily passed in appreciation of the
spring morning. Even the village seemed touched
with the magic of it. The air was clear, almost crisp.
Windows sparkled and flowers bloomed and the people she passed nodded and exchanged smiles. She
gripped the wrapped book in her arms and responded in kind.

Before she reached her destination, the inn that
served as a post house for the coach, she was hailed
by the two women she'd wanted most to avoid. She

sighed inwardly, turned and waited for them to approach her.

"My daughter tells me that you're off to London, Mrs. Esterly."

Sarah Harrington beamed at Margaret, her face wreathed in a look of approval. Anne Coving stood beside her. A casual observer might take them to be no more than friends. But they were sisters, for all their disparity in appearance.

Sarah was tall and slender, and favored dark colors. Anne was short and plump and tended to wear bright fabrics. Sarah's face, while narrow and thin was almost always graced with a smile. The expression on Anne's plump face made Margaret think she'd recently smelled something vile.

"Abigail says that it is an adventure of sorts," Anne said, her eyes narrowing.

"I'm going to visit a friend," Margaret explained. A lie by only the most strict interpretation. She had planned on staying with Maude and Samuel Plodgett overnight after transacting her business.

"It will be the second time you have returned to London since the fire, won't it?" Sarah asked.

"Such a terrible thing," Anne said, "to lose a husband that way."

Margaret nodded, but did not comment. Anne seemed to take great delight not only in tragedy, but in the repeating of it. If there was a tale to be told, the woman would be happy to relate it, the more sordid or distressing the better.

"Dorothy is progressing quite well in her reading," she said to Sarah. An almost desperate diversion. "I'm sure you are very proud of her."

Sarah's smile broadened in pleasure.

"Abigail has a great talent in drawing," Margaret said, turning to Anne. What she did not say to Abigail's mother was that her daughter was also most unpleasant. If one of the girls began to cry, it was because Abigail had pinched her. If an inkwell spilled, Abigail was the cause. The child also emulated her mother in that she was quick to spread tales, true or not.

Out of the corner of her eye Margaret saw the coach approaching from the end of the street. She bid farewell to the two women and walked to the inn with a sense of welcome relief.

Her traveling companions to London were a varied group. Two men dressed as gentlemen, an older lady who smelled of camphor and a young woman and her little boy whose antics were charming for the first hour but grating as the journey went on.

Margaret wrapped the ends of her shawl around the *Journal* to further camouflage it. Her hands clasped it tightly as if the secrets contained within its covers would seep out into the air around her if she did not. She smiled at her own whimsy, and concentrated on the view outside the window.

When Margaret arrived at the Earl of Babidge's house, she was led to the same room where she and the earl had transacted their business previously. Instead of asking her to wait, however, the manservant simply tapped once and pushed the door open. She entered the library, expecting to see the affable earl.

A small fire was laid against the early spring chill. A man sat in one of the burgundy wing chairs facing the hearth. At her entrance, he stood and turned. Not the Earl of Babidge after all, but the man who had occupied too many of her thoughts for the past weeks.

Montraine.

Her heart seemed to stop and then lunge forward as if making up for its laxity. Even her breath was uneven, coming in short, choppy breaths. She had gotten her wish, then. To see him once again. She'd not thought that the sight of him would be so startling, however.

She had thought him captivating in moonlight. It was nothing to how he appeared now in the light of day.

Beautiful.

What a silly word to use in conjunction with a man like him. Yet *handsome* seemed too feeble a description to contain his dark good looks. Perhaps she was destined never to think of a word suitable enough.

"Hello again," he softly said. "I have been waiting for you."

She halted where she was, gripped the book in her arms tightly.

Had Lucifer been a golden angel, crafted of sunlight and radiance before being cast from heaven? He should, instead, have possessed black hair and sapphire eyes, been blessed with a smile that hinted at wickedness. And graced with a voice that promised sin and absolution in its dark whisper.

"Were you?" she said shakily. "How did you know I would be here?"

"Babby is my friend," he said, "and eager to assist me in finding you."

"You looked for me?" How odd that her mouth was dry, and her breath seemed caught in her chest.

"Oh yes," he said, walking slowly toward her. "I have. You are a woman of great mystery, Mrs. Esterly. Tell me, does your husband know you're here?"

Run, Margaret. Take the Journal *and leave this place. This man is a danger. Or a delight.*

"I'm a widow," she said, her voice more tremulous than she wished.

"Are you?"

She nodded, feeling the caution vanish in that instant she looked at him. It faded beneath a greater fascination.

He met her gaze with his own intent stare. His look was one of speculation and curiosity. She did not fault him for that. She had enough of her own about him.

"A widow," he said, repeating it. "Your name?" he asked, with a smile that did not quite reach his eyes.

"Margaret," she said quietly, responding as if she were in a daze. "Who are you, then?"

"Michael Hawthorne," he said, bowing slightly.

"A duke?" She tilted her head.

"Alas, only an earl," he said, smiling sardonically.

"I would have thought you a prince," she said, startling herself with the admission. He only smiled at her comment.

"It seems we know little enough about each other."

Silence was the best recourse to that statement. She stared at the carpet between them.

"A few moments upon the terrace should not be so easily recalled. I wondered if you were shadow or substance. Or perhaps a ghost of my imagination."

"I am very real," she said, his words coaxing forth her smile.

"But more circumspect than before."

"You were only a shadow yourself," she whispered. "Now you are only too real."

He strode forward until he stood in front of her. He reached out his hand, pulled the book and her reticule gently from her grasp, set them down on the sideboard. She said nothing in response or protest.

Something was happening to her. Her mind was clouded in alarmed wonder. Her heart, already beating fast at his appearance, began to escalate, her breath tightening in her chest. This moment replicated that night of violins and breezes. A moment of sorcery so strong that she trembled in its spell.

"Come," he said, taking her hand and leading her to the fire. His hand held hers in a gentle restraint, much as he had that night on the terrace. But here there were few shadows, only the orange glow of a fire, and through the windows the gleam of sunlight breaking through the clouds.

"Have you traveled far?" A commonplace question, but his touch on her hand didn't seem at all ordinary. She could feel the warmth of his hand even through her glove.

"Not far," she murmured, wishing that he wouldn't stand so close. She could feel his breath against her cheek.

Suddenly, his hand reached up and brushed a tendril of hair back from her cheek. A lover's touch. Too intimate. Gentle, almost tender. His knuckles stroked down the edge of her jaw.

No one had ever touched her this way.

She reached up and stayed his hand, held it with hers. He studied her face as if he had never seen a woman before, the intensity of his gaze almost burning.

Run, Margaret. As fast and as far as you can.

She heard the admonition of her conscience, but another voice intruded. This whisper belonged to her and yet was someone just now discovered. This woman of secret dreams and hidden wishes slipped atop the person Margaret knew herself to be. This shadow spoke and moved and thought with her own will. *Stay. Touch him. Reach out with your fingers and trace the line of his jaw, that unsmiling mouth.*

She took a deep shuddering breath, dropped his hand, and stepped back from him. He, too, seemed to feel the need to separate himself. He walked to the sideboard, turned, and faced her. The width of a room was between them, yet she felt his presence as if he touched her still.

"You interest me too greatly," he said, "and I cannot afford distractions at this time in my life."

A statement so arrogant that it had the welcome effect of dissipating the strange spell entwining around them.

"How am I a distraction?" she asked, suddenly amused.

"First, by having a curiosity that equals my own," he said.

Her cheeks warmed. Did he know she'd read the *Journals*? How could he?

"I don't understand," she said carefully.

"You stood on the terrace, spying on a ball."

"Yes," she confessed, relieved.

"And today. Why didn't you leave the moment you saw it was me and not Babby?"

"I have business to conduct with the earl," she said in her defense. Not quite the truth.

"You stayed because of curiosity, Margaret."

She looked away, wishing that he would not speak her name in quite that fashion. It was almost a caress.

Perhaps he was correct. She should have left when she'd first seen him. Or when he'd touched her cheek. Drawn up her dignity, her pride, and departed the room. Perhaps scourged him with a look first, so that he knew she was not the sort to be enchanted with words and masculine perfection.

But it seemed she was not wise after all. Perhaps curiosity was a good enough pretense.

"Secondly," he said, smiling softly. "You are a distraction because you possess a mouth made for kissing."

She stared at him.

Her blood felt hot, as if it flowed through her body carrying fire. Her breath was captured and held in ransom for her good sense. *Leave this room, Margaret. Leave him.* It seemed as if the ghost of her Gran reprimanded her for her hesitation.

"It is better, perhaps," she said a moment later, still rooted to the spot, "to be congratulated for ordinary virtues. Neatness, some accomplishment."

"Kindness," he contributed with a smile.

She nodded.

"Are you kind, Margaret?"

"I believe I am." She studied the carpet beneath her feet again. "Are you?"

"Some would say I am not. Otherwise, you would not still be here. I should have allowed you to conduct your business and left you alone."

"Why didn't you?" She glanced up and discovered him watching her so intently that it felt as if he touched her with his gaze.

He walked back to where she stood beside the fire.

She looked away. The room was suddenly too warm; she felt almost faint.

"Because I want my kiss," he said flatly.

Margaret jerked her head up to meet his look. Her eyes widened and she licked suddenly dry lips. The words settled in a hollow spot inside her.

She turned and walked to the window, concentrated upon the view. Desperate in a way she had never been before to find herself in the flurry of her thoughts.

She marked the journey of a carriage, then focused upon a bird flying to the roof of a house. The morning sky had been gray, a dismal London day. She had often seen such. Yet now the sun was shining brightly. A transformation. Not unlike the one she felt within herself.

She turned and glanced back at him.

He had not moved, a statue of restraint, a muscle flexing in his cheek. He neither smiled nor eased the words with charm.

It would be unwise to allow the boundaries between them to be lowered, even for a moment. She knew that without understanding why. Yet she wanted to touch him. What sort of woman did that make her?

"One kiss," he said, as if he knew she wavered.

She should have left the moment she saw him in the room. Instead, they flirted with danger, and with each other.

"I don't know you," she said almost desperately.

"What do you need to know in payment for a kiss?" he asked, impatiently, frowning.

"Why me?" A question to hide the unsettling truth. Both the pragmatic, demure, quiet, and proper Margaret and this woman she had become upon meeting him wanted to kiss him. So deeply and completely that she could taste the flavor of it when it was done.

"I don't know." His scowl deepened. "It's a question I've asked myself for too many weeks."

"Have you come to no satisfactory answer?"

"Yes. One kiss."

"That's all?"

"Yes. When it's over, the bond will be severed, the fascination will ease. I will, blessedly, be able to concentrate upon my work and my marriage."

She glanced at him, shocked.

"I'm not married yet," he said, one eyebrow arching. "Nor affianced. You are a distraction to that also."

She turned back to the window. "So this might be an act of charity on my part, to enable you to continue your life unfettered by diversions," she said, unexpectedly amused.

"Margaret." His voice was so close to her that she jumped, startled. He stood behind her, his finger trailing at the collar of her spencer, barely touched the nape of her neck. Her indrawn breath was captured, held, then released on a sigh as he trailed a delicate pattern inside the material, against her skin. She shivered in response.

A taboo, that touch.

"Margaret, say yes," he whispered.

When she remained silent, he continued. "I want to know why I can't forget you."

She turned slowly and looked up at him.

"It's only a kiss, Margaret," he urged. "And once it's done, this fascination will be over."

"One kiss," she said, attempting to appear as worldly as he. In truth, her heart was beating a strange tattoo, one of skipped beats and sheer excitement.

Slowly, she tilted her chin up, closed her eyes. Waited in an agony of expectancy. A thousand starlings flew in her chest, and her cheeks were heated as if by a brazier. Her lips were full, expectant and waiting, and her breathing sounded too harsh, as if she had run a great distance.

But instead of the warm brush of his lips upon her

mouth, she felt the slow stroke of his thumb across her lips. She opened her eyes to discover him smiling down into her face.

"Not here. I want to kiss you somewhere where we will not be interrupted."

She blinked at him, suddenly uncertain.

Montraine smiled softly, almost dispassionately, turned, and walked to the sideboard.

Surreptitiously, she pressed a hand to her chest. Her breasts felt hard, achy.

He picked up her belongings, returned to her side. He handed her the reticule and the *Journal*, then helped her arrange the shawl around her shoulders.

At the door he turned and held out his hand. She stared wide-eyed at him. A look passed between them, one of questions asked and answered. Did she want to go with him? Almost desperately. Was it wise? No. Was he a man to trust? She had felt safe with him from the beginning, but trust was not what she felt at this particular moment.

One kiss. A lure, an invitation. An impossible attraction to resist. Desire was a word found only in the *Journals of Augustin X*, never in her life. One kiss, that was all.

Perhaps, after all, what she wanted was to build up a store of memories for when she was old. I kissed an earl, she might say to her students, and the young girls would giggle.

She smiled, stretched out her hand, and went with him.

Chapter 8

*A strong heartbeat, felt at a lover's elbow,
reveals his stamina and ability.*

The Journals of Augustin X

Together they left the Earl of Babidge's house,
encountering only the majordomo at the door.
Montraine nodded briskly at the man, and he stepped
back, deferential in a way he had never been to Margaret.

If she had been the butler she would have been
quelled by that look. As it was, she found herself fascinated.

Montraine walked to the hack, dismissed him with
a few words, then returned to her side. Silently emanating from him was an authority more effective
than another man's boast.

Without a word, he led her to a gleaming ebony
carriage drawn by four matched bays. A footman
jumped from the back and opened the door for her.

Montraine said nothing as she hesitated, simply stood aside for her to precede him.

She mounted the steps and entered the carriage. Montraine settled into the seat in front of her, his back to the horses. The curtains were open, but she didn't pretend an interest in the scenery. Instead, she met his gaze.

"A difficult journey to make with one footstep," she said. "From modest and proper to heedless." Abandoned.

"Are you feeling heedless, Margaret?" he asked, a smile curving his lips.

"Yes," she admitted. Danger. Why didn't she feel it? Instead, anticipation curled in the pit of her stomach.

"Are there any little Esterlys claiming your attention?" he asked suddenly.

"I have no children," she softly said. It was a sadness with which she'd learned to live.

"No maiden aunts, no uncles, no parents in reserve?"

"No," she said. Except for Penelope, there was no one. But the bond between them was one of friendship, not relation.

"No siblings?"

He was implacable in his curiosity.

"Why do you ask?"

"I only wished to know if there was anyone who waits for you."

"Only my students," she said. "And they do not expect me until tomorrow."

He looked surprised.

"I teach the village girls," she explained.

"Yet there is London in your voice."

"I was born and raised here," she admitted.

He sat angled against the seat, the better to make use of the space with his long legs. He commanded the interior of the carriage as he had the terrace.

"What do you teach them?"

She smiled. "To read and write correctly. A rudimentary ability in ciphering, some French, and some unremarkable talent in drawing."

"Why did you leave London?"

"I wished a change," she said, surprised at the ease she felt in telling him. "I suspect it is something contrary to my nature, that I should wish to live in the country while those in London have nothing but contempt for it."

"Is that why you're here now? Because of something contrary in your nature?"

Perhaps, she silently answered. Or because she very much wanted a kiss from him.

"Why did you let Babby think you were married?" he asked, as if he knew she would not admit to fascination. Or loneliness.

"Because men do not often wish to transact business with women. And it is safer to have a customer believe that a husband will protect against any unwelcome advances."

"Did Babby give you any difficulty?" His face tightened, his smile vanishing.

She smiled at him. "No. I had the distinct impression that it embarrassed him to deal with me. I confess to thinking the earl resembles a cute hedgehog. He would look excessively silly leering."

"Babby will not appreciate such a comment," Michael said, his good humor restored. "He fancies himself a man a with a great attractiveness to the ladies."

His hand clenched atop the walking stick, his eyes were a direct and piercing blue.

I want to know why I couldn't forget you.

A sentiment she had felt often enough during these past weeks. He felt the same as she. Her conscience whispered to her. She should be cautious. Discreet.

Instead, she smiled.

She was lovely. Her hair was auburn, a perfect shade against the ivory of her complexion. Her eyes were hazel, their hue a warm green at the moment. But it was her mouth that fascinated him. The upper lip was as full as the lower. A perfect pout, as if nature had crafted this one mouth for kissing.

One kiss. That was all he wanted. Then, he would be himself once more, focused upon his future. He would execute the Cyrillic cipher and pick out a bride. His thoughts would not be filled with an unknown woman who enchanted him. He would kiss her and she would be only a woman again. Not a Circe.

She seemed almost innocent sitting there. She had blushed when he'd spoken of her mouth. Yet she'd come to London to sell a lewd book to Babby. A contradiction, a duality of her nature, that she would be both daring and seemingly virtuous.

He'd been impatient for her arrival, irritated by the delay of it. When she'd entered Babby's library he'd watched her. There was something about the way she walked. When she'd turned from the window, straightened her shoulders, tilting her head up for his kiss, he'd heard a clarion call of warning.

This woman would be better forgotten. Except, of course, that he had been unable to do so.

"Are you wondering why I have not kissed you yet?" he asked. He smiled slightly at the look on her face. A curious combination of eagerness, anticipation, and surprise. He felt himself tighten, his caution being beaten down by a baser, more fervent need.

Instead of responding, she asked a question of her own. "Where are we going?"

To perdition, no doubt. But it was not the answer he gave her. "I would be wise to take you somewhere public," he admitted. "But it is either too early, or there are no amusements I would care to subject you to."

She sat, patient, waiting for him to complete his answer.

"I'm taking you home," he said finally.

"Your home?" she asked, wide-eyed.

He nodded. "A bachelor establishment," he said. "A house I share with a dignified butler and a maid I rarely see." There, he had laid it out for her. Blatantly and without adornment. He was taking her somewhere private, where he might kiss her for as long as a kiss lasted.

"Do you want to return to Babby's?"

"Should I?"

"An answer only you can divine, Margaret."

Her eyes were wide, but she remained silent. "Only one kiss?" she asked finally.

"Yes," he said, his tone harsher than he'd wished. "At the end of it, I will place you in a carriage myself."

He didn't tell her that if she opened the door or summoned the driver, he would use every means within his disposal to change her mind. He allowed her the illusion of freedom at that moment. But in fact, their destiny had been decided that night on the terrace.

Chapter 9

*A woman of pleasure understands the power
of both tenderness and passion.*

The Journals of Augustin X

When the carriage stopped, they alighted from
it in silence. As if neither could bear to speak
lest they break the spell of shimmering anticipation.

She looked around as Montraine walked to the
front of the carriage, spoke to the driver. There were
in a fashionable tree-lined square, absurdly quiet, as
if the cacophony of London did not exist only blocks
away. The house was not unlike the Earl of Babidge's,
but Montraine's home differed in that the steps were
banded by a black wrought-iron railing and the brass
knocker on the black door was in the shape of a large
fish.

"What did you tell him?" she asked Montraine,
when he returned to her side. The driver flicked the
reins, encouragement the horses did not seem to need.

"That I would not require him for a while," he said,

as he took her arm. He escorted her up the wide steps.
A bachelor establishment, he had said.

Now was the time for caution. If she wished to
leave, she should say so at this moment. She did not
doubt that he would call back the carriage, make arrangements for her to be taken wherever she wished.
Men like Michael Hawthorne did not need to force a
female.

But it was not coercion she felt. Only fascination.

She remained mute as he ushered her up the steps.
They were greeted at the door by a tall man with a
shock of white hair and a military bearing. His attire
was of somber black, with a stock so heavily starched
it looked almost painful to wear.

"Smytheton," Michael said, "you may have the rest
of today out."

The majordomo managed a wintry smile. "I have
no plans, my lord."

"I shall not need you," Michael said.

Only then did the man nod once, sharply, before
leaving them.

Montraine turned and stretched out his hand. She
handed him the *Journal* and reticule and he placed
them on the table beside the door. What more would
he take from her? Her will? No, it was her own decision to be here. An unwise one, she suspected. If he
was not the flame, neither was she a moth. Only
lonely, perhaps. And wishing an adventure to hold
secret and guarded in her heart.

The faint light illuminated the surprising foyer, a
rotunda created by twelve marble columns, each festooned with carved leaves and topped with an ornate
basket of engraved flowers.

Above them was a clear dome of glass rendered
golden by the bright sun. An array of brilliant white

marble statues decorated its outer curve. Women had been carved dressed in flowing gowns so sheer that the shape of their legs could be seen. Men were attired in swaths of material that barely shielded their loins before being draped over one shoulder. Each statue held a different pose, but each stretched out a hand, palm curved and fingers curled. As if to feel the sunlight that streamed in through the clear glass dome and fell in a perfect circle between the columns of the rotunda. A bird flew over the dome; his shadow fell on her before she was bathed by sunlight again.

She tilted back her head, closed her eyes. It was not unlike the experience she had in the Standing Stones. As if she were a very small part of a vast, unknown world.

She opened her eyes to find him standing there, watching her. His smile was slow, an oddly warming expression. She felt the effect of it down to her toes.

"A pantheon," Michael said, moving closer. "The original owner had a penchant for statuary and a love for antiquity."

She looked about her. Stairs curved around the rotunda like a bird's wing, soared two stories above them.

"Say something," he urged.

"What should I say?" Her question reverberated back to her. She stared, delighted, at the figures above her. "It has an echo."

"Whisper something," he coaxed, leaning against one column. "It's even more amazing."

"Montraine," she said. His lips curved in a smile as the sound of his name reverberated around them.

She looked up again, as if the whispers hid in the statues above them. "How wonderful." Praise that echoed back to her.

He came to her then, slowly untied the bow of her bonnet, his fingers trailing his hands down the length of ribbon. He bent his head, so close that his breath whispered against her cheek.

Now?

But instead of kissing her, he stepped back, his soft smile appearing to approve of her silence and her acquiescence. She could do little else, trapped in this moment, adrift in wonder beneath a pantheon. She was no longer the virtuous widow, the teacher, the friend. She became someone else in his presence, as if he saw beneath the façade to the person she wished to be. Secure from gossip, safe from censure, in this room and this moment she could be audacious and almost wicked.

His fingers slid beneath her bonnet and threaded through her hair.

Margaret's breath caught.

His palms rested warmly against her temples. She closed her eyes, waiting. But he only pushed the bonnet from her hair and it fell with a soft rustle of sound to the floor.

Her lips trembled in anticipation. Her lashes fluttered open finally. Her face warmed at his unwavering, almost fierce look.

"One kiss, Montraine," she reminded him in a whisper.

"Yes," he said curtly, removing her gloves from each hand as if she'd lost the ability to move. Perhaps she had.

He lay the gloves she'd borrowed from Penelope on the table, bent and retrieved her bonnet, and placed them beside it. Gloves, book, bonnet, reticule. A decorous tableau of accessories. A woman's presence in his bachelor home. How many other women had been here? How many had he seduced with an effortless smile and a bit of whimsy?

She didn't want to know.

He returned to her side, reached for her hand again, studying it intently. She tried to pull away from his grasp, but he would not allow it. Instead, he smoothed his fingers over the tips of hers.

"I still have your glove," he said absently, stroking her fingers.

"Do you?" she asked, surprised that she was able to speak without her voice trembling. "I wondered where it had gone," she said. A lie. She recalled only too well the moment of their dance, his tucking it into his jacket.

"I keep it in my desk drawer," he admitted with a smile as if mocking himself. "Like a schoolboy I study it from time to time. Why is that, I wonder?" He lifted his head, his gaze pinning her in place.

She shook her head wordlessly.

Time was suspended, the moments passing more slowly than normal. They stood motionless within the circle of columns. The sunlight streaming in through the dome's convex curve lifted the shadows. Silence was their accessory, their actions condoned and given absolution by the marble smiles of the gods and goddesses above them.

He took her hand, turned it over and rested it on his, and now trailed his fingertip from wrist to the tip of her thumb and back again. A journey repeated again and again with each finger.

She shivered.

"Are you cold?"

"Yes." There, another lie.

He threaded his fingers through hers, turned and walked with her across the rotunda. He opened the door to another room, turned, and smiled at her coaxingly.

The sitting room was surprisingly intimate. A settee upholstered in blue silk sat against one wall. Facing it were two wing chairs in a soft ivory and blue fabric. Between them was a large square table adorned with a bowl of spring flowers.

He led her to the small black granite fireplace against one wall, stood with her in front of it. He still had not relinquished her hand. His fingertip moved slowly back across her palm to the inside of her wrist, as if he measured the pounding beat located there. Then he traced a small circle in the middle of her palm.

Her fingers curled toward her wrist, and he gently pressed them back. It was a delicate touch, hardly shocking, but still she trembled. There was no moonlight, no sound of violins, no darkness to hide her response.

She suspected he would stop the moment she asked him to cease. Or if she pulled her hand away. A lesson then, in those moments. She could not dictate his actions, but she could curtail them.

Yet she remained silent and motionless.

"You are very sensitive," he said. "I will have to be gentle with you." His fingers linked with hers and he curled them into a fist, trapping his fingertips against her palm. He pulled her closer to him, an inch at a time. So slowly that she could have stopped him at any moment. Or spoken the words to halt him.

She felt his breath against her forehead. Trapped in wonder, she closed her eyes. His fingers traced from her temple to her chin.

Enchantment.

*   *   *

He stood so close to her that he could hear her breathe. He leaned his head down, rubbed his cheek against the softness of the hair at her temple.

Her hands reached out and gripped the sleeves of his coat. For balance? Did she feel as unstable as he?

"If I kiss you now," he said, forcing the words past the construction in his throat, "I will have to let you go."

"One kiss, that's all," she said faintly.

A gentle admonition. He swore silently to himself, wishing that he had not given her his word.

"Yes," he said grimly, "one kiss."

His hands brushed against her back as he eased her toward him. She took a tiny step forward, until one foot was wedged between his boots. Could they stand any closer? Each leaned against the other, eyes closed. His fingers fanned out, pressed against her shoulders, slid down her back slowly. He felt himself hardening even further, a physical response to a need that had been present since he'd seen her at Babby's.

She was a stranger. Yet he'd thought too much about the kiss she'd almost given him. Then why had he not taken it earlier, when she'd tilted back her head and waited for it? Because he wished to touch her as he did at this moment. Softly, with the hint of appeasement in the distance. Gently, his need vying with his curiosity.

He stepped back, dropped his hands to his side. A stoic denunciation of the anticipation he felt.

Her expression was bemused, her eyes wide, the pupils dark. As if she had just now awakened from sleep. Or been loved well and long.

He had lost his anchor somewhere between meeting her at Babby's house and this moment. He was no longer certain of what he should, or would, do.

One short and unremarkable kiss. It should not have attained such a degree of importance.

He moved closer to the fireplace, grateful that Smytheton had lit a small blaze. It gave him something to do, something upon which to concentrate other than her.

Still, he could not help but glance at her. He should not focus on that mouth. Instead, he should banish her from his sight, hie himself to his library and concentrate on the Cyrillic cipher.

How was it that a woman married once should have such an aura of innocence? An almost untouched quality?

Her glance was questioning, her silence an inquisition.

He held out his hand, and even though they were only feet apart, she took one more step closer. He touched her lips with the fingertips of his other hand. They were surprisingly warm. Almost hot.

She said nothing, as if she knew how tenuous was his restraint. He had not thought that touching her would affect him the way it did. He pulled her closer to him again. He leaned down, until he was only an inch away from her mouth.

"This is not a kiss," he said. He placed his fingers beneath her chin, tilted her head up. "Not a kiss," he murmured. His lips moved closer, until they were only a breath away. If she had sighed, their mouths would have touched.

She remained motionless, almost breathless. Until his tongue reached out and touched the sloping curve of her bottom lip. The taste of her. Only that. Her breath hitched then, a gasp of surprise. It might have faded from his consciousness, eased his growing arousal, might have assuaged his curiosity had she not reached out with her own tongue and touched the tip of his.

For a second they were frozen in intimacy, daring and teasing. Testing the very edges of restraint.

It was difficult to hold her so close, and not kiss her. Why had he not done so on the terrace? They might, then, be more familiar in this moment. He might take her upstairs to his chamber and love her in the brightness of an afternoon sun.

Instead, he was held to his honor. To his word. One kiss, that was all, and he would release her.

He pulled back from her, framed her face with his hands. His thumbs stroked across her eyebrows, the warmth and blush of her cheeks. Her eyes fluttered shut, a slight gasp emerged from her parted lips, a pulse beat strong and heavily at her neck as if her heart raced as swiftly and uncontrollably as his.

His fingers threaded through the hair at her temples. Tendrils were coming loose from her careful braid. He found the pins at the nape of her neck, removed one, and let it fall to the floor.

Margaret's eyes opened; her hand flew to her hair. He brushed it aside, pulled the braid from its coil, and draped it over her shoulder. His fingers played with the end of it, all his concentration fixed on one tress.

He wanted the braid loosened, the curls flowing over her shoulders. An improvident wish. He curled his fist around the braid, over and over, until his hand was against her scalp and her head tilted back.

Her gaze was steady on him, her look clear and without guile. She did not ask him to release her, nor charm him with words. She did that too well with silence.

Outside a carriage no doubt passed. The steps of an

adjoining townhouse were being swept, one of London's ubiquitous bells rang. In this room, however, there was only the sound of the fire, the brush of his breath and hers. The moment framed in utter stillness.

His other hand reached up and traced the sweeping line of her throat.

He could smell the scent on her skin. Something light and flowery that reminded him of spring. Her skin was warm, her pulse fast.

He should have argued for more of her. Two kisses. A hundred. More than one. It was an idiotic thing to do, to bring her here. Why had he done so? Because he had wanted more than to simply kiss her. He wanted to take her to his bed. There, the truth.

Once done, it would be over. She would be placed in a carriage and his life would return to normal. He would spend hours on the Cyrillic cipher and not on wondering who she was. He would select his bride and be about his marriage.

Normalcy, something decidedly missing these past weeks.

He reached out and cupped her face. Lowered his head. She closed her eyes. He wished her lips did not tremble. One hand reached behind her neck as if to hold her to him. He lowered his head until his mouth was only an inch from hers, breathed against her lips, priming them for his kiss.

Instead, he traded the kiss for words. "Stay with me," he said.

Her hands gripped his arms. Her eyes flew open. Her breath, heated and rapid, bathed his lips. He wanted to know what she thought, why she looked so panicked at this moment. Yet it was not all fear. She would not hold him so tightly, nor would the blush on her cheek be deepening in color, if it were.

"I cannot," she said tremulously.

"Why not? There is no one to know, Margaret. No one but us."

He was not celibate by nature. It was caution more than inclination that had prevented him from forming a long-term alliance with any woman. Yet there were few alternatives. He'd not the inclination to take advantage of the offers from bored wives, some of whom were married to friends of his. Nor did he use the services of those poor women of the street. Consequently, he had been almost a monk in the past year.

That was the only reason he felt this way.

He should take her to his bed, submerge himself in the femaleness of her. Indulge himself in an afternoon of seduction. And when it was over, he would be himself once again. A man of order, systematic reasoning, detailed logic. Not a beast with but one thought on his mind.

He smoothed his fingers from both shoulders to wrists. Slow, gliding strokes. He wanted to put his hands on her skin, feel the texture of it. Forbidden wishes. He was as far from civility at this moment as he was from rational thought.

Slowly, giving her time to protest, he placed his palms on the front of her spencer. Felt the warmth of her, the pounding beat of her heart. Not unaffected, but still silent. Was she afraid? Or simply willing?

"This garment is too tight for you," he said. "Your breasts feel constrained."

The dress was the same one she'd worn the night he'd met her. At the time he had thought it a costume. Now he recognized it for what it was. An indication if not of penury, then of careful pride. He had not recognized the signs of poverty before, so captivated with the woman. Now he could not ignore it.

She was defenseless, alone in the world. With no relatives. No one to protect her from salacious earls with lust on their minds.

Her silence added to his shame, bringing into sharp relief the inequities of their stations in life. He was a noble who, although necessity dictate he wed an heiress, still possessed an income far in excess of hers. She was a poor widow. Perhaps her silence was fear and the secrets she held in her eyes merely a resigned acceptance of his actions.

He dropped his hands, walked away from her. The fact that he had to force himself to do so was a further indication of the danger of this moment.

"Forgive me," he said, staring into the fire. His booted foot braced on the fender, both hands fisted on the mantel.

"It would be better if you left this room right now," he bit out. Give him a moment to calm. Simply leave, and he would be himself once more.

Margaret stood watching him, her heart beating so loud she felt as if her chest trembled with it. She fingered the button at her neck. Although she had never swooned in her life, at this moment it felt possible.

She had wanted a kiss. Something to put into her storehouse of memories for those times of loneliness. A recollection of an afternoon when she had become scandalous and thoroughly reckless.

Instead, he had placed his hands on her, touched her softly, his fingers imprinted forever on her breasts.

What was she doing? She was both excited and frightened. She wanted to be exactly where she was and far from here. She wanted him to touch her again, train her in wantonness, and teach her desire.

Leave now, Margaret. It is still not too late. The world would condemn you for your foolishness, but you have not yet been labeled whore.

She didn't care. Wasn't that a silly answer? She didn't care. She repeated it again in her mind, realizing that her conscience was silent, muted beneath the wonder she felt. She didn't care. A third time. If Sarah Harrington knew what she was doing, she and her sister would go from house to house condemning her with their whispers. The shopkeepers along Stanton Street, where their small bookshop had been, would be hard pressed to recognize her. Where had proper Margaret gone?

He turned and glanced at her, and she realized that part of what she'd hungered for was being answered in his look. She had never been desired. Not in this way. This feeling was harsh and wild and too compelling to ignore or deny. An awareness of him thrummed through her, a heady feeling as if she'd drunk too much wine.

She knew that what she was contemplating was unwise. But who was to know? No one was here; no one would tell. There was the door. She could walk through it. He had invited her to do so. Almost urged her to take her dignity and her reputation and run from him.

He stood in profile to her. A man still mostly a stranger. Yet how many times had she stared at a painting resembling him, stroked her finger across a muscled back as if to feel the texture of his skin beneath her trembling finger? How many dreams had she had of a man who looked similar to him, and awakened wishing he was real and alive and close to her?

Now he was.

Tomorrow, or next week, or a year from now, she

was not going to cloak this moment in mystique and claim it had been seduction. It was, instead, complicity.

She placed her shawl on the settee, looked in his direction once again.

One kiss? No, more. Much more.

Chapter 10

*A direct and uncomplicated mutual
understanding is a requirement of great passion.*

The Journals of Augustin X

He waited for the sound of her departure. But there was no click of the key in the lock, and the door didn't open. Long moments later he turned and she was still standing there in the same position, her lovely mouth solemn. Her hands were clasped before her, but her chin was firmly tilted up at him.

He was right to think her a country princess. She had the arrogance of a monarch.

Her next action released him from self-condemnation, threw him once again into confusion. She began to open the buttons of her spencer.

His gaze flew to hers, only to trap him in the openness of her look. He felt stunned into admiration for her. She was like no other woman he'd ever known. Direct and demure, shocking yet innocent. Captivating.

He walked to where she stood.

"If you stay, Margaret, I will do more than kiss you. Is that what you want?"

"Yes." A whisper of assent.

"I will love you," he said softly. "With great deliberation and absolutely no hesitation. Is that what you want?"

"Please."

He smiled.

The spencer unfastened, he pushed it off her shoulders. It fell to the floor with a whisper. The sleeves of her dress were puffed, gathered in small tucks on the shoulder, then tight from elbow to wrist.

He heard a stitch rip as he pulled one sleeve down, exposing a shoulder. He wanted to tell her that he would buy her a hundred such dresses. But at the moment, there were other concerns in his mind. The sight of her skin creamy in the sunlight. Smooth to his touch. She shivered where his fingers stroked.

The dress had a rounded neck. From her neck to where the material began, her skin was bare. Anyone might see it. But not anyone would do as he did now.

He bent down and murmured against her skin. "This is not a kiss, Margaret." But his lips pressed in the hollow between her breasts, even as his fingers pulled her bodice lower.

He thanked Providence that she was not an innocent. Or a wife.

The bedroom was too damned far away.

She might change her mind, or convince herself it was not wise, or his own logical thought might come to the forefront. His chamber was simply not an adequate destination.

He led her to the settee. When she sat, he arranged the cushions behind her. He draped her shawl over her shoulders, even as he reached behind her to undo the top button of her dress. She said nothing to his actions, but her eyes widened.

He was seduced by her silence.

He pulled down her bodice just a little. A few inches, no more. Enough so that the rosy edge of her aureole peeped below the material.

He touched her breast with one finger. A slow, exploratory touch. She closed her eyes, kept them shut as he reached into her bodice and gently pulled the material down, exposing her breast. Her nipple puckered, grew tighter in anticipation.

He dusted small kisses over her neck, shoulders, then traced an invisible line to her breast. It seemed acutely sensitive to his touch. His fingers plucked at her nipple, gently elongating it. Then his tongue replaced his fingers, circled it slowly, tenderly. Margaret placed her hand at the back of his head, urged him forward.

A moment later, he opened his lips, the nipple bathed in the heat of his tongue and mouth. He pulled on it strongly, teased her with the barest edge of his teeth. He heard her softly gasp, her hands falling to her sides.

He pulled back, wished there was some way to preserve the picture of her as she sat there. Now was the time to wish for some talent in drawing. He would have sketched her, perhaps rendered her in oils.

She sat on the settee, a virtuous pose in her clean and serviceable cotton. Her hands were clasped tightly together on her lap, her eyes downcast, her gaze fixed on the carpet at her feet. However, her cheeks were stained with color, and her breath was rapid. Afraid? She glanced up at him and he realized he was wrong. The languid expression in her eyes was arousal, passion. Not fear.

Beneath the shawl, one breast lay exposed for his touch, the nipple erect and hard.

He would, if he were a painter of some renown, choose titian for her hair, the subtlest rose high upon her cheeks, a darker green for her eyes. And her lips. A color to match that one exposed nipple. As if nature itself had marked the shade in order to render it the same.

A courtesan, someone a king might treasure. Let alone a lowly earl.

The expression on her face was neither censorious nor embarrassed. Instead, there was stillness to her, as if she waited for him to continue. He wanted to enchant her, beguile her so completely that she would no longer be silent, but as needy as he.

He was so hard that he hurt.

He traced the slope of her breast with his fingers. She shivered. She was so still that he could see the fine tremors on her skin. Placing his hands on her waist, he brought her forward a little, then bent his head. His mouth encompassed the tip of her breast, sucked it tenderly.

Her hands clenched into fists; her breath was exhaled in a sigh.

It had been less than an hour since he'd seen her at Babby's house. In that time he'd given her his word, questioned the fabric of his honor. Promised her a kiss. But now he wanted more.

Her surrender.

He moved closer to her, pulled back the draped shawl. Her face lifted and her gaze turned to him. His eyes were a blaze of blue, his mouth solemn, his face intent. He exposed her breast, tucked the shawl around it. His palm pressed against her nipple gently. His fingers fanned out to encompass her breast even as he watched her. That was the most startling sensation of them all, his intensity. As if he measured her response to him. Approved of her slight sigh, knew and sanctioned the feeling of heat traveling through her body.

He was a master at seduction. It was bright in the room and she had never loved in sunlight before. But it didn't seem to matter.

She felt an aching hollowness inside her. As if it was expanding, obliterating before it all those rules she'd learned about proper behavior, altering her. It was an intriguing feeling, this loss of herself.

A moment later, he leaned forward, reached for the glass bowl of flowers, then snapped off a daffodil, and an early spring rose. He twirled the daffodil slowly against her nipple, the bright yellow color a colorful contrast against her flushed skin. She closed her eyes at the feeling. Exquisite delight.

She had never known that it was possible to feel so much with her breasts, or that her nipples could harden until they almost hurt. When he pulled the flower away, a slight dusting of pollen appeared on her breast.

"If I were an industrious bee," he said, smiling, "I would be thrilled at this discovery."

He reached over and pulled down the other side of her bodice, exposing her other breast, then sucked gently on her. Margaret reached out and placed both hands flat against his hollowed cheeks, held him in place. She felt as if she were swimming in something dark and liquid, heedless and uncaring and maddened by him.

He didn't ask, didn't coax. Nor did he request her permission, or seduce her with words. He simply pulled her from the settee, onto her knees and then to the floor. His hands, eager in anticipation, stroked from shoulder to waist, thigh to ankle, as he undressed her.

His fingers found each separate curve, her inner elbow, the place where shoulder and neck joined. He learned her, the indentation of her navel, the soft, fine hairs on her upper thigh. The line of leg, the curve of an ankle. His fingers teased her, brushed against intimate curls. His longest finger slid between her thighs. She was slippery, her intimate folds gently swollen. Her head turned as his fingers touched her slowly, her soft moan an enticement.

He wanted to gently bite her breasts, stroke her to pleasure with his fingers. And do more. So much more, that it didn't seem fair that there were only hours left to the day. Perhaps he would keep her with him for a week. A month, perhaps, and by the time the days were done, he would understand the woman behind the mystery. All ciphers could be solved, all puzzles could be reduced to their most understandable. People were the same. All it required was a control over emotions, a rational discourse. Logic. Sensibility.

Some other time, perhaps.

He was too fervent, he knew that. His actions were almost those of an uncontrolled youth. Or the acts of a starving man. Before him on the carpet lay his feast, the voluptuousness of her body a lush invitation.

He nearly ripped off his clothes, behavior unlike him. He knelt over her like a predator. But then, he did not feel quite human at this moment.

She looked up at him, her eyes languid, her mouth

a lure. A naked angel's welcome. How odd that he thought of his honor at this moment. Her fingers fluttered on his shoulders, her nails scraped against his skin, and then all thought was lost.

He entered her slowly, the moment almost unendurable, it was so close to ecstasy. He had never before been so aroused, so hard. The sensation was not simply in his loins, but seemed to spread throughout his body. His attention, his logic, his very sensibility had been supplanted by anticipation. At the same time, he wanted to make it last longer. For hours, perhaps. For days.

Her hips rose up to meet him and he almost moaned with the feeling.

He looked down at her. Her head was turned, her profile lovely and sunlit. Her hair lay in disarray upon the patterned carpet, her braid dislodged by passion, not intent. One hand was clenched into a fist and pressed against her mouth. He didn't want her to stifle any sound. He wanted to hear them. Moans and gasps. Pleas and sobs.

His hand played between their bodies, plucked gently at a nipple with his fingers before his mouth replaced it. He withdrew, then entered her again.

Her body tightened around him. An invitation as demanding as her fingers drumming a tattoo on his hips. Her hips rose as she welcomed each of his strokes. Her breath was held tight, then released on a gasp.

Not long enough, damn it. It wasn't going to be long enough.

His breath hitched, the back of his throat closed up, his fists clenched on the floor as he drove into her. Some atavistic, not entirely human response roared through him. He wanted to make her scream in pleasure, sob in his arms.

He held onto the last of his control, determined.

She closed her eyes, pressed her fist against her lips. He wondered if she felt as he did, strung so tight on the edge of pleasure that it was almost pain.

He knew the instant it happened.

Her arms flung out, her body bowed beneath him as if she were a tightly strung string, or supple wood. A sound emerged from between her lips. A plea, a cry, a warning. He felt what she was experiencing. A sudden blindness, deafness to the world. A death, perhaps, to the consciousness that was each of them. Did she feel the same? Michael heard the question in his mind. But then again, it could have been only a thought, lost in the instant before his vision grayed.

Chapter 11

*A courtesan selects her lovers with great skill,
preferring those men with large ears,
an indication of vigor and drive.*

The Journals of Augustin X

What had she'd done? Margaret closed her eyes,
wished herself somewhere else.

He lay beside her on the carpet of the sitting room.
He'd taken her on the floor and she had not noticed
until now, she'd been so desperate in passion.

She was new to this matter of decadence. She'd had
no training in it, no sense of what was right or proper
within the boundaries of this sinful behavior. Should
she tell him that she had never felt this way before?

For a shattering moment, she had been turned inside out, rendered as sparkling as a star. Sent hurtling
to a place she'd never been before, linked to earth
only by his hands and the whisper of his words.

She wondered if the women of the *Journals* had ever
faced such confusion. But then, they had been

courtesans, trained in the way of giving pleasure, counseled in the method of receiving it. Each knew her exact and precise role with all its attendant complexities.

What would one of those women do in a similar circumstance? Praise Montraine for his skill? Confess her bewilderment? What could she say to him?

You frighten me. There, the truth. And one other. *I frighten myself.* He had lured her with a promise, and she had known when he'd given it to her that it was a dangerous attraction. Yet she had come with him all the same, in trembling uncertainty and expectant wonder.

One kiss, that was all she had wanted. Just that, and no more. For all the nights she'd lain awake staring at the ceiling and wondering at the course of her life. A memory, that was all she'd wanted. She should not have wished for something so dear. So dangerous. Margaret knew now that she would recall him for the rest of her life. And this loving? It was burned into her mind.

She turned her head to find him watching her.

His hand reached out and pushed back a damp tendril of her hair. Then one finger softly stroked down her throat to her breasts. His knuckles brushed between them, as if he would brand her there.

But he didn't speak, nor did she, enmeshed in silence and wonder.

A moment later he rose up, and bending his head, touched his lips to hers. He kissed her slowly, as if he savored a delicacy. His lips coaxed hers open, his tongue explored her. An unhurried, almost maddening, kiss.

Finally, he pulled back, smiled down at her upturned face, then stroked his finger softly against the fullness of her bottom lip.

"I was right to think your mouth made for kissing," he said teasingly.

She closed her eyes, reached up and slowly cupped the back of his neck with her hand. *Unwise, Margaret.* But she wanted another kiss. She brought him down to her, felt his lips touch hers. Again. Once more. More.

"Kissing you last was wiser, I think," he said long moments later. "I would never have been content with one."

In her mind she answered him. *Neither would I.*

She sat up, watched him even as she began to assemble her clothing. He did the same, dressing quickly. The silence between them was awkward and telling. It forced them back into their proscribed roles as nothing else could have.

He stood and walked to the hearth, watching the fire. She glanced at him, thinking that he was as engrossed in his study of it as she was of him. She wondered if he commanded it to burn brightly, and the fire simply fell beneath his will. Indeed, he might be able to decree that the wind blow and the sun shine. Stand upon the headland and dictate to the sea. Mystical thoughts for a woman versed in practicality.

Words did not seem to be allowed in this almost secret room. As if the spilling of one would let loose a torrent of thousands. Perhaps it was better if they remained silent. Michael wanted no recriminations, no tearful confessions, no wishes to turn back the clock.

He stared at the fire, his attention on the woman behind him. Each rustle of material was furnished a mental image by his mind. A curious bit of imagination that had been dormant until now.

What had he done?

Acted entirely unlike himself, for one. Taken a woman on the floor in the morning room, for another. Used little finesse. He had been like a callow boy with his first woman. Eager to impress, but more intent upon his own pleasure.

At least that was not one sin not on his doorstep. If she had not fainted from pleasure, she had come close to it. He turned his head and looked at her. She sat on the settee, her cheeks still flushed. Her hands stilled in the act of donning her cotton stockings. She made no move, however, to cover herself.

He hardened in unrepentant response. He wanted to remove the shift she'd donned, and take her dress off again, stroke her exquisitely sensitive breasts, kiss her until she fainted from it.

And if that wasn't enough of a dangerous thought, he wanted to know what she was thinking at the moment. What caused that small smile on her lips? Embarrassment? Or acknowledgment of this silent stretch of moments between them?

It wasn't wise to solicit her thoughts. Doing so would reveal too much of his inner nature, betray the curiosity that refused to remain quiescent even now. He had already surrendered a certain measure of vulnerability to her in his reaction.

An apology might be in order. He had been too hurried. Too feverish. Was it wise, however, to admit to such a thing? The uncertainty he felt was an irritant. But then, he had never before been in this circumstance.

He turned away, concentrated on the fire again. She was going to be impossible to forget.

In a matter of months he was going to give up his autonomy, his privacy in order to recoup a fortune that would not be in ruins save for the selfishness of others. Keeping Margaret with him would soften having the marriage foisted upon him.

The thought brought him up short.

A mistress? He'd never thought to have one. But then, he'd never thought to love a woman on the floor of his morning room, either.

He turned to her, the words voiced before he knew he was going to speak them. "Stay with me."

She looked surprised. As well she might be. His behavior since he'd seen her at Babby's house had not been entirely normal. Decidedly irrational.

She stood and came to him, turned her back, an artless and silent request as she held up her hair and bared the nape of her neck to him. A smile curved his lips as he buttoned her dress. He placed a small, almost discreet, kiss there before he finished his task.

She turned and raised her hand to his face. Her palm felt cool, her eyes lambent. There was something in her expression, some emotion he could not decipher. Perhaps she was adrift in the same bewilderment he felt, albeit stripped of its annoyance.

"No," she said.

He felt a spurt of irritation at her easy refusal.

"I've no mistress," he said. Nor a wish for one until now.

She looked away, began to braid her hair.

"Will you consider the post?" he asked, deliberately smoothing his face of all expression. He would show neither his eagerness nor his annoyance.

"You make it sound as proper as a governess," she said. "But I regret that I cannot comply. I was not raised to be a mistress, however my actions indicate it."

"You might come to like me, Margaret Esterly."

"No doubt I would," she effortlessly agreed. "But no."

"My visits to you would be scheduled. They would not be oppressive. I have patterns in my life. Restraint. I am normally not ruled by my loins."

"But you are by your obstinacy?"

"I don't know what you mean," he said, annoyed.

"You should be seeking your wife, Montraine. Not a mistress."

She rebuked him with a soft smile.

"You would never have to worry," he said stiffly. How stern he looked standing there, frowning at her. Autocratic and insistent. Yet this was the same man who had loved her so passionately only a few moments ago.

"No," she said, slipping her feet into her shoes. In that one word she put all her revulsion for the role. But the fact that he had offered it to her neither offended her nor was a surprise.

He was an earl and the nobility often acted with arrogance. That very attitude was an indication of the chasm that stretched between them.

"Do you regret this afternoon, Margaret?"

She glanced at him, smiled ruefully. "No," she said, "but perhaps I should." A truth for him, and a warning for herself. She finished braiding her hair, then stood.

"You really are leaving, aren't you?" He looked surprised.

She turned and smiled gently at him. "Why should I stay? So that we might argue about this further? We cannot be friends and we must not be lovers."

She walked to the door, turned, and glanced at him. One more look for her memories.

He'd not donned his jacket, but stood there attired in shirt and trousers, his feet bare, his hair disheveled. His face was carefully expressionless, but his eyes were filled with irritation. Or was it regret? If so, she felt the same. Not that this afternoon had happened, but that it must end here. Now.

A wise and sane voice, kept muted beneath desire thrust up into her confusion, chided her. *Leave, Margaret. Before he stretches out his hand and you take it. Before he asks again and you agree.*

She turned and left him.

Chapter 12

*A courtesan who experiences pleasure at the
giving of it excels in the art of love.*

The Journals of Augustin X

"Montraine, I'm so pleased you could attend!" His hostess, Lady Dunston, smiled
brightly up at him.

He stared at the crowd of people milling through
the house. He'd forced himself to this gathering for
one purpose alone, that of singling out his bride. By
summer's end he had to be married. An explicit
enough goal.

"We've some delightful entertainments planned,"
Lady Dunston said. "I do hope one of your sisters will
honor us and play. Such beautiful young ladies."

"Yes, it is warm," he said, distracted. "It's the time
of year for it, however, and to be expected."

Leticia Enright was to be present tonight. In addition, Arianne Mosely had told Charlotte that she
would be in attendance. If they did not suit as bridal

candidates, then Jane Hestly certainly did. Then, all this hesitation about picking a bride would be over.

"Oh, but I was talking of your sisters, my lord. Such talented young ladies."

He frowned down at the woman standing beside him, unwilling to admit that he had not paid any attention to her comments. She was fluttering her fan at him as if it were eyelashes. Women had a habit of doing that. He had no control over his appearance, but the content of his mind was his to choose. However, most females did not seem to care a flying farthing what he thought. Their main interest in him appeared to be how he looked in his blacks.

"Do you not think so, my lord?"

Only one woman of his acquaintance had ever questioned him, challenged his conclusions. Margaret, again. She had an insidious way of slipping into his thoughts.

Get out of my mind. It had been long enough. She should have vanished like a vapor before now. Instead, Margaret Esterly was proving to be a recalcitrant phantom.

"I beg your pardon," he said, attempting to be sociable. "I was distracted by the number of guests."

"We are quite overflowing," she said happily, tapping him with her fan. "Almost no one declined."

"Indeed," he said, forcing a smile to his face.

She said something else, but his attention was captured by a woman on the opposite side of the room. Her hair was auburn, her laugh intriguing. He narrowed his eyes and stared across the room, motionless. It couldn't be her. She lived in the country. The woman turned, revealing a pleasant enough face. But not, however, Margaret's. The disappointment he felt was unwarranted and unwelcome.

He had respected her wish for privacy and some degree of anonymity, evidenced by her fleeing from him that day. He had followed her, intent upon offering up his carriage for her use, but she had disappeared. From that day forward he had not attempted to find her.

His thoughts, however, were another matter.

His morning rides were filled with images of Margaret's remarkable smile. A mouth that almost begged to be kissed. Even his morning boxing matches had been marked by a curious distraction of thought. So much so that he'd almost been leveled twice.

If he believed in Fate, he might well countenance the idea that she had been delivered to him as a test of sorts. *Do you believe in logic, Michael? Then here is a woman who will be in your mind incessantly. Discover logic in that. Order, Michael? Her incursion into your life will bring only chaos. You will stop your work too often and think of her, wonder where she went, who she truly is. Or, if those fascinations are not enough, here is one more. Why can't you forget her?*

She declined to be his mistress, but she did quite well as a wraith, refusing to leave his thoughts even at the most inopportune moment.

His hostess looked affronted, folded up her fan, and muttered an excuse to leave him. He stared after her, wondering what it was he'd said.

For the last month he'd been unable to focus his thoughts on the Cyrillic cipher or his financial difficulties. He insisted upon quiet while he worked. But the cacophony that prevented him from concentrating now was that of his own thoughts. Snippets of memory flashed into his mind like sparks. He remembered her smile, the curve of her lips. The sweep of her lashes against her cheek, her mouth. Michael stared at his hand. Even now he could recall how her skin felt, as if the memory of her resided in his fingertips.

"Enjoying the party, Montraine?" He turned and nodded to an acquaintance. What the devil was the man's name?

"Warm evening, isn't it?" he asked, but before the man answered, he'd moved on.

He found himself repeating every word he'd spoken to her. Every nuance of speech, every inflection was examined in close detail. What had convinced her not to take advantage of his offer? *We can never be friends and we must not be lovers.* It had been a sensible notion to make Margaret his mistress. It simply possessed order. She would be a part of his life. He would pass a portion of his week with her. Grow to know her. He would provide for her and she, in turn, would . . . his thoughts halted as he stopped. What was happening to him? It was the very worst thing he could do. She occupied too much of his mind, too deep a corner of his concentration.

Someone spoke to him and he raised a hand in greeting, smiled.

He glanced over the assembled crowd. People were seating themselves in the drawing room. A few of the female guests had been prevailed upon to play before dinner. His sister, Charlotte, had begged off, to his immense relief. Elizabeth, the only one of his sisters with any musical ability at all, had slipped from the room a few moments earlier. She disliked these amusements as much as he.

Unfortunately, he was trapped by good manners and the fact that he had already been noticed. He smiled at Leticia Enright, among the first to agree to perform.

She sat, hands poised above the keys, and sent him

a particularly lovely smile. Moments later, Michael wished he'd been able to follow Elizabeth's example. What Leticia was doing to Mozart should not be visited upon Satan himself. She came to a particularly difficult passage, sent the audience an apologetic glance as her fingers fumbled on the keys, then simply skipped over the rest of it.

He frowned at the ceiling. A giant disk carved of plaster accentuated the baroque chandelier that emerged from it. A centerpiece for his attention.

Did Margaret play? He closed his eyes, not to mute out the sound of Leticia's music as much as to blank out thoughts of the Widow Esterly.

When Leticia was roundly applauded, he suspected that it was due more to the fact that she had finished playing than out of any appreciation for her talent.

He stood and approached her.

"I ruined it, did I not?" Her voice quivered and her fingers trembled as she gathered up the sheet music. She studied the piano, the carpet, the candles, the flower arrangement. Anything but him.

"It is a difficult passage," he said, attempting to put her at ease.

She nodded jerkily, gripped the music to her bosom, and stood before him as if she expected punishment for her poor rendition.

"My sisters could not have done better," he said.

She blinked back tears. "But you sat there the whole time and *frowned* at me."

"My sisters tell me I do that often," he said, finding it odd that he should have to apologize for his facial gestures. What people construed as ferocity was more often than not absorption. He was simply thinking out a puzzle.

She gulped back a sob and nodded, then walked from the room so swiftly that it was almost a run. He stared after her. Did he frighten her that much? If she was so fearful now, what would she be like if they wed?

The image of Leticia Enright cowering in his bed, sobbing through her days, was enough to strike her from his list.

I will love you. With great deliberation and absolutely no hesitation. Is that what you wish?

Please.

Bloody hell. Not now!

He went to speak with his hostess. At his request, she raised one brow, haughty in her pique.

"I am trusting you with my difficulty," he said with a conciliatory smile.

She unbent enough to glance at him speculatively. "A bridal candidate, Montraine?" she asked.

Any other time, he would have demurred from answering. But his inattention had annoyed her and he'd bridges to mend.

"Very well," she said. "I will seat Arianne Mosely next to you."

He smiled his thanks, knowing that before morning, word of his intentions toward the woman would be common knowledge.

Gradually the assembled company moved into the dining room and Michael made his way to his place. Arianne Mosely sat delicately against the back of the chair, her right hand toying with the silverware while her gaze focused on the elaborate centerpiece.

She was a very agreeable young woman he'd met at Babby's house. He remembered her as kind, exceptionally pleasant, graced with an agreeable nature.

When the first course was removed, Arianne leaned toward him. "Too spicy, don't you think?"

He smiled and sipped his wine.

After taking two bites of fish in white sauce, she frowned and lay her fork against the plate. "The sauce tastes too much of flour," she said, her voice too loud for such a critical remark.

The breaded oysters, sweetbreads, and peas were all treated to the same derision. Everything within sight or hearing was subjected to her remonstrations. Michael began to count her complaints.

"Lady Dunston is too old to be wearing pearls. They are a young woman's adornment."

"That gown is not appropriate to a matron of her years."

"Whoever suggested those absurd-looking flowers for a dinner table?"

"The candles must have drippings in them. They sputter too much."

"I would sack any servant as slow as her footmen."

"Those girls are laughing entirely too loudly."

Her observations, while issued in an agreeable voice and meant, he was certain, to sound witty, managed only to be petty. Michael intensely disliked people whose character thrived on the disparagement of others.

Nor did she seem to notice that two of his sisters were in the group of women she criticized, a fact she laughed off when he pointed it out to her. And she did not appear to care that his mother was a friend of their hostess and had advised her on the decorations. However irritating his relatives, they were his and not to be subjected to criticism by other people.

"Thank heavens this dreadful meal is over," Arianne said.

He seconded the thought and erased her from his shortened list of wifely candidates.

There was only one woman left. Miss Jane Hestly was of an agreeable nature and seemed ideally suited to be a wife. She barely spoke above a whisper and if she had a few grating mannerisms, Michael reasoned, then so did he.

An hour later in the ballroom, he decided. He would settle on her, then. Get over this idiotic fixation about Margaret Esterly. He would forget her. Completely. Absolutely. An admonition he'd already given himself for a month. How much longer until he believed it?

"Please do not fix any more studied looks upon Jane Hestly," Elizabeth said, coming up to him. She frowned at him and pursed her lips. A unique experience, to be chastised by his youngest sister.

He raised one brow.

"You object to her?"

The look she sent him was part commiseration, part irritation.

"She is such a prig, Michael. She speaks in that nasally tone all day long. It's enough to make the hairs on the back of my neck stand up. Everything, positively everything, she says is in Latin. Then, just when you're ready to announce that you don't understand, she gives you that patronizing look. As if she thinks you're some sort of imbecile for not speaking Latin. As if anyone does," Elizabeth said, frowning at him. "Then, she utters that perfectly horrid giggle that's meant to sound sweet and apologetic, but resembles a pig's snort, instead."

He grinned at her, amused.

"You're perfectly handsome, Michael. Surely there are other women better suited." Elizabeth looked suddenly shamefaced. "Do not tell me that you have some fondness for her. Is that why you're considering her? I could understand it if you did. We cannot always choose whom to love."

This wisdom set him aback. Because of the affection he felt for her, and because she looked at him with such hope in her eyes, he almost lied. He did not wish to disabuse her of the notions she held dear.

"No," he said, "I do not love her. I choose to live my life not with an excess of emotion, Elizabeth, but with organization and logic."

For the longest time, his youngest sister simply looked at him.

"Perhaps you and Jane will suit each other well, after all." Elizabeth smiled at him—pityingly, he thought. "And I thought *I* was lonely sometimes," she said, and left him.

He stared after her.

Love was not necessary in most society marriages. In fact, it was a decided disadvantage. Love was what young girls felt for their kittens. What boys felt for their dogs. It rarely existed between husband and wife. And when it existed between a man and woman it was demanding. And destructive.

His father had taught him that.

"Quite a success, your sister." Michael turned his head. Babby stood there, looking uncomfortably corseted and tucked into his blacks. "In fact, all your sisters seemed to be doing extraordinarily well this season," he said.

"My mother will be pleased," Michael said wryly.

The Countess of Montraine did not hesitate to let it be known that she had great things in mind for her daughters, regardless of what any of them wished for themselves.

He wondered what Elizabeth truly wanted in life. A certain security, certainly. Love? Evidently, from the nature of Elizabeth's comments.

Would Margaret feel the same? Or would she be more realistic because she'd been married before? How odd that the thought of her husband grated on his nerves.

The two men stood together, looking out over the assembled dancers.

There was only one thing to do to end this. Find Margaret.

"How is your new secretary working out?" he asked.

"Man's got the most decided way about him. Almost frightens me. Wouldn't be at all surprised if he organizes the linen presses next," Babby said.

"Has he been able to make sense of your correspondence yet?"

"Finished cataloging the library. He's got a great respect for my collections. Says it's one of the finest he's ever seen."

Michael restrained his irritation. Babby never got to the point by a direct line. It was more often than not a circuitous journey.

"He's working on my files now. Oh," he said, suddenly smiling at Michael, "you want that letter. I'll see if I can't hurry him up a bit."

"Merely a thought," Michael said blandly, wondering if he was successful at hiding his impatience.

"Am I at least going to get the second *Journal* out of it? If you recall, I was supposed to have purchased it the last time."

Michael nodded. An oversight. The last thing he

had been concerned about was Babby's purchase of an erotic book.

Babby smiled knowingly. "An attractive woman, as I recall," he said.

Michael only smiled.

Chapter 13

*Loving in the energy of the rising sun brings
about stamina and a balance of energy.*

The Journals of Augustin X

Margaret closed the cottage door quietly. Penelope looked up, smiled a welcome, and returned to her cooking.

She'd been walking this afternoon. Thinking, too. She'd not come to any answer for the greatest of her questions, but she had decided to tell Penelope.

Margaret looked around the cottage. Here she had grieved for Jerome, and finally found acceptance. Within these four walls she'd felt loneliness, too, learning to live with the fact that her future stretched out in an unending fashion for the rest of her life. But it seemed she had been granted another future. Not loneliness, but joy.

"I'm with child," Margaret said quietly.

Penelope turned, wide-eyed, from the cookfire. The spoon she was using to stir the stew dangled from her fingers. At least, Margaret thought wryly, they had chicken in their meals lately. The problem was that she could not bear the aroma.

"You're with child," Penelope repeated dully.

Margaret sighed, feeling as if she hung on the edge of a cliff. Perched somewhere between disaster and exhilaration.

"I've been ill five mornings in a row," she said. "And in the afternoons as well." She sat heavily on a chair.

"I thought it strange, but . . ."

"You'd no reason to think I had lain with a man?" Penelope nodded.

"I have," Margaret said. There, a confession. "I met him when I sold the books."

"Yesterday you almost fainted," Penelope said.

"Yes, not the first time I felt that way," Margaret said. She'd heard enough talk among her London friends to know the signs of breeding. But the greatest one was last week when Penelope had lain on her cot, holding a heated brick wrapped in toweling to her stomach, cursing women's fate and the plague that visited them once a month. Except, of course, that she had been exempt this month. And would for many more to come.

"You're with child." Penelope repeated incredulously once more. The spoon wavered in the air.

"In all those years I was married to Jerome, I never bore him a child," Margaret said, her voice faint. It was the strangest thing, but she could not seem to understand it fully yet. She was not barren, after all.

"One of the women in the village says that it is the rooster, not the hen, who is to blame if there are no eggs," Penelope said.

Her comment startled a laugh from Margaret.

"What will you do?" Penelope asked.

Margaret smiled. "Become a mother," she said.

"The villagers will talk, you know," Penelope said worriedly.

Margaret nodded. "Yes, they will," she said. One of her greatest concerns. Her child would be labeled a bastard for her actions, and it was the one thing that disturbed her in this sudden and unexpected joy. But how did she prevent it? That question remained unanswered.

"Will you let him know?" Penelope asked. "The man, I mean?" Her voice was tentative, the question one Margaret had asked herself enough times.

Should she tell Michael of their child? What would he do if she sent word to him? She did not doubt that he would wish to support her, make her his mistress. Doing so would label their child, just as Jerome had been. He had been deeply ashamed of his illegitimacy.

She placed her hand on her waist. Even now, her child grew inside her. She must find a way to protect him from scandal, a cruel world, and even his mother's foolishness.

"No," she said, answering Penelope finally. "There is no need to tell him."

"What say you, Duke?" the Earl of Babidge said. "A fine acquisition, is it not?"

The Duke of Tarrant nodded. It was remarkably warm in Babidge's library, but he felt ice coat his backbone.

He held the book he thought destroyed in his hands. One of three he'd received seven years ago.

He remembered even now the pride he'd felt. The government had not comprehended the enormity of its mistake. He alone had understood what the Empire would suffer if things were left as they were.

"Good God, Babby, where did you find such a thing?" A masculine laugh over his shoulder startled Tarrant. He turned and frowned at the man before lowering the book to the table. Perhaps it was a copy. They had shared a number of jests about the type of books they'd used. Certain to inspire interest, but those who read it would never think to look for anything deeper.

He opened the book to the middle, thumbed through it with fingers that trembled despite his resolve, noted the faint marks. It was the same.

He opened the front cover of the book and saw the newly inscribed name. *Jerome Esterly, Bookseller*. His finger trailed over Jerome's flowing script as he mastered his rage. His bastard brother had always had a tradesman's cleverness. Or a thief's.

"Are you willing to sell it?" he asked, turning to the Earl of Babidge. The man was a bumbling fool. An inveterate gossip. The worst person in the world to be in possession of this book. What if someone noticed the marks?

"I haven't read the thing through yet," Babidge said, grinning at him.

Tarrant reluctantly surrendered the book to the man waiting beside him. An after-dinner entertainment, the viewing of Babby's newest acquisition. How many people had already seen it?

Tarrant moved closer to his host. "Have you had it long, Babidge?" he asked.

"A few weeks only," Babidge said.

"A most fascinating acquisition," Tarrant said, forcing a smile to his face. "Where did you get it?"

Babidge's face seemed to close up, his interest in the glass in his hand intent. "A delightful woman sold it to me. I intended to buy the second book from her as well, but the sale was interrupted," he said with a smile. "She's caught the fancy of a friend of mine."

"A woman?"

Even as he asked, he knew. There was only one person who could have had access to the *Journals*. Margaret. The shopgirl his bastard brother had married. The woman with the insolent eyes.

It was only a matter of time until someone discovered the link between them. Or that the books were his.

Tarrant turned away, his mind racing. A man's recitation of one of the passages in the book incited a great deal of laughter. The book was more than simply risqué. It was so much more than that.

He could be hanged because of it.

There was a heritage to protect. His own. A lineage to continue. One of proud men and prized accomplishments. He did not regret his actions seven years ago. He would do the same again if such an opportunity were placed before him.

History would judge him well, even as his contemporaries would not understand. Those with narrow minds and the vision to match would not conceive of his original intent.

But the *Journals of Augustin X* must not be allowed to surface. Not now. Not ever.

"What on earth could Michael be thinking of? Jane Hestly? He can't be serious. She's got a fortune, all right, but she also has protruding teeth and that ghastly whiny voice. Not to mention that nose of hers."

The Countess of Montraine looked irritated.

The sitting room in the Hawthornes' London home was a cheerful place to be. Decorated in bright yellow with green accents, it spoke of springtime on even the dreariest of days. Today, however, the atmosphere was most definitely not sunny, Elizabeth Hawthorne thought. Not as long as her mother was in a mood.

"He's found the plainest girl in England." Her mother frowned at Elizabeth. "My grandchildren will be unpresentable."

"I believe that he simply wants it done and over."

"Oh, mother, he cannot get married now! That will spoil all our plans. All the balls will be in her honor. It isn't fair, truly it isn't," Charlotte whined.

"If he doesn't wed soon, you won't have a dowry, Charlotte. It will be used to support Setton," Elizabeth said—a bit of truth that horrified Charlotte into silence. "Besides, you're only eighteen. It isn't as if you're going to be left on the shelf."

"Well, I'm nineteen and I do not care if my dowry is spent upon a new roof," Ada said. "Marriage is but an enslavement of women."

"There will be no talk of a Hawthorne woman on the shelf," the countess said, with a frown at Elizabeth. "You shall all procure wonderful husbands. Viscounts, at the very least. Earls, however, are preferred."

"There cannot be that many, surely," Ada said.

"I have deduced that there are well over two hundred," her mother said, eyes narrowed. "There are, however, only twenty dukes."

"We need an emancipator for Ada and a blind man for Charlotte. That way he can free Ada from her imagined slavery and Charlotte can be assured of eternal devotion," Elizabeth said, smiling.

"You are quite horrid, Elizabeth. Simply because you will probably remain forever a spinster does not mean *we* shall be." Charlotte frowned at her, but only fleetingly, in order not to mar her features permanently.

"Your sister is not at all doomed. Elizabeth is only seventeen. The one thing she needs to do is curtail her opinions. Of which she has many," her mother said, sending an irritated look at her youngest daughter. "It is quite off-putting, my dear."

Elizabeth smiled at her mother's pronouncement. She'd heard the same criticism every day of her life.

She used her scissors to cut a dangling thread, and then replaced them in her embroidery chest. In truth, the embroidery was a way of keeping her thoughts restrained. She did wish her sisters and mother were different, people she might truly enjoy. She loved them, but before an hour was out, they had irritated her so deeply she felt like screaming.

Charlotte looked at her, apprehension furrowing her brow briefly. "He wouldn't truly offer for her, would he? Oh, how horrible it would be to have an ugly sister-in-law! One could never talk about gowns or admiring glances or anything female."

"I think it would be refreshing to have an ugly relative," Ada said. "That way, the men would not concentrate so on a woman's appearance, but more on thoughts. Thoughts are a mind's path to greatness."

Elizabeth rolled her eyes.

"Besides, she is an intellectual, Mother," Ada said. "She would be a welcome addition to the family. I quite like her."

"You would," Charlotte said. "You've studied Latin."

"It is a shame that a woman must marry at all," Ada said. "But perhaps our brother can be convinced to be a fair husband."

Elizabeth sighed. Ada was forever going on about

the unfairness of women's plight. Elizabeth doubted, however, that her oldest sister truly felt that way. Ada espoused different causes with the same frequency with which she changed her frock.

"I shall talk to him about this Hestly woman," the countess declared.

"You know how he gets when he's working, Mother," Elizabeth warned. A bit of caution. Michael did not like to be disturbed.

"He would not allow me to address him on the plight of the Bedlam women the other day," Ada said.

"You have a tendency to go on and on about your causes, Ada," Elizabeth said. She glanced over at Charlotte. "And your giggling gives him a headache."

"That is not at all the way to speak to your sisters, Elizabeth."

She nodded. It did not do to argue with her mother. Not only because Elizabeth was unlikely to win any such match, but because the countess did not like to be challenged.

Michael had ascended to the earldom at the age of fourteen. Barely more than a child. He'd been left three estates, none of them prosperous, a dwindling fortune, and the responsibility of all of them. It was not an inexpensive proposition to launch three girls into the Marriage Mart all at once, but Michael had never said a word about the cost.

The only significant change he'd made, once he'd ascended to his majority, was to establish his own residence. Not for privacy, she suspected, than the fact that the cacophony of this house made it impossible for him to work.

"Is it true," Elizabeth asked, "that the Kittridges are planning a huge event next week?"

Her mother frowned at her. "It does not signify."

"The Kittridge ball will be huge," Charlotte said plaintively.

"I understand that the theme is ancient Rome," Elizabeth said. For the first time, Ada looked interested.

"How do you know such things?" Charlotte asked.

"I listen," Elizabeth said simply.

"Women should talk," Ada said, frowning. "Instead of remaining meek. Otherwise, men believe them to be devoid of the capacity to do so."

Elizabeth rolled her eyes again.

Babby's new secretary had forwarded Margaret's letter to him yesterday. Michael had studied it so intently that he knew each detail of it. A copperplate signature, a studied hand. In that, Margaret was more adept than his sisters. Her a's and o's looked too much alike, a slight imperfection that he nonetheless found intriguing.

It was a businesslike letter, one that searched out intent.

I have been led to believe you might be interested in a volume in my possession.

Her address was listed in the care of a Mr. Samuel Plodgett.

A further mystery. A puzzle. An undeniable temptation to a man who solved ciphers. That's what he told himself as he stood in front of the address she listed, holding her letter in his hand. As if he could not bear to place it in his desk, but must carry it about with him.

He surrendered to his inquisitive nature with some irritation. He should be working on the Cyrillic cipher, his mathematical engine, sending letters to his stewards. If nothing else, he should be penning a note to Jane Hestly. A necessary task, one of matrimonial pursuit. *It is my sincere wish that we might meet again.* A dance of words to warn her that he was embarking upon a serious mission, that of marriage.

Instead, he stood in front of a draper's shop, frowning.

He opened the door and was immediately greeted by a friendly voice, one that belonged, evidently, to the shopkeeper. A round-faced man with a bright smile came forward from the back of the room.

The shop was crowded, evidently prosperous. Several women eyed him over bolts of cloth. It had not escaped his notice that he was the only man among the customers.

"How may I assist you, sir?"

"Are you Samuel Plodgett?" he said.

"I am, sir. How may I be of service to you?" He rubbed his hands and smiled expectantly.

"I wish to find Margaret Esterly."

"I want that book," Tarrant said, addressing the window. He didn't bother to look behind him. He could see the reflection of his servant in the darkened glass. Night had fallen over London, obscuring the scene before him, darkening his own mood.

"Your Grace?" There was surprise in the other man's tone. It was unusual for Peter to show any emotion at all. It almost interested him.

"The Earl of Babidge is in possession of a book, Peter. The first volume of the *Journals of Augustin X.*"

The silence was telling.

He turned, his smile thin lipped. "I see you remember them. It seems they weren't destroyed after all,

Peter." He took a deep breath, attempted to quell his rage. "The earl has it, and you must acquire it again," he said. "By whatever means necessary."

A bow. A nod of agreement.

"When you have completed that task, I have another for you. As important, if not more so. I want you to find Margaret Esterly. Quickly, Peter. Do whatever you have to in order to convince her to surrender the other two books to you."

There was a message implicit in his directions. By Peter's small smile, it was evident that the other man had captured his meaning clearly enough.

Had she sold the other two books? He felt a spurt of fear, then rage that she should dare to do this to him.

Chapter 14

*A woman's whisper is more powerful
than a shout.*

The Journals of Augustin X

Margaret stood within the Standing Stones, listening to the silence. She'd dismissed her students and remained behind, feeling like a penitent in this place of awe and wonder. A warm breeze blew against her cheek, teasing the tendrils of hair at the nape of her neck and temples, pressing the skirt of her dress against her legs.

Between the stones she could see the valley below, her small cottage and her closest neighbor, Malverne House. It was there that Tom, Penelope's husband, worked, in the home occupied by Squire Tippett and his family. The squire raised terriers and was an occasional sight on the Downs, the dogs nipping at his heels. Beyond Malverne House was Tom's small cottage that he shared with his new bride and his mother. Further still was Silbury Village. A small and intimate place viewed from so high a vantage point.

She knew, finally, what she was going to do. The answer had come to her a few moments ago. She would remain in the cottage for another month or two. After that, and before people in the village were aware of her condition, she would move away. She would find another village, pretend that Jerome was recently deceased, and this child born after his father's death. A poignant tale rather than a shocking one. In this way she would protect her child from her folly.

The decision to leave her students had not been an easy one, but there was one child who needed her more than the girls of Silbury Village. Her own.

She descended the hill and began to slowly walk back to the cottage. A rabbit amused her by sitting on the path and twitching its nose at her. Almost as if he chided her for her preoccupation. There were flowers in the lane, a bit of delft and yellow. She bent down and plucked one, twirled it on its stem, thinking of another yellow flower in a London sitting room. She closed her eyes, feeling herself warm.

Only to open them to find him standing there.

Montraine.

She almost fainted with the shock.

Was she a witch? Had she summoned him to her with the power of her thoughts? She felt rooted to the spot.

He stood beside a carriage in front of her cottage. Silent, motionless, staring at her as if he had all the time in the world to do so. He was dressed in buckskin trousers with a linen shirt laundered to a bright white and topped with a stock. A waistcoat of midnight blue covered it, and over that a double-breasted coat to match. There was not a crease on him. Nothing to indicate that he'd traveled any distance at all.

Had he married? The question brought with it the usual regret. Not that she had spent an afternoon with him. Nor even that she carried his child. But that he was not an easy man to forget.

She walked slowly toward him, managed a smile. "Should I ask why you've sought me out? Or even how?" She marveled at the fact that she was able to speak.

"It required a bribe," he said tightly.

A surprising response. But it seemed that he was not going to elaborate upon it.

"Why are you here, Montraine?" she asked carefully. "To ask me to be your mistress again?"

"You would do better than this place," he said, looking around him.

"It is not the equal of your London home, I agree," she said. "But it suits me well enough."

She approached the door, fitted her thumb in the latch. Would a closed door act as a deterrent to him? She had the distinct impression that it would have no affect on him at all.

"I could provide you a better place to live, Margaret," he said.

She turned and faced him.

"I do not wish to be your mistress, Montraine. Why did you think I would accept? Because I had acted the part? Perhaps once, but not again."

"Why not?"

An autocratic question. One that startled her in its baldness. "Why not? Because I was not raised to be a whore."

"A harsh word, Margaret. *Companion* is better."

"You can call an onion a flower, Montraine, but it does not make it so," she said, amused.

There was a small smile on his face now, reminis-

cent of another time. It made her wish to press her
fingers against his mouth, to chide him for his words.
Instead, she focused on the sight beyond him, on the
pattern the wind made in the grass. On the sky. The
leaden gray clouds had been moved aside by a brisk
wind, and a patch of light blue peeped through. A bit
of optimism.

He reached out, brushed a tendril of her hair back
from her cheek. She moved away from his touch.
"There are certain benefits to being my mistress," he
said.

"There are more benefits to living here," she said.

"Would it do to regale you with a list of advantages
I could provide?"

He took one step closer. A lesson she should have
learned earlier, perhaps. Michael Hawthorne was not
a man easily stopped. Or stayed in the course of any
action he chose.

"No doubt you would offer me a house," she said,
burying her trembling hands in the folds of her skirt.
"A coach? A wardrobe, no doubt. Perhaps even a
crate or two of books for those times when I am
bored? To while away the hours when you are with
your wife? What else will you give me?"

"I would give you me, Margaret. Does that not
count for anything?"

Too much a temptation. After Jerome died, it had
been two years until a man had touched her. But these
weeks since she'd lain with Montraine seemed somehow even longer.

"Can you not find a willing woman in London?"

"I am more entertained, evidently," he said testily,
"by chasing after one particular female."

She glanced away, feeling an unwise amusement at
his pique.

"I would have thought you busy selecting a wife."

"My entire list of candidates has been rejected for one reason or another. I am left with one, but I cannot summon the enthusiasm for it."

A statement that had her looking at him again.

"I pity the woman who bores you so much that you cannot even ask for her hand in marriage."

His smile was too charming. She looked away again.

"I will not be your mistress. No matter how convincing your argument."

"Then will you accept a bargain between us?"

"What sort of bargain, Montraine?" A wickedness, to feel such curiosity now.

"A week," he said surprisingly. "A week of your life."

"In exchange for what?"

"An end to this," he said harshly. His mood changed suddenly. As if a summer storm had blown across his smile. Or perhaps his agreeable nature had been a ruse, and he'd been angry all this time. With her?

"Even my work has suffered, Margaret. Instead, my concentration is fixed on the memory of a woman who let me love her in sunlight."

She felt her cheeks warm.

"Give me a week, and at the end of it, I shall never disturb you again. Your life will be yours to live."

"As it is now," she said.

He shook his head. "No," he said. "I've not yet had my fill of you."

The remark was so utterly overbearing that for a moment she didn't know how to respond to it.

Finally she found her voice. "Don't you realize that even widows are not exempt from scandal?" she said angrily. "Even living in a country village, I have a reputation to protect. It's why I used Samuel to forward my mail, and why I was so careful to keep my name withheld when I wrote about the *Journals*."

"Except for one day when you forgot yourself, Margaret."

Her breath caught. "How utterly uncivil of you, Montraine."

"To mention that day, or to speak the truth? I'm remarkably tenacious, Margaret." There was that agreeableness again, but it was balanced by the sharp look in his eyes and the tightness of his smile.

"It sounds not unlike another bargain," she said, her cheeks flaming. One kiss. A simple kiss that had led to an afternoon filled with sorcery.

"I did not break that agreement, Margaret. I let you go."

True enough. She had spent a restless night at Samuel's house, anticipating Montraine's arrival any moment. But he had not come and she'd gradually accepted that he had not followed her.

It was safer never to be in his company again. Not only because the chance of her surrender was too great—the afternoon in London had proven that. But also because she was more lonely now than she could ever remember being. Penelope was newly wed; the cottage seemed empty and echoing.

"I want you in my bed." A frank admission. One that did not please him to utter, from the look on his face. One brow rose sardonically, yet his gaze was shuttered.

"We cannot always have what we desire," she said wryly. "Sometimes we must accept what we're given."

"Fate?"

"Why not?"

"Perhaps what we call Fate is no more than choice. If a man races a horse across a cobbled road, the horse will eventually lose a shoe. Fate? Or the rider's choice?"

"Exactly what point are we debating, Montraine?" Should she feel so amused?

"You being in my bed," he answered. "The result of a choice, not fate."

"I believe I have already chosen."

"Unwisely, as it happens," he said huskily.

"Are you that arrogant by nature? Or are nobles trained in such behavior from the cradle?"

"I merely state the obvious," he said. "Come with me, Margaret. One week."

"I remember being cajoled in a similar fashion about a kiss, Montraine."

"I will not do anything to you that you do not wish, Margaret," he said carefully.

Oh, but that was the problem, wasn't it? She wanted it all.

"And when it's over, you'll leave me alone?"

"Only if you want it."

Did he think that she would be convinced to stay with him after their week?

Yes.

Here they were again with another bargain. Except, of course, this meeting was fraught with so much more. The secret she held from him. Conjoined memories of an afternoon that evidently neither of them could forget. His words heated her. If she was so susceptible to his words, what would a touch bring? Instant surrender. An answer that came too quickly to be false.

A week of kisses. A week of fascination. In the end,

it was too much. Too much danger. Too much attraction. She might well succumb to his role for her, but her child deserved more than a fool for a mother.

"Say yes, Margaret."

"No," she said, and turned to open the door.

"Why did I think that's exactly what you were going to say?"

His tone was amused. But she'd no chance to wonder at it. Before she could open the door, he had picked her up and was striding away from the cottage. Even his coachman seemed enlivened by the scene, for he smiled broadly when he saw Michael approach the carriage with her in his arms.

"Montraine!" She scowled at him, but he didn't even look at her.

She grabbed at his cravat. He kept walking. She pulled harder. He halted, glanced down at her.

"Are you trying to throttle me?" His grip tightened as he looked down at her, then away, a wickedly sensual smile dancing on his lips.

"If it will make you put me down."

"I will, as soon as we reach the carriage."

"You cannot abduct me!"

"I seem to be doing so," he said reasonably, resuming his progression toward the carriage.

"Montraine," she demanded, "put me down!"

"Certainly," he said. "Once we are inside."

He reached the carriage, shifted her in his arms, and opened the door. She placed her feet on the steps and ducked beneath his arm. He calmly pulled her inside the carriage, ignoring her struggles to get free. He merely sat with her on his lap, her arms trapped by his.

"Surely you are not so desperate that you are forced to abduct women," she said, scowling at him.

"I seem to have this odd compulsion about one particular widow."

"Has no one ever denied you?"

"Do you think this a sign of self-imposed indulgence?" He didn't look at all pleased. She had the thought again that his surface affability hid a deeper anger. But it was not, oddly enough, directed toward her. Almost as if he was irritated at himself.

She herself had felt the same warring emotions. Passion versus prudence. She stared straight ahead, determined not to soften toward him.

He picked up his walking stick from where it was propped in the corner, tapped on the roof of the carriage with the end of it, then dropped it again. All without releasing her.

She frowned at him. He smiled in response, studied her in the dim light of the carriage. "I was wrong. My memory of you did not serve you well."

She wasn't quite sure whether she was being insulted or complimented. The former would fan her irritation; she had no reason whatsoever to wish for the latter.

"You are much lovelier than I remember."

It would be better, perhaps, not to feel a surge of warmth at his words.

"Are you going to send me that fulminating stare the entire journey?"

"I see no reason to feel amiable about you at the moment," she said. "This is not wise, Montraine."

"You are no doubt correct, Margaret."

"Then why are you doing it?"

"I believe it's the only way I can remove you from my mind. You've been a constant visitor there."

"I have no effect on your thoughts, Montraine."

"On the contrary, you seem to have a great deal to do with them."

She focused her concentration upon the floor of the carriage. She didn't even have her gloves. Or her bonnet. He, on the other hand, looked sartorially perfect.

A difficult man to forget. But then, she had not truly tried.

"What do you want from me, Montraine?"

"An understanding," he said.

He stroked one finger down her bare arm, from elbow to wrist. Her dress was a summer frock, green cotton with short sleeves. She looked down at his hand, then at the expression on his face. His attention was to the inner curve of her elbow, then the slow movement of his finger along her skin.

"Montraine." Her voice was softer, her tone inquisitive rather than admonitory.

"I remember you sitting in the sunlight, your beautiful breasts bared for me. You trembled when I touched you." He glanced over at her, smiled softly.

How could he do this to her?

"Shall I tell you how many times I've walked into that room? Smytheton looks at me oddly, as if he knows I've lost my senses. But the room has a ghost now. A woman who sits quiet and demure with naked breasts, their nipples wet from my kisses."

She closed her eyes.

He'd released his grip on her arms, but she still sat motionless on his lap. She was trapped by words, instead.

"I've thought of you ever since you left me. You make me smile, Margaret, and think of things I've never considered before. You have an aura of mystery about you. I found myself wondering how you spend your days, where you live, why you seem so innocent and yet not. I find myself thinking that if I can only kiss you again, this fascination will ease."

"But you don't want just a kiss," she said breathlessly.

"No," he softly said.

He reached out and turned her chin. His hand moved to the back of her head, urged her forward one inch at a time.

She stared into his eyes as she came closer, then let her lids flutter shut.

His mouth was hot, the kiss soft and alluring, coaxing her lips open. Once more. Once more and that was all. She would be satisfied never to touch him again.

Liar.

His kiss became the stuff of her dreams. Deeper. Openly carnal, impatient. His tongue invaded her mouth. He gripped her chin with one hand while the other pressed against the back of her head, held her steady.

He broke the kiss long enough to murmur against her lips. Soft words that sent a bolt of heat through her. "A week of kisses, Margaret." His mouth descended on hers again, stripping her of breath and inclination.

She had vowed not to think of the shape of a man's shoulders, or how it felt to have her breasts touched. Or the deep emptiness inside her. She had lain awake at night with closed eyes, clenched hands and forced herself to think calming thoughts.

It had not worked. Instead, she had imagined feeling just this way again.

Her hands wound around his neck, stroking the hair curling softly at the nape of his neck.

She should pull back, say something to him that would caution him, urge him to remember the restraint he claimed was part of his nature. Instead, her hands fumbled on his shoulders, kneading them.

He cupped her cloth-covered breast, strummed his thumb over a suddenly erect nipple. "Like a little stone," he said silkily.

Heat pooled in her body, warmed her cheeks. Quickly summoned desire. She was a true wanton, then.

He kissed her again. Her hair had been left unbound this morning. He gripped handfuls of it, pulled her closer still. His palms were hot against her temples, her cheeks.

Again. Another kiss. And another. Her hands pulled him closer, a sound emerged from her throat. A plea, a moan. A sigh of surrender.

They kissed the entire way past Silbury Village. When he finally pulled back, she sank weakly against his chest.

"A week," he said, his voice deep, almost harsh.

A week of him. Surely a week would be safe. A week to last her for the rest of her life. When that week was over, she would commence her plans.

A voice filled her mind, one that sounded like her Gran's. A stern tone, one that chided her. *Margaret, do not be a foolish girl.* But she was very much afraid that she was.

"I want to love you again," he murmured against her ear. Gently, he bit on the lobe. "Don't you remember how it was with us?"

Excitement rippled through her. How could she forget?

"When it's over will you let me go?" she asked on a sigh, eyes closed. Her cheek pressed against his chest; she heard the pounding of his heart beneath her ear.

Unwise, Margaret. Foolish girl.

"Yes," he bit out, brushing his chin against her temple. "Kiss me."

A command. A decree. A summons.

How could she deny him? Or herself?

He pressed both hands on either side of her head, slanted his mouth over hers, inhaling her breath and her will. Her fingers gripped his wrists, then slipped behind his neck to hold him in place.

Montraine. A name. Or an enchantment.

Long moments later, his hands slid to her back. She fell forward, rested her cheek on the cradle of her arms. His breathing was as harsh as hers.

"Just a kiss," he said, sounding stunned.

Should she be feeling so amused? Not simply that, but pleased that he felt as lost as she. Prideful that she could render him as needy.

Now, *that* must truly be a sin.

He made no pretense of subtlety as his hand slipped beneath her skirt, traveled up until he reached her stocking top. Above it, her skin was bare, and his fingers played there, stroking softly, intrusively upward until he found her, damp and swollen.

"You're ready for me," he said, a note of surprise in his voice.

She nodded against her folded arms. She felt as if the air was thick around her, that time itself slowed in its execution, each second having a full measure of beats. His fingers explored her intimately in a rhythm of arousal. His palm pressed against her, his thumb rotating slowly.

"Now," he said. "I have to be in you now."

"Yes," she said, the word uttered through lips that felt oddly numb.

She should be shocked at being loved in a carriage.

Horrified at it. But all she could feel was that time was too slow, and he must end this. Now. Not in a bed, or on a floor. But in this moment. Later would be time enough to be horrified at her actions.

A moment, a second, an eternity later, he freed himself, lifted her, spread her legs. She sank down on him, a gasp escaping her. Her body welcomed him, molded itself to him, an invasion of the senses as well as the body. She felt a flush travel from her toes to the top of her head, carrying with it an almost unbearable tingling sensation. Her breasts peaked almost painfully.

She fumbled with his cravat, pulled the neckcloth off, baring his throat so that she could kiss him there. Touch her tongue to his skin, inhale his scent. Her face was buried against his neck, her eyes clenched shut. Her body urged her mind's silence as he raised and lowered her.

What was she doing? Now, please now. Paradoxical thoughts. Or cautions and wishes, entwined.

Her face was hot, her lips heated against his skin. Even her breath was warm as if there was a furnace inside her. Molten coals.

He leaned back against the carriage seat, spread out both arms until his hands braced against the walls. Her knees were on either side of him, her arms wound around his neck, her cheek pressed against his, eyes closed. He lifted one booted foot, then another to the other seat, deepening his penetration.

The sensation was exquisite. Delight and an almost pained wonder. Her breath came harshly, her body urged completion, while her mind demanded that she end this. *Be proper and wise and Margaret.*

He gripped her by her waist, raised, then slowly lowered her over him. Over and over until the sheer joy of the feeling was simply more than she could bear.

Suddenly she was there. Not in a carriage all along the road. But in another place where her body splintered and shattered and the sound she made was close to a moan or a prayer. And his oaths, rough and heartfelt, accompanied her on the journey.

Michael couldn't believe he had done it. He had taken a woman in a carriage. He, Michael Hawthorne, irritatingly known as the Code Master, Earl of Montraine, had just swived a woman in a carriage.

And done a remarkably good job at it.

Margaret slumped against him, her breath short and fast. If her heartbeat was anything like his, it was a wonder they hadn't both succumbed to apoplexy.

He stared over her shoulder at the opposite side of the carriage as if witnessing the man he had become. How much of an idiot was he?

Not a rhetorical question at all, he thought wryly. His hand pressed against her back, held her against him. He had lost his senses. Forgot where he was, who he was. A few kisses and he had been maddened. No. More than that. The fact that he could not quite describe what had come over him concerned him.

Margaret sat up finally, brushed the tendrils of hair back from her face. She wouldn't meet his eyes. It was just as well; he doubted he could meet hers. He helped her arrange herself, straighten her skirts, move back to the other seat. Their fingers met, then their gaze, and both separated quickly.

She fascinated him, an interest normally reserved for the most complex of ciphers. Perhaps it was because she posed the most difficult puzzle he'd ever been given. She amused him; she irritated him; she disturbed him. This craving for her had translated into behavior he would never have ascribed to himself. One look at her and he was a randy goat.

He didn't feel the lassitude he normally did following lovemaking. But then, he had never engaged in the act in a traveling carriage. He wondered if his coachman knew what had transpired.

He was going to keep his hands off her, he vowed. Ration himself. He would see her only once a day. Become used to her the way he'd learned to drink brandy. A sip here and there before imbibing the entire snifter.

The next time would occur in the bed. A nice, soft bed with clean sheets. He would impress her with his skill. He closed his eyes. Bloody hell. He'd taken her once on the floor and once in a carriage. At this point, she probably didn't think he possessed any skill at all.

"Are we going to London?" she asked. Her attention had been directed to the scenery for the last quarter hour. There was nothing much to see other than a flattened landscape and a few verdant hills. However, it seemed to serve as a fascinating diversion for her. Somewhere to rest her gaze other than in his direction.

He nodded, studying her as if his memory had somehow faded in the weeks since he'd seen her. Her cheeks bloomed with the faintest shade of pink as if striving to match her lips. Her auburn hair gleamed with highlights and her eyes were green today. Not a bright hue, but a subdued one.

What was it about her that fascinated him? Her perfume? He didn't think she wore any. The way she wore her hair? Today it was loose, curling down and over her shoulders. Even now it seemed to entice him to spear his hands through it, find all the separate gold and red colors.

When he'd seen her stop along the path and pluck a flower, he'd found himself enchanted all over again. The sun had touched her hair as if it had found the one thing of beauty and delicacy there in that poor place.

What kind of woman made him smile, feel an overpowering lust, then made him wish to guard her in the next breath?

Had he shamed her? It had not been his intent. But then, he'd not known he would become a rutting beast with a kiss. Perhaps if he did not kiss her the next time, he might retain a little sense.

A week with Margaret was perhaps too much. It would be wiser to return her to her cottage in a day or so. Or three. Very well, a week. But only that.

After this week, he would concentrate on the Cyrillic cipher. What time was left would be devoted to his mathematical engine. Perhaps if he buried himself in the problems associated with gears and levers and metal tolerances, he would become himself once more.

She sat in the corner of the carriage and clasped her hands together so that he would not see that she trembled. Arousal or its aftermath?

He had felt her shatter in his arms, her internal muscles clenching him so tight that the pleasure had been intense. Mindless. Yet they sat together now as if such abandon had embarrassed them.

Twice now they had reacted the same way. Perhaps she was not unlike him, unused to being lost so completely in pleasure.

He moved, restless. He was not a man, however intense his study of puzzles and codes and ciphers, who was familiar with self-reflection. He knew who he was, what his duties were, what his responsibilities were. They defined him. They did not allow for any doubt or self-questioning.

Yet every time he was with her he found himself doing exactly that. Becoming someone else, acting in a manner that was unlike himself.

He had no experience whatsoever in postcoital moments in a carriage. Although he doubted that he should be feeling so damn smug.

Chapter 15

*A woman who would know her body
must first know her mind.*

The Journals of Augustin X

When the carriage stopped and they alighted
from it, she looked about her, recognized his
house. They mounted the stairs together, neither
speaking. The door opened and Smytheton appeared,
perfectly attired despite the lateness of the hour.

Margaret smiled at him. He seemed taken aback at
the gesture. He nodded in return, frowned at Michael.

"Get to bed, Smytheton. It's late."

"My lord, if I may be of service?"

"Only if you retire for the night," Michael said.

Smytheton looked at him disapprovingly. Margaret
wondered if Smytheton was aware of what had transpired in the carriage. Was that why Michael was being chided with a glance? They stared at each other,
majordomo and earl. Smytheton finally bowed

slightly, left the foyer, and went to his room, his lone candle lighting the way.

Margaret stood silent as Michael lit a branch of candles, walked beside him up the steps. At the second floor, they followed a corridor to a set of double doors.

Margaret had the strange thought that it was a gate through which she must pass. What lay on the other side?

Any protest against his abduction of her had been adequately silenced by her behavior in the carriage. She had been wild for him.

The room was furnished with a large armoire, two candlestands, and a set of wooden steps that led up to a wide bed draped in an ivory counterpane. A fireplace dominated one wall, its elaborately chiseled mantel of marble a subtle indication of wealth.

She moved to the end of the bed, curved her hand around one of the thickly carved mahogany posts, turned, and glanced to where he still stood. Even after traveling so long he barely looked mussed. Wrinkles would cringe before Michael Hawthorne.

Should she be in awe of him? An indication of his power, perhaps, that the thought entered her mind. Or a sign of her stubbornness that she refused to be quelled by him. It was, after all, not the man she had to fear. But the way he could make her feel. Her own nature was at fault, not his.

"I was wrong again," he said. "I thought you lovely in the sunlight. But candlelight suits you more."

A compliment, to bridge the silence between them. She offered him a comment in return. Perhaps conversation might ease the memory of their abandon.

"My Gran used to say that beauty was overrated. That what counted was a person's character, not his appearance. But then, she was old when I was born, and her beauty had long since faded."

"Did she raise you?" he asked.

She nodded. "My parents died of influenza when I was just a child, and she was my only relative." She sat on the end of the bed, her hand still curved around the post.

"An only child, then. I might have bequeathed you my sisters. I wished often enough to be rid of them."

She smoothed her left hand over the counterpane.

"How many siblings do you have?" she asked.

"Three sisters. No brothers, and a mother."

He leaned against the door, indolent, effortlessly handsome. She should not be so transfixed by the sight of him.

"What would you read?" he asked.

At her questioning look, he continued. "Earlier," he said. "When you asked if I would send you a box of books to while away your time. What would you choose?"

"Something about Rome," she said. It was evident he had not expected her answer. Had he thought she wished to read only novels? "Or India," she said. "One of the *Journals* takes place there, and it seems an altogether exotic locale."

She had thought, once, that it might be a wondrous thing to see the world. To feel the sea wind on her cheek, and spy mountains that scraped the sky. Or travel a river filled with white-flecked eddies. Perhaps stand, awestruck, at the base of a waterfall and witness the rainbow in the mist.

Other people had seen such things, and written about them with words that had speared her heart. Each sentence had driven inside to the deepest part of her and tied itself to her longing, made her wish to be more than herself.

But her world had narrowed, her wishes and wants more elemental. When would the drought end? Who would buy the *Journals*? How would she protect her child? The world was, somehow, not as important as that last question.

"I'll show you my library, then," he said. "Perhaps you can find a volume there to please you."

She smiled. They were so utterly polite. Hours earlier they had clawed at each other. She felt her cheeks warm.

"I can arrange for a bath, if you like," he said. A surprising offer.

She had never wished to live among the nobility. She could not remember having a single thought of envy for their large houses and their well-sprung carriages. But at the moment, the thought of a bath was almost enough to make her wish herself a duchess. It was a luxury in her small cottage, one she granted herself as often as she could. But it meant endless trips to the well and hours heating the water.

She nodded. "I would like that," she said.

He left the room then. It felt as if the air changed, became less charged. Her imagination.

She leaned against the post, closed her eyes. Perhaps it would have been better for her to choose sleep instead. An effect of her condition, perhaps, that she was tired so often.

But she stood, walked around the room, found herself in front of the armoire. She pressed her hand against the door, wondered what she would find inside if she was so ill mannered to invade his privacy. His shirts, perhaps, carefully folded? A selection of cravats, perfectly shined boots?

What was she doing here? She was indulging in a whim. A reverie. A sorcerer's dream. She was his apprentice in this flight of fancy.

It would be wiser to be gone from here. She could go to her friends, the Plodgetts. She would borrow the coach fare from Samuel. He and Maude would talk to her of commonplace things. The three of them would recall days in which she was wise and solemn and had her wits about her.

Her eyes closed, she breathed in the scent in this room. Something that smelled of herbs and woods. And Montraine.

A tap on the door and it opened. She whirled, feeling awkward that he'd caught her acting besotted in front of his wardrobe.

"It seems that today is the maid's half-day off," he said, smiling slightly. "I believe, however, that we can manage."

He led her out of the room and down the stairs, through the foyer and a series of corridors until they reached the kitchen.

The room was a cheery place. A well-scrubbed wooden plank table stretched the length of the space. Cupboards and shelves painted white lined the walls and were filled with cooking implements. The windowsill was laden with red pots of green herbs. There, in front of a newly fueled fire, sat a copper bath half filled with water.

A large, black cauldron of water sat simmering in the corner of the kitchen fire. Michael poured the boiling water into a smaller bucket, then into the bath.

"Can I help?" she asked, standing there with hands clasped before her.

"Do you doubt my ability, Margaret?"

"Not at all," she said. "You seem quite competent at the task."

He grinned, an expression that she'd not seen before. A bit of boyishness peeping out from beneath the role of earl.

"The truth of the matter is that I'd prefer not to wake Smytheton again," he confessed. "Besides, I'm not incompetent."

"Is it customary to have such a forbidding butler?"

"It's not customary to have Smytheton at all," he said wryly. "Most major domos work their way up from the ranks, beginning at the post of footman. Smytheton has only been in my employ these last seven years. He served with Wellington. With distinction, I understand. I could not turn him away when he applied for the post. But I never knew that he would hold me in such disdain." He poured another bucket of boiling water into the tub.

"Does he truly?"

Glancing over at her, he smiled. "I have the feeling at times that he has taken on the role of father protector."

"He does not approve of my being here," she said. She had not missed the look the butler had given Michael the first time she'd come to his home. Nor on this occasion.

"It suits him to feel superior. I regularly perform in ways that give him that opportunity."

"Have you done this before?"

"Prepared a bath?"

She smiled. "No, brought a woman here."

He straightened. "No," he said simply, and returned to the fire.

The silence was not uncomfortable, but it seemed filled with comments better left unsaid.

She looked around the kitchen. The ceiling was decorated with cherubs in the corners. Small, impudent, smiling, they seemed to look down at them in inquisitiveness.

"Are the cherubs another oddity of the builder?" she asked.

His glance followed hers. "This part of the house was originally public rooms. I had it changed to make it easier for the staff. But I had the workers leave the cherubs intact."

"They no doubt annoy Smytheton."

He grinned again. "No doubt."

He filled the bucket with hot water again.

"It's a great deal of bother," she said watching him pour it into the bath.

His sleeves were rolled up to the elbows, his shirt dotted with water. A lock of hair had fallen over his brow. He appeared intent on this chore and she could not help but wonder if he approached everything with such single-minded directness. As if he focused his entire energy on each separate task to the exclusion of everything else.

She warmed, thinking that he had been the same during their lovemaking in the carriage. He had been as fevered as she and as lost to their surroundings.

"Have you changed your mind, then?" he asked, turning.

"I would not dare to," she said, smiling. "Not after all your efforts on my behalf. I simply meant to express my appreciation."

"Enough to let me stay and watch you bathe?" One side of his mouth curved. A thoroughly charming expression of mischief.

"Is that what mistresses do?"

"A companion," he corrected, his smile slipping. "My companion."

"No," she said, admonishing him with a look. An answer to both questions. One asked, one hidden.

She turned away, reached behind her, and began to unfasten the buttons of her dress.

She heard a hollow sound as the empty bucket was placed on the floor, then felt his hands releasing the rest of her buttons. She turned her head and glanced at him, holding the bodice of her dress close to her chest.

He stepped back and dropped his hands, caught in the same silence that enveloped her.

Margaret felt exposed, and absurdly vulnerable. She had bared her body to this man in the bright light of a spring day, loved him in a rocking carriage. Yet she had not felt as naked then as she did at this moment. It was as if he could see all of her insecurities, and worries and knew how they battled with her pride.

"I will be in my library if you need any assistance," he said, his eyes suddenly filled with a stormy intensity.

Margaret nodded, said nothing to him as he left the room. She removed the rest of her clothing, folding it carefully and placing it on the small table beside the door.

The tub rose high in the back, where it was heavily embossed with roses and daisies, then sloped to a blunt point at the foot. Almost like slipping into a shoe, she thought with a smile, as she stepped inside it.

She sighed in bliss as she sank down into the hot water. A stool beside the tub was piled high with toweling. Atop it, a small container that she picked up and opened to reveal a soap fragrant with herbs. It reminded her of Michael. An intimacy, to bathe herself with his scent. But then, she had crossed the boundaries of proper behavior so many times since she'd met him that she would be hard pressed to find the line now.

It was not wise to admit to infatuation. It was most assuredly not sensible to admit that he occupied too much of her mind. She could easily admire him. There were many things to commend him. The fact that he so obviously respected his surly butler. There was his humor, and his tenacity, his way of looking at the world as if he'd dared it to interfere with his plans. Coupled with a self-reliance she had not often seen among nobles.

She smiled at herself. The only other acquaintance she had with nobility was the Duke of Tarrant, a man she could never admire.

She placed her hands on her waist wondering how long it would be before there were signs that she was with child. If she had not decided to leave Silbury, this week would ruin her, scandalize the villagers, label her a whore. Carrying the Earl of Montraine's child would render her a pariah to all those people who spoke so approvingly of her subdued demeanor and proper ways.

She didn't feel the least proper now.

A week. Let it be too short a time to become captivated by him. Let her leave here in a week and return to herself.

She leaned her head against the back of the tub, closed her eyes. It sounded almost like a prayer.

He stood in the doorway, watching her. She was asleep, the washing cloth bunched into a ball between her hands. The candlelight flickered over her face, dancing over the hollows created by cheekbones and long lashes. Firelight tinted the room yellow, summoned forth the red and gold highlights in her hair.

He was lax in his knowledge of Greek and Roman mythology, but surely there was a goddess appropriately similar? A being with the light of humor in her eyes, who disappeared in springtime to become a fawn, perhaps. Or emerged in summer adorned in leaves of gold. Someone with a nature as changeable as the seasons and as eternal as womanhood itself.

If so, her name should be something commonplace, to counterbalance the fascination of her character. Margaret, perhaps.

He smiled at his whimsy. He had come to see what was delaying her only to become adrift in thoughts of myth and Margaret.

"I am only grateful Smytheton has gone to bed," he said, retrieving the toweling from the table. "Otherwise, you might give the poor man a heart seizure."

She blinked open her eyes, watched him even as her lips curved in welcome. Her expression was quickly overlaid with one of more caution, but not before he'd felt the full effect of that warm and tender smile.

Her eyes, those lovely eyes that seemed to change hue depending upon what she wore, were now simply hazel. Tired, with a look to them that solicited his concern.

He unfolded the toweling, held it out for her.

She crossed her arms over her breasts. He smiled at the evidence of her modesty. She had been as fervent as he this morning in the carriage. And that one afternoon nearly two months ago when they'd loved on the carpet in a room a few feet from here. But now she hid herself from his sight.

"The water's cold," he said, finally, when it was obvious she was not going to stand. "I shall avert my eyes if you wish," he offered.

"Please."

He smiled, but turned his head to the side. He heard the sound of the water, glimpsed a view of her fire-lit silhouette out of the corner of his eye.

He wrapped the toweling around her, stroked his hands over her arms, chiding her with a look. Retrieving the candle, he handed it to her, then bent and scooped her up into his arms.

"It is not necessary for you to carry me," she said. He said nothing in response.

"I shall not run away," she promised.

"You are cold."

"But not infirm," she said.

"You are not that much of a burden, Margaret."

His left hand was pressed against her shoulder, while his right curved against her bare thigh. But that was not what incited his sudden foul humor. It was his erection, hard and joyous at the feel of her. As if he'd been celibate for a decade.

What was happening to him?

She looked up into his face, then glanced away.

At the top of the stairs, he lowered her before a long table. "If you put the candle on the table," he said, "you can open the door."

"If you'd set me on my feet, I could do so more easily."

"Just do it, Margaret," he said tersely.

She placed the candle on the table, then reached out and obediently turned the handle of the door. He pushed it open with his foot and entered the room.

Watery light streamed into the chamber, touching upon the four-poster bed, filtering in through the opened curtains. A bower of moonlight.

He set her on her feet beside the bed, then walked to the hearth and knelt before it.

He had taken her from the cottage without giving her a chance to pack a valise. Not an entirely reasoned move. But he vowed to buy her what she needed. Clothes, most definitely. Either that, or keep her in his chamber for the next week, slake his lust, bury his tumescence where it most longed to be. He turned and glanced at her.

She yawned. Just that. A simple gesture, but one that tempered his mindless hunger even as it grew.

He stood, walked to the armoire, and retrieved his dressing gown. He returned to her side, placed it on her shoulders, helped her arms into it. The garment was silk, only marginally thicker than the thin toweling she wore now. But it fostered the illusion of cover. He tied the belt around her waist, smoothed the lapel, found himself staring at the curves his dressing gown now boasted.

He tugged at the toweling and she allowed it to drop to the floor. He retrieved it and threw it on a nearby chair.

"It will be something for you to sleep in," he said. He himself preferred nakedness to the cumbersome nightshirts fashion dictated.

"Thank you," she said, her voice soft and tremulous. Her look held no condemnation. It was simply as if she had accepted her circumstances and had decided to endure them for as long as it lasted.

He wanted ask her, suddenly, if that was how she accepted what life gave to her. Poverty, loneliness, the grief of losing her husband.

Yet this woman with her quiet dignity and her small smile was not his captive. There was nothing truly binding them together but the will to be bound. At least for a week.

She yawned again, hiding the gesture behind a raised hand. A surge of tenderness, coupled with lust, surged through him. An altogether uncomfortable pairing of emotions.

"Get some sleep, Margaret," he said, kissing her softly on the forehead. An almost avuncular gesture. Hardly a way to treat a woman he wished to make his mistress.

He left her then, before he could change his mind.

Margaret awoke at dawn, feeling as if she'd slept upon a cloud. The mattress was soft and fragrant with herbs and the scent of lemons. She turned her head and he was there beside her, asleep.

A curious feeling, waking beside a man again. Especially one who looked like Michael Hawthorne.

She propped herself up on one elbow and studied him.

His face was oddly commanding even in sleep, as if his features, proud and strong, needed no animation. A smile, however, normally warmed that line on the side of his mouth, created a dimple from it. A look in his eyes made his brows appear less fierce. His habit of brushing his hands through his hair contained that one unruly lock on his forehead.

He lay on his back, one arm flung above his head, the other resting at his waist. His legs were splayed wide so that he took up most of the bed. The sheets bunched on his upper thighs revealed a well-defined chest, muscular arms, both furred with black hair. A thoroughly imposing man.

Had she been captivated by him because of his appearance? Or because of her own loneliness? Or had she simply been angry about the future decreed her and it had spilled over into defiance? Was that the reason she had gone with him that first day?

And this week? What was the answer for that?

He had not come to her last night. She didn't know quite what to make of that. She lay down on her side, watching him sleep, feeling remarkably content to do so.

Her stomach was blissfully steady, she was pleasantly sleepy, and the dawn sky over London was a reminder that her country hours could well be ignored for this week. She stretched out her hand until her fingers almost touched him.

Sleep came and brushed a smile over her lips.

Chapter 16

*A woman of pleasure
will praise her lover often.*

The Journals of Augustin X

When she awoke again, Michael had left her. But on the end of her bed were the clothes she'd left in the kitchen, now cleaned and pressed. She dressed and went in search of him.

"I believe, miss," Smytheton said at the bottom of the stairs, "that you will find his lordship in his library." A curt nod was his only direction. "The morning room has been cleared for your modiste," he added, a severe frown settling over his face.

"I am not properly a miss anymore," she said, clasping her hands together. Why she should care what he thought of her, she didn't know. But it seemed somehow important that he realize she had not totally ruined herself. "I am a widow, you see. And I know nothing of a modiste."

He bowed slightly. "His lordship has sent for one, madam."

She crossed the foyer to the library door, watching as Smytheton glided into the shadows. Michael's voice answered her knock and she pushed open the door.

She had thought the rotunda magnificent. But it was nothing to this chamber, as a taste of sugar is lacking when compared to a cream-filled pastry.

The library was easily four times the size of her cottage. It soared two floors, the upper story reached by curving iron stairs at either end of the room. Mahogany bookcases filled with volumes lined both the lower and the upper levels. Arranged in front of a fire were a settee and two chairs. A perfect place to curl up and read.

But the greatest wonder was above her. She tilted her head back, surveyed the painting.

She had heard of cathedrals built to revere God and palaces designed to ennoble men. Places that would inspire awe and a sense of reverence. But she'd not thought to feel such emotions in a man's library.

No shelf had ever lain empty in their bookshop, and they'd had orders from all over England. Still, there were more volumes here than their shop had ever carried at one time or perhaps altogether.

"Your eyes are as wide as moons, Margaret."

She glanced at him. He sat at his desk watching her.

"It's a wondrous place. And a very large room."

"The house has only one bedchamber because of it," he said. "The others were sacrificed in order to enlarge the library."

"I have never seen so many books," she confessed. "Have you read all these?" Her fingers brushed against the spines of the volumes as she passed from one bookcase to another. He had diverse interests. There were topics ranging from ancient civilizations to animal husbandry.

"A majority of them," he conceded. "I read quickly."

"Is that what occupies you in this room?"

He seemed to measure the words in his mind before he spoke them.

"I primarily do ciphers here."

"Ciphers?"

"Puzzles. Codes, if you will. I unravel secrets that other people do not want read."

The knowledge surprised her. It seemed alien to the nature of the man he had shown himself to be. But then, he had remarked on more than one occasion that he was restrained. Orderly. Wished to live by a certain structure. But the Montraine she knew had always been a volatile mix of impatience and passion.

"Why ciphers?" she asked.

"The easiest explanation is because they need to be solved. But it's not the only answer. I'm intensely competitive," he said, an admission made with a mocking smile. As if he gave her the truth and ridiculed it at the same time. "A deplorable facet of my character," he said. "I hate to be bested by anything."

"Is that why you found me? Because you did not like to be bested?"

"You were a puzzle," he conceded with a smile. "A fascinating one."

She thought about it for a moment. "So, this week is to allow you time to reason me out?"

"I doubt you would be that quickly solved," he admitted, his smile surprising her. "Even though I'm exceptionally good at puzzles."

Her look must have been questioning, because he

continued. "There's something orderly about them. Numbers have a purpose, a reasoning, a pattern."

"Are you working on a cipher now? Other than me," she added.

"Right at the moment I'm involved with overseeing the mundane details that occur on a weekly basis."

"What mundane details does an earl oversee?"

He smiled, his expression lightening. "Do you truly wish to know?"

"Very much so," she said truthfully.

"I read and approve the accounts of three stewards, assess the inventory of three estates, give orders to plant, harvest, or lay fallow acreage. There are forty-three people whose lives are entwined with Montraine interests here and abroad. I approve their salaries and their employment and adjudicate grievances when they occur. There is the upkeep of foreign investments, there are horses to be purchased, buildings to be maintained. Not to mention paying the not inconsiderable bills for my sisters and mother."

"Three estates?" she asked, surprised.

"Setton, the largest, which is entailed. Haversham, which was brought into the family by my mother. And Torrent, which is a smaller farm on the border. It sounds a great deal more than it is."

"Yet you still have time to do ciphers?" she asked in amazement.

"I confess I recited all that to impress you," he said, looking not at all like a man who needed to resort to braggadocio. "I handle a little of it each day. That way it's manageable."

"Order, again."

"I have always believed it to be of some value," he said.

She walked slowly to a table in the corner. On it

was an odd device that looked to be nothing more than bits of twisted black metal.

She turned and he was there beside her. "A mathematical engine," he said. "An invention of mine."

"What does it do?"

"It will not harm you," he said with a smile. She glanced at him. "You look very cautious of it."

"I've never seen anything quite like it before."

"That's because there isn't anything like it," he said, smiling. He reached past her and turned a large crank. All the various parts began to move in harmony, wheels rotating and clicking. Finally, a rectangle of slate flipped onto a small metal bed.

"What does it do?" she asked, spellbound.

"It writes ciphers," he said proudly. "But I believe it can do much more."

"I can see why you have not yet selected a wife," she said. "Courtship would take too much time from your work. Perhaps you can simply abduct a bride."

"Have I truly abducted you, Margaret?" he asked softly from behind her.

Instead of answering, she walked away from him, concentrated on the contents of another bookcase.

"Smytheton says that the sitting room has been cleared for the modiste. What modiste?" she asked, staring at a title in a language she did not know.

"Don't women like clothes? My sisters have always given me that impression," he said, following her.

"I won't be here that long, Michael," she said, glancing at him. She knew full well how much time it took to sew a dress. "We came to a bargain, you and I. A week, and that is all. No more than that."

One eyebrow rose.

"I've already received word from the modiste, Margaret. She will attend you this afternoon."

"So I am to fetch water from the well in a newly crafted dress? Something silk, with a bit of lace, please," she said in disgust. "So the rabbits and squirrels are not offended. Or teach school in a ballgown?"

"Or you might attend the theater with me."

"By all means," she said sardonically. "I must be seen in order to attract my next protector."

"It is my fault that you have no other clothing to wear, Margaret." His eyes narrowed even though his tone was agreeable. She'd been afraid of the emotions he made her feel, but never the man. But if she had not felt the tenderness of his touch, she would have been cautious of him at that moment.

"If you're in the mood for grand gestures, send your coachman back to my cottage for my clothing, Michael."

"How many dresses do you have, Margaret?" he asked.

"It's none of your concern, Michael. Don't you see that? In a week . . . six days, it will not matter. My wardrobe, how I live, even where I live will not be a concern of yours. You cannot offer me inducements to remain here. I will not."

"Very well, Margaret," he said, the words clipped. "I will send the modiste away. It was an act of reparation for taking you from your home so precipitously. An apology, if you will. I never thought your pride so unbending that you would refuse to accept anything from me."

"It would be better," she said softly, "if there were no more links between us. Not your kindness, Michael, nor your generosity."

They were already entwined by an emotion that neither accepted with good grace. A combination of passion and desire coupled with a curiosity that had not yet been appeased. Or perhaps they simply ignored its presence.

Her hands reached out and brushed his cuff. The material of his shirt was as soft as it appeared. Another measure of wealth, if he only knew it. The stiffest, scratchiest linen was reserved for the poor, the quality of it inferior to that of lawn.

"It's the last thing I will give you, Margaret," he said. "I promise," he said.

His words shamed her. He had given her far more than a dress. His greatest gift was a child whose existence would remain secret from him.

Tell him, her conscience whispered. But she could not. He was a man of power, influence. She had no wish to be his mistress and would not allow her child to be used as leverage.

One eyebrow rose imperiously. "It's only a dress, Margaret. A nightrail, perhaps, nothing more."

He leaned forward to place a kiss on her cheek. His fingers rested beneath her chin.

Her head tilted back, her lips opened. The softest sigh emerged from between her lips as he kissed her. There was so much pleasure even in a kiss.

"Let them fit you," he said, the words spoken against her lips. Then his mouth covered hers, his smile adding a uniqueness to his kiss.

She pulled away from him and nodded, words beyond her.

Chapter 17

Patience in passion leads to
greater joy than haste.

The Journals of Augustin X

Michael had always attempted to separate himself from those activities of women that were meant, by their very nature, to be grating. A week ago he would have fled from the very thought of a modiste and her coterie of seamstresses, or fittings. He would have labeled the man a liar if anyone had told him that he'd be sitting in the morning room amidst a group of giggling women and having quite an enjoyable time.

He sat on the divan, arms outstretched to either side. A pose of indolence. Small dolls, attired in the latest fashions, lay sprawled on the floor in front of him like a miniature harem of exhausted coquettes.

His attention was on Margaret standing on a pedestal, slowly being stripped of her green dress.

He crossed his legs to hide his sudden jubilant tumescence. It did not help that Margaret stared directly at him, her cheeks growing more pink as she stood there, bared to her shift.

He should have known that the sight of her would affect him. He was not necessarily sane around her. Yesterday in a carriage had proven that.

He should be about his work again. There was the Cyrillic cipher to solve. Less nonsense and more rational discourse, that's what he needed. More a semblance of normalcy. A bit of logic in this sudden world of confusion.

"You must remain perfectly still," the modiste complained. "Else we'll never get the proper measurements."

Did she know that he grew hard at the sight of her? It seemed as if she did, what with that glittering look she gave him. He sat up fully, realizing suddenly that it was not anger in her eyes, but humiliation.

Bloody hell. He stood, strode to her side.

"Give us a moment," he said, turning to the modiste.

The modiste, a woman of some advanced years, stepped back, away from him. The three women who had accompanied her left the room with remarkable quickness.

In only a moment, it seemed, he and Margaret were alone.

"Must you do this?" Margaret's arms spread wide to indicate the bolts of cloth, ribbon.

"I never meant to embarrass you," he said, honestly.

"There are so many of them," she said, staring at the floor.

"And you've never been undressed among a group

of women?" he asked, feeling an absurd bout of tenderness.

"There has hardly been an occasion," she said. "I've sewn all my own clothes."

"Then I have erred again," he said. "Forgive me."

She met his look with one of her own. He wondered if she knew that there was an almost imperious tilt to her chin sometimes. A decidedly fascinating quality of challenge about her.

Michael rarely obeyed impulses unless they were of a cerebral nature. He was highly creative within the structure of his thoughts. But never in his actions. He was almost never impetuous.

Except with her.

The room was empty except for the two of them, the door was closed; she stood on her pedestal.

He looked up at her face. She glanced at him, then away. Did she know what he wanted? Her shift swathed her from neck to knee and was tied in tiny bows down the front. His fingers reached out and pulled open the first bow.

"Please let me," he said softly, asking for absolution for his eagerness and permission in one breath. He wanted to see her. Wanted her naked before him. An odd wish, perhaps, but one that had kept him rooted to the room, to this ritual of women.

The second bow was loosened. Her hand reached up and flattened on his. Her gaze did not relinquish his.

"Please," he murmured.

After a moment, she dropped both her hand and her gaze.

Slowly, he untied the bows, reached inside with both hands, and spread open the fabric revealing her beautiful breasts. He brushed his thumb over her nipples.

She closed her eyes in response.

The bows only reached to the waist. Slowly he pulled the shift up, revealing her thighs, her hips. Her bout with modesty was lost as he raised the shift above her head, threw it to the floor.

Her figure was lush. Full breasts, hips that curved enticingly, long legs.

She stood there without moving or attempting to shield herself from his gaze. He reached out a finger and trailed it from between her breasts to below her navel. An arrow of sensation.

She uttered a soft, choked sound.

He explored her with fingers and thumbs and palms, hearing the slight sounds she made as he did so. Her nipples were exquisitely erect, sensitive. Michael traced his fingers over the swell of her buttocks, the hollow at the base of her spine. She trembled at each stroke of his fingers.

He savored the column of her throat, felt the rapid beat of her blood beneath his skin.

"The women are waiting," she murmured, breathless.

"Let them wait," he said.

She stood before him, her eyes closed, lashes fanned against her cheeks. Her hands were flattened against her thighs.

He placed his hands on her hips and stepped forward. Because she was on a pedestal, her breasts were at the perfect height for his mouth. He tongued a nipple, drew it into his mouth. When she sighed, he smiled against her skin.

"To be powerless in passion is both maddening and arousing," she murmured.

"True," he said, teasing the nipple with his tongue.

"Something I read once," she offered, her words ending in another sigh.

"In the *Journals*?"

She nodded, a slight, almost imperceptible gesture.

He anointed her breast with another soft kiss. "Did you like reading those books, Margaret?"

She smiled with her eyes still shut tight. But he noted that a flush warmed her cheeks.

"Yes and no," she admitted.

"Why yes?"

"I learned a great deal," she said. The last word trailed off into a gasp as he opened his mouth, closed it softly over a distended nipple.

"Why no?" he asked, pulling back and tracing a circle around the damp flesh of her breast with his fingers.

She didn't answer.

He looked up, smiled. Her blush had deepened.

"Why no?" he asked again.

She opened her eyes, looked at him. There was only silence between them. Michael had the absurd feeling that she dared him in some inexplicable way.

"I had certain questions," she said. "But there was no one to ask."

He recalled only too well the graphic nature of the illustrations in Babby's book. "Or practice with, perhaps?"

Her eyes closed, as if she could not bear his scrutiny.

"I would have volunteered to assist you," he said.

"Another act of charity?" Her eyes flew open and she smiled at him. There was that look again. A definite enticement.

"A good cause, the education of innocents," he replied.

In a gesture he had not anticipated, in a movement he had not expected, she stepped down from the pedestal and placed her palm flat against his trousers.

His smile faded beneath his surprise.

"You might be an acceptable candidate," she said.

She measured the length of his arousal almost in judgment. Was he large enough for her? Hard enough?

"Will I do?" A harsh question. She looked bemused at it.

"Yes," she said. Almost a breath of sound. Barely more. Her cheeks deepened in color. "Oh, yes."

He swelled even harder. An ardent and almost joyous response to her touch. He felt himself to be not unlike a cobra, tantalized and teased into making an appearance by the soft sounds of a flute. The instrument of his seduction was her hand, and the gaze that studied his body with infinite care.

"If you would consider me," he said, entering into her game, "I would be happy to oblige. What must I do?"

She held out her hand and he took it. He thought later that he should have recognized it for what it was, an invitation to ecstasy.

He stood in front of her, effortlessly handsome. He might have modeled for one of the statues in his pantheon. A god standing with nonchalant arrogance. No, not a god. A man altogether too human.

Hers.

The word trickled over her in a wondrous spirit of possessiveness. How fascinating that she'd not realized it. She had borrowed him for a time. A week. A few days.

The sense of power she felt was intriguing. It lifted a corner of her lip as she watched him. One of his brows arched in tandem.

She might do anything with him. Anything at all.

All the questions the *Journals* had sparked might be answered in this week.

"You have quite an interesting look on your face, Margaret," he said. "Is this where I should cry off? Be restrained and return to my library?" His smile seemed to mock his words.

"If you wish," she said, pulling back.

"God forbid you should think me a foolish man."

Stubborn, arrogant, impossibly handsome. But not foolish.

"No," she said. "But you do not like to be bested and you do have an affinity for numbers," she said. She didn't elaborate at his quizzical look.

She took one step toward him. "I have read that it's possible to see colors at certain moments of pleasure," she said.

"The *Journals*, again?"

She nodded.

She walked to him, reached up and began to slowly unwind the stock from his neck. His hands remained at his sides; he made no move to stop her or to halt her actions. Exactly in the pose she wanted him.

Margaret stepped back, pulled his arms from his sleeves one by one, then pushed the coat off his shoulders. Picking it up, she flung it atop the chair in the corner. His only response was a quirk of his lip.

She slowly unfastened the cuffs of his shirt. "Passion is not simply a physical state, but one of the mind," she said, focusing her attention to the gold links that kept the two edges of material together.

She looked up. His stare had narrowed, but he said nothing further. His smile, she was pleased to see, had disappeared.

His shirt removed, he stood there bare chested. She ran the palm of her hands up and down his skin, wondering why it should be that a man's chest should be so utterly fascinating. She explored the texture of his nipples half-hidden beneath the soft curling hair. "Does it give you pleasure, Michael, to have these stroked?"

"Not as much as I receive from touching yours," he said, his smile back in place, but altered in character. It seemed tighter, less amused.

"Even kissing them does nothing?" She added the gesture to the question.

He shook his head. Information, then, that she added to her store of knowledge about him. "But you like it when I touch you," she said, rubbing his bare arms with the palms of her hands. She followed the contours of his chest, fingers splayed.

"Yes."

Her hands trailed up to his shoulders, down to the waistband of his trousers. Her fingers traced a path from his abdomen, over his arm, to his back as she walked behind him. The muscles seemed as well defined there as on his chest. Her hands smoothed from the indentation of his spine up to his shoulder blades.

She moved to the front of him again. Her fingers reached out and began to unfasten his trousers. His boots were removed with a joint effort. Then his stockings and the remainder of his clothes. A few moments later he stood in front of her, naked, and gloriously tumescent.

Her hands reached out and cradled his erection.

"Blue," she said, stroking both palms up and down his length.

"What?"

"The first color. You should think of blue. Close your eyes," she said, not looking up to see if he did so. Instead, her focus was on the hardness cradled between her hands. "Blue is a cool color," she said, "the shade of deep water and the sky. Think of something blue and cooling," she instructed him.

"I doubt that will work," he said dryly. "Not at long as you're touching me."

She glanced up at him. His face had darkened in hue, as if the warmth between her hands traveled throughout his body.

She reached out with one hand and placed her hand upon his stomach. Her other hand remained holding him, a selfish pleasure.

"You must think blue," she said softly. "The blue of your eyes, perhaps."

"Colors are beyond me at the moment," he said.

She removed her hands from him, the message implicit. "Blue," she said gently chiding.

"Blue," he conceded after a long moment.

Margaret smiled gently, realized that his restraint was formidable to allow her this play. A word would stop it, a gesture halt it, but he stood mute in front of her. A participant in her game.

Waiting.

"Blue," she said, moving behind him again, trailing her fingers down his back, "is the color of invitation. The opening of the senses. The beginning of awareness. To think of blue," she said, kissing a line from his right shoulder to his left, "is to make oneself open to the possibilities of life."

"All this from blue," he said. His voice sounded rough. Her smile deepened.

"Whereas green," she said, moving his arms so that she might extend her own beneath them, "is the color of readiness. The bloom of spring, the emergence of nature. Ripeness for feeling."

She pressed her cheek against his back, extended her arms around him. She stood there for a long stretch of minutes, her cheek flattened against his back, her palms pressed to his chest. She could feel the booming beat of his heart beneath her fingertips.

She drew her nails gently along the sides of his stomach, heard his indrawn breath.

"What's the next color?"

"Are you ready for it?"

"More than you know," he said dryly.

She moved to his side, glanced down at him, fully erect. "If I had been a maiden," she said, "I would have been terrified of your size. It doesn't look as if it would fit at all."

The muscle in his jaw clenched but otherwise he did not move. Such restraint. Admirable. She smiled and reached out and circled the head of his erection with one gentle finger.

He closed his eyes.

"Orange," she said. "The color of a fire's core. The color, they say, belonging to passion itself."

"Not red?"

"Red is for later," she said softly. Her finger traced a line down his turgid length, back up again. His hands unclenched and he rubbed his palms down his thighs.

"Touch me," he said. "With both hands."

Fire traveled through her, made her skin feel tight.

Her nipples contracted, her body felt as if it would burst into flame.

"Not yet," she said. "Perhaps later. Think orange," she said. She bent over, blew a warm breath on him, watched as his erection responded by seeming to grow larger, to reach for her lips. His hips arched as if he wished her to swallow him.

"Orange. Red. Blue. Green," he rasped. "What else?"

"Patience," she said, smiling.

She stroked him softly with fingers that were growing more adept at the task. With each of his harsh breaths, Margaret felt more skilled, more competent.

"A magnificent instrument of pleasure," she murmured. "That is what one of the women in the *Journals* said."

Montraine muttered something, a curse, a moan she wasn't sure which.

The modiste had brought a selection of ribbons and laces. Margaret walked to the case, and withdrew a long blue ribbon, returned to his side. She knelt in front of him on the floor.

He stood above her, aroused and heavy, his flesh hot. She reached out and slid one trembling finger up the length of his erection. "Why do clerics say that Eve tempted Adam?" she asked. "Adam was the one with more allure."

"The true meaning of the serpent?" he asked, his voice tight.

Her smile broadened.

"Perhaps Eve seduced him with words," he said. "And colors," he said.

He bent and pulled her up by both arms. Her head tilted back. Their kiss was a melding of open mouths, entwined tongues and heat.

"No," he said harshly, a moment later. "It was Eve."

She looked up, met his glittering gaze. His cheeks were flushed, his smile thin.

"Lie down on the floor," she said, her breath tight, her blood thrumming through her body in a flush of heat. "Please."

He stared at her for a long moment, a silent stretch of seconds. She was surprised when he complied, so fierce was his look.

He lay on the floor in front of her, a banquet for her lips, a feast for her senses. One arm was bent beneath his head, one leg slightly drawn up. A picture of indolent perfection. Except, of course, for his tumescence. Exquisitely large and almost throbbing.

"Put your arms over your head," she told him. "And cross your wrists."

One eyebrow rose. He smiled, a particularly rapacious expression and held out his wrists to be tied. Margaret only shook her head. She pressed his arms back into place over his head, then leaned down and began to lace the ribbon around him, the ends wound around each of his thighs and tied with a bow. Her fingers were exquisitely gentle, barely touching him. The ribbon's placement pulled his erection upright, a magnificent phallus adorned in a spiral of blue.

She glanced at his face. His eyes narrowed, but his hands remained crossed over his head.

"The most experienced courtesans in the *Journals* had a challenge," she said, slowly tracing the spiral of ribbon with one gentle finger. "It was only offered to the most talented of lovers."

He remained silent.

"It's called the Hundred Licks of Love," she said. "Shall we test your stamina?"

Her tongue traced around the ribbon, up and around the head of his erection. She circled it slowly, deliciously prolonging the pleasure. Finally, Margaret raised her head, looked at him. "That's one."

Michael closed his eyes.

A few minutes later, she pulled back. His hands had flattened against the floor, the muscles of his arms flexed. His eyes were still closed; there was a look of such fixed purpose on his face that he appeared almost pained.

"A lover who thought himself skilled could master only ten licks," she said, returning to her exquisite task. A moment later she spoke again. "A man learning to prolong his pleasure could achieve thirty. But only the greatest and most proficient lovers could achieve forty or more."

She counted out each lick as she finished. At twenty-eight, she heard him moan, then cut off the sound with ruthless restraint. At thirty-three his hips arched up from the floor. His feet pressed against the floor and he pushed himself against her lips. She admonished him with a particularly intense thirty-fourth lick.

"Thirty-seven," she said a moment later, speaking against his flesh, trailing her lips and tongue across him.

"Margaret," he warned gutturally.

"Thirty-eight," she murmured.

He was so hot that it was like touching fire. Her fingers slid to the base of his erection, felt how tight his scrotal sac. The ribbon was damp now, straining against his hardness. It felt as if he'd grown longer and harder in the intervening moments.

"Forty," she said a few moments later, raising her head and congratulating him with a smile. The expression on his face was feral, unrestrained. This was not a man who spoke of restraint and planning and schedules.

"You wanted to know what the meaning of red was," she said at fifty licks. She trailed her hand from his thighs to his chest. His eyes opened, his narrowed gaze focused on her face. "It's the color of ecstasy."

He lunged at her.

Michael had the loathsome thought that he would spill his seed trying to pull off the damnable ribbon, he was that desperate for her. His fingers fumbled on the bows. Finally, it was off and he was free.

There was nothing of skill in this urgency. All he could feel was the pounding need to be inside her. Desperate for her as if she was water for his thirst and food for his hunger. He rolled with her until she was beneath him. When he entered her she was slick and hot, so tight that he thought he saw white suns beneath his closed lids.

Supporting himself on his forearms, he trailed the tips of his fingers through the hair at her temples. Margaret, he was pleased to see, looked nearly as stunned as he.

Her inner walls rippled against him. An intimate imploration. A beckoning to a distant place, one far removed from this sunlit room. His body was eager and more than willing to follow. His will wanted to surrender in the face of this clawing wonder.

"I can feel you tighten around me," he said roughly. "As if you're trembling inside."

His fingers traced over her mouth and she opened her lips. An artless invitation he could not deny. He bent forward and kissed her, inhaled her trembling sigh as he withdrew and then slowly entered her again. Finally, he broke off the kiss, his breath tight, his blood pounding.

He rose up, pulled slowly out of her. An excruciating pleasure. She made a choked sound of protest that he answered by entering her again.

The sensuality of it, the ecstasy of the moment, was almost too much.

Please, please, please. A mindless petition. He didn't know to whom he pleaded, or for what. An end to this? It was too acute, almost too much sensation. Please. A breath escaped him and he stilled, captured on the spike of sanity. A moment. A moment, that's all he wanted.

Desire had an edge to it. The need became waves, undulating currents that swept through every part of him. He wanted this, needed this. Wanted her. More, he needed her.

His fingers gripped her hips tightly and he counted out a cipher in his mind. Something to soothe him, calm him. Prolong this exquisite moment.

He forced himself to still, bent his head and breathed harshly against her neck until he gained some command over his body.

He heard himself murmur against her skin. Idiocies and foolishness. He was being catapulted someplace he had never been before. A world of mindless darkness and pleasure so acute he held his breath.

He began to breathe rhythmically, slowly. The kind of breathing she'd read about in the *Journals*. Words emerged from between his lips. No, numbers that he exhaled against her ear. "17, 35, 14, 49, 12, 57, 6, 97."

"What are you saying?"

"I'm reciting cipher patterns. Do not, I beg you, ask me why," he said tersely.

The surge of tenderness she felt startled her. It was so powerful that it was almost painful.

She placed her palm against his face, turned so that she could kiss him. Her internal muscles clenched against him. A sharp feeling so sweet that it was almost pain surged through her.

He moved suddenly, no longer calm and restrained. His face was fierce, almost pained. He began driving into her again and again. Finally, she uttered a soft, helpless moan as she felt her body arch instinctively, her arms flung out as if to hold onto the sky. The sensation captured her and made her a prisoner, blinded her.

So intense was the feeling that it was an eternity of exquisite pleasure. She was insensate, reeling from the blackness, lost in it. Captivated by him.

Michael Hawthorne, Earl of Montraine, holder of properties and three estates, Code Master, rewarded with honors by the Crown for his contributions to his country, lay on the floor and felt an almost sotted wonder.

His toes curled in absolute bliss. Dear God, he felt good. He turned his head and watched her. He wanted to kiss her lips off her face, and hold her so tight that there was no clear definition between where he left off and she began.

A warning bell sounded in his mind.

He was a descendant of a long and proud line. An earl. A man of some reputation. He had an obligation to his family to marry, and soon, an heiress who would provide for the financial stability of his earldom. He couldn't keep doing this.

He was being driven mad by lust.

In addition, he was becoming very familiar with the

ceiling of the morning room. Perhaps he should have it painted, at least, like the library. Some vista upon which to concentrate when he lay here, exhausted, sated, and incapable of moving.

"I have a perfectly good bed upstairs," he muttered, disgusted.

He turned his head, glanced at her. Her eyes were closed, her arms flung above her head. Her soft smile transfixed him.

The knock on the door was a shattering jolt back to reality. "My lord?" Smytheton's voice. "The modiste wonders if you are ready for her now."

Margaret sat up quickly, staring in horror at the door. Michael instantly began to formulate a way out of this situation. Unfortunately, his mind refused to obey. Instead, it was a numb, gray fog.

Anyone entering this room would immediately comprehend exactly what they had been doing. The fact that he had forgotten the place, the circumstance, and everything other than Margaret was one more peal of the warning bell in his mind.

"There's nothing else for it," he said, the truth raw and inescapable. "We're going to have to brazen it out, I'm afraid."

A few moments later, dressed, he opened the door. Margaret stood beside him, her garments similarly restored. He smiled at the modiste and nodded at his butler. It seemed to him that Smytheton scowled even more furiously, and the modiste appeared more than scandalized. Affronted, perhaps.

"You'll have to use the measurements you have, madam," he said, his voice curt. He left the room with Margaret at his side. Once in the foyer, he turned and beckoned Smytheton to him. A quick instruction, and the butler nodded, returned to the modiste.

"What did you tell him?" Margaret asked, after they had sought sanctuary in his library.

"I paid her for the ribbon," he said, grinning at her.

They had, no doubt, provided enough fodder for the rumor mills of society for months to come. He should have been irritated by his own behavior. Or cautious about his apparent lack of control when it came to Margaret.

Instead, he began to laugh.

Chapter 18

*The journey to ecstasy is one that
begins with a thought.*

The Journals of Augustin X

"**P**eterson says he cannot spare the cook, your lordship," Molly said, bobbing a curtsy.

"He did, did he?" Michael frowned at the young maid. His irritation, however, was not addressed at her, but at his mother's butler.

"The countess is entertaining, your lordship, and he says that he can't spare him. He says that since Smytheton thinks he can do everything in a household, there's no need for him to borrow the cook."

He raised an eyebrow and frowned at her. She bobbed another curtsy.

Evidently Peterson hadn't understood. Between Molly and Smytheton, they did quite well normally, but Michael wanted tomorrow night's dinner to be something special. The fact that Peterson was acting peckish annoyed him, especially since he employed the man.

"You will have to return, Molly," he said. He finished the note he was writing and handed it to her. It was a tersely worded suggestion that Peterson find some way to accede to the request, that it had come from him, not Smytheton.

She bobbed yet another curtsy and left the room.

Entertaining again?

His mother saw nothing wrong with going through her entire quarter's allowance in a month and then expecting him to be responsible for her subsequent bills.

Wedding an heiress was becoming imperative. A leisurely courtship would not suffice. He needed an influx of capital now. Knowledge gleaned after he had gone through this month's expenditures. Shoes, hats, gowns, flowers, a host of odds and ends purchased in order to impress or flatter.

If he didn't wed soon, there would be no money to pay all these bills.

But the thought of being sacrificed upon the matrimonial altar, while once acceptable, now seemed particularly repugnant.

He couldn't, for example, conceive of being as abandoned with a wife as he had been with Margaret two days ago. Jane Hestly floated through his mind. She had pale blond hair and rather pinched-looking features, thin lips, and cheeks that sagged like premature jowls. He doubted if she would care to know anything about the *Journals of Augustin X*. Nor could he imagine her wanting to wind a blue ribbon around him.

Margaret delighted him, and amused him, intrigued him, and incited his curiosity. More, he became someone he particularly liked in her company, as if she brought out his better nature. True, that man was unrestrained and decidedly irrational, but he'd never before felt so alive.

There were some women destined to remain in a man's mind forever. He had the somewhat unsettling thought that Margaret was one of them.

But he couldn't marry Margaret. He scowled down at the bills in front of him. For the first time, he was angry about his fate. Trussed up and delivered to the bride wealthy enough to purchase his title and his family lineage. A damnable future, one that stretched out almost interminably before him.

London life had acquainted Margaret with noise, an almost endless variety of sounds. As if the world visited the City and finding it to be delightful, remained there. But here, in Michael's house, it was almost as if she were in the country again, it was remarkably quiet. In the morning room it seemed doubly so. Her only companion was the faint whir and click of the mantel clock.

The knock came only seconds before Michael opened the door.

"I am so glad it's you," she said, looking up. "I had thought for a moment that it might be that dreadful modiste."

"Cannot bear to be measured again?" he asked, smiling and entering the room. Today he was dressed in black trousers and a pristine white shirt, neither of which looked the worse for wear, despite the unseasonably warm day. But then, he always looked perfect.

"I don't think I can ever look at the woman again," she admitted.

They shared a conspiratorial smile. It had been a difficult moment, but they had weathered it. The only result was that Smytheton had been even more formal ever since.

"She no doubt feels the same way about us."

Margaret shook her head. "There is a rule in commerce that personal feelings do not matter. The fact that you may not like a customer is not important. You must still sell to him."

"A odd parallel to society," he said. "Many times you may not wish to converse with an individual, but are compelled to by good manners."

She smiled. "What, then, is the comparison when there is but one book and two customers wishing to purchase it?" she asked.

"That's easy," he said, smiling. "One dance, two partners."

"Not enough money to pay for a purchase?" She entered into their game with a smile.

"A suitor who does not come up to snuff. There is nothing to do but put the goods back on the shelf." His smile broadened.

"A book that has not yet arrived, and a customer who is anxious?"

"You really must give me a more difficult challenge," he chided. "A spinster waiting for a suitor. Regrettably, her eagerness is wasted."

She thought for a moment. "An author whose book does not sell?" she asked, smiling.

He smiled. "An anxious mama with one season wasted and a daughter still to be wed."

"I give up," she said, laughing.

"Whatever her personal feelings," he said, still smiling, "the modiste has sent one of your dresses," he said.

"One? There is more than one?" She shook her head at him.

"I confess," he said, not looking at all repentant. "I ordered a few."

He studiously ignored her look. Instead, he strode to the settee and bent over to kiss her lightly. "I was feeling very generous," he said huskily.

Heat traveled through her body at memories of that day. She had never done something so wanton. So thoroughly brazen. Her own wickedness had surprised her, almost as much as the stunning enjoyment of their loving.

"What are you reading?" he asked, glancing at the book in her hands.

"Something entitled *Biographia Literaria* by Samuel Coleridge. He calls himself a poet but styles himself a critic. But I think him rather impressed with the sound of his own words, more than with their meaning."

"Why do you think that?"

She opened the book, and glanced up at him. "Listen to this. 'Every reform, however necessary, will by weak minds be carried to an excess, which will itself need reforming.' That is only chapter one. He does go on. 'No man was ever yet a great poet, without being at the same time a profound philosopher.' I do think he is talking about himself."

"I know little of poetry," he said. "I have studiously avoided it in the past. But it seems to me that there are only two types of poems. Either the meandering ode that doubles as the poet's search for himself, or poems dedicated to nature, urns, and Homer."

She closed the book and smiled at him, amused. "And you think neither is worthy of merit?"

"A soul is an intrinsically personal thing," he said. "God is too vast to be contained within meter and rhyme. And once a tree has been mentioned, it needn't be expounded upon again."

"And love? A great many poems are dedicated to love."

"Love is one of those emotions that differs in the experience of it."

"And is therefore incapable of being described?" she asked.

"Doesn't it have a different definition according to the person you ask?"

"Perhaps it is better simply to look into someone's eyes and know that despite whatever failing or fault that person has, you will never turn aside or betray him."

"Acceptance?" he asked.

"Unconditional," she said.

"As a definition of love? Not entirely logical," he said.

"Life itself is not always logical, Michael."

"No, it isn't," he agreed. "Else I would not be here now, arguing the merits of love. Instead," he said smiling, "I've come to take you boating."

"Boating?" Her eyes sparkled, her mouth curved in an altogether delicious smile.

"Henry the Eighth did it all the time."

"Should I be reassured? I seem to remember that he had a penchant for disposing of women."

"Only wives," he countered.

It was the wrong thing to say. It reminded him of his duty, the shortness of a week. Very well, he would restrict his remarks to those of an impersonal nature. They would simply enjoy today and think of nothing more solemn than the shape of the clouds in the sky.

The directions for their outing had been furnished to him by Smytheton, who had consented to address him for the first time in a day. Despite his forbidding scowl, he had prepared a hearty lunch for them, a heavy affair in a straw basket.

A picnic, then. It surprised Michael to realize that he had never before done something like this.

They took the carriage to a small town about an hour's ride outside London. There, along the gently sloping bank, exactly where Smytheton had indicated, was an inn where Michael was able to hire a flat-bottomed skiff.

Both of them looked at the vessel dubiously. Margaret, however, was the first to express doubts.

"It doesn't look like it will hold us," she said.

"You must be more confident in my abilities, Margaret," he said.

"I have faith in your abilities, Montraine. It's the boat that concerns me."

He pulled it closer by the rope, glanced up at her. "Politeness decrees that you enter first while I steady it."

She sent him a quick glance of remonstrance. He grinned.

"I would much rather be impolite and have you test whether or not it will float," she announced.

"So the gentlemanly thing would be to go down with the ship?"

She nodded vigorously. "Absolutely," she said.

Margaret stood on the bank, her hands clasped behind her. He had never heard her giggle. The sound seemed unlike her, almost girlish. One thing he could most definitely verify was the fact that Margaret Esterly was no girl. But the sound charmed him all the same.

He stepped into the skiff and held his hands out for her. The boat rocked beneath his feet. For a moment, Michael thought he was going to be overturned.

She placed her hand trustingly in his, a gesture at odds with her sudden laughter. Together they stood in the boat as it shivered beneath them. If he leaned one way the boat rocked in that direction. He tested it only to have Margaret grip his sleeves for balance.

"Don't you think you should sit down?" she asked, laughing.

"Why should I sit when I can have a beautiful woman holding onto me?"

"I am not beautiful," she countered.

"Are you certain?"

"Most assuredly."

He stroked his finger down her nose, tapped the end of it gently. "Perhaps it's because of your nose. I've seen more aquiline noses."

He stared into her eyes. "And I will confess that your eyes are an odd shade. Sometimes I think they're hazel. Sometimes they seem almost pure green. Perhaps if you had different-colored eyes you would be considered truly beautiful."

Because they now stood so still, the boat only rocked gently with the current. Even so, her hands still gripped his upper arms tightly.

"And your hair . . ."

"What about my hair?" she asked, indignant.

"It could be a more normal shade. Something blond, perhaps. Less red."

She narrowed her eyes at him. "Is this a lesson, then? Not to question compliments?"

He smiled, amused.

"On the other hand," she said, studying him, "I have often thought you beautiful. Almost lovely. A very pretty man."

He began to laugh, thoroughly routed.

A moment later, both of them seated in their proper places, he began to row away from the inn's dock.

The inn itself was a squat building, perched on the edge of the river like a broody hen. It had been painted red years ago, the color now a shade that reminded him of burgundy. From the carriages parked in its side yard it did a brisk business. In addition, there were several boaters out on the river. Couples, for the most part, the ladies shaded with their parasols, the men acting with more skill than he possessed at the oars.

After a while, however, he managed the rhythm of it, drawing away from the bank and heading into the river. Here the Thames was surprisingly clear, the current strong, not yet affected by the tides.

It was a perfect day, the blue sky only occasionally dotted with fluffy white clouds. Trees lined the river and the sloping green banks attested to a wet spring. A scene of bucolic beauty.

Margaret leaned back, let her fingers trail in the water. Closing her eyes, she tilted her face to the sun. He had the sudden feeling that she had not spent many moments in indolence either.

The moment was perfect, silent and hushed.

"Do you ever wonder what the rest of your life will be like?" Margaret asked.

The question surprised him, but he answered her

honestly. "Not really. My life is ordained within certain strictures. I have a duty to my family, and an obligation to my country. It leaves few opportunities for extemporaneous living."

Such as choosing his destiny.

"That can be both very comforting and very constraining."

He had been rowing steadily. Now he rested the oars and sat with one knee drawn up as he removed his coat and waistcoat.

It occurred to him that he would never have been in Jane Hestly's presence similarly dressed. But then, he wouldn't have carried her from a cottage and loved her in a coach. And he doubted he would be laughing much in her presence.

"What of your own life, Margaret? What will your future bring?"

She looked discomfited by the question. As if he had pried into a province that was none of his concern. Her attention was directed to a tree not far from the shoreline. She looked at it as if she'd never viewed a tree before. Nor even seen a bird like the one that flew from one of its branches.

She turned suddenly and looked at him, her direct glance rendering him vaguely uncomfortable. "What happens when something occurs in your well-planned life that you do not expect? What do you do then?" she asked.

"Nothing has," he said.

"You live a charmed life, Montraine," she said, smiling enigmatically.

Was he destined to think her forever a mystery? The more time he spent with her, the more puzzling she became.

There were only three days remaining to them. He

was all too aware that Margaret was intent upon returning to her cottage on the Downs. If she did, he would have no reason to seek her out again. After all, he'd given his word.

Unless, of course, he convinced her to remain with him.

Chapter 19

⚜

*A woman who embraces pleasure
accepts all of her senses.*

The Journals of Augustin X

He picked up the oars and began to row again.
Even the act of doing something so obviously
unfamiliar was performed with grace.

"Do you like the rain?" she asked.

He glanced over at her. "I like storms."

"And cider?"

"Cider?" A smile curved his lips. She felt proud of
herself for coaxing him to amusement. Even if it was
a little at her expense.

"Cider."

"All in all, I prefer brandy."

"What is your favorite color?"

"Blue," he said, and surprisingly winked at her.

"Do you like sweet foods? Or sour?"

"I haven't thought about it," he said. "I like lobster
soup. And those little tarts cook used to make. I don't

care for mutton," he said, obviously considering the question. "But I do like roast beef."

"And Christmas pudding?"

"I like currants best," he said smiling. "Is there a reason for this litany of questions?"

"A lamentable curiosity," she confessed.

She had studied him avidly these past days, marked things in her mind that she would recall when they were no longer together. He was a man capable of focusing on one thing to the exclusion of all else. When he laughed it was almost with a sense of surprise, as if his levity was so rare that it startled him. There was a scar on his left knee from when he was six and mean to his sister's cat. A confession he had made ruefully last night. The cat had retaliated by digging its claws into him. The scar was both a lesson and a punishment, he'd admitted.

"Is my curiosity equally acceptable?" he asked.

She smiled and replied. "My favorite color is green."

"And your favorite foods?"

"Something easy to grow," she admitted. "Other than that, I have few preferences."

"Storms?"

"They seem lonely to me," she admitted.

"They needn't be," he said casually. "I could always arrange to be with you in inclement weather. If I were loving you when it thundered, I doubt you would know it."

She wondered at the surprising hurt she felt by that statement, and its most apparent answer. "Unless your wife needed you," she said quietly. "Or you were away at one of your estates. Or your child was ill and needed you at his side. Or your horse went lame and you couldn't reach me in time."

He stopped rowing. The gentle lapping of the river's current carried them closer to shore as the boat nosed up against the gentle embankment of an island.

"You have thought of only the worst things that could happen, Margaret. It doesn't have to be that way."

A confession, then. She could not bear being on the periphery of his life, being an afterthought, a casual moment.

She smiled brightly. "One of the things that intrigues me about you, Michael, is the fact that you are unlike most peers I've seen. You work for the government when most nobles lead indolent lives. You employ a formidable butler because he is a war veteran. Yet you would have me believe that it would be easy for you to have a wife and a mistress and think nothing of it. Perhaps in the beginning. But it would only be a matter of time until you began to deplore the circumstances. And despise yourself."

There was silence while he considered her. The only sound was the lapping of the water against the shore. Even the birds had quieted, as if to eavesdrop on their conversation.

"And you? Would you hate me?"

"No," she said, smiling faintly. "But I would despise what I had become."

"Is that truly how you feel, Margaret?'

"Yes," she said. "It is. And I've no doubt you would come to feel the same."

"I had no idea you had studied me so well."

Her thoughts had been too often on him. Even when they were separated she had spent hours thinking of the Earl of Montraine. Wondering what he would do in certain situations. Dreaming of him, picturing him in all sorts of situations.

Her answer divulged nothing of that. "You forget, Michael, that I was in trade. It is important to be able to gauge people quickly. Especially if you wish to make a sale."

"You were very successful, I imagine," he said evenly.

The truth was somewhat different. Jerome had often struggled to pay their bills. Too often, he had solicited assistance from his brother. Even when she had asked him to consider any other available option.

"I confess to studying tradespeople less closely than you have nobles," he said, his face somber.

"I do not doubt that you pay your bills in a timely fashion. I used to dread obtaining the trade of a peer. It meant that a bill would not be paid for months."

"Perhaps they did as my mother does: hides them in her hatbox until the top will not close. Only then does she proffer them to me," he said dryly.

"Then on behalf of all tradesmen in London, may I implore you to pay them with great dispatch? It sometimes makes a difference between having coal for the fire or freezing in winter."

His wry smile surprised her. "Exactly the reason I must marry," he said. "But then, I haven't told you I need an heiress, have I?"

"You?" she asked, surprised. "But you have three estates."

"That are doing badly at the moment. However," he said, jumping from the skiff, "the day is lovely and I am not at all disposed to think of debts and obligations at the moment."

The place where he'd chosen to have their meal was a small island, a picturesque setting, remarkably serene. It was also very private. From the waterline, the ground sloped upward to a small knoll and then farther to a line of trees.

"Not in the middle of a river, Michael. Surely you have no plans for that," she said, chiding him with a look.

He began to laugh, the sound carrying over the water and echoing back to them. She stood, hands on hips, glaring at him. But his laugh was so infectious that she could not hide her own smile. A moment later he reached out and grabbed her by her waist, lifted her effortlessly up from the boat, and set her on the ground.

"Now you think I go around fornicating in the fields. Tupping in the trees. Even I have more restraint than that. I think."

She felt a flush warm her cheek.

"Although," he said, "the thought does have merits."

"You are incorrigible," she said.

He only grinned and reached into the boat for the basket.

They settled on a knoll not far from the water's edge. Together they set out the linen cloth Smytheton had provided.

"He's very talented, Smytheton," Margaret said, laying out the foodstuffs he had packed for them. "Is it customary for a man in his position to know so many things?"

"I think it has more to do with being an old campaigner," Michael said. "His only flaw is that he's a deplorable cook."

He glanced into the basket. "A bit of roast beef, some cheese, and some sort of crusty bread," he announced. "And," he added, reaching into the bottom of the basket and retrieving two clay jars, "ale! Not an elegant meal, but a fortifying one. Perhaps even Smytheton didn't want to exceed his capabilities today."

"I'm surprised that your household is so small."

"Not the home of an earl? My work requires that I have some degree of privacy."

"But you will be married soon, and circumstances will change." She traced a pattern on the edge of the plate with her finger.

"Yes," he said simply.

A moment later, she looked over at him. He caught her glance and returned it. "You weren't correct, you know. I'm not as honorable as you think. I would keep you with me and feel no regret about it at all."

He looked away, then, concentrating on the horizon.

He had surprised her with his revelation. Until now she'd thought his wish to make her his mistress had been because of their divergent roles in life. Now she realized it was not so much a function of aristocracy as necessity. He was as trapped as she. She would forever be the Widow Esterly and he was duty bound to marry an heiress.

She reached out and touched his arm in wordless understanding. He glanced down at her hand, placed his own upon it.

"Having you with me has made the thought of marriage possible," he said, his voice low. She tightened her hand on his arm, feeling a spike of pain at his tone. He was not a man to whom confession came easily. "A week with you is not enough, Margaret. A year, perhaps, or two. Perhaps a decade. But not a week."

She felt a surge of panic at his words, at the tenderness they invoked, then sought a refuge in irritation. It was an easier emotion to feel, and one that guarded her. It would be too easy to fall victim to his charm, to accede to his request, to begin to understand his needs and join them with her own.

The most dangerous thought was that it would be almost effortless to become his mistress.

She looked startled.

"Is such arrogance a function of your nobility, Michael?" she asked, irritated. "Do you never listen? Do other people's wishes not have *any* meaning to you *at all*?"

"I suspect that you have a prejudice against the nobility, Margaret." A genial comment, one that gave her no hint of his thoughts. She made no secret of her anger at him. He almost admired her the freedom of her emotions. Perhaps it was easier than the restraint he felt at all times.

She shook her head. "I don't know many. But what I have seen has not endeared me to them."

"I shall attempt to convince you that one particular earl is not that onerous," he said, smiling at her.

"To do that you would have to consent to cease asking me to be your mistress."

He raised one knee and propped his wrist on it, then looked out over the river.

"What would you like to discuss, then?" An offering of himself.

She did not hesitate. "Why do you work when most nobles do not?"

"What would you have me do? Become a dilettante?" He frowned at her.

"Why are you not involved in Parliament?"

"I take my seat in Lords when some piece of legislation interests me," he said. It was odd that he divulged so much of himself to her. Was it because they had been so intimate? Yet a pairing of bodies did not necessarily lead to a joining of minds.

"Ciphers give me a way to be of value," he said, oddly compelled to justify himself to her. "Some way of being of service to my country."

"Is that important to you?"

"I could not serve in the war," he said. "My family needed me. Perhaps I felt the lack."

"Did you do code work during the war?"

For a long moment he studied at her.

"I did," he admitted.

"Then you were better placed there than to be cannon fodder," she said. A bit of protectiveness that charmed him.

"Why did you come with me that first day?" A question he had always wanted to ask her.

It was her turn to study him. He could not help but wonder what she saw. A man who was too curious about her? He was certainly that. And one who chose not to reveal the exact extent of his fascination.

"Because I wanted a memory," she said finally. "Or perhaps because I wished to be someone I was not for a little while. Someone daring and improper."

"And now you're content to be Margaret Esterly of Silbury Village?"

"It's a role I am comfortable with," she answered. "It holds no surprises, and no expectations."

"No danger, but no delight. Is that how you wish to live your life?"

She slanted a look at him. "Most people do. Common lives, only rarely interrupted by joy or tragedy."

"I know your tragedy," he said, thinking of her husband. "What is your joy?"

"Simple things," she said. "The sound of birds. Squire Tippet's terrier puppies. The sight of snow. Being in the middle of the Standing Stones and listening to the wind."

"None of those activities involves other people," he said.

"Neither do your ciphers," she countered.

"So we each find joy in solitary ways."

He had the disconcerting thought that there were probably more similarities between them than differences. It was not wise to consider the links he had with this woman. It was perhaps dangerous enough that he found himself lusting for her continually.

"Shall we change that? Come to the theater with me tonight. *Macbeth* is playing and we shall immerse ourselves in tales of Scottish tragedy."

"I have never seen it," she said, and there was a trace of wistfulness in her tone.

"Then come with me."

She nodded, then smiled.

"In the meantime, perhaps we should choose only safe topics of conversation. There is the weather," he said. He looked up at the sky. "It looks to be a very pleasant day."

"Yes," she said, following his lead. "It does. No wind. No rain. Only a few clouds."

"That topic is sufficiently exhausted, I believe," he said.

She only smiled.

"Of the two, which do you prefer? Your cottage or London?"

She suddenly frowned at him. He felt chastised to his toes. "I am only curious. There is no underlying motive," he quickly added.

"Are you always so?"

He thought about it for a moment, realized that his life had always been marked by his search for answers. "Yes. But I note that you are the same. After all, you have read the *Journals of Augustin X*."

"A vastly improper thing to do. But they were the only books in the cottage."

He didn't attempt to hide his amusement at her sophistry. A flush on her cheeks was an admission that she knew her words were foolish.

"I think that I should explain codes to you," he said. "Or number patterns. Or something that you might find exceedingly dull. A topic not related to you or me or this week."

"I have never seen patterns in numbers," she said, removing her bonnet and placing it beside her.

"If I were to say the numbers 1-7-13-6-12-18-11, what would you say?"

She thought a moment, repeated the first four numbers aloud. He knew the moment she understood. "Take a number, add six, add another six, subtract seven and then repeat it."

"You have just solved a code," he announced.

"It cannot be that easy," she said dubiously.

"It is when you take it in small bits." He looked away, wondering if he could find a way to explain it, surprised that he wished to try. "It's similar to thinking of all the tasks you must accomplish in a year. It's unwieldy to try to manage that much knowledge. But you can conceive of a day. Even a week. Add that together, and it becomes a sennight, month, a quarter.

"The greatest difficulty in solving codes isn't finding the pattern, but breaking it down into manageable sections."

"How does an earl become a code breaker?"

"He must first be a little boy interested in number games," he said. "I invented codes to use when communicating with my closest friend. It was a way to confound my sisters, then it became a fascination all its own."

"Your childhood sounds as if it was a happy one, despite all those sisters."

"It was not," he said simply, toying with a piece of grass beneath his hand. "My father shot himself when I was fourteen." He heard the words with a kind of horrified wonder. He never spoke of his father. "What about your childhood?" he asked, in an effort to change the subject.

"I seemed to spend it forever at my lessons," she said. "My Gran had been a governess once, and she was determined that I should learn everything she knew."

"Your Gran would not approve of your being here," he said, before she spoke the words. An unsafe topic.

"No," she agreed, "she would not."

The silence between them was not as companionable as before.

"We might discuss Parliament," she said finally. "I used to have rousing discussions with Samuel Plodgett."

"Your friend the draper?"

She nodded.

"Or poetry. But then, I recall you do not like poetry."

She walks in beauty like the night. There was something wrong about a man who quotes to himself. And Byron, of all people. Wordsworth had said it better.

A perfect woman, nobly planned, to warn, to comfort, and command; and yet a spirit still and bright, with something of angelic light.

He was becoming, he realized, decidedly foolish.

Chapter 20

Lovers who share their hearts share their souls.

The Journals of Augustin X

Their luncheon finished, they packed up the dishes. They stood, began to walk inland. It was, as they had each decreed, a perfect spring day with no hint of rain in the sky.

It was difficult to tell that he was an earl. Or that she was a poor widow. On this forested island, rank and role did not seem to matter. A curious silence had overtaken them. Not one of expectation, as it had often been in the past with them, but one of appreciation. As if they knew that times such as these were precious and rare and all too soon gone.

She tilted her head back to look up at the trees. From here the branches appeared like a canopy of emerald against an azure sky.

He had the oddest ability to capture her emotions. To incite her to amusement, or to irritate her. And, at the core of it, perhaps, the most disturbing emotion of all. Desire? Or a ceaseless lust? Whatever the word, it was always present.

The temptation was there to tell him her secret, to make him understand why she could not stay. But in the end, it was more prudent to remain silent.

Just as it was wiser to hold something of herself back. Until today, she'd been able to convince herself that he hadn't wanted anything from her but abandon. That, she could give to him in full measure. But companionship? Amusement? They trod on shaky ground, hinted at more. She had measured the boundary of their relationship once. *We cannot be friends and we must not be lovers.* But somehow, they had become both.

The trees were thick, so dense they could barely see the water. By the smile on his face, this site was exactly what Michael wanted.

He turned his head and studied her, his gaze both inscrutable and direct. He had that way of looking at things, as if he focused all his attention upon that one instant in time. He had done it often, but she had never found herself quite so pinned by a gaze before.

Slowly, he began to walk toward her. Just as slowly she backed away, a smile curving her lips.

Did he know that she had never experienced anything like what she felt with him? An instant delight and desire. It was better if he did not know. Her future was at stake. Hers and her child's.

Her back hit something solid. She had backed up against tree, a venerable oak.

He smiled at her, a particularly teasing grin. She reached out her hands and braced them against his chest. He curved his hand around one of hers, brought it up to his mouth, and gently kissed her knuckles. The sweetness of the gesture charmed her.

"I've fallen into your plans well, haven't I? Here, Michael? In the forest?"

He cupped his hands around her face, his thumbs brushing from the corners of her mouth to her cheeks. As if he wished to memorize the shape of it. She could only stand and stare at him.

"I only wished a kiss. Some men are addicted to brandy," he said slowly, studying her mouth. "Some like to wager too much. It seems that my besetting obsession is kisses from Margaret."

The expression on his face was one she had never seen before, something approaching tenderness.

All those moments in her life that had been precious to her, those times she would recall when she was an old woman, had taken place in this same odd serenity. As if nature itself recognized the import of these moments and hushed the world around her.

He dipped his head and kissed her. Sweetly, almost innocently. As if she were delicate and rare and precious to him.

She should not feel sad. An odd emotion to have coupled with such yearning. Her emotions felt held not in her heart but on her skin, and even the brush of air was enough to stir them.

The days were passing as quickly as seconds. The week too soon gone.

She extended her arms around him, pressed her cheek against his shirted chest, her eyes closed tight. Each second of this embrace was to be remembered, recalled. Every sound. A gentle breeze in the branches above them, the whispering of leaves being stirred by forest creatures. The faraway call of a boatman, a laugh. The lapping of the river not far from where they stood.

She drew in her breath and held it, the better to

keep this one moment crystal and pure. Yet prudence spoke in that instant. *Do not do this to me. Do not make me love you.*

It might already be too late.

"I cannot see you without wishing to kiss you," he said harshly against her temple, his voice at odds with the gentleness he held her. "And I cannot kiss you without wishing to touch you. But when I touch you, all I want is to be in you. To feel you around me. To hear you cry my name in that soft voice of yours."

He pulled her tighter against him.

"If you said the word," he said gruffly, "I would take you now on the forest floor. In a boat." He laughed mirthlessly. "I would no doubt love you up against a tree." He lay his cheek against her hair, his hands pressing against her back. The beat of his heart seemed to be an echo of her longing for him, translated into sharp, stinging tears.

"For the love of God, stay with me, Margaret," he whispered hoarsely.

A tear fell and dampened his shirt.

She wanted him. Not for a moment, an hour. Or even a week. There, a confession. A purging of the soul. She wanted all of him, not the dregs of his life. Not the odd moments when he could spare the time.

"No, Michael," she said, pulling back slowly, the effort more difficult than she believed. She turned away from him, lowered her head, stared at the ground. "Would it be better if I left now, returned home?"

"A threat, Margaret?"

She glanced over her shoulder at him. He had become the stern and unapproachable earl once more.

"No, Michael. Only a question. Would it be easier if we simply said good-bye now?"

"No."

"Then please, do not make this more difficult on both of us. The agreement was a week, and after that, you would forget me."

"And if I cannot?"

"You must," she said simply.

He said nothing, only began to walk toward the shoreline.

She followed him in silence.

The Duke of Tarrant stood before a fire in his library. If his servants thought it unusual that he asked for one to be laid on this warm spring day, they did not express it to him. He would not have cared.

He had envisioned leaving behind the *Journals*, wondering perhaps if there would come a time when a grandchild, or even a great-grandson, would stumble onto the secret. A time distant from now, when sentiments were not so inflamed and when people would measure history with detachment. His actions would not be reviled in that distant age. Instead, they would be understood, and perhaps even applauded.

His descendants would have marveled at the courage of the twentieth Duke of Tarrant. Whether they agreed with his philosophy was unimportant. They would have felt, nonetheless, a pride that he had acted upon his convictions. As had all the men who had come before him.

Because of Jerome, and now his widow, that was all changed.

Now not one person alive would know what he had done. What he had single-handedly accomplished with his money and his brilliance.

He opened the book and tore the frontispiece from

it, threw it into the fire, and watched it curl, a writhing paper snake. Consumed to ash all too quickly. Another few pages. It took nearly an hour for it to burn. With each page, his bitterness mounted.

Chapter 21

True lovers do not fear the loss of self.

The Journals of Augustin X

He had ordered that the sconces in the stairway be lit, along with those in the foyer. He had dressed earlier, placed the key grid for the Cyrillic cipher and his translations into the leather dispatch case to take to Robert tomorrow. He had, finally, solved it this afternoon.

At first he thought the sender was in the employ of a man of some repute. Count Ioannis Antonias Kaponistrias had been a member of the Russian diplomatic service, one of the chief advisors of Czar Alexander I. But in recent years, his interests had changed. He'd become active in the cause of obtaining Greek independence from Turkey. What Michael deciphered indicated that he'd been betrayed by a woman, no doubt someone close to him. She had been so successful in her machinations that the conflict be-

tween Greece and Turkey would probably only escalate.

Not the first time he'd uncovered a woman's involvement in matters of state. As operatives, women
were often overlooked, thought gentle and weak. His
experience indicated just the opposite. They were fre-
quently the most successful of spies, only because
they were underestimated.

Smytheton crossed the foyer, disappeared into the
hallway. "I am waiting for Margaret," he almost said.
An explanation that was wholly unnecessary. But perhaps he only wanted to voice the words, hold fast this
moment.

Upon their return from the river, she'd remained
silent. An odd and disconcerting experience for him.
He was familiar with a woman's tantrums. Screams,
shouts, wails of despair, anything but an almost sad
serenity. It had consumed his own irritation.

When Margaret descended the stairs, his breath
stilled. Her face was luminous in candlelight. Her
mouth, that beautiful mouth, was curved in a soft be-
guiling smile that mirrored the sparkle in her eyes.

"You look radiant," he said, a bit of honesty offered
up with a smile.

"If so, I am only a fitting partner for you," she said
softly.

It was a simple day dress of deep blue silk, a shade
and fabric that Michael had chosen because he was
partial to blue. Across the top of the high bodice and
puffed sleeves was a row of gathered lace. The full
skirt fell to her ankles in a cascade of folds.

He wished now that he had gone against her protestations and ordered a formal gown. She would not
be dressed as ornately as most of the women attending the theater. His gift would have to suffice.

"I was wondering if you needed any help dressing," he said, smiling up at her. "You've no maid."

"I have never had one," she said.

"Still," he teased, "I should have offered."

"And you? Do you not miss having a valet?"

"Harrison says I should. But living in this house is a recompense. The modiste did well," he said, reaching out his hand to her.

He twirled her in a slow circle, approving of her appearance. They left the foyer and walked down the hall to the dining room.

The table was covered with china, cutlery, and crystal arrayed upon a white tablecloth. A silver epergne designed in the shape of one of the new clipper ships stretched nearly the length of the table, candles protruding from every available orifice.

Her eyes widened as she stared at it.

"Smytheton borrowed that monstrosity," Michael said in his own defense. "I had nothing to do with it."

"It does have one advantage," she said. "The room is as bright as day."

He helped her into her seat, to the right of his at the head of the table. Smytheton entered with the first course, a lobster soup. It was very rich and heavily seasoned. No doubt the reason Margaret ate so little.

"There seems to be a great deal of cutlery," she said, fingering a fork.

He understood in that moment, and cursed himself for a fool. He had thought, somehow, to make the night magical. All he'd done was to illuminate the differences between them.

"I admit," he said, forcing a smile to his face, "that it looks overwhelming. But think of it as if it were a puzzle. All the various utensils are used for a specific purpose. Such as this, for example," he said picking up an odd-looking fork. The tines of it were curved at the end, almost as if it were the bowl of a spoon. "A fish fork," he said.

Again he picked up another item from the table and held it aloft. This fork was as strangely shaped as the other. But the tines were half the length of its handle.

"A fruit fork." When he proffered a knife that matched the fork in size, Margaret smiled.

"I suppose it would be too common to simply pick up an apple?"

"Exceedingly," he said with a smile. "Then you would have no reason for this plethora of silverware."

He held up a large spoon crafted in a perfect oval. "But it is in the spoon that we truly have fine mastery. This is the soup spoon," he said. "Not to be confused with the dessert spoons." Another piece of cutlery joined the first. "There is also the custard spoon, and the pudding spoon."

"So many?" she asked, amazed.

"Oh, yes," he said, smiling at her. "It's a ceremony of entrance, you see. Once you have mastered the dinnerware, you are considered one of the initiated." He returned the cutlery to its place.

"When did you become initiated?"

"I was eight, I believe," he said. "And a very well-behaved child."

She tilted her head, surveyed him. "I doubt that's entirely true," she said. He only smiled in response.

One by one the courses were consumed. He noticed that Margaret only managed a taste of some of the dishes. She was unconsciously emulating those most proper of society matrons who thought it common to partake of every course.

When the meal was over, and Smytheton summoned to convey his appreciation to the cook, they left the dining room. Margaret remained in the foyer, standing silently beneath the shadowed dome while he retrieved his gift from the library.

"I have a surprise for you," he said upon returning. His words echoed back at him, and he drew her away from the rotunda.

"More than the dinner or the theater?" she asked, surprised.

He nodded, and unfurled the shawl. Its paisley pattern was enhanced by delicate gold threads woven into the design. She reached out her hand, and stroked it softly. Even in the darkness it glittered.

He placed the shawl on her shoulders, discovering in that instant that he liked giving her things. It pleased him on an elemental, almost visceral, level.

Her expression of surprise muted to become pleasure.

"I should not take anything else from you," she said faintly.

"The nights can be cool," he softly said, feeling an absurd tenderness. "I would blame myself if you became chilled. Then you would have to remain longer."

"You make it difficult to refuse you, Michael," she said, smiling up at him.

"Then you should not," he said, smiling.

"I will miss you when I leave," she said. An artless comment, one that he could see she had not meant to say. But it hung in the air between them, lengthening the moment.

"My lord," Smytheton said, stepping inside the door. "The carriage is here."

Michael nodded, and held out his arm.

Chapter 22

When tranquility and relaxation are in
abundance, passion is sublime.

The Journals of Augustin X

The theater was so brightly lit it looked to be on fire.

They had to run the gauntlet of street peddlers from the carriage to the doors. Young girls sold oranges, flowers, and matches, while two or three older women hiked their skirts up on one side to indicate their status as prostitutes. But they weren't the only ones plying their wares or begging for coins on this night. There were pickpockets, grizzled war veterans, and small boys who offered to dust the street or hold a lady's pattens.

The entranceway, the stairs, and the corridors of the theater were as crowded as the square. A few people greeted Michael. His only response was a quick smile, a wave, intent on their destination. He deliberately did not stop to introduce Margaret. His sudden discomfiting thought was that he did not know a way to do so that would not ultimately shame her. She was not a relative, nor his fiancée. If he simply omitted her status or declared her a friend, the association would be assumed to be one of an illicit nature. By being polite, he would label her his mistress, but by refusing to introduce her, he declared her the same.

As they walked up the stairs, the crowd became less dense. One by one, they parted, as if word was being passed of their arrival in front of them. A few people turned and watched them as they passed.

Once they entered his box, Margaret sat, remaining silent and seemingly unaffected. If she felt it difficult to be watched by so many people, he couldn't tell. He himself was growing more and more aware of the heads turning in their direction. There were enough interested gazes meeting his that he doubted *Macbeth* would be as much discussed as he and Margaret.

"Have you ever been to Covent Garden before?"

She glanced at him, nodded. "I saw *Don Giovanni* once, a few years ago."

"Did you enjoy it?"

"I think it would have been better if it had been in Italian. It seemed a little silly hearing it in English."

Her smile should not have made his loins tighten. That's all he needed, he thought in disgust. To prove himself a debauched fool in front of thousands of interested spectators. He stared at the stage floor and concentrated on a Trithemius cipher, then a polyalphabetic substitution code.

The whispering began. Like the faintest breeze, it seemed to float through the room, careening from one guest to another. It seemed he had underestimated both society's curiosity about him and possibly the modiste's volubility.

Margaret sat, her attention on the stage. There was a look on her face, one of resolve coupled with an undeniable dismay. Wasn't that the definition of courage, the ability to persevere even when one did not wish to do so?

He had never before had anyone to defend. His sisters had fashioned themselves into a triumvirate early on, protected one another. But Margaret had no such armor of rank or relation.

Her words came back to him. *I must be seen in order to attract my next protector.* His mood worsened. He had done nothing but ensure that she was the object of censure and gossip. Why the bloody hell hadn't he realized it before now?

Because you weren't exactly thinking with your mind, Michael. He frowned at that wry thought.

He had always believed that he was aware of his faults, knew them, attempted to lessen them. However, at this moment, he discovered another niche to his character, one that did not please him one whit. He had only seen his wishes and his wants, an insufferable arrogance. Not once had he considered what might happen to Margaret in these circumstances. Arrogance has a price, one that demanded payment. Unfortunately, in this instance, the bill was not presented to him.

His box was to the right of the stage, selected because of its view of the performance, not those attending it. He knew, however, that until the candles were extinguished, that they would be a focal point of countless interested stares.

"Have I ever told you about the Duchess of Wiltshire?"

She turned her head and glanced at him. "No," she said softly, "you haven't."

"She is an old, crotchety woman who insists upon a diet of cabbage and turnips. No one, however, has the courage to tell her that her company is unbearable for more than a few moments. The Earl of Stonebridge is a man of medium years who loves his port with such fervor that he can be counted upon to drool in his soup and get ill in the bushes. The Marquess of Binsnoble has an affection for his pugs. He kisses them on the snout and insists on carrying them about with him at all times."

There was an expression on her face now, something other than that frozen stillness. It was confusion mixed with the dawning of amusement. "Is there a reason you're telling me this?"

"They're only human," he said, looking out at the theater. "Each one of them has his flaws and can be expected to exhibit them, given enough time."

He sought out the interested gaze of more than one old biddy. His frown, however, had not one deleterious effect. Another example of how he'd misjudged a situation. On the whole, he was not adept at failure. He discovered that it irritated him to be wrong.

"The Countess of Rutledge is ensconced in another century and insists upon revealing her sagging breasts down to the nipple, but everyone politely averts their eyes when she comes close."

"Are you going to recite all their failings to me?" she asked, her smile broadening.

"If necessary," he said, perfectly prepared to do so. "Why?"

"To help you understand that it does not matter what they say."

"Even if they whisper that you are here with your mistress?"

"I rarely attend the theater," he said. "People are

naturally curious about the woman who accompanies me tonight. I simply misjudged the degree of their interest."

"Are you considered an enigma, Michael?"

"You look fascinated at the thought."

"I do not perceive you as being mysterious," she said.

"I have divulged more to you, Margaret, then I have to any other living soul." A bit of honesty that silenced him. He realized that she knew more about certain aspects of his life than any other woman of his acquaintance. But more than that, she was privy to thoughts he had not shared with anyone else.

"It is all right, Michael. I knew it would happen, you see. A man and his mistress often cause talk. This is what you want for me, and it's a life I cannot accept."

He stared at her, incapable of uttering a word in his defense.

The chandeliers were finally lowered, the candles extinguished by waiting footmen. A few moments later, the curtain rose and the play began. *Macbeth*. A play dour enough for his mood.

He watched Margaret's profile in the near darkness.

She leaned forward, had her elbow propped up on the curving wall of the box.

His attention was only peripherally drawn to the play. He had seen it many times before. His reason for being here tonight was not so much to view it again as it was to give Margaret the experience.

Instead, he had only subjected her to ridicule.

He was a debauched fool after all.

Thunderous applause marked the entr'acte. Margaret sat back in her seat, enchanted. Greed, ambition, and murder. Perfectly horrible, and utterly delightful.

Michael ordered refreshments for them, another surprise. As the chandelier was lowered, then raised again, its candles lit, she found herself once again the object of attention.

She turned and glanced at the circle of boxes, at the faces that were turned in their direction It was a unique experience, being the subject of so much discussion. She wondered what held such fascination for them. The fact she was here with Montraine? Or that she was not one of them?

Suddenly, she found herself staring at the Duke of Tarrant across the expanse of the theater. He looked as stunned as she felt.

The Duke had not changed. He still reminded her of a gaunt bird of prey, one who looked at her with loathing. She preferred the curious gazes of the other onlookers to his vitriol.

She heard Michael speaking and she glanced up when he appeared at her elbow. A footman left the box as Michael handed her a glass and a linen napkin.

The privileges of rank, she supposed, to be served while attending the theater. She took the glass from him, stared down at the contents. Something pink and frothy. She couldn't drink it.

"Are you not feeling well, Margaret?"

She shook her head slowly. "Would you be very disappointed if we left?"

"If that is what you wish," he said. It surprised her that he offered no objection. Perhaps he thought she wished to leave because of the whispers. She looked over at Tarrant again. Not gossip, but hatred. It marred the rest of the evening.

"Yes," she said, turning to Michael. "I would very much like to leave."

She didn't look at Tarrant again, but she felt his gaze on her back as they left the box.

Aphra Hawthorn, Countess of Montraine, was exhausted. Her feet ached abominably; her face felt as if it were cracking. Charlotte would not cease prattling on and on about the many eligible gentlemen who'd asked her to dance. Ada looked as tired as she felt. Only Elizabeth seemed blissfully untouched by the night's events. Her youngest daughter did not look as if she'd literally danced until dawn and was now saying farewell to the last of the guests.

Youth. It seemed a weapon at times.

The ball had been a decided success in terms of masculine interest in her daughters, but the sun was on the horizon. Aphra knew that if she didn't reach her bed straightaway she would simply collapse where she stood. As she waited for her carriage to be brought around, she heard the tittering sound of laughter from the group surrounding Helen Kittridge. She drew herself up to her full height, surreptitiously patted the tendrils of hair at the nape of her neck back into place, and girded herself for war.

Ever since she'd come to London all those many years ago, the woman had been a nuisance, an irritant. They had been courted by the same man, each led on to believe he would offer for her. Aphra had long since decided that she had won that particular skirmish and lost a larger battle. If Edward married Helen then perhaps the other woman would have spent the last twenty years being as miserable as Aphra had been.

In thirty years she had rarely spoken to Helen. She had wed a marquis, a delightfully happy union, Aphra was told, and from that had born a litter of children. Their rivalry was currently being acted out between their daughters. Sally Kittridge, Helen's only daughter, seemed to be a well-mannered, genteel sort of girl with a shy smile and washed out features. The same might be said of her character. The girl was simply bland.

But then, Aphra acknowledged, she probably didn't worry Helen as her own daughters did. For all her love for them, Aphra was not blind to her children's idiosyncrasies. Charlotte whined, Ada droned on about her causes, and Elizabeth said every thought in her head the instant it arrived there.

She glanced at the group surrounding Helen Kittridge. The ball was attended by the very same people she'd seen only last night. There simply was not enough time between social engagements to have done something notable enough to mention. Evidently, however, they had found something interesting to discuss.

Aphra studiously concentrated on her gloves, pretending a disinterest she did not feel. She was not only curious but mildly alarmed. From time to time several people in the group would glance at her and then look away, tittering.

What had Charlotte done now? Had Ada solicited funds for one of her causes? Or had Elizabeth offended someone with her honesty?

Where was her carriage? She frowned at the footman, who bowed in response. His servility did not, however, render the line of carriages shorter.

"You're looking well, Aphra." She turned her head to discover Helen Kittridge standing beside her.

"And you," she said courteously, nodding.

Behind Helen stood three women. Far enough that it was not obvious they were eavesdropping on the conversation but close enough so that it would not strain their ears to do so.

The fact that Helen Kittridge approached her now was an omen of the worst sort. Aphra waited impatiently for the revelation that she was certain to come. Some news that absolutely delighted the other woman.

She nearly broke her fan when she heard.

Chapter 23

❦

*Violent emotions are disruptive
to physical pleasure.*

The Journals of Augustin X

Michael hesitated in the doorway of the morning room, almost as if he didn't wish to leave her.

How utterly handsome he was. How perfectly splendid, attired in a deep blue wool coat and trousers, white shirt, and silk cravat. His black leather boots had been polished to a shine. The picture of sartorial elegance. An earl about the business of the Empire.

"I'll only be an hour or so," he said, studying her. "Perhaps even less than that."

He didn't disclose the reason for his errand, but she suspected that it had something to do with the leather case he held. Even this week of hedonism had not exempted him from a sense of responsibility. Each day he worked in his library for a few hours.

"I shall take advantage of the time to read a bit more," she said, smiling gently at him.

"Our friend Coleridge?" he asked with a smile. "Or some other volume you chose?"

She smiled. "A tale of a knight," she said, fingering *Ivanhoe*.

"Nothing along the lines of the *Journals*?" he teased.

She shook her head. The *Journals* offered no further interest. Instead, memories of him would easily suffice.

"Will you be all right here alone?" he asked.

"I shall sit here on the settee and be as quiet as a mouse," she promised.

"If you wish anything, do not hesitate to ring for Smytheton."

"I would much rather fetch anything I needed for myself."

"Has Smytheton been rude to you?" He frowned at her, a glower she'd come to associate with him. Not so much an expression of his mood, she suspected, as his concentration. At the moment, she was the subject of it.

"No. He has been almost punctilious in his regard."

"You are certain?"

She had the distinct impression that he would not leave her until she reassured him. She had rarely been so cosseted.

"I shall be fine, Michael," she said.

He crossed the room, leaned down and kissed her. A long, lingering moment later, he stepped back.

"I should leave," he said huskily.

"Yes," she conceded, lifting her gaze to him.

How could she bear the moment when they parted?

"I shall be fine, Michael," she said again and forced a smile to her face.

He nodded once, then left the room.

*   *   *

At the doorway, Michael turned and glanced back at the morning room, torn between his duty and his wishes. A surprising conflict, one he'd rarely felt.

"Take care of her, Smytheton," he said as his butler handed him his top hat and walking stick. Smytheton only nodded, his face carefully expressionless. Michael never quite knew what the man was thinking when he chose to be inscrutable.

As for himself, he was all too certain of his thoughts.

He entered his carriage, resigning himself to the errand before him.

He had not considered what the role of mistress would cost her, both in pride and dignity. Not once had he envisioned being in public with her, but keeping her to himself.

Like a caged animal, Michael?

The thought ate at him.

It had been nothing more than selfishness. An arrogance of thought and deed. He'd wanted her with him because his life seemed somehow more exciting with her. But he had never truly understood what it would mean to her. Their conversation on the river, the night at the theater had both been lessons in his overweening pride.

She had been right all along. What had she said to him that first day? Something about not being raised to be a mistress. Being with him would be the worst thing he could ask of her.

He respected her quiet dignity, was curious about the look of reflection in her eyes sometimes. She was his companion in abandon yet she was equally at home in silence while he worked.

The truth was that he didn't want Margaret hurt, nor did he ever wish a repeat of what had happened at the theater. As long as he lived he would remember the sight of her sitting there, a queen in restraint and demeanor while people whispered about her. Never again, he vowed.

A terrible realization to make, that his fascination for a woman was capable of harming her.

A moment ago, he'd not wanted to leave her. What would it be like to do so in two days?

Alan Stilton stood at the window gazing out at the parklands of Wickhampton. A wandering stream curved through the garden, led to a walkway bordered by pleached limes. He could turn his head and view the landscape at the rear of the house, a verdant lawn graced with a long reflecting pool.

The lavender fields to the south of the estate scented the air. The drone of bees and the soft, melodic sound of the breeze rustling the leaves were the only accompaniments to his thoughts.

A legacy, Wickhampton. His sons would continue his lineage, and down through time the name of Stilton would be revered. For the grand deeds of his ancestors, perhaps but never for his own.

It didn't concern him that he had ordered people killed. Soldiers were never deemed murderers, and he'd been involved in nothing less than war. He had tried to save the Empire and in doing so had placed his own heritage in jeopardy.

Tarrant had come to Wickhampton because he needed to be free of London for awhile. Or perhaps he just wanted to be reminded of his family's five hundred years of service to England. He could not forget that. It was for his heritage that he had acted in the way he had, for the very glory of England.

"Enter," he said, softening his voice deliberately, so

that it appeared almost avuncular. There were those who believed him to be so. He had long accepted the premise that perception is truth. What people convince themselves they see, they believe. Therefore he was rarely without a smile or a kind word. Easy deceptions that cost him little.

He turned and watched as Peter came closer. A greeting, permission asked and granted.

"You needn't search for Margaret Esterly any further, Peter. I have seen her myself." A small smile curved Tarrant's lips, hiding the fury he felt. "She has a protector, evidently," he continued. "The Earl of Montraine."

The Code Master. What an exquisite and horrifying irony. The last man in England who should read the *Journals of Augustin X.*

The moment he had seen Margaret with the Earl of Montraine, he knew that the situation had taken another dimension, become infinitely more dangerous.

"It is he who concerns me, Peter. He's a man equipped with an intrusive curiosity. If she has the other two books in her possession, it might prove to be an altogether uncomfortable pairing."

Peter remained respectfully silent.

"She has been a thorn in my side for years. She offends me and I would have her plucked out." An order couched in a biblical parlance. "But he is the one who concerns me the most."

"You wish him killed, Your Grace?"

Tarrant frowned at his coachman. "A nasty word, Peter. Let's not use it again. It is enough that you and I understand each other. It is not necessary to speak of certain things. If both the earl and his newest fancy disappeared, I would be pleased."

Only then would his world be secure once again.

* * *

Margaret felt oddly sad at Michael's departure, then forced herself to turn back to the book. But the tale of *Ivanhoe* could not interest her for long. Instead, she kept envisioning him as Michael, tall, with black hair, blue eyes and an arresting smile.

She set the book down on the settee beside her, propped her chin in her hands and stared out the window.

There might come a time when she regretted this week. But she could not imagine that moment. She had expected to spend the time with him in passion, but had not suspected that they might find companionship together, also. Twice they had sat on the settee in the library together, each involved in a book. One afternoon it had rained hard while they were reading, the comforting patter on the cobbles adding a coziness to the scene.

Last night, however, had proven that this week was foolish. She played with disaster, all the while pretending that they lived in a world apart. They did not. The life each lived was all too proscribed. The experience at the theater had proven that.

She glanced toward the door, the sound of voices intruding on her thoughts.

"Mama, he will ruin everything. No one will be remembering the ball. They'll be talking about this scandal. I will be ruined."

"You are the most frivolous girl, Charlotte. All you can think of is yourself."

"Elizabeth, you will not speak to your sister in such tones. It does not augur well for your manners. Such stridency will no doubt set your suitors to running."

"I do not see why women seek out marriage at all. 'Independence I have long considered as the grand blessing of life, the basis of every virtue.' "

"Please no, Ada. Must you forever quote Wollstone-craft?"

"She is a perfect martyr to the cause of women's vindication."

"Oh, pish, she's not a martyr at all. You only quote her when you want to stir up an argument. I doubt you feel half of what you say."

"I, for one, would always want the companionship of an amiable suitor."

"Where is my son, Smytheton?"

It was bedlam; a bevy of female voices, all talking over each other.

Smytheton's voice. "I regret, my lady, that the Earl has gone out."

"It does not signify, Smytheton. We shall wait until he returns. Bring us chocolate in the morning room."

"I shall not have chocolate, Smytheton. It spots my face."

"I do think that it has something in it like lauda-num. It leads one to feel enormously content and everyone knows that such is not the natural state of mind."

His mother. Dear God, the Countess of Montraine. And Michael's sisters.

Margaret stood, brushed her suddenly damp hands down her skirt, composed herself, and waited.

The door opened and she was face-to-face with a woman of middle years, expensively attired in a high waisted bronze colored silk. A matching bonnet, tucked and pleated in the same shade of silk and adorned with ivory silk peonies was perched over startling red hair.

The countess slowly removed her leather gloves,

tanned to match her dress, all the while staring at Margaret with narrowed eyes.

"Who, may I ask, are you?" she asked sharply.

Before Margaret could answer, the countess turned and addressed her question to Smytheton. "Who is this woman?"

The majordomo looked at a loss for words.

"Margaret Esterly," she said. She swallowed hard, clasped her hands together, determined not to be intimidated by this formidable woman.

There was not one wrinkle on her face. It was so smooth that she barely seemed to frown.

It was a well-known fact that red flannel, dampened in hot water, and then rubbed over the lips could impart a pink hue for hours. A cloth soaked in blackberry tea and laid across the eyes could reduce puffiness. Coal ash carefully applied could darken blond or graying lashes and brows. Egg white, beaten with just the barest touch of honey, could smooth the face and eliminate all traces of age.

Margaret couldn't help but wonder if the countess used egg white on her face, along with a bit of red flannel and coal ash.

For a long, uncomfortable moment they simply stared at each other. Smytheton slipped from the room like a tendril of smoke.

"Can you explain your presence in my son's house? Or shall I make the necessary assumption?"

"I'm afraid it is," Margaret admitted quietly, "exactly as you think." And this meeting was the very worst thing that could happen.

"You admit it?" the countess asked. Surprise flickered over her face.

A slender young girl with brown hair and Michael's

sapphire blue eyes peeked around her mother then stepped forward.

"Hello," she said warmly. "I'm Elizabeth," the girl said. "I'm Michael's youngest sister." she explained. "And that is Charlotte, the middle one," she said, pointing to a girl of her height with blond hair and brown eyes. "Ada is the oldest and never this silent normally."

"Elizabeth," the countess said tightly, "have you no sense at all? You've just introduced your sisters to a woman of ill repute."

"Are you a soiled dove? Has Michael rescued you from a life of poverty and despair?" Ada asked Margaret curiously. Her brown hair was pulled back severely into a bun, as if she wished to make herself plain. Her eyes were a light brown; her gaze was as intent as her brother's.

"His whore? We've just been introduced to Michael's whore?" Charlotte wailed.

Margaret flinched, then held herself still.

"Where did you learn that crudity, Charlotte?" her mother asked, glaring at her. "That is not a word you should know, let alone speak." She held up her hand. "Get in the carriage, girls," the Countess said. "I have no intention of allowing you to be sullied by this creature."

"But Mama . . ." Elizabeth's protest was cut short by her mother's look.

Once they had left the room, the countess turned and surveyed Margaret slowly from toe to nose, a slow, measured, and thoroughly disdainful look.

Margaret willed herself to appear nonchalant. The countess, however, was as intimidating a personage as the Duke of Tarrant.

"My daughters are innocents. I, however, have had

experience in dealing with women of your ilk most of my life. Can I infer from your presence here that my son has lost his senses? Or has he taken a leaf from his father's book and become enamored of his mistress?"

"I am not his mistress," she said. Not exactly.

Smytheton appeared at the door once again, this time carrying a silver tray laden with two silver pots, a covered container, and an assortment of cups. The countess ignored his presence, never turning her gaze from Margaret. The butler carefully lowered the tray to the table and then looked at both women before choosing to leave the room rather than interrupt the awkward silence.

"Where is my son?" the countess finally asked.

"I'm not entirely sure," Margaret admitted.

"Do you not know how to speak, young woman? You address me as my lady. And you are respectful of your betters."

Irritation nudged aside the humiliation of this moment. Or perhaps it was pride, finally coming to the forefront.

The countess was not unlike those she had served at the bookshop. The women of the nobility traveled in black lacquered carriages, not seeming to notice the squalor they passed. Not for them the bone-jarring journey across the cobbles or the stench of London's streets. Their carriages had springs to soften their backsides, and they carried nosegays to perfume the air. They rarely saw her when she served them or made remarks in her hearing that were insulting. Effortless rudeness performed condescendingly.

"If I erred in not addressing you properly, I apologize, my lady," she said, tilting her chin up. "But should you not also apologize for your rudeness? Or are you simply an arbiter of manners and do not bother to abide by them?"

"You are as you are, young woman. I will issue no expression of regret for it."

They stood facing each other across the table.

"You think to insinuate yourself into Michael's life, no doubt," the countess said caustically. "Your ploy will not succeed. I will see to it that he sends you packing back to the docks, where you can ply your trade with those who appreciate your no doubt considerable talents."

Margaret knew full well that her presence in Michael's home was not considered proper by anyone's standards, either tradesman or noble. But neither was she a common doxy. However, not one protest came to mind. Instead, she was subjected to the other woman's silent and all encompassing contempt.

The bitter tang of the chocolate wafted upward from the tray. She had never cared for the drink in the best of times, but today it seemed especially horrid. Perhaps it was because of all the rich food she ate last night, or simply the tension of this meeting. Or, perhaps her child was simply making his presence known in the most awkward and inopportune moment. For whatever reason, she felt suddenly and acutely nauseated.

She closed her eyes, waited for her stomach to settle, all the while breathing deeply. It was the only way to counter the discomfort. But it seemed as long as the chocolate was there, so was the feeling of sickness.

"What is wrong with you?" the countess demanded.

Margaret shook her head, pressed her hand to her waist, lowered her eyes and walked determinedly toward the doorway.

"Where do you think you're going?" the countess demanded. "I have not yet dismissed you."

She didn't turn, didn't answer, intent only on the chamber she shared with Michael and privacy.

Chapter 24

If you would know another, know yourself.
If you would love another, love yourself.

The Journals of Augustin X

Robert was his usual reticent self when Michael turned over the results of the Cyrillic cipher to him. He had not expected anything else. But he knew his friend well, and could tell from the sheer absence of expression on Robert's face that he was excited about the translation.

From this moment forward he wouldn't know what happened to the cipher. Should any additional messages come into the Foreign Office's possession using that same key, the code could be unscrambled by someone else. His involvement was only in deciphering the pattern. How it altered history was often unknown.

He returned home to discover his mother's carriage waiting on the curb. The first sign that something was wrong. The presence of his oddly silent sisters inside the vehicle was the second indication. In addition, Elizabeth looked concerned, an expression that warned him of the confrontation no doubt taking place at this moment.

He confronted Smytheton at the door. "Where are they?"

"In the morning room, my lord."

His feeling of dread accentuated with each footstep. The door opened just as he reached for it. Margaret swept by him, her face parchment white. She brushed away his staying hand and raced for the stairs.

He turned to face his mother.

"What did you say to her?"

She frowned at him, jerked on her gloves.

"It's what I have to say to you that's important, Michael. Is that the same woman you had the temerity to bring to the theater last night? At the height of the season? Have you no thoughts for my standing? Or your sister's reputation? If you must behave in such a deplorable fashion, then you should comport yourself with the grace your father did, and hide the trollop!"

"Is that what you told her?" he asked, his anger mounting.

"It does not signify what I said. Everyone is talking about what you have done, Michael. I had to be informed of it by Helen Kittridge!"

"So you thought it important to come here today," he said, as dispassionately as possible. "And see for yourself."

"No, Michael. I came to protect the reputation of this family, which is evidently not one of your concerns," she snapped.

"Why, Mother, because I chose to have a companion at the theater?"

She narrowed her eyes at him. "No, Michael, because you chose a strumpet to accompany you." Twin dots of fiery color appeared on her face.

"She is not a strumpet," he said tightly. "Merely a woman with no family to protect her." The truth startled him. Another bitter recognition of his own idiocy. "Her presence here is not her fault. But mine."

"You're very loyal to her, Michael," his mother said, her lips tightening. "More so than to your own family."

"Perhaps because she is more deserving of it." He turned and left the room, intent on finding Margaret.

"Is it because of the child?"

He turned and stared back at his mother. She stood in the doorway, the picture of wealth and position. "What are you talking about?"

"Your absurd protectiveness for this woman. Is it because of the child she carries?"

At his silence, she frowned at him. "Surely you knew? She's breeding."

Michael felt as if a brick had struck him. "Did she tell you that?"

"No," she said, "but she didn't have to. I've had four children of my own, Michael. I know the signs well enough. She has that look, for one. And the smell of chocolate made her ill. I was the same with Charlotte."

She glided across the foyer as if she didn't see him standing there, dumbstruck. Smytheton opened the door for her, bowed. She turned and glanced at Michael. "But do not take my word for it," she said sharply. "Ask her yourself."

Michael took the stairs two at a time. Whatever he expected to find, it was not Margaret seated at the end of the bed, wearing her faded green cotton dress. Her hands were linked together on her lap, her feet crossed at the ankles. Beside her on the bed was the blue dress she'd worn earlier, topped with the shawl he'd given her.

He entered the room, closed the door behind him. She didn't look up as he approached her, only fixed her attention on her linked hands.

"Why didn't you tell me?" he said, his voice too loud. He stood before her and attempted to calm himself.

Her head jerked up and she stared at him wide-eyed. If anything, she grew more pale.

"Tell you what?" she asked. A paltry attempt at brazening it out, he thought.

"About the child. My child." His look dared her to deny it.

It seemed to him as if the moments thudded past with their own sound. A drumbeat, heavy and ponderous.

"How do you know?" she asked finally, her voice faint.

A confession couched in a question.

"My mother informed me. Evidently, having four children has given her some insight into life," he said dryly. "Perhaps I should be grateful for her timely interference. Were you bloody well going to tell me, Margaret?" He continued to gaze at her, hoping that he appeared more calm than he felt. "Or were you just going to fade away into nothingness? Never letting me know? Never telling me that I sired a child?"

"Why?" she asked, standing. "So that you could label him your bastard?"

He was taken aback by her anger.

"I never wanted you to know," she said, and the

truth of that statement rang out in her words. Idiotic to feel a spurt of pain at her comment.

"Why not?" There, a rational enough question.

She gripped one of the posts, studied the carving intently. "Because you would never stop trying to convince me to stay with you."

"You're right," he said. "I won't."

She frowned at him.

"At least he would be provided for," he said. "Or do you intend to raise him in your cottage? Educate him as well? I do not doubt that you are a good teacher, Margaret, but I could provide him with better schools."

"You probably could, Michael," she said, turning aside. "But then he would be forever known as the Earl of Montraine's bastard."

Another startling blow. How adept she was becoming at delivering verbal wounds.

"Better than being poor, Margaret," he said, in an effort to ward off the effect of her words.

She narrowed her eyes and stared at him. "Is it? My grandmother earned money by tatting lace and taking in washing. Her knuckles were so red and swollen that sometimes she wept in her sleep. I was called Margaret Long Toes because my shoes never fit. I'd cut out the toes so that I could keep wearing them. There were days, Michael, when there was not enough to eat and I went to sleep early in order to dream of food. Do not try to teach me about being poor."

A formidable woman. She had lost what stability she'd had with her husband's death, yet had transformed herself. A teacher, a woman of the country. Now a mother, dedicated and protective even before her child was born.

"The poor have pride, too, Michael. Perhaps more than the rich because it means more to us."

Anger gave her some color. At least now she was not so pale.

"You can't leave me, Margaret," he said stubbornly. Reasonably. He was waging a war of wills and words, one he'd never expected to have. But then, he'd not thought that she would come to mean so much to him. Or that she would be carrying his child. Nor had he ever considered that the realization would create yet another emotion inside him—an ebullient pride.

"Do you remember Covent Garden, Michael? The women who strutted about the theater district with their skirts pulled up, the better for the world to see what they were? Is that what you wish to make of me?" Her eyes flashed at him.

"Bloody hell, Margaret." He strode to the fireplace in order to put some distance between them. He needed time to think, to marshal his arguments. She had effectively punctured his logic and shown him the weakness of his reasoning.

"My husband was a duke's bastard. The nobility of his sire did not make his illegitimacy easier to bear. Is that what you want for your child, to be mocked at school? To be called bastard?"

"Do you really think that now is the time to bring up your damnably sainted husband?" he asked caustically.

"Stop swearing at me," she said testily.

"I want to do more than that, Margaret," he admitted. "I want to strip you naked, tie you to this bed and force you to remain there until you start making some bloody, damnable sense!"

Her eyes widened. Good. She should be a little wary of him at the moment. Rage had a cleansing effect, Michael noted. He felt as if it burned from the inside out, the fuel being all the petty exasperations of his days, the irritants he'd buried for years.

"Why are you so angry?" she asked him, courageous enough to look at him again. He wanted to warn her that he was changing as the moments passed, becoming someone not quite himself.

Why was he so angry? Because she was slipping away from him and there was not one damn thing he could do about it. Because she was right, and he saw that just as he saw his own actions in a kind of magnifying glass. The shame he felt warred with other, more dominant emotions. Need, desire, a possessiveness that shocked him.

He stood at the fireplace, fists clenched, fascinated to discover that rage was bringing forth a new man. This man wanted to throw the new gowns his mother had purchased on dubious credit out in the street, trample on the bonnets his sisters nonchalantly ordered, flail his arms like a madman and rail at every damn woman on the face of the earth. But more, he wanted to keep her with him no matter the cost. No matter what he had to do to ensure it.

"Is it pride, Montraine? Is that all this is?"

He glanced over his shoulder at her.

She walked toward him. He stiffened, looked away from her, furious. Instead of anger, there were tears in her eyes. "Let me go, Michael," she softly said. "This will not aid us at all. It will only ruin the memories of these past days." When she reached him, she reached up and pressed four fingers gently against his lips.

"There is nothing you can say to me that will convince me," she said softly. "It is perhaps not a shocking thing for a man to have a mistress. Quite another to be one. I find that I do not like being called *whore*. And I could not bear it if our child was labeled a bastard as he surely will be if I stay."

It felt almost as if a door was swinging shut, slowly. An odd reaction to repudiation. The pain of it surprised him.

"I don't want to be your whore, Michael. I don't want you."

That was new. Something altogether innovative. He forced a smile to his face to mask his sudden surprised hurt.

"I'm supposed to simply accept your decision, Margaret? Walk away and forget?"

"You have no choice," she said simply. "I was only a challenge to you, Michael," she said. "And you told me yourself you don't like being bested."

Let her go. Settle an amount of money on her. Ask her to inform him when the child is born. Marry your heiress and send more money on an annual basis. Arrange to do so through his solicitor. Arrange for the child's schooling. His conscience had a hundred suggestions. If he wished to handle the situation in a pragmatic fashion, there were options available to him.

How strange that they were all unacceptable.

He didn't know how to say all he wished to say to her. The words should have come easier than they did. Instead, they crouched, cowardly, in his throat.

I admire your strength, Margaret, your wit and the way you look at the world. I glory in your mind and cherish your thoughts. Even your anger fascinates me.

When had this enchantment with her happened? When they'd laughed together on the river? Or in the theater when she'd sat so still and proud while everyone gossiped about her? Or on a terrace when she'd almost kissed him? Did it matter when it had happened? It had. Simply put, it had.

"Can you so easily forget me, Margaret?"

"I will have to," she said softly. But he noted that she did not quite look him in the eye.

"What are you going to do, Margaret? Will your villagers not think it a little strange that a woman two years widowed is bearing a child? It will be a little difficult to convince the villagers that the child is the sainted Jerome's." At the look on her face he bit back an oath. "That's exactly what you're going to do, isn't it?" The words she'd said to him a week ago resounded in his mind. She'd hinted at it then. *Even where I live will not be a concern of yours.*

"Perhaps," she said.

He turned and fingered one of a pair of Staffordshire dogs resting on the mantel. "So, you are going to have to go away. Create a new existence for yourself. Pretend yourself newly widowed and claim the child Jerome's." He turned and glanced at her. "Is that it, Margaret?"

Her silence was assent enough.

"I should be happy you wish to leave me. I would be well suited with Jane Hestly as a wife." She would not be easily coaxed to amusement, his bride. She would be solemn and serious and exceedingly proper. Nor would she have a way of tapping her fingernails on the cover of the book as she read, a habit that had made him smile. She would not have the ability to make him doubt himself. And she would not, he realized, possess the capacity to wound him.

Margaret stood silent behind him. Waiting for his assent, his agreement. Patient while he brushed aside this surprising pain so that he could speak.

He had avoided sentiment all his life. Because it

was his nature. Because, too, he'd been surfeited with it. Yet now he felt buffeted by the force of it. Strangely animated in a way he'd never been. Rage and euphoria, a curious combination.

He had thought of words such as enchanted or captivated to describe his reaction to her, but they did not measure exactly what he felt. The emotion Margaret sparked in him seemed difficult, almost impossible, to place in a net of words. If it was a number, he would call it infinity. And the very poetry of that thought shook him to the core.

The realization slid into his mind with the ease of a breath.

Surely a logical man would have understood long before now? A man whose life revolved around puzzles and ciphers and codes would have comprehended what had happened to him? It shouldn't have taken him this long to understand.

He loved her. Not simply, not easily. It wasn't a friendly, passive emotion. It changed him, this feeling, made him a different man. One who wasn't certain or sure. One not at all reasonable as much as alive.

There was only one thing to do.

"I want to go home," she said again from behind him.

He turned and looked at her, almost bemused with the realization of what he was about to do. He couldn't hold it within, couldn't restrain himself one second longer. Without his conscious thought, his arm reached out and grabbed the china dog and hurled it against the window. It shattered in an explosion of sound, an odd counterpart to the buoyancy of his own emotions.

Her gaze flew to his, her mouth open in shock.

He smiled at her, feeling an exuberance that was

unlike him. "I will be delighted to take you home, Margaret. Pleased beyond all measure. Happy to do it. This afternoon, in fact. Will that be soon enough?"

She nodded silently, her gaze fixed cautiously on him.

The fissured glass sent faceted shafts of sunlight into the room, illuminating the shards of porcelain littering the floor. Kicking away the larger pieces in his path, he strode to the door.

He turned and surveyed her, thinking that she still looked shocked. Well she might be. And later, what would her reaction be? He began to smile, then chuckle. Gradually, his laughter overcame him, giving life to the jubilance he felt.

Margaret only stared at him as if he were a madman.

Indeed he might be.

Chapter 25

*Pleasure can be as soft as the breeze of a
butterfly's wing or as shattering as a
mountain crumbling.*

The Journals of Augustin X

A brief burst of rain had freshened the air earlier
leaving the sky a brilliant blue without a hint
of clouds. The leaves of the trees in the square were
a glossy emerald. Even the cobbles seemed a different
color, now a bright and glaring orange.

Michael stepped into the carriage, settling opposite
Margaret. Her hands lay folded in her lap, her shoulders squared.

They had not spoken since he'd left the chamber a
few hours earlier. But his strange mood seemed to
have dissipated. Now Michael seemed intent upon the
passing scenery or else captured by his thoughts.

Mayfair offered an illusion of calm. As they traveled further into London, the noise level increased.
The clatter of carriage wheels across the cobbles, the

whinny of thousands of horses. The street peddlers, barrow girls, shouts, cries, laughter—they were all part of the cacophony of the city.

The buildings began to change as they traveled further west. Here they were built closer together, blocking out the brightness of the day. Even the air seemed thicker, almost sulphurous. As early as it was, shadows puddled in the streets. Soot covered the bricks and rendered the world monochromatic.

Gray was the color of poverty.

Finally, they were quit of London completely, the landscape appearing as if by magic, unmarred by buildings and the noise of thousands of people.

Michael clenched the gold head of his walking stick so hard his hand must hurt. A muscle flexed in his jaw as he stared out at the view.

She might have been wary of him after the scene in the bedchamber, if other memories had not intruded. Not a man of rage, but one who laughed with her on the floor of the morning room. A diligent man who worked beneath a dawn-painted sky, showed her the echo of a pantheon with the delight of pride. A man who had carried her upstairs after she'd fallen asleep in the bath.

It was true he was obstinate, supremely logical. He sought patterns in numbers and meaning in codes. Yet he had abducted her from her home for a week of passion, laughed with her and been boyish. An inconsistency. A fascination.

I expect a certain order in my life.

She recalled his words only too well. Yet, he'd not acted rationally, especially this morning. He'd been furious.

The afternoon advanced as they traveled west, but

other than a few questions posed and answered, they barely spoke.

"Would you like to stop at an inn?" he asked at one point.

"No," she answered as politely. "I'd rather travel straight through."

An hour later—"Are you comfortable?"

"Yes, very."

She blinked her eyes against the spike of tears, lifted the leather shade with a fingertip, and pretended an interest in the countryside. They were growing closer to Silbury.

In a few moments he would say good-bye to her. Forever.

What happens when something occurs in your well-planned life that you simply do not expect? What do you do then?

She'd asked him that question the day on the river. The answer to it had been remarkably simple, but not particularly easy. He had spent hours in his library, writing to his solicitor, giving him instructions that would set into motion the destruction of his heritage.

Torrent had not been producing well for the last decade, but the land was scenic and the hunting was good. Haversham was less well situated, but the property had potential. Surely both estates could be sold easily.

Although Setton was entailed, the furnishings were not. There were some Chinese bowls and Delft pottery that hadn't been shattered in his parents' marriage, along with works of art and some fine pieces of statuary collected by his grandfather. Also, there were a few pieces of jewelry neither wished to wear nor pass on to his sisters. Rubies were unlucky, she'd always said. Perhaps, in this case, they might bring him some good fortune.

But he was adamant about retaining the London houses. He would not live with his mother and sisters, and he could not banish them to Setton. At least not until his sisters had a chance at a season. The expenses for that would be paid by the sale of a bibelot or two—a silk screen his grandmother had fancied, or a gold snuffbox dating back a few decades.

Nor would he have to touch their dowries if he was careful. They would then all be able to make advantageous marriages even if word of his financial reversals got out.

He tallied up his possessions like a man standing before the judge at debtor's gaol. The complete sum was not an enormous amount, even considering that he might receive a fair price for Torrent and Haversham. But it would be enough to live quietly, if economically, for the rest of his life. A subdued existence, one that pleased him to contemplate.

The greatest change would be to send word to his creditors that he would no longer pay for any of his mother's extravagant shopping sprees. In addition, he was going to cut down on her staff, and establish a great many other economies not previously instituted. The days of profligacy while waiting for an heiress to be wed was over.

His mind whirred with possibilities.

The one true regret he had was being forced to sell the few parcels of land in Scotland left to him by his maternal grandmother. He'd always thought it would be a legacy he, himself, could pass down to his child independent of the entail.

In a way, he thought, glancing at Margaret, perhaps it was.

*   *   *

The coach slowed and turned into the lane before the cottage.

The day had grown overcast, but the clouds could not render this moment more somber. The carriage stopped in front of the cottage, rolled a few feet, and finally remained still.

They looked at each other. A last honest glance, perhaps. What did he see? A woman teetering on the edge of acquiescence? One who clutched her pride and her dignity around her as if it was a tattered cloak and prayed that she would not cry?

He preceded her, kicked down the steps himself and jumped to the gravel path. He turned and held his hand out for her, his glance as inscrutable as before. She stepped down from the carriage silently.

She had half expected him to add weight to his earlier argument. To convince her to stay with cajolery and promises. But it seemed as if she'd rendered him silent. Or his rage had burned out any further protestations he might make. Perhaps he had simply realized that there were times when words were simply not enough.

The seconds ticked by as if they were hours. There was so much she wanted to say to him and nothing that was safe. How, for example, did a woman thank a man for passion? For teaching her the meaning of desire? For treating her with delicacy and joy?

He walked her to the door in silence. She steeled herself for his departure, hoping that he did not delay the moment of their parting.

Please. Leave me now. She heard the words so loudly in her mind that it was as if she'd spoken them. She turned, placed her hand on his chest. A wordless plea for his kindness. *Leave me*. She did not want him to see her cry.

He placed his fingers beneath her chin and raised her face. She expected a kiss. A last, poignant embrace to be forever remembered.

Instead, he studied her face, traced the line of her bottom lip with his thumb. Drawing out the moment until time was so thin she could almost see through it.

"Marry me," he said softly.

She stared at him, stunned. "What?" The word emerged as a croak.

"I can't marry you," she said.

"Why not?" His tender smile was muted somewhat by his irritated frown.

"You're only asking because of the child," she said breathlessly.

"If it makes you feel better to think that, then by all means, do so."

She blinked up at him.

"Is there another reason?" Her heart stilled, waiting.

"I find myself excessively emotional around you," he said, raising one eyebrow at her.

Margaret found it difficult to breathe. His blue eyes were direct, without a hint of humor.

"Marry me," he said again.

She glanced over her shoulder at the carriage. The coachman looked entirely too interested in their conversation. She turned, hooked her thumb in the latch, pushed open the door.

He followed her, looked around. "It is," he said, "exactly as I had pictured it."

She waited for the criticisms, but instead he began

to pace, a restless movement from doorway to wall, shooting her a fierce look as he passed.

She watched him. "Are you going to throw something again?"

"I might," he said unrepentedly. "I'm in the mood for it." He stopped, stared down at the floor once, then continued. "You are not going to make this easy, are you?"

He most definitely was not acting himself. But then he had not since he'd thrown the porcelain dog at the window. He'd looked almost pleased then. Now the light of battle was in his eyes.

He walked to the door and lifted his arm toward the coach. She followed him, watched as the driver nodded and climbed down from the seat, a valise in hand.

"What is that?"

"A few belongings," he said calmly. "I knew this might be a long siege. After all, you've made your feelings about the nobility all too clear."

"You can't stay here, Montraine!" She stared at him, horrified.

"And you wouldn't stay with me," he said agreeably.

The sound of another vehicle approaching the cottage drew her attention. Wide-eyed she stared at the wagon. It was piled high with furniture, pillows, a mattress or two. If she wasn't mistaken there were even a few pots tied to the top. But the greatest surprise was Smytheton perched stiffly on the wagon seat beside the driver, his white hair askew, his black suit dusty, and an expression of extreme annoyance on his face.

"Smytheton?" she asked weakly.

Michael nodded. "He'll act as your duenna if you

will. Hardly a proper chaperone, I agree, but it's better than remaining in London." He turned and fixed her with a fierce look. "Isn't it?"

She waved both hands in the air, backed up as if to forestall everything he was saying. And doing.

"I have no intention of allowing you to remain here, Margaret," he announced. He surveyed the cottage, the paucity of furniture, the lone west window. "It's small, but I don't doubt that Smytheton can make something of it. I hope the old boy doesn't snore. Unless, of course, you have a lean-to where he can sleep?"

She found herself nodding. "For the chickens," she said, then realized what she was saying. She shook her head, stepped back.

"Or you can simply marry me," he said.

"You can't be serious." It was too preposterous. Earls did not marry poor widows.

He came closer, put his hands on her shoulders and drew her closer.

One hand tipped her chin back, the other threaded through the hair at the nape of her neck. "Oh, but I am. We can live here or we can live in London."

"You can't marry me," she countered, breathless and absurdly hopeful. "You need an heiress."

"I've already arranged to sell almost everything I own," he said. "We'll have to economize, but we should survive."

"I'm a commoner," she said, almost desperately.

His smile was quick, amused. "I'm not royalty, so it doesn't matter."

"Your mother will be displeased."

"Now *there's* a reason," he said, wryly, pulling her slowly closer.

"I'm a tradesman's widow. I don't know anything

about being a countess." She felt a frisson of horror at the thought. "I only know about books and sales and inventory. Or teaching. I know that," she said, fumbling with her thoughts and her words.

One eyebrow arched. "Which only proves you're intelligent," he said. "You know how to read and reason. A decided advantage to most females of my acquaintance."

"Montraine . . ."

He gave her shoulders a quick, impatient squeeze. "I'm declaring my love," he said, "and you're arguing with me. Why did I know this would happen?"

"You are?" she said, blinking up at him.

"I am," he said somberly.

"Oh." She was left completely without a response. Even if she had thought of something to say, she doubted she would have been able to utter it. The air had been pulled from her lungs and her heart had stopped beating.

"Be quiet, Margaret," he whispered against her lips, and kissed her.

Long, exquisite, delighted moments later, a gasp made her pull back. Margaret blinked, dazed not only by Michael's words, but by the passion of their kiss.

She turned her head, saw Smytheton in the doorway. In front of him stood a few of her students. Dorothy had a bouquet of wildflowers clutched tightly in her hand. Little Mary stood with her hands behind her back. Both of them looked surprised. No, shocked. Abigail, however, wore an expression of unholy glee. Before Margaret could speak, all of them melted away.

"Who was that?" Michael asked. "Your students?"

Both her hands were still clutching Michael's coat. With great precision, she released them, smoothed the wrinkles on the fabric. She found herself patting him, as if she wished to reassure herself that he was real.

"Margaret?"

She looked up at him. "Yes," she said, sighing. "Abigail is the daughter of the village gossip and will fill her mother's shoes quite adequately one day."

He arched one brow and smiled down at her. "Your reputation is sealed, then."

"You needn't look so pleased," she said.

"You are plunged into ruination," he announced. "Even if you move, the gossip is sure to follow you. You're a fallen woman. Irretrievably compromised."

She closed her eyes, leaned her forehead against his chest, feeling his arms surround her. It was such a pleasant place to be, here in his arms.

"Will you marry me, Margaret?" he softly asked.

Their worlds occasionally collided but rarely merged. The truth was, however, that she loved him. Simply. Completely. Absolutely. Totally.

"Yes," she murmured, capitulating.

"To protect your reputation?" he asked softly. She pulled back, studied his sudden frown. Clearly the idea did not please him.

"No," she admitted.

He stood there silent. Waiting, no doubt, for an answering declaration from her. How strange that she felt almost shy with him at the moment. "The idea of your marrying another woman is most definitely not appealing," she said, her palms pressed against the fabric of his coat. She smoothed them across his chest to his arms and back again.

How did she tell him that he was like the air she breathed and the sun on her face? Necessary delights of living.

"Jealousy?"

She shook her head.

"I have been given to understand that a woman in these circumstances is not so reticent about her feelings," he said tautly.

"Are you going to throw something again?"

"Why do you look so delighted at the prospect? Does my momentary insanity please you?"

She stroked his arm. "I should not confess to such a thing, should I? But you're very attractive when you're enraged."

His brow rose even further, his grin thoroughly wicked. "Then is it my manly form, Margaret?"

Until she'd known him she'd never experienced sorcery. Never known what it was like to feel passion. For the sheer blinding alchemy of that she would be forever grateful. But being with him was oddly more. It was the taste of an orange, the smell of a rose, the touch of the first spring raindrop expanded and multiplied and folded over itself. The meaning, perhaps, of joy.

She stood on tiptoe and breathed against his ear. "No, Michael. Love." The most fervent of avowals gently whispered.

The reward for her honesty was a soft laugh and a long kiss.

Chapter 26

*A courtesan speaks softly and with wit,
smiles with genuine mirth and promises
pleasure with her glance.*

The Journals of Augustin X

Michael Hartley Hawthorne, Earl of Montraine,
and Margaret Lindlay Esterly, widow, stood
before the vicar the next morning in the small stone
church in Silbury Village.

The faint sunlight barely lit the one stained glass
window over the altar. The air smelled damp, an odor
common to the old stone structure. The day itself was
one of mist and melancholy, contrasting sharply to
Margaret's dazed delight.

No special arrangements or permissions were required since she had lived in Silbury Village for more
than six months. All that was necessary was for Michael to pay for the required license and also the sti-
pend to the clergyman. She did not doubt that
Michael had promised an additional generous sum to

the vicar if the ceremony was kept private and short. Consequently, Penelope and Tom were the only guests.

Smytheton had been sent back to London in the wagon, a journey that displeased him almost as much as the abortive one to Silbury Village, if his glower was any indication.

The vicar's voice droned on, but she paid only half an ear to his opening sermon. From time to time Penelope would glance at her, then at Michael. As if she were as stunned as Margaret at the very fact of this wedding.

"Is he the one?" Penelope had asked this morning, when they were packing her meager possessions into Michael's valise. "The babe's father?"

Margaret nodded.

"You'll be a countess now, Miss Margaret."

"I know nothing at all about being a countess, Penelope," she said, not quite able to hide her fear at the thought. "I doubt I'll do well at it."

"You'll do better than well," her friend said loyally. "So will the babe. Ever since you found those accursed *Journals*, we've been plagued with bad luck. Maybe this marriage is a change from that."

Those accursed *Journals*.

Margaret looked up at the rafters where the strongbox was hidden.

A few moments later, Penelope stood on the table while Margaret held it steady. She reached up to grab the dusty box from the rafter with one hand while she pressed the other against the wall for balance. She handed the box to Margaret, who set it to one side while she helped Penelope scramble down from the table.

"I hope you'll be taking those books with you," Penelope said. "I wouldn't want my Tom to get any ideas." She leaned close to Margaret, as if they weren't the only people in the cottage. "There are things in those books, Miss Margaret, that are surely wicked."

Deliciously so. Margaret quickly stifled that thought. Instead, she reached inside, retrieved the two remaining *Journals*, and placed them in the valise. She left the money inside. Closing the strongbox, she handed it to Penelope.

"I want you to have it," she said. "The money will give you and Tom a good start on your marriage."

Penelope looked stunned. "I could not, Miss Margaret."

"I insist," she said adamantly. The proceeds from the sale of the first *Journal* would be enough to rent a small cottage of their own. Or perhaps even purchase this one from Squire Tippett.

Penelope had been flabbergasted ever since Margaret's announcement.

As for herself, she appeared appropriately solemn. She hoped the calm expression on her face was an adequate disguise for her sudden terror.

What was she doing? A thought that repeated itself over and over, an accompaniment to the vicar's voice. She couldn't marry this man. He was an earl. What did she know of earls?

You're just as good as anyone, Margaret. Her Gran's voice echoed in her mind. Her Gran would have been pleased by this marriage. But her grandmother had been a governess, a woman familiar with the dealings of the rich. She knew how to comport herself in the homes of nobles. Her only experience had been a week of passion. She knew nothing of dances, and dinners, and morning calls.

Michael turned his head and studied her, his gaze uncomfortably direct. Then he smiled as if he'd heard her fears and wished to ease her mind.

In that moment she knew. It came not in a rush of awareness, but in a whisper. The true meaning of love was not simply gentleness and sharing, but also the violence of surrender, the relinquishing of pride and fear. And the faith of stepping into a blackened abyss lit only by one faint star.

He reached out and took her hand and she held it tight, reassured.

A very large orange colored cat sauntered into the church and sat on the stone floor beside the vicar. His tail whipped around, his eyes fixed on Margaret as if to question her presence in a house set aside for worship. She had no doubt it was the clergyman's cat, what with that look of condemnation in his feline eyes.

The vows performed, the prayer lingered on. The diatribe on sin and redemption was halted by Michael's frown, a particularly quelling look that had the cleric stammering to a halt.

She stepped away from the altar, turned to Penelope, bewildered at the speed with which her life had changed.

"Well, if you had to do something so foolish, Miss Margaret," Penelope whispered, looking at Michael, "at least you chose a handsome nob."

"He is quite agreeable, isn't he?" she said, smiling.

"Does he always frown so?" Penelope asked.

"Always." Margaret's smile broadened as Michael's scowl deepened.

"That might take some getting used to," Penelope said. "Do you think the babe will look like him?"

"I sincerely hope he does not frown as much," Margaret said.

"Are you quite finished discussing me?" Michael asked sardonically.

He looked so aristocratic standing there, so desperately out of place in this tiny church. Utterly handsome. Hers.

She reached up and brushed a kiss on his cheek. He looked startled for a moment, then his arm reached out and encompassed her waist. He escorted her to the front of the church where they signed the parish register, signaling an official end to the wedding ceremony. She was now Margaret Hawthorne, wife of Michael, Earl of Montraine. Or as Penelope might say in one of her more vulgar moments, cor, she was a bleedin' countess.

Michael had dreaded his wedding day for years. In all his thoughts of it, he'd never believed that he might be experiencing what he was at this moment. Happiness, a tinge of fear, and an almost visceral possessiveness coupled with another, less discernable feeling. Triumph. She was his.

An entirely confusing range of emotions.

Then again, he'd never thought that he would have to convince a woman to wed him with the assiduousness he had Margaret Esterly. Correction. Margaret Esterly Hawthorne, Countess of Montraine. A role that seemed, oddly enough, to suit her, if that regal little tilt to her chin was any indication. Nor had he thought that he might have to beggar himself to gain a bride. He should perhaps have felt something about that development, but the fact was that he was too happy to care.

He placed his hand on the small of Margaret's back

and escorted her from the church. He had paid the vicar well, not only to execute the marriage ceremony without delay, but to ensure some measure of privacy and to protect Margaret from gossip.

As they left the church, he realized that while the marriage might have been intimate, the speculation had already begun. Standing on the street before them were a group of women, each holding tight to the hand of a girl. At their appearance in the doorway, the assembled mothers began to mutter. Not unlike, he thought, a gaggle of disapproving geese.

A tall, angular woman with a long face stepped forward. She glanced curiously at Michael and then away, as if dismissing him.

"I've come to tell you, Mrs. Esterly, that you'll not be teaching my Dorothy again," she said. "I don't want her near the likes of you."

"It seems as if your Abigail wasted no time in circulating her tale," he said in an aside to Margaret.

She nodded.

"Nor I," said another woman. Her face was round, her eyes narrowed with an expression of repugnance "Harlot."

He felt Margaret wince beside him.

He didn't give a flying farthing what the world thought of him. His experience was that society would talk about him whether or not he participated in their discussions. But he had no intention of standing here and listening to them revile Margaret. Perhaps the two of them had been unwise, but they had not sinned against these women who had set themselves up as moral jurists.

He stepped forward, in front of Margaret.

"You are speaking of my wife, madam," he said sharply, "the Countess of Montraine. And as her husband," he warned them, "I am not disposed to hear your insults."

The announcement had the effect of a bolt of lightning. They silenced as one, utterly transfixed.

Penelope and Tom moved to his side. "I'll have you know, Anne Coving," Penelope said, in a voice that carried well, "that Miss Margaret was married this morning. And I'll not allow you to ruin this moment with your vicious tongue."

He guided Margaret from the steps, the women falling back as they walked through the group to the carriage. An oddly silent crowd now.

He turned as Margaret bid farewell to her friend, then waited as she entered the carriage. He frowned at the assembled group, smiled his thanks to Penelope and her still silent husband and entered the carriage, sitting beside his wife.

Margaret glanced at him, a small smile curving her lips.

"Well, what did you expect?" he said, still irritated at the group of harpies outside the church. "For me to tolerate their insults to you?"

"I was only thinking," she said, "that this is the first time I have seen your arrogance directed at another. On the whole, I prefer not being the recipient of it."

"You're well quit of this place, Margaret," he said, still annoyed. "Little minds in little places."

"London will be better?" Her quizzical look chided him.

"Very well, it's true. We've fueled the gossip mills well. I do not doubt that there will be nothing but rumor and innuendo for months to come."

"Do you mind?"

He sat back, tossed his walking stick to the opposite seat.

"Not one whit," he said, honestly.

He had his share of friends who were his rank, but his closest association was with Robert, a man without a title. In addition, he labored beside men in the Black Chamber who were measured not by their rank, but by their abilities and intelligence. Was that why he saw the boundaries of his society as more fluid than most? Because he admired men not for what they had inherited, but for their reasoning? Or for their ability to dwell in an abstract world few people understood?

Perhaps. But he was well aware that there were those who would find great pleasure in ensuring that Margaret's entry into society was difficult. By keeping the walls high and the moat deep, the inbred xenophobic *ton* kept itself pure and unsullied.

He would have to protect her from the more vindictive members of society, his mother included.

Chapter 27

*The love of pleasure must never be mistaken
for the pleasure of love.*

The Journals of Augustin X

It seemed to Michael that he and Margaret had spent an inordinate amount of time in a carriage together. Night had fallen by the time they entered the outskirts of London. His carriage was well sprung, a vehicle built for uncertain roads. The London cobbles could barely be felt. Margaret had long since succumbed to sleep.

He should have done the same. He had not slept well the night before, having taken shelter at Malverne House. He would not have insinuated himself into the squire's good graces had Silbury Village boasted an inn. A concession to Margaret's reputation. He would have sacrificed far more than being nipped and barked at for half the night by Squire Tippett's six terriers.

His wife lay against him, a small unearthly smile

wreathing her lips even in sleep. He wanted to kiss it gently from her lips.

Only a sign, then, of how half-witted he was becoming. To find the one woman in the entire world who could render him idiotic. Then to turn his world upside down to marry her.

Another indication of his foolishness. He was a rutting beast. A man clearly out of his element. Even in sleep she aroused him.

They halted, finally, before his home. Michael thought the sudden cessation of movement would wake her, but Margaret slept on, so deeply that he thought it a pity to disturb her.

He leaned forward and placed his hand against her cheek. Margaret's eyes flew open as if he had called her name.

"We are home, Margaret."

She nodded drowsily and sat up. His hand dropped away as she straightened her skirt and checked to see if her hair was orderly. It occurred to him that he had never before seen a woman perform such gestures so matter-of-factly. There was no cry of distress, no fumbling for a mirror, no lamentations as to fatigue or the tedium of the journey. Simply a pat and a smooth of hand, and that was all.

He descended from the carriage and held his hand out for her, a role better suited to footman than earl, but he was concerned for her footing. It had evidently rained earlier from the sheen on the cobbles.

He took Margaret's valise from the coachman. It seemed a foolish thing to summon Smytheton at this late hour. Especially since the man was still irritated at him for making him travel to Silbury. He hefted it with a grunt and glanced at her.

"What have you packed in here, Margaret? Bricks?"

"Just my things," she said, covering her yawning mouth with both hands. "Oh, and the *Journals*."

"I will have to read them one day," he said.

She said nothing in response to his remark, only smiled slightly. He left the valise on the table, watched as she walked slowly up the stairs. It would be better to allow her to rest. Certainly he could restrain himself for a little while. One night, after all, was not *that* many hours.

"Margaret," he said, stepping forward. His hand was on the banister, his gaze intent on her.

She smiled, tenderly. An expression that should not have made his heart thud in his chest. She held out her hand to him, answering his unspoken question.

He reached her quickly, his breath coming in a piercing rush as he kissed her.

The journey up the remaining steps was easily made, but not quickly executed. Twice he stopped and kissed her until their breaths came shallow and fast. Twice, he thought that the chamber was too far away and the stairs, although uncomfortable, would make an adequate trysting place.

It was his wedding night. An occasion that called for some restraint. He managed to reach their room before he lost his senses. Again. Forever.

Once in their chamber, Michael turned to her. His fingers flew over fastenings and buttons, removing her dress, his coat, her chemise, his cravat, her stockings, his trousers. She began to laugh as he threw each piece into the air to land where it would.

"Wait," she said, before he pulled her to the bed. "Stand there, Michael, just for a moment."

"Why?" His cheeks were flushed, his eyes seemed to glitter.

Her hand flattened against his naked chest, moved slowly up until her thumb rested in the well at the base of his throat, fascinated at the rapid beat of his pulse there.

"I have to warn you, Margaret," he said tightly. "I am decidedly impatient at the moment."

He had always spoken of his regimented life, the order he craved. Yet she'd never witnessed the control he claimed ruled his world.

"There is a certain value in waiting, Michael." Her fingers moved slowly to his shoulder as if giving him time to protest the exploratory touch. Her palm curved around the ball of his shoulder measuring it.

"Not tonight there isn't," he said, reaching for her.

She smiled, amused.

"You should have modeled for the statues in your pantheon. You are so utterly beautiful."

For a moment he seemed at a loss for words, but he quickly recovered from his surprise. "Shall I make you pay for my favors, then?" he asked, as he led her to their bed.

"I hope not," she said, watching him. He moved to the bed, lay down upon it, and stretched out his hand for her, seemingly impervious to his nakedness.

He lay there, pasha-like, a feast for her eyes. Lit by the candlelight and shadowed by night. A man blessed with a physical attractiveness that lured her and a mind that fascinated her. A man who made her smile even as he seduced her.

Yet this was not seduction. It was, perhaps, an alchemy of the spirit. A sharing that occurred whenever they came together. Something rare and extraordinary, as if God himself had given him to her. *For your grief and your tears, I give you something wondrous. Some-*

thing to be treasured for the rest of your life. Guard it well, you'll not see a love like this again.

"I doubt I could afford you," she said, a smile curving her lips. "You look as if you would be worth your weight in gold. All the richest women in the world might wish to purchase you for their pleasure."

"There are commodities other than money, Margaret," he said, his teasing smile a match to hers.

She lay on the bed, turned to face him.

Heat was in the center of her, spreading outward until even the tips of her fingers felt on fire. "Truly?"

He reached out a hand and pressed it against her hip, slid his palm across her stomach.

"When will your body begin to change?" he asked.

The question surprised her. "Soon. I think."

He drew a circle around a nipple. "Your breasts will grow larger," he said.

She nodded. His gaze lowered; he traced a line from the middle of her breasts to her navel.

"I find you eminently worthwhile," he said, his smile soft and alluring. A gentle smile with only the barest touch of wickedness to it.

"No payment necessary to enjoy you?"

"A kiss?"

He rolled onto his back and reached out for her. She leaned over him, placed her hand on his cheek. His skin was hot beneath her touch. She traced his lips with her fingers before lowering her mouth to his. Something opened up inside her. A sweetness, a poignancy, not unlike the moment just before tears.

She could not remember a moment as exquisitely beautiful as this one. The room around them was hollowed out by shadows, the only spot of illumination the single candle. Its flickering light made the rain-streaked windows appear diamond encrusted.

Could time itself be halted? If so, she would wish to savor this instant when she lifted her head and his gaze held hers.

His face seemed to change. His hand reached up, cupped her face, his fingers threading through her hair. Teasing desire had been replaced by tenderness. Heady and sweet, passion filled, it promised more than simple fulfillment.

She felt spellbound.

This man was her husband. Bound to her by ritual and God. He was the man who had fathered her child, who had promised to protect her and shield her and worship her with his body.

He turned her and raised himself over her, entered her slowly, as if he knew that she was ready for him. Needed him. There was hollowness inside her, an emptiness only he could fill.

His eyes remained open, watching her. She reached up with both hands and curled her fingers within his. Was this aching delight she felt shared by him?

She could see herself reflected in his eyes. If she looked deeper, would she see the man he truly was? Overpoweringly male. An earl who laughed with abandon and loved with intensity. A man of arrogance, dedication, pride. A noble who loved his country, honored his family. Loved her.

The candle sputtered, the seconds lengthened as they gazed at each other. The rhythm of their breathing slowed until they breathed in tandem. His fingers loosened, then tightened on hers.

It was a strange and disconcerting experience she had at that moment. As though she surrendered herself completely to him. He filled the void, becoming part of her in a way she did not fully understand.

Perhaps the boundaries of self, rank, world had simply disappeared.

The moment was timeless and trembling.

Unable to bear it a moment more, she closed her eyes. A tear slipped from beneath her closed lids, fell to the pillow. He bent his head and kissed its path.

She reached up, placed her lips on his, sighed inwardly as he deepened the kiss. A feeling began in the core of her, as if all the disparate parts, once cohesive and complete, were being separated from the person she knew herself to be. And he gathered up the pieces and held them safe.

Slowly, he pulled out of her. She closed her eyes and waited an eternity for him to enter her again. Her body bowed in joy when he did.

She began to anticipate his movement, her body arching toward his. A dreamy, achingly slow possession, unhurried and exquisitely timed, their bodies in rhythmic tandem. The feeling washed over her in waves, becoming stronger with each prolonged stroke of his body in hers.

It was too much. It was too intense, too much to endure. She arched beneath him, lost in bliss. Margaret clung to him, her breath captured in a startled scream. The rest of the world dropped away until there was only him.

All that she needed.

Michael propped his head on his palm and studied her. Margaret lay on her side, facing him.

Dawn was making an appearance on the horizon. The sky was growing lighter; its midnight blue fading reluctantly like a reveler not ready for his bed. Across the horizon streaks of pink, a hue to match the color of Margaret's cheek, warned of the sun's approach.

His fingers gently traced the curve of her jaw, then traveled upward to her mouth, nose. One fingertip dusted across her eyelids, marked the thick line of her lashes, then returned to trace the shape of her mouth.

"You are not asleep," he whispered. "Else you would not be smiling."

"I am," she said firmly. "It's only that you're tickling me."

He placed his hand on her shoulder, traced a path to her hand. Her fingers were long and slender; the nails gently rounded and clean. But there were calluses at the end of her fingertips. Until he'd seen her cottage, he'd not thought of the way she lived, had not considered that she had been on the edge of penury. Yet she had refused to take from him. Neither money nor security. A woman of independence and pride.

His wife.

"Margaret." They lay so close that the speaking of her name was no more than a breath on her cheek.

Her hair was the color of autumn; her mouth curved easily into a smile and bestowed kisses with the flavor of eternity. The words were not his usual ones; they were almost poetic.

He'd thought he understood desire. Had experienced it, shared it with women in his past. He had tucked it into his mind along with other necessary emotions. Something to be understood and accepted. But Michael was beginning to recognize the depth of his ignorance.

She opened her eyes and looked at him. Her expression made him smile. Irritation, and sleepiness. She didn't rouse easily.

The words must be said before another moment passed, before another second clicked upon the clock.

"I accept you, Margaret," he said, looking at her beloved face. "Unconditionally. Madly."

Margaret looked startled at his declaration, but then it seemed she remembered their earlier conversation. "I accept you, too, Michael," she murmured, her smile luminous. "Unconditionally. Madly."

A realization occurred to the Earl of Montraine in that moment. He had not entirely believed in love, but it was all too evident that it truly did exist. He had never understood, however, that love flowed outward, from the soul of one person to another. Until this moment, he had never realized that it was an all-encompassing thing, an emotion that blessed both the recipient and the giver.

Not at all a sensible thing, love.

She cuddled against him. He wrapped his arms around her as she buried her head against his shoulder, nuzzling his neck with her lips. A moment later her breathing was rhythmic, soft. She'd fallen asleep again. He smiled and held her there safely in his arms.

Chapter 28

Silence will stifle pleasure
while gentle words will encourage it.

The Journals of Augustin X

Smytheton was waiting for Margaret at the base of the stairs.

"Allow me to convey my felicitations to you, my lady, on the occasion of your marriage," he said stiffly.

"Thank you, Smytheton," she said. She wondered if he knew it was the very first time she had been addressed so formally.

He reminded her, oddly enough, of what her father might have looked like if he'd lived. He'd been a soldier, too. Her Gran had told her that he had big, strong shoulders and a broad face. She had been only a baby when he'd died, but sometimes she thought she remembered his wintry blue eyes. Or maybe it was just from all of Gran's stories.

Smytheton had the same light blue eyes, and a

shock of white hair that made him look altogether very distinguished. The perfect majordomo for an earl's home.

A more proper accessory than she was, certainly.

She went to the table, picked up the valise.

"Where is Michael?" She revised the question at Smytheton's frown. "Where is his lordship?"

"I believe, my lady, that he is in his library," he said, bowing.

Not the same the respectful gesture he showed to Michael. This unctuous effort seemed to say that he knew well enough where she had come from and that she did not quite deserve his reverence.

If he had been disposed to listen, she would have gladly informed him that she disliked the trappings of rank. It was perfectly acceptable to her if he never bowed again. However, that would have made him frown once more, and she had had quite enough of Smytheton's glowers.

She knocked on the door, pushing it open at the sound of Michael's voice.

He sat in the middle of his library at his desk. A majestic setting for a man of similar appearance.

She smiled, feeling unaccountably shy.

"Good morning," she said.

He smiled at her. "I was wondering when you would awake."

"I'm sleepy all the time lately. But I understand that it is normal when one is carrying a child."

She walked toward him. "Are you happy about becoming a father, Michael?" A question she'd never asked.

"I am," he said. "But even more so about becoming a husband."

Her smile was born deep inside her where secret
wishes were stored.

"Are you preparing to leave me again?" he asked,
eyeing the valise in her hands cautiously.

She placed the bag on the desk. "I've brought you
the *Journals*," she said, taking them from the case.
"Where else to keep books but in a library?"

"I never asked where you got them," he said, his
attention directed at her, not the *Journals*.

"I found them in the strongbox. It was the only item
I was able to save the night the bookshop burned
down."

"Tell me about it," he said, standing. He pulled the
chair in front of his desk to the side of it.

"There isn't that much to tell," she said, sitting beside him. She related the story of that night, and when
she was finished, his scowl was even deeper.

"Did no one ever determine how the fire started?"

She shook her head.

"You're lucky to be alive," he said. He stood,
walked to her side and scooped her up in his arms.
He returned to his own chair, still holding her.

"Don't frown so, Michael. I did survive it," she said,
looping her arms around his neck. "It's all right," she
murmured, laying her head against his chest, and
heard the booming sound of his heart.

"I've never sat on someone's lap before," she admitted a few moments later. "It is a thoroughly pleasant experience."

He smiled, brushed a kiss over her forehead. "I was
just thinking that my work cannot compete with such
temptation."

"Could I truly tempt you from your work?" An intriguing notion.

"At this moment?" He smiled and shook his head.

"I need to get the harvest figures to my solicitor if he is to sell my properties."

"Is it a very grand sacrifice?" How could he do it? How could he sell his birthright and seem remarkably calm about it?

"Not a sacrifice at all," he said with equanimity. "We shall have to practice some economies, but we'll still have candles and coal."

"Penelope used to say that I could make a meal out of a pea," she offered.

He laughed, the sound echoing in the large room. "There isn't a need for such drastic measures," he said. "Except, perhaps, as an example. I do not think my mother or sisters are going to take the news at all well."

"That we have married, or that I am not an heiress?"

"Perhaps both," he said. She smiled at him, grateful for his honesty. "In the end they will have no choice in the matter."

"Do you think it's truly that simple? Your mother makes me think it will not be. Besides you cannot simply decree that people act in a certain way and expect them to obey your command."

"Can't I?" His smile was altogether too charming.

"The only place people are orderly and silent is in a graveyard, Michael."

He smiled, amused. "*Orderly* and *silent* are not words I would use to describe my family," he said. "But on this, they will have no discussion. It is done, Margaret. Do you worry that it might be undone?"

She sighed. "I know nothing of being a countess, Michael. I am frankly terrified to attempt it."

"Do you not remember the examples of nobility I recited to you, Margaret? There are countless others.

The *ton* is simply a collection of people, all with their own eccentricities."

"So if I stumble over someone's toes, or drop my fork, or spill my wine, I will just be seen as endearingly clumsy?"

"No," he corrected. "You will be the endearingly clumsy The Right Honorable Countess of Montraine. Therein lies the difference."

"Then I should consider myself fortunate that I chose an earl, shouldn't I?"

"I have a feeling you'd be happier if I were a mere knight."

"Or a tradesman, perhaps," she offered.

"Being in society is not that onerous, Margaret," he said with a smile. "As long as certain rules are obeyed, you should have no difficulties."

She smiled at him, wondering if she should mention that her Gran had educated her in propriety. Perhaps he did not remember, since they had broken so many rules together. "Such as?"

There was silence for a moment, as if he chose the words to say.

"You are never to be in the company of a man," Michael began. "Unless, of course, I approve of him. Or to speak to those men who seem too coarse or have a roving eye. Bachelors are to be avoided, as well as recent widowers."

Margaret didn't mention that she had never heard of such dictates. True, an unmarried woman or one beneath the age of thirty was limited severely in her contacts with the opposite sex. But she had never heard of a wife being so constrained. However, she said nothing, simply looked at him with what she hoped was an earnest expression. It would not be wise to reveal her amusement.

"When we travel together, you will procede me into the carriage, while I leave it first."

A rule she knew well enough.

"While traveling, I will sit with my back to the horses or sit at your side. But again, if you are ever in a closed carriage with another man, he is never to sit beside you."

She only nodded, fascinated. Not with the rules he intoned, but with him. She had never considered him proprietary. But it seemed he was.

"In public you will always walk close to the wall of building or a structure, so that I may protect you from ruffians."

"It would be easy enough to formulate a set of restrictions for you, also, Montraine," she said.

"Did you know that you call me that only when you're annoyed?" He lowered his head, kissed her gently.

"Not fair," she murmured against his lips. "I forget everything I'm thinking when you kiss me."

"Nice to know it's not simply one sided," he whispered, kissing the edge of her ear.

She smiled, pushed him gently away.

"You are never to smile at another woman the way you do me," she said, tapping a finger on his chest as if to accentuate each point. "Nor are you ever to touch another woman. Or remove her gloves or her shawl, or stare at her bodice."

He leaned back in the chair, obviously amused.

"When you are in a carriage with another woman, you must not stare at her intently. Or talk to her in that voice of yours, one that promises almost wickedness."

"Almost wickedness?" he asked, grinning at her.

"Sometimes I think you are too alluring, Montraine."

"I shall immediately transform myself into a troll," he promised.

"Please do not," she teased. "I will endeavor to tolerate it."

For several long moments they looked at each other. A sharing of selves not unlike their loving the night before.

He smiled, a slow dawning smile that curled her toes.

"If I were you," he said, "I would not worry about being a countess."

"I have no idea what countesses do," she confessed, sighing.

"They spend money," he said. "That has been my experience. But with our newly instituted economies, that proves unwise."

"I have learned how to thatch a roof," she offered. "And how to repair the chinks in the mortar between bricks."

"A valuable wife," he said, obviously amused. "We shall always have a roof over our heads."

"I do not suppose there are any chickens about that I might feed? Or eggs to gather?"

"Nary a one."

"I am quite good at milking."

"Regrettably," he said, "there is not one cow in the house. You could always visit the modiste for the final fitting of your dresses," he suggested.

"A countess-like occupation?"

His nod confirmed it.

"I shall ask Molly to go. And frankly, I do not care whether or not the dresses fit. I never wish to see the woman again."

"You have entirely too many sensibilities," he said, grinning. "You cannot be a truly arrogant countess unless you've mastered the insouciance necessary to carry it off. You must simply appear as though scandal has no effect on you. Besides, didn't you mention that it makes no difference what your feelings are in the matter?"

"That was when I was attempting to make a sale," she said. "I find it's somewhat different being a customer. Besides, that attitude was ascribed to by the Margaret who was willing to be your mistress for a week. This woman has lapsed back into propriety."

"Yet, I do not doubt you can be coaxed from it," he said, nearly leering at her.

She began to laugh, willing to admit he was indeed correct.

She stood, kissed him lightly. As she left the room, she retrieved a book from the shelf. A treatise on the dignity of man. It would make for heavy reading, but it was something that would occupy her mind.

Until, of course, he could join her again.

Michael watched as she left the room, wondering if it was altogether wise to be so enchanted by a wife. But then, he had little choice.

The crop figures completed, he made a package to send to his solicitor.

He leaned back in his chair and surveyed the library. It was a pity that he hadn't the money to begin renovations. The third floor now had rooms only for Smytheton and Molly. They needed a nursery, perhaps another room for a nurserymaid.

It might be more feasible simply to sell this house and find something larger in a less fashionable location. But he would not, he vowed, occupy the family home as long as his female relatives were in residence.

His fingers trailed over the edge of one of the books. But for the *Journals*, he and Margaret would never have met. She would have remained in her cottage and he would be married to Jane Hestly. But for a moment upon a terrace he would not be sitting here now. But for that single space of seconds when he'd turned, hearing the brush of her shoe against the bricks, he might have missed her entirely.

Perhaps there was something to Fate, after all.

He smiled at himself again, opened the cover of the first *Journal*.

> *Oh reader, it is my intent to divulge all, to keep nothing hidden from you. For I am a traveler and a wanderer through the world. These tales I impart for education and enlightenment and joy. This second volume begins my tale of the land of the Manchu.*

Michael smiled and turned the first page. He was amazed at the breadth of topics addressed. But Augustin X's greatest fascination seemed to be all the various women he'd bedded in the course of his journeys.

As he began to read, Michael noticed the annotations beside each chapter heading. Babby's volume had been distinguished with the same marks.

It was second nature to jot down comments that interested him while reading, or to make notes that he could pursue at a later time. Michael made a listing of the marks as he continued to read, but the sheer eroticism of Augustin X's tale diffused his interest in the marginalia.

An hour later, he sat back in his chair, realizing that it had not been the wisest thing to read this book. It was one thing to have an inkling of the man's licentious life, quite another to read each salacious detail. To say that the Augustin X had a way with words was an understatement. Either he had an incredibly rich imagination, or the man had been able to hold sway in the beds of more than a few supremely accomplished women.

There was carnality in abundance, written in such precise and unremitting detail that Michael did not doubt the skill of the writer or the lover. Yet reading the *Journals* had left Michael feeling oddly empty. There was more to passion than what Augustin had described.

Even as a stranger, Margaret had made him laugh, had incited his curiosity. He had, oddly enough, liked her from the first.

His attention was captured by one of the paintings. The woman lay on her back, her hands clenched in the sheets beside her. There was such an expression of delight on her face that he was immediately intrigued. Her lover was intent on bringing her to pleasure with his mouth.

He smiled, shut the *Journal*, and went in search of his wife.

Chapter 29

~~~~~~ ∞◯◯◯ ~~~~~~

*Moderation must be practiced
in sexual congress.*

The Journals of Augustin X

"**W**e can stay at home if you wish," he said, leaning toward her. A tendril had come loose from her hair and he pushed it behind her ear. "We truly do not have to go to Vauxhall Gardens. You can claim a headache, or your condition, or some female indisposition."

"A female indisposition?"

He bent down and kissed the tip of her nose. "I have three sisters, madam. Do you think I have no idea of female complaints? I've been surfeited with them all my life."

"While I have never been indisposed, Michael." She recanted that statement with a wry smile. "Very well, I do detest the smell of chocolate. But I truly would like to see Green's balloon again. I saw it a few years ago at the King's coronation celebration and have never forgotten it. To think that someone could really devise such a thing or wish to fly like a bird."

"If you're sure you're up to the outing," he said.

She slanted a look at him, then reached up and kissed his cheek. Smytheton made a noise behind them—no doubt to remind them of their decorum.

Michael tapped his walking stick idly on the front step as they waited for the carriage to be brought around.

He glanced up to see his carriage approach, coming up behind another carriage on the street. He noted distantly that the coach with its four matched horses had no coat of arms or other markings to indicate its owner. Not unusual, especially in Mayfair.

This afternoon Margaret was wearing one of her new dresses, a soft green that made her eyes appear emerald. He stood below her, held out his hand.

Once again he was struck by how lovely she was.

"You have a radiance I've never seen before," he said, studying her. How absurdly besotted he was becoming. "Is it something particular to women with child? Or is it simply you, I wonder?"

One moment Margaret was smiling teasingly at him, about to respond to his comment. The next, an expression of horror flickered over her face as she stared at something beyond him.

"Michael!"

He turned his head at the sound of her warning. He glanced behind him, saw the driver of the coach pull a pistol from the folds of his coat. Everything registered within a few seconds. His mind, trained to see patterns, instantly recognized danger.

It felt as if time itself had slowed in order for him to see each movement, each gesture, each futile second. He couldn't reach her, was inches from protecting her.

It was only then that Michael heard the report of a gun. Instead of the pain he anticipated, there was only Margaret's soft, surprised gasp. His mind searched for understanding even as she crumpled in front of him.

Michael heard Smytheton's shout of alarm, the clattering wheels, the sound of the whip as the carriage sped away. But all his attention was on Margaret. She lay unearthly still, blood seeping from her wound to mark the steps in a hideous crimson stain.

In moments he had scooped her into his arms and brushed past Smytheton, through the front door, and up the stairs to their chamber, where he lay Margaret gently on the bed.

She made a sound; her eyes fluttered open. There was so much pain there that he could almost feel it himself.

"It will be all right," he said. Nonsensical words. "Don't worry, Margaret. It will be all right." A reassurance he found himself repeating over and over.

Help her. For God's sake, help her. His mind issued instructions that his body fumbled to obey. He tore off the bodice of her dress. The bullet had entered her right shoulder, the sight of her torn and gaping flesh making him wince.

He pressed his handkerchief to her wound. "It's the only way to stop the bleeding," he told her, when she gasped and her body stiffened with pain.

Smytheton brought him a length of toweling that he used to replace his bloody handkerchief. Michael thought of all those books he'd read, treatises on diseases of the body, books detailing the theories of ill humors, since proven unreliable. A thousand years of knowledge, and none of it adequate for this moment.

Smytheton spoke from behind him. "We can summon a surgeon, sir. But I've some experience with battlefield wounds."

Michael glanced over his shoulder at his majordomo. Smytheton met his gaze steadily. "I served with Wellington, sir, on the Peninsula." A reminder of his experience.

"Can you help her?" Please God.

"I believe so, my lord," Smytheton said calmly. "In the meantime, sir, we can send Molly to fetch the physician."

He did so, and shortly afterward Michael found himself relegated to the position of observer. There was competence in Smytheton's manner as he probed the wound with meticulous care, removing the wadding and the traces of shot.

It looked as if Smytheton's skills once more extended far beyond that of an average majordomo. A valuable man to have in his employ, and a blessing at the moment.

Michael was not a man given to prayer, an admission that did not seem entirely proper given the circumstances. He was not entirely certain how he felt about the Almighty. His existence was something in little doubt, but His exact interference in mundane mortal activities was grounds for some speculation.

There had been times when, as a young man, Michael had prayed to God to rid him of his sisters' presence if only for a few moments.

Had he wasted his invocations to God? Was a being, upon his birth, given only so many petitions? Had he spent his on mundane irritations? If so, he called them all back now in order to have two remaining. *Save her, and spare her from pain.*

Margaret moaned and he winced at the sound. "Can you not hurry, Smytheton?"

"I must be certain the wound is clean, my lord. There is nothing more to be feared than a gangrenous limb."

Finally, it was done. The bits of metal had been excised, the wound dusted with Anderson's Powder, packed, and bandaged.

During the last hour, Margaret had floated in and out of awareness. Now her eyes opened just for a moment. He wished them closed again, there was such an expression of pain in their depths.

Michael had recognized, years ago, that he was a maze thinker. When confronted with a wall, he immediately postulated alternatives. But he discovered in the last few moments that emotion could halt his mind's thoughts. He felt as if he were trapped in the maze, but instead of being able to figure out how to escape, he could only concentrate on the huge, impenetrable hedge before him.

An evidence of the power of fear, perhaps.

Ease her pain, God. It was less a prayer than a dictate. Would God punish him for his admonishment?

The physician arrived just at that moment. Michael left the room and looked down into the rotunda. The man was coming up the stairs, his frown indicating his displeasure.

"I was in the middle of my luncheon, my lord," he complained. "Surely, it cannot be as much a crisis as your maid gave me to believe."

"My wife has been shot," Michael said tersely. "I don't know what could be more important than that."

The physician entered the room, peeled back the bandage, and gave a cursory examination to Margaret's wound. He did not treat injuries as much as distributed nostrums, but had he not been satisfied with the results of the treatment, Michael didn't doubt he would have called for a surgeon.

"The wound to her shoulder seems to have been treated well. She will have some pain for a while, but I shall prescribe some tonics for her." He wrote something on a piece of paper, handed it to Smytheton. "The apothecary will be able to provide you these treatments."

"And the child?" Michael asked.

Both the physician and Smytheton appeared surprised.

"If you will step to the side of the bed, my lord, I shall ascertain her condition."

Smytheton left the room as Michael waited, watching as the physician examined Margaret above the sheets, patting her stomach and placing his hands on either side of her hips. "Nature has a way of protecting her own, my lord. If she has suffered no ill effects up until this moment, I doubt she will.

"You will need a good midwife when the time comes, but I expect she'll have an easy enough time at delivery. She has the hips for it. You should count yourself lucky, my lord. You should fill up your nursery with children in no time."

To that surprising pronouncement, Michael had no answer.

"If that will be all, my lord, I'll be on my way," the doctor said, his good humor restored, no doubt, by the thought of returning to his meal.

A moment later the door closed sharply behind him.

Chapter 30

~~~~~~~

*A woman of pleasure experiences great
joy from a man's enthusiasm.*

The Journals of Augustin X

The bookshop was on fire. The door to the hall was a
few feet to her left. Billowing smoke poured into the
opening and the rough boards of the floor were warm beneath her bare feet. Hands reached out and gripped her
arms. Then someone began slapping at the burning hem of
her garment. Michael.

The scene changed again to a field filled with clouds of
wildflowers. Michael stood there. Clasping each of his
hands was a child with his blue eyes. A little boy with black
hair and a bright smile pulled away and raced toward her,
while a little girl with auburn curls followed.

"Look, Mama!" The children darted from flower to flower
like industrious bees. Gathering a bouquet so large that
their childish arms could not hold them all, and the blos-
soms fell to mark their path through the meadow. Their
images faded away to the sound of laughter.

*   *   *

Margaret blinked her eyes open. The room was quiet, the morning well advanced, evidenced by the sunlight streaming in through the folds of the curtains. Michael was asleep in a chair beside the bed. His face rested on the mattress, his arm outstretched, as if he reached for her even in his sleep.

She moved, but the surprising pain in her arm rooted her in place. Slowly, she traced the bandage on her shoulder, measuring the dimensions of it. Events were blurry from the time she'd seen the gun in the driver's hand. She'd been shot, then.

She glanced once more at Michael. He didn't look injured, a thought that was followed by another one. The baby?

She leaned back against the pillows, closed her eyes, and pressed her hand against her waist. The only pain was in her arm and shoulder. Surely the absence of any other discomfort meant that all was well?

She opened her eyes to find Michael awake, watching her.

There had never been less than perfect order about his attire. His shirts were never wrinkled and his trousers always appeared perfectly creased. She'd never seen a spot of ink on his fingers, or a speck of dust on his boots. This morning, however, he looked decidedly mussed. It rendered him even more attractive.

"How do you feel?" he asked, his voice a rasp. His hands reached out to touch her, pressed against her leg as if needing the contact.

Instead of answering him, she asked a question of her own. "The baby?"

"Is fine, the physician says," he said reassuringly. "And you?"

"I'm a bit sore," she admitted.

"An understatement, I suspect."

She conceded the point with a nod.

"Why do I feel so odd?" she asked. "My head feels as if it's not quite attached."

"The physician gave you something for the pain," he answered.

She leaned back against the pillow, unaccountably tired. The questions she had, however, prevented sleep.

"Who would do such a thing, Michael?"

He reached out and picked up her hand, studying each separate finger intently. "Are there any secrets in your past, Margaret? Anyone who would wish to do you harm?"

"No one but Sarah Harrington," she said with a wisp of smile. "And I believe you routed her and her sister quite adequately."

He waited, patient.

"I've no secrets, Michael." She sat up, felt her face warm. "Only that I've read the *Journals*, and I've already confessed to that."

"I doubt if that act will rank as a great and onerous sin," he said, his quick smile banishing the look of fatigue on his face.

"I don't know," she countered, leaning back against the pillow. "It felt exceedingly daring to read Augustin's words at the time.

"I have led a remarkably simple life other than that," she said.

He smiled, absently she thought, as he studied her hand. She wondered if he truly saw it or if he was simply lost in his thoughts.

"What are you thinking?" she asked. Her free hand

cupped his cheek, her palm abraded by his night beard.

He glanced up, smiled more genuinely this time. "That I don't know where to begin," he admitted. "The carriage wasn't a hired hack. It was of good quality, as were the horses. But I've never seen the man before and I don't know why you were shot." He frowned, his concentration fixed again on his thoughts. "Unless, of course," he said, "the bullet was not meant for you at all, but for me."

"For you?" She felt a frisson of fear for him.

"Some of the codes I've solved have had foreign implications," he said enigmatically. "There might be someone who wishes to punish me, if for no other reason, for solving them."

He released her hand, then stood and walked to the window. Smytheton had, in his usually capable way, had it repaired recently. The smell of the glazier's putty was still strong in the room.

"I will not go to one of your properties," she said, guessing at the tenor of his thoughts.

He turned, surprised, then caught her glance. "I have no properties other than Setton, but it might be a good idea. It might be safer," he added.

"How can it be safer for me when you're here?"

"I have not protected you very well so far," he said wryly.

"But you didn't realize there was a need to do so," she argued. "Now that we are forewarned, we can be more cautious." She sat up more fully, wincing at the unexpected pain. The look on his face made her wish she had not done so.

"I will not leave you," she said firmly. "I'm afraid I'm tenacious on that point, Montraine."

"Is this the woman who was afraid of being a countess?" he asked dryly.

"It did sound rather autocratic, didn't it?" she asked. "Regardless," she said, her gaze on him, "I will not leave."

"It would be safer," he said again, his gaze not leaving her.

"You cannot know that," she argued.

"What I cannot do," he said huskily, "is to see something happen to you again."

"It will not," she said determinedly. "You will solve this puzzle soon enough. Until then, we shall be on our honeymoon."

"Batten ourselves in the house? The idea has merit." He came to sit at her side. "You should rest for now."

"An autocratic decree, your lordship," she said.

"I'm an earl," he teased. "And my wishes are always obeyed."

He was so handsome sitting there bathed by the morning light that she wanted simply to watch him, study him for hours.

"Is there a portrait of you?" she asked suddenly.

"A portrait?" He looked surprised at the question. She nodded.

"At Setton," he said. "It was painted when I became earl. But I was only fourteen at the time."

"So young," she murmured. It didn't seem at all fair that he'd had to assume all the responsibility he had at such a tender age.

"It was a long time ago," he said, bending to kiss her cheek. She moved her head and kissed him on the lips, instead.

"You should rest now," he said, pulling back finally.

"I'm a countess," she decreed, "and not at all tired."

He only raised one eyebrow at her as if he knew the truth. She *was* unaccountably weary.

A little while later she fell asleep again, feeling comforted by his presence, and the feel of his hand in hers.

The Duke of Tarrant frowned at his coachman, enraged. Until today Peter had never failed him.

Tarrant walked away from him, needing to put some distance between the two of them. Peter simply hung his head, waiting in silence for the verbal whipping. An indication of his slavish obedience. Peter loved him the way a beaten dog loves a kind master. Until today, Tarrant had never been anything but gentle with him.

"She isn't dead," Peter said again. "But I believe I wounded her."

"You fool," Tarrant said softly. "I told you to kill her. Or kill him. Two targets, Peter, and you still managed to fail?"

"Yes, Your Grace," Peter said, glancing up at him. His face was pale, but he didn't look away. A point in his favor. "Shall I try again?"

"Do you expect them to allow you the chance?" the Duke asked sardonically. "If I were the Earl of Montraine, I'd be searching for the assailant. One look at your ugly face, Peter, and you're found out."

He smiled thinly, stood and walked to the door. "No," he said opening it and standing aside for his coachman to leave his presence. "We shall wait a while, until they do not expect it. And then you will not fail, Peter."

He closed the door on the man's heels then turned and faced his library. Another irritation caused by

Margaret Esterly. If the woman was within his reach he would have throttled her with his bare hands.

Elizabeth stood on the doorstep, staring at him for so long that it began to be an irritant.

"I have not changed that much since we last saw each other, surely," Michael said dryly.

"No, Michael," she said slowly. "I was just thinking that you look terrible. As if you've not slept at all."

"Not that much lately," he admitted.

"Mama has taken to her bed with a sick headache, but not before forbidding me to come," she said, striding into the foyer. Smytheton stepped back from the door, bowed slightly. She smiled brightly at him, an expression that had the effect of easing his glower somewhat.

"Then why have you?"

"To help, of course, Michael," she said, stripping off her gloves. "Mama is moaning words like *scandal* and *financial ruin* in addition to repeating Helen Kittridge's name over and over. She thinks your marriage is shocking."

"How did she find out so soon?" He shouldn't, perhaps, have been surprised. Gossip traveled through the *ton* at breakneck speed.

"The physician was quite voluble when he attended Charlotte. She's been in her room for the last week sneezing. He says," she whispered in an aside, "that Charlotte might actually be sensitive to the London air. Of course, that only made her cry more."

"Do you feel the same about my marriage?" He looked at her steadily, fully prepared to oust his favorite sister from his home if she said one unkind word about his wife.

She was equally direct in her look, but then Elizabeth always was. She smiled after a moment. "You must answer two questions before I say, Michael."

"Perhaps." He folded his arms and waited.

"Does Margaret know any Latin?"

His smile felt unused, almost rusty. "No," he said.

"And do you love her?" Her smile was charming. Inquisitive, but charming.

"I'll stop at one," he said, smiling reluctantly.

"You do!" she declared. "Or else you wouldn't be so secretive. You never talk about things that matter to you."

He raised one eyebrow as he stared down at her. She simply continued to smile, all the while advancing on the staircase.

"Where do you think you're going?"

"To see my new sister-in-law, of course. To be a better nurse than you've been, no doubt."

He followed her up the stairs. There was no other choice short of bodily carrying _her_ back down.

"Was she very badly hurt?" she asked, glancing back at him.

"Her shoulder," he said shortly.

"Why would someone shoot your wife?"

"You've learned that from the physician, I suppose?"

"Oh, yes," she said blithely. "Plus the fact that you're going to be a father. All whispered in an undertone to Mama, of course. I was not supposed to hear."

"But you didn't allow that to stop you," he said dryly.

She halted on the stairs and stared down at him. "You're going to be a wonderful father, you know. But you are entirely too secretive, Michael. It comes, no doubt, from doing nothing but ciphers for years."

"You shouldn't know about that, either," he said, no longer surprised by her sources of knowledge. He would prefer to think his occupation somewhat secret, but perhaps Babby's idiotic name for him had eliminated any hope of discretion.

"Nonsense, there is no secret in London," she declared.

He shook his head, opened the door, and escorted her inside.

"Margaret, this is my meddlesome sister, Elizabeth."

"I am the most charming of people," Elizabeth countered.

Margaret, sitting up in bed, turned and smiled at both of them.

"I have come to be your nurse, and to offer you some companionship."

"I never told you how arrogant my sister is, have I?" he asked.

Elizabeth frowned at him, then turned and smiled brightly at Margaret.

"The only proper topics for visits are the weather and one's engagements," she said. "But I've just finished the most delicious novel," she whispered. "And I do so want to hear how you and Michael met."

He looked at Margaret. She glanced at him and then away.

It struck him then, so hard that it was almost a hammer's blow. *I cannot live without her.* How strange that he should remember his father's words at this moment. Or begin to understand the depth of his father's love for one woman.

He wanted to banish his sister and take his wife in his arms, attempt to explain to her why he couldn't speak and his breath was oddly trapped in his chest.

The force of his need and his recognition of it was a blinding fact, one that did not need nor require his sister's rapt audience.

"We shall be quite all right on our own, Michael," Elizabeth said, gently pushing him from the room. "Margaret needs a friend and I'm perfectly prepared to be one."

Margaret's expression was the only reason he allowed himself to be thrust out the door. She looked bemused. Curious.

He halted halfway down the stairs, turned and glanced back at the door to his room. Female laughter was not often heard in this house. It was a strangely appealing sound.

He stood in the foyer for a long moment, looking up at the ceiling, thinking that he had become as idiotic as any besotted fool. He'd given up his estates for her and his heart, willingly. The force of the emotion was staggering.

He must keep her safe.

He had sent Smytheton around with inquiries as to a strange coach and four, but none of his neighbors had seen anything. Robert was away from London, no doubt involved in something to do with the Cyrillic cipher, and he didn't wish to discuss the shooting with another individual in his office.

He had taken the precaution of destroying all his cipher worksheets, especially those relating to the most recent codes he'd solved. His memory would furnish the details he needed.

He had limited his activities, preferring instead to stay at Margaret's side. Guarding her had become of paramount importance.

But there was nothing about Margaret's life that could not be closely examined. She had lived circumspectly, an almost cloistered existence. Until, of course, she'd stood upon a darkened terrace one night months ago.

Her only secret had been a curiosity easily confessed. *It felt exceedingly daring to read Augustin's words at the time.*

He opened the drawer where he'd left the notes he'd transcribed upon reading one of the books. He began to read the *Journals* again. Without being drawn into Augustine X's words, he completed his annotations, flipping from the beginning of the book to its end until he'd written down all the margin notes.

His eyes scanned the column of numbers and letters, noticing a pattern. A code? It may be nothing. The volumes could simply be used as printer's proofs; the marks meant for the binder.

Then again, books were often used to transmit coded messages. Normally the method utilized was to underline selected words in a passage. Placed together they formed sentences. Not altogether a secure system of encipherment.

But perhaps he had been too hasty after all. He began to work, finding himself immersed in the possibilities before him.

Chapter 31

The greatest mystery is that of
a woman's smile.

The Journals of Augustin X

Because of her bandage and the soreness of her arm, Margaret required help in dressing and undressing. Michael had served as her maid, doing so with a rather forbidding scowl, and then absenting himself from the room until she was asleep.

Tonight he was evidently intent upon doing the same. She sat on the side of the bed and studied him.

She was filled with a particularly languorous feeling, one that had the oddest effect of making her fingertips tingle. All because of him, of course. His frowns amused her, while his smiles had the ability to alter even her heart, seeming to stop it for a beat or two before it raced to catch up.

He was a man of intelligence and logic and tumultuous emotion, for all that he tamped it down. A being capable of great tenderness, protectiveness, and the granting of exquisite physical pleasure. Now he stood looking at her with solemn blue eyes that measured the silent moments between them.

Hers. Once before she'd had the thought. But then she'd only borrowed him. Now he was hers for a lifetime.

"Is it true that they call you the Code Master?"

"Where did you hear that?" he asked sardonically.

"Elizabeth, I believe. Or perhaps Smytheton. Both are very impressed by your consequence," she teased. "They tiptoe past your library door in case they disturb you, and talk about you in a hushed voice."

"Everyone does," he said amicably. "I'm quite an ogre." He walked slowly toward her. "Everyone but you, of course.

"Did you know there was a code in the *Journals*?" he asked, threading his fingers through her recently brushed hair.

"No," she said, turning. "Is there really? What does it say?"

"I haven't the slightest idea," he admitted. "I've just begun to sort it out."

"Should I feel pleased that you've broken your concentration to help me undress? Or is that why you've come?"

"Unless you choose to wear your dress to bed," he said.

"And then you'll go work in your library until I'm asleep? Again?" she asked, studying him.

One of his brows rose imperiously.

"I was shot in the arm, Michael," she said. "You mustn't think I'm all that delicate."

"Else you will tell me of the roof you thatched and the bricks you mended?" He smiled.

"I truly am better, and it has been more than a week. I've missed you," she said. There, a hint and an invitation in one.

She didn't need *that* much cosseting.

For a moment they simply looked at each other.

She stood and closed the distance between them.

"You have a dangerous mouth, Margaret," he said, bending his head to kiss her. Softly at first, then deepening the kiss until she saw only darkness behind her closed lids. She leaned into him, wanting to be touched. To be held by him. More kisses, please. A day's worth. A week. A lifetime.

He pulled back finally, his breathing as harsh as hers. They leaned against each other. For support, she thought, smiling.

She could remain this way for the rest of her life. Enthralled by this man. First he'd captivated her curiosity, then her body. Now her mind, her heart, and perhaps her very soul.

He slowly withdrew something from his waistcoat, held it up for her to see. She smiled as she realized exactly what it was. A long length of pink ribbon.

"Where did you get that?"

"I took it from the modiste's supplies," he said, coming to her. He wound the ribbon behind her neck and around her throat. "But do not think me a thief," he said. "I had Smytheton pay her for it."

"You've had it all this time?"

"I keep it with me always."

"Waiting, perhaps, for the propitious moment?" she teased.

He moved his hands behind her back and with great deliberation opened the first three buttons of her dress. The gaping bodice allowed him to press his lips against her collarbone, the curve of her shoulders.

He gently helped her off with her dress, his eyes narrowing as he viewed her bandage. He bent his head and kissed the edge of it just as he did every night.

He did not, however, remove her shift. He simply grabbed it at the hemline, began to tear it. Her hands reached out and rested on his wrists.

"I will buy you another one," he said.

"You said we should practice economies," she said softly, her voice tinged with humor.

"I'm too impatient," he said. "Besides, I think our fortunes can survive a shift," he said. He continued to tear the garment until it parted at her neckline.

Naked, except for her bandage, she stood in front of him. He gently pressed his palm against her bare breast.

"The sight of my hand against your skin arouses you, doesn't it?"

She nodded. She felt as if she could barely breathe.

The back of his fingers slid along the tip of her nipple. Her breasts were extremely sensitive lately, so much so that even that smallest movement was enough to make her gasp. His fingers imprisoned the nipple gently, elongating it. His other hand wound the length of ribbon midway around the fullness of her breast.

His gaze was intent upon her face. Knowing exactly what she felt. Aware, always, of her response to his touch.

He pulled on the ribbon gently with both hands, sliding the satin along her flesh slowly until he reached the tip. The gentle friction against her engorged nipple was an exquisite delight. Back and forth, slowly and delicately, until she caught her bottom lip with her teeth, trapping a moan between her lips.

"Which of your breasts is more sensitive, I wonder?"

He moved the ribbon, repeated the gentle torture.

"Both," she murmured slightly.

"Are you certain?" he asked. "We can try it again."

"I'm certain," she whispered.

So, it was to be seduction again. Overpowering and enervating. Fire traveled through her at the thought of it. Anticipation laced with desire.

Always for him.

"Kiss me, Michael," she said.

"No," he said. "Your kisses are too intoxicating."

"Please." A pretense of a pout.

"Later."

"Now."

"No," he said, a light of wickedness in his eyes and enchantingly talented fingers.

"Another question, then," he said, leaning close to her. She could feel his breath on her cheek, his inquisition one spoken only between lovers. "Do you like my lips on your breasts, Margaret? Or my fingers? Which brings you more pleasure?"

"Both," she said again, smiling slightly.

"You can't have both right now," he said, pulling back. "You must choose."

"Your lips."

"You want my mouth on you?" he asked softly.

She nodded. The heat in her body was increasing.

"Show me."

She pulled the ribbon free, handing it to him silently. She lifted her breast, then reached up and hooked her other hand behind his neck, pulled him down to her. "Here," she said, lifting her breast up for his anointing tongue. She felt fierce and demanding in passion.

"Valkyrie," he said, and placed his mouth on her.

Her hand kept him in place, the sweet and gentle suction too much a sensation. A moment of exquisite delight. She closed her eyes in order to savor it and him.

Long moments later, he pulled back.

"Is that what you wanted?" he asked.

"Yes. It's been so long," she sighed.

"Only days," he said, stroking his finger from the center of her breasts to her throat.

"Eons," she argued.

"An eternity?"

"Yes."

His thumb gently stroked over a nipple.

"You're trembling," he said.

"Yes." It seemed to be all she could say.

He bent and carried her to the bed. She really should protest, but his mouth was too close to hers. She kissed him instead. First, a short darting touch of the tip of her tongue. But then, he pressed his hand to the back of her head and held her there, deepened the kiss.

When she pulled back, he pressed his lips against her throat as if he wished to measure the pulse of her heart.

He lowered her to the bed, stood beside it looking down at her.

She wanted to be beautiful for him. His eyes answered her wish, made her feel like a goddess.

He removed his own clothes, smiling at the intensity of her study.

He moved around the bed and lay beside her. Only then did he reach for her again, pulling her atop him. She spread her legs until she straddled him, understanding immediately that he didn't want to hurt her shoulder.

"I've never done this before," she said helplessly.

"It is not that difficult. I shall volunteer to serve as your tutor," he teased.

He moved his hands, one resting on her buttock, the other against her stomach. Another sensation, strange and carnal and certainly wicked made her open her eyes and stare at him.

He grinned at her, the expression in his eyes intent.

In each hand he held the end of the ribbon. He had wound it between them. She felt it being pulled, slowly between her legs. It was blissfully decadent, almost too intense a feeling.

"Retaliation?" she asked, finding it difficult to speak.

"I do not like to think that I allow a debt to go unpaid." Another long stroke.

"Is that what it was, a debt?"

"A most glorious one. The memory of it will fuel my dreams for my lifetime."

He pulled the ribbon so that his fingers were against her intimate curls. His fingers stroked along its path, tucked it among soft and swollen folds. Gently. Tenderly.

"Do you think we can die of this?"

"Pleasure or each other?"

"Either or both." Her lashes were too heavy. She let her lids flutter shut. His hands, those talented, wonderful hands, continued to slowly pull on the ribbon, tease her with his touch.

He lifted her slowly, wound the ribbon once around himself, and then entered her slowly. A wanton, that's what she was. A wanton wife. She bent and murmured the words against his lips, feeling him smile in response.

He pushed her back so that she sat upright on him, the feeling of being so completely filled almost too much to bear. He pressed the heels of his feet on the bed and surged upward into her then shockingly pulled on the ribbon again. The sensation was almost unbearable.

"I cannot touch your breasts if I continue with this," he said. "Do you wish me to stop?"

"Indeed no," she said. A very proper response. One couched in the most decorous of phrases. In fact, she was adrift in a sensation of pure sensuality. Totally and beautifully sublime. Feeling. Nothing but feeling. And around it, holding her safe, was the image of him. His slight smile, the intensity of his eyes.

"Your breasts are lovely," he said, his voice husky. "I would like to kiss them."

She opened her eyes, her gaze on his face. He seemed imbued in a soft haze, as if the pleasure she felt colored even the sight of him.

"Would you?"

"Yes," he said, and licked his lips.

She looked down at herself. Her nipples had drawn up, the areolas puckered. She placed one hand beneath each breast. "Do you think them too large?"

"No," he said, smiling. "I have noted, however, that your nipples are . . . arrogant."

He smiled and gently pulled on the ribbon. A sharp and exquisite sensation traveled through her, harnessing her breath, holding her quiescent. She closed her eyes at the sensation and trapped a moan with her teeth.

"Very arrogant," he said, leisurely.

She blinked open her eyes. "Perhaps I am learning

to be a countess after all," she murmured.

His face was flushed, his eyes glittered at her. "My countess," he said.

She bent forward, raised herself to him. His mouth closed over a nipple and he began gently to suck.

His hands gripped her hips, began to push her down on him, establishing a rhythm. It seemed as if there was too much pleasure, all of it originating with him. More. Please. More.

He pulled back, his lips wet and hot as he pressed her forward and kissed her. A soft moan emerged from her lips, was captured in his kiss.

"Margaret." Her name was an odd and enchanting refrain. An urging to bliss, completion. And finally paradise.

Chapter 32

Anticipation is to the art of love
what amusement is to the soul.

The Journals of Augustin X

Michael glanced at the letter from his solicitor.
An offer had been made for Torrent, one surprisingly generous.

He glanced over at Margaret seated on the divan
reading. She had been so quiet in the last hour that
he had forgotten she was in the library at all. She was
attired in another of her new dresses, a deep blue
frock with a matching scarf wound around her neck
and under her wrist to support her injured shoulder.
He smiled at the sight of her, her cheek pressed
against the side of the couch, her eyes shut. Napping
again.

Tenderness surged through him at the sight of her.

He stood and went to her, scooping her up into his
arms before she could wake. She nodded at him sleepily. "You're carrying me again."

"I am," he admitted. "To our bedroom," he added.

"To have your wicked way with me?" She almost purred the question.

"No. For you to nap," he said, still smiling.

"I'm forever sleeping."

"Yes, you are," he agreed. "But then, it's for a good cause." He had grown accustomed to the idea of becoming a father. So much so that he was alternately enthralled and terrified at the prospect.

He tucked her into bed and kissed her lightly. She smiled, turned, and curved into the pillow at her side. She was asleep again before he left the room.

Returning to his library, he stared out at the fog-shrouded view from his library. The garden was obscured by an unusual afternoon mist. Fog was more prevalent in autumn or winter, rarely so in summer.

He moved back to his desk, forcing himself to work on the Augustin code. His mood was oddly somber this afternoon, the reluctance he felt unlike him.

He sat, opened the book and took out his notes.

Key codes were nothing more than language, albeit rendered more obscure and therefore more difficult to learn. All that was required to read this specialized code was a translation key, one of repetition, symbolism, or pattern. Perhaps the keyword in the Augustin Journals was separate for each chapter, which would explain the differing notations on each heading.

He opened the book to the first chapter. The margin notes were b 2 3. He selected the second paragraph, located two words beginning with the letter "b." The third letter in each word was an "o."

He sat back, stared at his annotations.

"She is recuperating, Mama. It is not the time for visitors." Elizabeth's voice.

He turned his head toward the door, jerked out of his concentration by the interruption. He stood, irritated by his mother's effrontery.

"I mean to have my say with this chit, Elizabeth. Get out of my way."

"Michael will not be pleased," Elizabeth said.

"She's right," he announced, opening the door and glaring at them. His mother was halfway up the stairs, his sisters trailing behind her.

"My wife is not receiving," he said curtly.

"I tried to stop her, Michael," Elizabeth said helplessly.

One quick nod was his only response. He knew only too well what his mother was like when she was set upon a certain course of action.

"I'm afraid I must end this visit," he said calmly, surveying his mother and sisters. "And insist that you not return in the future unless you are specifically invited."

His quick nod at Elizabeth rescinded that order for her. She smiled lightly, obviously relieved, and began to walk down the stairs.

"Is it true that you're selling Torrent?" his mother demanded, frowning down at him.

"And Haversham. We cannot afford them."

"We could have kept all our properties if you'd married an heiress," she countered. "Instead, you married your whore."

He strode across the foyer, enraged.

"My wife will not now, nor ever, be called that word," he said, his voice echoing through the rotunda. "Nor addressed in that tone."

"Are you even certain the child is yours?" His mother's face was mottled with color, her lips nearly bloodless with anger.

"I have tended to see you as an irritant," he said curtly. "But I have never thought of you as idiotic. Until now."

"How dare—"

"Not now, Mother," he said sharply. "I do not want to hear any more of your diatribes.

"Smytheton," he said, addressing the ever-present butler without removing his gaze from his mother. "Open the door. My mother and my sisters are leaving.

"Perhaps if you retreat to Setton," he said curtly, "you might be able to survive the horror of my marriage." His hands rested on his hips; his fingers drummed an impatient tattoo.

"But it's the middle of the season!" Charlotte burst out.

He glanced over at his sister. "You should have thought of that before you were tempted to be intrusive. Or rude," he said, turning to his mother. "Don't come again, Mother, until you're specifically invited."

She stared at him, taken aback by his order. An altogether welcome relief to have her reduced to silence. She turned and descended the stairs, pinning him with her gaze the whole time. At the doorway she turned. "You are acting decidedly unlike yourself, Michael. Has she bewitched you as well?"

She proceeded through the door, waving her arm as she did. "Come, girls." Ada and Charlotte followed her without a backward glance. Elizabeth darted to him, stood on tiptoe, and placed a kiss on his cheek.

"Now I know you love her," she whispered, smiling. Before he could respond she had disappeared through the doorway. Smytheton bowed, left the foyer.

"I used to think that nobles were insufferable,"

Margaret said. He looked up to discover her standing at the landing.

"You're supposed to be napping," he said.

"But then," she said, ignoring his comment, "I met you. You aren't like most earls are you?"

"While my mother remains the quintessential example of all that is to be avoided. Didactic, haughty, arrogant," he said ruefully.

"Was your father the same? Or was he a charming rogue?" She halted a few steps above him.

He gripped the banister, and pulled himself up, brushing a light kiss to her lovely mouth.

"The memories of my father," he admitted, "are mainly those of his shouting at my mother and her responding in kind."

He chuckled at her look of surprise. "My mother is not, for all that she would like to appear so, an example of propriety and rectitude. She has only become this way following my father's death. Prior to that, her lapses of decorum were legendary."

"Are you certain we're talking of the same woman?"

He nodded. "She took a riding crop to my father once. He retaliated by shooting out one of the stained glass windows in the chapel." His grin widened at the look of stunned surprise on her face. "My father's explanation for the act was that he was mad at God for creating woman in the first place, and my mother specifically. My childhood was not uneventful," he admitted.

She tilted her head and studied him. "Is that why you claim to be so restrained?"

"Claim?"

"I've never seen it."

He reached for her, clasped her hand, and walked

her down the rest of the stairs. He stood at the base and wound his arms around her waist. "I confess that my mother might be correct in this instance," he said. "Perhaps you *have* bewitched me."

He almost always wanted his hands on her. The curve of her back was beautiful, so fragile and feminine that he wanted to put his lips there right at this particular moment. In the center of it, and lower, where it curved to her buttocks. He felt himself swelling even now at the thought.

Like an impatient and unwise suitor, he walked Margaret gently back against the wall.

Her smile seemed tipped with merriment. A thoroughly enchanting look. He adored everything about her. Her laughing face, those fascinating eyes, that beautiful mouth.

"Raise your head," he said. "I want to kiss you."

Her eyes sparkled with amusement.

He leaned down and brushed his lips against hers. A teasing touch. Too soon transformed into something else. Whenever he kissed her he seemed to lose part of himself. As if he were falling down into a darkly hued cavern where thought was superfluous. Only physical sensation remained intact. The passage of time had not altered the sensation. If anything, it had heightened it.

The desire was there. God knows the need was.

Both his hands slapped against the wall on either side of her. His erection, eternally tumescent and almost boyishly eager, strained against his trousers.

His next kiss was openly carnal. Into it he infused all the instant hunger he always felt, and all the enduring fascination. But most of all, their kiss was filled with love, the power of which still awed him.

His hips arched forward involuntarily. Restraint managed by only a thread of thought.

"Excuse me, my lord." Smytheton's voice as he passed through the foyer. There was a distinct note of amusement in the majordomo's voice.

Michael jerked back from Margaret and stared straight ahead at the wall. A feeling unlike any he'd ever known slid through him.

He leaned his head against his arm, felt the burning sting of embarrassment. "Dear God, I've been a rutting bull in front of my butler."

Michael opened his eyes to find Margaret suffused with merriment. Every time she started to speak, another choking laugh emerged instead. He closed his eyes again.

"Have pity on my consequence," he muttered against her ear.

"We really should move," she teased. "He might come back again and it will only be worse."

He retreated with his wife to their chamber, the sound of her laughter echoing through the pantheon.

The Duke of Tarrant was watching his foals. Not an unknown pastime for him. They ran for their freedom the way all young things do, with a gusty expectation of long life and a rosy future.

Pity that it did not often come to pass.

He stood against the fence, watched the mist covering the ground. A summer oddity. As if even nature warned him of the danger that loomed.

Peter came and stood beside him. A master and his servant. Not quite as innocent a portrait as they appeared.

"I have a new plan," he said. "We can lure both of them to us and obtain the rest of the books."

Peter glanced at him. "You want me to take his wife."

"Exactly so," Tarrant said, turning and smiling. "See that it's done quickly," he said. "I want this over."

Peter nodded.

He donned his trousers, slipped on his dressing gown on, and leaned over the bed.

"You're leaving me," she complained sleepily, her eyes still closed.

"Do you mind?"

"Yes," she said, opening her eyes reluctantly. She reached up to grip the lapels of his dressing gown, pulled him down for a kiss, then sighed as he stood again.

"Less than a few weeks wed," she said, sighing dramatically, "and I've already been replaced by work."

"Never," he said, kissing her again. "But you should rest regardless."

"An obvious ploy to placate me," she said.

"Is it successful?" he asked with a smile.

"Yes," she admitted. "But I feel remarkably decadent sleeping in the afternoon."

"The prerogative of a countess," he teased.

She heard him leave the room and smiled.

Love is learned thing, perhaps. She had learned love at her grandmother's knee, from Jerome in a friendly, easy marriage. Michael, however, had taught her that love involved all her senses, that she could feel passion as well as delight. More emotions strung together than she had ever felt.

One other element to love that she had never before known. It fed on itself, and grew each day.

Michael was working at his desk when a tap on the door interrupted him. He called out to Smytheton, who entered the room in his usual somber way, crossing the carpet soundlessly and bowing unsmilingly in front of him. He picked the message up from the tray, opened it and scanned it quickly. Robert was back in London and inviting him to participate in a night of debauchery.

He penned a reply, inviting his friend to dinner instead, and informing him of his wedding. Margaret's existence would no doubt come as a shock to the man who believed he was privy to all manner of secrets. Michael smiled in anticipation, and returned the message to Smytheton.

"See that it gets off straight away, will you, Smytheton? I've invited Adams to dinner."

Smytheton only nodded and crept away on silent feet.

When he began solving a code, Michael sketched a grid upon a sheet of paper. As he began to fill in the deciphered letters, the grid helped him identify those missing. If he was fortunate, he could determine early on exactly what kind of code was used, what patterns were missing.

He had already deduced that the cipher in the *Journals* was a poly alphanumeric cipher. A surprisingly difficult one to solve, often requiring both the recipient and the sender to utilize a word key. It could be a phrase, one word, or a combination of words and numbers. But in the past few days he discovered that he didn't need the word key after all. His experience in solving the Cyrillic cipher proved invaluable, the two codes were so alike. One of the *Journals* could easily serve as the other's word key. All he had to do was compare the extractions.

Four hours later, he speared his hands through his hair and stared at the deciphered code in shock.

The mantel clock chimed softly. A reminder, then, of Robert's imminent arrival.

He stood and walked to the window, his mind silent, an empty cavern that resounded with only one thought. What he had read was an act that had altered history. One single deed that had changed the world and resulted in the death of thousands.

How was Margaret involved?

The lesson of the Cyrillic cipher was difficult to ignore. A woman's treachery had ended a man's career, made him suspect in a country he only wished to serve.

Had he been a fool? So blinded by his love for Margaret that he had not seen the truth before his eyes?

No. He banished that thought quickly. However she was involved, it was innocently, he was certain of that.

How do you know? A last, almost desperate, rational thought. The answer was simple. *Because I love her.*

He needed to turn the cipher over to Robert. It was imperative that the Foreign Office know what he had discovered. But not yet. Not until he could protect Margaret.

Chapter 33

⌒〜◯◯〜⌒

Anger spoils passion.

The Journals of Augustin X

"Do not tell me that he's never spoken of his fish?" Robert Adams asked.

Margaret shook her head, carefully moving her fork to the crystal rest as Smytheton replaced her bowl with a plate.

Surreptitiously she traced her fingers over the ornate silvery cutlery, stared down into the reflection of an almost translucent china plate. As a London shopkeeper's wife, she'd felt prosperous. Yet her utensils had been of commonplace steel, her bowls and cups and plates crafted of creamware.

An enormous gulf to cross from a tradesman's wife to countess. Margaret wondered if she would ever become used to it.

She was grateful for the dinner she and Michael had shared the night of the theater. His humor had made the experience less daunting. His effortless introduction to all those forks and spoons had made this night a little less difficult to endure. She did, however, watch both men carefully, in case she'd erred in some rudimentary fashion. Twice she had picked up the wrong fork, and she'd not known the purpose of the fingerbowl. But neither man had noticed her errors.

She glanced over at Michael. Robert had done most of the talking tonight. She'd thought, initially, it was because his was a voluble nature. But she suspected, as the evening advanced, that he was simply attempting to fill the void created by Michael's silence.

"Well," Robert said, leaning toward her, "he always wanted a dog. But his mother would not have one in the house. So he decided that if he was to have a pet at all, it would be a fish. He and the gardener made a net and caught several fish in the river near Setton, bringing them home in a bucket.

"He named each one of those ugly carp after kings of England. His mother was furious with him. The carp ate everything in the pond and grew to be huge." He glanced over at Michael. "You swore that they knew you and could do tricks."

"I was six at the time and allowed to be somewhat silly," Michael said, smiling slightly.

"His mother relented finally, and let him have a puppy," Robert said.

"It chased my sister's cats as I recall," Michael contributed, before lapsing back into silence.

"I think Smytheton has improved as a cook," Robert said. "Don't you agree, Michael?"

He didn't answer. Only after the second repetition of the question did Michael nod absently.

She turned and looked at him. He appeared preoccupied, stroking the stem of his wine glass with two fingers as if it held more interest than their conversation.

"Michael?" He looked up at the sound of her voice. He must have realized he was being inattentive, because for the next several minutes he attempted to concentrate on their conversation.

"Did you tell her about your first pony, Michael?"

"I doubt that Margaret truly wishes to be informed of every event in my childhood, Robert," he said.

Margaret glanced over at Michael, then at their guest. "On the contrary," she said softly, "I would be very interested to hear." What sort of little boy had he been? Brave and daring? Or shy?

Robert smiled at her across the table. He was an exceedingly charming man. His brown hair was the exact shade of his eyes. The expression in them had been kind from the moment he and she had been introduced.

He was untitled and not unaware of the state of poverty, she suspected. The fact that he was Michael's friend was not a surprise. For an earl, Michael seemed to have a surprisingly egalitarian outlook on life. Especially valuable, since he had just married a poor widow.

But his sidelong glances were making her uncomfortable. He had remained in his library the entire afternoon. The only time he had left the room was a few minutes before his friend had arrived. Little time to spare for dressing or conversation. She wondered, now, if the delay had been calculated.

"He spent most of his childhood trying to escape his sisters," Robert said.

Michael only smiled, but didn't speak.

She studied her blackened roast beef. She didn't think she could eat one more mouthful. Nor had Michael touched much of his dinner, even though he had consumed an inordinate amount of wine this evening. Another change. She had thought him temperate in his habits.

"Where do you hail from, Margaret?" Robert asked. "There's the flavor of London in your speech, but then I hear certain words that have a touch of Wiltshire about them."

"She has lived for the past two years in a place called Silbury Village, Robert," Michael said. He held up his wine glass. Smytheton instantly refilled it, but his face was a mask of stiff disapproval. "One could almost believe that there were fairies in the land, for the charm of the place."

His voice was mocking, and the precise, deliberate nature of his speech led Margaret to wonder if he was becoming affected by the wine. She felt a flush of embarrassment for him.

"I was born in London," she said quietly to Robert.

"Margaret's childhood is an infinitely more interesting topic of conversation than my own," Michael said, and took another sip of his wine.

Robert looked as if he wished to say something, but before he could comment, Michael suddenly stood. He threw his napkin down on his chair and stepped away from the table. At the doorway, he stopped, his back to the room.

"Unfortunately, I am not very good company this evening. Please, continue with your meal and your tales." With that he disappeared.

As the moments passed, it was all too evident that he was not going to return.

"Shall I regale you with tales of Michael as a boy?" Robert asked, without seeming to notice Michael's absence. "Or shall we be quit of him as a topic of conversation altogether?"

"What was he like as a little boy?" she asked. Robert smiled at her as if he knew what the effort had cost her.

"Not appreciably different," Robert said, settling back in his chair. "A smaller version of the Michael we know. Just as autocratic. I remember when Elizabeth was about to be born. He came to my home, disgusted. The process was taking entirely too long, he said. I think he believed that God was taunting him with the hope of a brother."

"What did he say when he discovered that he had another sister?" She propped her hand on her chin, imagining Michael as a child.

Robert laughed, the sound of it echoing through the room. "He refused to talk to his mother for weeks. When he did, he demanded to know where he took this new sister to exchange her for a worthwhile boy." He smiled, evidently recalling that moment. "As it is, Elizabeth is his favorite sister. I have always found that a bit of irony."

She looked down at her place setting. Smytheton bent low on her left side. "Would you like me to remove your plate, my lady?" His tone was, for Smytheton, almost friendly. She glanced up at him, surprised, only to be greeted with a slight smile. She nodded, bemused, and he did so, retreating into the kitchen.

She tiptoed around the subject, hoping that Robert would understand the question she dared not asked. "The Countess is a formidable woman," she said.

"You realize, of course, that you outrank her now. She is no longer the Countess of Montraine. You are.

She has been relegated to being Dowager."

She looked at him, horrified. It was something she had never considered.

"If you do not mind me saying so, Margaret, you have the most fascinating look on your face at the moment. As if I have said something altogether horrible."

Politeness prevented her from divulging her thoughts. Her former mother-in-law had been a rather demure woman of middle years. It had been difficult for Margaret to equate the retiring woman with a girl who had attracted a duke. Even her death, three years after Margaret had married Jerome, had been quietly done, almost apologetically.

This mother-in-law, however, was proving to be quite a personage, even in Margaret's thoughts.

"I myself," Robert said, "have avoided her at all possible costs. She terrified me as a child. She does so equally as an adult."

That information was not at all reassuring.

Robert took his leave finally, a rather self-conscious departure. He glanced more than once at the closed door of Michael's library, but he expressed no desire to see his friend again.

After Robert had left, Margaret stood in the foyer, uncertain. To her left was the curving staircase. Ahead, the library.

"Would you like a bit of spiced wine in your chamber, my lady?"

She glanced at Smytheton. "Is he often like this?"

The barrier between a newly made countess and a majordomo was not quite as solid as that of a woman born to the nobility. The question she asked breached that wall but, to her surprise, Smytheton answered her.

"Only when he is involved in a cipher. Then, he is impatient with interruptions." She understood the meaning well enough. It would not be wise to go into that room.

"Are you certain you would not care for the spiced wine, my lady?" The barrier was back in place.

Margaret shook her head. But instead of mounting the steps, she headed for the library. The man she had come to love so deeply had altered in the course of only a few hours. In his place was a man he had always claimed to be. Restrained, reserved, a man of logic and sensibilities.

Cold.

She was going to find out why.

Michael was standing by the wall of windows when she entered the room. She closed the door behind her and leaned against it as if needing a bulwark.

"What is it, Michael? What's wrong?" she asked.

His reflection in the window was of a stern faced man with watchful eyes.

"I do not like feeling powerless," he said finally.

She frowned at him. "Do you?"

"With you I do," he admitted. "Perhaps I should be like my father and shoot out a window whenever I lose control."

"Yet tonight you were too restrained."

"A ruse," he said dryly.

"One that served its purpose," she said, coming closer. "I was convinced of it. And your rudeness," she added.

"I apologize for that," he said, turning to face her. "I was distracted by my thoughts." He seemed to study her face in the faint light. "I've solved the code," he said finally.

He walked to his desk, picked up a sheet of paper and handed it to her. "It was only an accident that I was able to solve most of the code with two of the books. But then, my knowledge of the Cyrillic cipher helped, too."

She read the translated code once, then again, attempting to find some meaning in it.

Captain Athir has been assured that the Navy will not interfere. Therefore, our package can proceed safely on Feb. 24 to the southern coast of France to be met by Lady C.

"What does it mean?" she asked, glancing up at him.

"There is an island not far from the southern coast of France. And the date would be correct."

"What island?"

"Elba."

She stared down at the paper in her hand. "But wasn't it on Elba that Napoleon was imprisoned?"

"More correctly, he was awarded sovereignty over Elba when he went into exile. But someone helped him back to France. Someone with wealth and influence."

"Is this why you've been so distant tonight?"

"No," he said. "It was because I was trying to think of a way to protect you."

"Me? Why?"

"Because both Babby and Robert know you have the *Journals* and at the moment you're the only person associated with them. Grounds enough for charges of treason."

She looked up at him, stunned.

"Treason?" She stared down at the paper in her

hand. "Do you believe I had anything to do with this?"

"No, I don't," he said firmly. "But my word wouldn't be enough to save you. Nor the fact that you were shot."

"You think someone shot at me because of the *Journals*?"

He nodded. "It's a possibility."

"But why?"

"Perhaps to silence you, even to obtain the *Journals*."

"Or to prevent you from learning this secret?" She felt a frisson of fear as she realized it made sense.

His slight smile acknowledged the truth of her words.

She sat on the edge of his desk, suddenly feeling light headed. Normally Fate hangs on the swing of a pendulum. But never so clearly. She had never before been able to say—this is where it happened. This is where I erred. I should have turned left, or said no, or gone to the market, or chosen blue. Yet Margaret saw the moment Fate swung in her direction in perfect and unremitting clarity. The moment she'd thrown the strongbox out the window minutes before the bookshop was engulfed in flames.

Because of those stupid books, she had brought danger to Michael and to her unborn child.

"Penelope always said they were cursed," she said dully, "and now I'm beginning to believe her correct."

"I think we're dealing with something or someone more tangible than a curse." He closed both books and returned them to the safe. "I can't even ask for help from the Foreign Office, Margaret, until I am certain you will not be charged."

"Would they truly think I'm a traitor?'

"Not if I can prevent it," he said somberly. "Who else knew you had the *Journals*?"

She thought back. "There was a list of men tucked into one of the volumes. I wrote to three of them," she said, repeating their names.

"Was your note like the one you sent Babby? Without giving many particulars?" he explained.

She nodded. "I didn't want to hurt my reputation," she said, smiling ruefully. "I thought that if I sent the letters through Samuel no one would know it was me."

"I wonder if he's had another visitor," he said. "Someone who convinced him to divulge your identity?"

"As you did?" she asked wryly. "I doubt it. Samuel is a very careful man. He must have trusted you to do so."

"Less trust," he admitted, "then the fact that I purchased three bolts of cloth from him."

"A bribe?" she asked, smiling silently.

He only nodded absently in response. She knew that look well. He was concentrating upon the problem, sorting out the solution in his mind.

"It would have taken a massive effort to get Napoleon off Elba," he said. "Jailers were bribed and a ship arranged, acts that required both power and money. Perhaps one of those men is involved."

"What are you going to do, Michael?"

"I need the first *Journal*. There's a chance that the first book might hold a clue to the identity of the traitor."

"Why three books? Wouldn't one have sufficed?"

"It's a question I've asked myself. Less dangerous, I think, to have the information spread between three volumes. They were, no doubt, sent at different times to the recipient in England." He glanced over at her. "Where did Jerome get them?"

"I don't know," she said, thinking back to the day of the fire. "I had never seen them before."

She glanced at him, startled by the thought that occurred to her. "Do you think Jerome might have been involved?"

He shrugged. "At this point, I don't know who to suspect."

"We're both in danger, aren't we?" she asked, afraid for him. By the look on his face she knew she was right.

"Be careful, Michael," she said softly.

He enfolded her in his embrace and for long moments they remained that way, needing the closeness.

"I will not see Babby until the morning," he said against her hair. "I will be safe enough. And I'll set Smytheton to guarding you," he said, in an obvious effort to lighten their mood.

"He will do nothing but scowl disdainfully at me," she said, looking up as she wrapped her arms more tightly around him. She forced a smile to her face. An expression to ease his mind and hide the sudden chilling taste of fear.

Chapter 34

⌒◦⌒◦⌒

*A loving embrace is important
in the early days of a union,
in order to eliminate anxiety.*

The Journals of Augustin X

Michael discovered Babby at home, and was gratified to find that his friend was not entertaining, nor was he regaling some intimate friends with newly discovered gossip.

The safest course was to ask to look at the book, giving Babby as innocuous a reason as possible, something that wouldn't spark his curiosity. The last thing Michael wanted was Babby speculating about the *Journals* publicly.

Unfortunately, his caution wasn't necessary.

"I'd let you borrow the book, Montraine, but I haven't got it," Babby said, looking crestfallen.

"Do you sell it, Babby?"

"Stolen, Montraine. Can you imagine? I get my library in some semblance of order finally, and the

deuced thing's stolen. I would think my life cursed if
I hadn't found the most wonderful lady love in the
past months. I must recommend her to you." He wiggled his eyebrows and grinned at Michael.

"I'm married, Babby," Michael said, smiling
slightly. Stating it to Babby was the equivalent of
sending a notice to the new Sunday *Times*. "And due
to be a father," Michael added.

The news didn't even halt Babby in mid-breath.
"Do I know her, Montraine?" Babby squinted up at
him.

It was the first time Michael realized that his friend
did resemble a hedgehog, albeit one with a waistcoat
of bright yellow and embroidered with orange flowers.

"You do, Babby. It's because of you that we met at
all. Margaret Esterly, if you'll recall."

Babby's eyes widened. "A plebeian marriage, Montraine?"

"Not at all," he said easily. "Margaret is the least
common woman I know."

"A love match, then?"

Michael grinned, thinking that Babby, for all his sil-
liness, had cut to the core. "Very much so," he said.

"About the book, Babby?" he asked, to get his
friend back on course again.

"It was the damnedest thing, Montraine. They
didn't steal all my books, just the one. I wouldn't have
minded so much if I hadn't just had the whole place
catalogued. Don't think I would have even discovered
it missing without that new secretary of mine. Every
damn volume was on the floor. Took days to put it
back together. I say," he asked, his eyes brightening,
"I don't suppose that wife of yours has any more of

those books for sale? I'd offer to lend them to you at any time, of course."

"I'll ask her," he said.

It was the easiest answer. But he had every intention of asking Margaret to give the books to the Foreign Office. It was, he reasoned, the safest place for them.

At first Margaret thought it was Molly returning from the market. But then, it was the maid's half day off, and it would be unusual for her to return early. She walked out of the library, where she had been reading a thoroughly wonderful novel, and stood in the foyer.

"Michael?" His name echoed back to her from the dome. She looked up and smiled. It was a French blue-and-pewter kind of day. The sunlight streaming into the dome had a silver cast to it as if the threatening rain had dimmed the sky.

"Smytheton?"

She turned at a sound and her heart nearly stopped.

A man stood there, a stranger with a face like a bag of rocks. A giant of a man with huge hands. And in one of those hands he held a pistol aimed directly at her chest.

"Come out of the room," he said. His voice was low, absurdly soft for a man of his size.

She remained frozen in the doorway.

"I've orders to take you somewhere," he said, pleasantly. "If it's necessary to shoot you first, then I will."

Reluctantly, Margaret moved into the foyer.

He stepped into the library, gun still pointed at her, then took an envelope from his pocket and threw it inside the room.

"Whose orders?" Margaret marveled that she could speak.

He didn't answer. Instead, he walked toward her, pressed the barrel of the pistol against her back. She began to move where he directed her, toward the rear of the house.

"Where are we going?" That elicited no response either.

Where was Smytheton?

"Where are you taking me?"

"Move along," he said, pressing the pistol against her spine.

Slowly, Margaret walked down the hall and into the kitchen. Smytheton lay on the floor, his head bloody.

She ran to him, knelt at his side, but the giant grabbed her arm and pulled her out the door.

At the back of the townhouse a carriage was waiting. The man reached past her, opened the door, and pushed her inside. She struggled, pulled away from him, but he gripped her injured shoulder so tightly with one hand that she almost fell to her knees in pain. He pulled her up, threw her roughly back into the carriage. Margaret stumbled, righted herself, and sat heavily.

A moment later she heard the crack of a whip and the vehicle was in motion.

It concerned her that the driver had neither bound her nor blindfolded her. She peered through the curtains as they traveled quickly west. Evidently, he didn't fear that she would speak of this abduction. Why? Because she was not expected to return from it?

She pressed her hand against her throbbing shoulder, leaned back against the seat and closed her eyes. Where was she going, and why?

Margaret knew her destination soon enough. They headed further west, then north, her suspicion realized with each passing landmark. They were headed toward Wickhampton, the Duke of Tarrant's estate.

She licked suddenly dry lips, attempted to calm the frantic beat of her heart as Michael's words came back to her.

It would have taken a massive effort to get Napoleon off Elba. Jailers were bribed and a ship arranged, acts that required both power and money.

Was Tarrant the man behind Napoleon's escape? If so, what did he want with her? She didn't have the *Journals* with her, nor had the driver demanded them. Suddenly, she knew. She was only bait. And the prize? Michael.

The carriage pulled into the gates of Wickhampton, but instead of circling in front of the main door the vehicle halted in front of one of the wings.

The door was opened by the hulking driver once again. This time she didn't struggle or call for help. She was no match for the man or his pistol. She simply kept silent as he retrieved a large iron key from his pocket and opened the vine-covered door at the end of the building. They climbed up a small set of steps to another door, one that opened into a corridor.

Evidently, this wing was not often used. The late afternoon sun streamed in through the windows and created a sunny tunnel of dust-laden light. But there was no sound other than their footsteps echoing on the bare wooden floors. No servants, no clink of dishes, no chattering maids. Nothing to indicate that there was any other occupant in this part of Wickhampton.

The burly driver still held tight to her arm and seemed to be counting the doors they passed. A moment later he opened one to reveal an empty bedchamber, the furniture adorned with dust sheets.

He pushed her into the room, then closed and locked the door. The sound of heavy footsteps in the hallway indicated that he had left her again. To tell the duke that she was his prisoner?

She wasn't about to remain meekly in place and wait until the Duke of Tarrant decided her fate. She began to tear off the dust covers one by one, revealing two chairs, a table, and the dust laden counterpane of a fourposter bed.

There was nothing sharp, nothing pointed. No fireplace tools.

The windows were coated with a dulling layer of dust. The view they revealed was that of an immaculate lawn beneath a darkening sky. Not one servant or gardener in sight. She pulled at the windows, but they wouldn't open.

She turned away, saw the bulge beneath the counterpane, and felt a surge of triumph.

A bed warmer. The duke's maids were evidently not very industrious. The one who had last tidied this room might well be called lazy. Bedwarmers were normally removed in the morning, emptied of their coals or embers, and stored beneath the bed. This one had been left in place. Margaret blessed the lazy maid even as she realized what she'd found.

Her weapon.

Margaret's arm was still so weak, she doubted she would be capable of more than one good swing with the bedwarmer. The one asset she had was the element of surprise.

Standing in front of the door, Margaret practiced

hefting the warmer. It was heavy even emptied of its long dead coals. If she aimed it at the middle of the door, she might be able to smash the pistol out of the driver's grip. No, that was silly. She hadn't the slightest idea how to fire a gun. She suspected there was a good deal more to it than simply pointing it. She'd be better off aiming for his head. She'd never coshed anyone before, had never had the idea of doing so.

To save Michael, Margaret realized she was capable of almost anything.

Michael took the precaution of visiting the draper before returning home. Samuel had not been contacted by anyone wishing to find Margaret. But he was all too happy to give Michael a few more bolts of cloth in honor of his marriage.

It was full dark by the time Michael reached home, armed with congratulations from the draper and his and his wife's best wishes to Margaret. Michael decided that he knew just the way of delivering such affectionate greetings.

Despite the fact that his errand to Babby's had been futile, Michael felt an almost exultant joy. An emotion not difficult to trace to its source. While he had been pleased with the tenor of his life and proud enough of his accomplishments in the past, it felt as if that man had been only a shadow of who he was now.

His life had been given over to Margaret's care sometime when he was not looking. Not to patterns, nor ciphers, nor puzzles, but to Margaret. She had awakened in him something he had not before known. Sensuality, and an eagerness to explore his mind's imaginings. He'd known companionship with her, a most definite clash of wills coupled with amusement, tenderness, and wonder.

The only thing marring his happiness was the mystery of the *Journals.*

Light from the gas lamps around the square pooled on the cobbled streets, illuminated the doorway. But Smytheton didn't silently open the door as Michael walked up the steps. Nor did he stand there, stiff as a sergeant-major. Michael found that odd, since his majordomo often anticipated him. What concerned him even more was the fact that the door was ajar.

He called out a greeting, but silence was the only response. Lighting a candle from the sideboard, he took the stairs two at a time. Margaret wasn't in their chamber. He called out her name, but there was no answer. No smiling presence.

No Margaret. And no Smytheton.

He walked down the stairs again, entered his library. Perhaps she had become involved in a book and had not heard him. But she wasn't in this room, either.

It was then that he saw the letter. He bent and picked it up, a sense of dread spreading through him as he opened and read the words. He was a man unused to fear; it was an emotion he'd felt little of in his lifetime. But he experienced it now as he flicked open the red ducal seal and read the words:

Your wife is my guest. If you wish to see her, bring the Journals of Augustin X *with you.*

Margaret, in exchange for the *Journals.* The Duke of Tarrant. They had been correct, then. He folded the note slowly, slipped it inside his waistcoat. He walked to his desk, lit a branch of candles, and retrieved the

Journals from the bookcase, slipping them into an empty dispatch case, all his actions done in a silent kind of fog.

He found Smytheton in the kitchen, leaning weakly against a wall. The blood from his head wound streaked his face and pooled on the floor. Michael bent and helped him to his feet, walked with him to the table. The older man sat heavily, his hand pressed on his still bleeding wound.

"Can you tell me what happened, Smytheton?"

"I only had a chance to see him, my lord, before he hit me with the butt end of his pistol. More than that I don't know."

"How long ago?"

"I was getting ready to prepare dinner, my lord. An hour? Perhaps a little more."

An hour gone.

"I need your help, Smytheton."

The old soldier's training came to the fore. Smytheton neither whined nor offered his injury as excuse. He simply straightened his shoulders. "What can I do, my lord?"

"We must get word to Robert," Michael said, and related the information he needed to convey.

"I will, my lord," Smytheton said, and almost saluted him.

Michael left the front of the house, grateful to discover that his carriage had not yet been taken to the stables. He signaled James, gave him directions before climbing into the vehicle.

The journey seemed achingly slow to Michael, as if the horses' hooves were mired in mud. He had never been to Wickhampton. But all he knew was that it was taking too long to travel there. Each rotation of the wheels seemed to resound with a curious warning.

Not soon enough. Not soon enough. Not soon enough.

An eternity later, the carriage turned into the broad iron gates that led to Wickhampton. A mile further and the road finally curved in front of the structure. Darkness favored the great house. It was so enormous it seemed to block out the moon. The drive was covered with crushed stone that glittered in the moonlight. The carriage slowed, then halted before the tall front steps.

The structure that faced him was less home than monument. The original building, topped incongruously by a tower that seemed medieval in origin, was flanked by two wings. They jutted toward the front of the house as if to embrace a visitor.

He mounted the set of wide steps that led to the tall front doors.

His knock was answered almost immediately by a man of exceedingly large stature. He opened one of the enormous double doors without any seeming effort and stood aside as Michael entered.

The foyer was the size of his library, brightly lit, the task being performed by a white-gloved footman attired in blue-and-gold livery. Wickhampton was impressive, if not for its size, then for the floor-to-ceiling works of art being illuminated one by one. Right at the moment, however, Michael didn't give a flying farthing for Tarrant's taste in Italian artists.

He was led to the duke's study without a word by another silent footman. An indication that Tarrant cared little that his actions were witnessed by his servants. It should have reassured Michael as to his safety and Margaret's fate. Strangely enough, it didn't.

The chamber Michael entered was dark, lit only by one branch of candles mounted on a tall stand. A tall, hulking man stood in front of a desk, his face heavily scarred. It looked as if he'd been badly beaten many times and the bones in his face had never healed properly.

But it was the other man who drew his attention. Tall and almost unnaturally thin, he had a narrow ascetic's face. His eyes were dark and penetrating, his smile thin lipped. Almost as if he mocked the gesture, but made it nonetheless.

"Tarrant?"

How odd, that he had never met the man. The *ton* was not large, their greatest complaint the boredom fostered by meeting the same people repeatedly. But then, most of his time was spent immersed in codes.

"Alan Stilton, at your service." The duke's palm pressed against his chest as he bowed. A courtly gesture, one reminiscent of a hundred years earlier. "I have, of course, the privilege of addressing the Earl of Montraine."

"Where is my wife?" Michael asked curtly, in no mood for pleasantries.

His question obviously surprised the duke. His smile thinned even more. "So you married her? The woman holds a decided fascination for you, Montraine. My brother felt the same. Pity she never interested me."

"Where is Margaret?"

Instead of answering him, the duke turned and spoke to his companion.

"That will be all, Peter," he said. "You must take care of that other matter we discussed."

"Where is my wife?" Michael said again. Louder.

He stood, feet braced, opposite the desk. In his right hand he held the dispatch case. His left was clenched tightly as he measured the distance to Tarrant. The rage he felt was so dark and disturbing that he easily defined it. He was capable of killing this man.

"You have a decidedly limited repertoire of questions, don't you?"

"Where is Margaret?"

Tarrant ignored his question, nodded instead at the dispatch case in his hand. "Are those the books?"

"Yes," he said curtly.

"Did you solve the code?" The duke looked up at him, smiled again. "But of course you did."

Tarrant's hand stretched out, but Michael only shook his head. "Not until I see my wife."

"Lovers united?" The duke's thin lips curved.

Michael remained silent.

"I regret I can't accede to your request," Tarrant said. "But then, you can't imagine it to have been this easy. The man who just left this room has gone to kill her."

The candlelight illuminated the duke's pale face, rendering it a caricature. One of an evil monk, or a zealot. "And when he's finished, he will come back and kill you."

Margaret heard a noise in the corridor. A man's shout, accompanied by the sound of running footsteps. Finally, muted thunder. A pistol?

She stood behind the door, watching as the handle turned slowly. She was trembling, but she still gripped the bedwarmer tightly between her hands. The door creaked open. She clenched her eyes shut, prayed, and swung as hard as she could.

The weapon was halted in mid-swing.

She opened her eyes, blinked several times, but the vision did not change. The smile was warm, the brown eyes friendly. Robert stood there, both hands firmly gripping the handle of her impromptu weapon.

"I do not believe, Robert," she said, almost reduced to tears, "that I have ever been so happy to see anyone."

"I am happy to oblige, Margaret."

"Michael is in danger, Robert," she said frantically, feeling as if time itself were an enemy. "We must get word to him."

"Not to fear, Margaret," he said, smiling at her in a brotherly fashion. "Reinforcements have arrived."

They both heard the noise. Michael knew the sound well enough: a pistol being shot in close quarters.

Michael hurled the books at the branch of candles. The room was instantly catapulted into darkness. He threw himself at the duke, skidding across the desk, the impact so hard that his shoulder lifted the other man a few inches off the floor. When Tarrant fell, Michael was on top of him.

The rage Michael felt made him someone else. A primitive man lost in grief and betrayal, and an anger so fierce that he wanted to choke the man with his bare hands. He needed to feel the moment his death occurred. Slowly. In agony.

Someone lit a candle, and suddenly the room was filled with people.

"Let him go, Michael," a voice said. He glanced up. Robert.

The glow illuminated the duke's contorted face, but he didn't release his grip on the man's throat. Instead, he tightened his hands, watching in satisfaction as Tarrant struggled for air.

"She's alive, Michael."

"He shot her," he said hoarsely.

"It wasn't Margaret who died, but his servant. We

caught him just as he was entering her room."

He heard the words from far away. But the heels of both hands still pressed hard against the duke's neck.

"But he won't be alive much longer if you don't let him go." Michael felt his arms being grabbed, but he pulled away easily. His strength seemed greater and more deadly than that of any two men.

"She's alive, Michael." Robert's voice again. "I've seen her myself."

Slowly, he eased the pressure of his hands. The duke sputtered and coughed beneath him.

Another candle was lit. He glanced up. People were entering the room. Not liveried servants, but Robert's men.

"Michael?"

He stared at the apparition in the doorway. *Margaret*. The candlelight seemed to render her almost ethereal. Or perhaps it was simply his mind, illogical and wishing she was here.

He stumbled to his feet just as she ran to him. He closed his eyes and held her tight, inhaling great gulps of air as if he'd held his breath from the moment he'd read Tarrant's note.

She was safe. Alive and safe.

Finally he pulled back, still holding her close. Margaret surveyed the clutter of the room, the fallen candles, the scorched carpet, the *Journals* lying on the floor.

"Have you been throwing things again, Montraine?"

"Just so," he said, amused.

"A very touching scene," Tarrant rasped, being

helped from the floor. He massaged his throat and glared at them.

"The man is a traitor, Robert," Michael said, and proceeded to tell his friend about the code.

"You fool," Tarrant said bitterly. "I worked on England's behalf. If Napoleon had been left to molder at Elba, he would have become the focus of a rallying cry. A martyr for the cause of French independence. He was defeated soon enough."

"How many English soldiers died at Waterloo because of your treason?" Michael asked bluntly.

"They were casualties of war," Tarrant spat out.

"As easy as that? Thousands upon thousands die and you can't even see your own complicity? You must have felt some guilt, Tarrant. Otherwise you would not have been so secretive about your participation."

"I knew the world would not understand."

"Why keep the books, if they held such a dangerous secret?" He answered his own question as he stared at the duke. "An act of pride. One that you have had time to regret, no doubt."

"How was I to know that that fool bastard brother of mine would steal them from me?" Tarrant sneered. "I thought he came to borrow money. I should have suspected something when he looked too damn cheerful at my refusal."

"You killed him, didn't you?" Margaret asked softly. Michael could feel her tremble beneath his arm. But she took one step forward and glared at the duke.

"An apt punishment," Tarrant said tersely. "A thief should expect no less."

"And the bookshop? You set fire to that as well?" He only sneered at her.

"There's nothing noble about your nobility, Tarrant," she said angrily. "You're depraved."

"Now is not the time to express your disdain of the peerage, my love," he whispered, pulling her back.

Tarrant suddenly moved, so quickly that the two men standing in front of him were unprepared for his action. Picking up a pistol hidden beneath a sheaf of papers on his desk, he pointed it deliberately at Margaret. "You always were insolent."

Michael shoved her behind him.

"How protective you are, Montraine. Is she worth dying for?"

"Yes," he said simply.

From here Tarrant could not miss. This time there would be no doubt of the assailant nor the victim. But the other man surprised him. He smiled and slowly raised the pistol, placing the end of the barrel against his temple.

Michael turned and pulled Margaret through the doorway. He didn't flinch, nor did he turn back at the sound of the shot. He didn't care about the Duke of Tarrant or his self-imposed fate.

Only three things mattered to Michael Hawthorne, Earl of Montraine. The woman beside him, the child she carried, and their future together.

Epilogue

～⌒♾⌒～

A happy and joyous life depends upon
conjugal harmony.

The Journals of Augustin X

"There is a spot on your shirt," Margaret said,
amused. He stood in the morning room, the
picture of sartorial elegance. Except, of course, for that
coin-sized stain on the front of his white shirt.

He plucked the offending material out with two fingers and stared at it. "Veronica was excessively vig-
orous."

"I suspect it was her father," Margaret said, smiling.
"You mustn't jostle her so soon after her feeding."

"Nonsense," he said in his own defense. "She thoroughly enjoys it."

"As much as when you recite code patterns and
numbers to her?" Her look teased him. "She's much
too young to understand."

Margaret had fixed in her mind what type of father he might be. He would take some interest in the rearing of his child, she'd decided. But she had honestly not thought he would be so doting. He was in the nursery so often that the nurserymaid had complained. The baby, too, seemed enraptured at the sound of his voice. The sight of them, father and daughter, was enough to bring tears to Margaret's eyes.

"She's an exceptionally intelligent child," he said, raising one eyebrow at her.

"She's only three months old."

"Not too young for her superior abilities to be measured," he said proudly.

Margaret stifled her smile.

Sometimes, in deciphering a code, Michael was in the middle of it before the beginning was revealed clearly. He needed to test various patterns before discerning which one made more sense.

It occurred to him that his life had been like that.

He was a man who'd been familiar with a solitary schedule, one he'd devised for his peace of mind. Silence had been a necessity. Now laughter, and crooning, and the sound of a lullaby, filled the air most times, along with soft footfalls upon the stairs and a sweet voice. He found himself stopping to listen for all the various noises of his world, then returning to his tasks with a smile on his face.

The past year had seen many other changes.

His valet had left his employ in a huff a month earlier, declaring that he'd been hired away by another man, a toff, a gentleman with a great care for his wardrobe and his person. One that did not—and here Harrison had sniffed at him—smell so much of infant.

Now his sleeping schedule rotated around not his ciphers but his daughter. He hadn't been boxing for weeks, and he doubted his horses would recognize him lately. His entire life centered on two individuals, Margaret and Veronica. Yet, instead of his world narrowing, it seemed to expand.

His thoughts, heretofore engaged in a routine and predictable pattern, now seemed fixated on the concept of happiness as a goal, in addition to furnishing his wife with smiles.

The enchantment that had settled over his house was not limited solely to his person, either. The nurserymaid hummed constantly, Molly smiled, and even Smytheton did not look quite so fierce lately.

The only thing disconcerting about his world was today.

"It's them," he said, hearing the knock on the door. "Do we have to do this?"

She brushed a piece of lint off his coat. "It's better to get it over with," she said, smiling.

"I don't see why."

"Because families should not be parted by unkind words," she said. "And it's time we healed the breach. There's Veronica, after all."

"Remember that I warned you," he said, walking into the foyer beside her.

Smytheton reached the door, opened it.

The Dowager Countess of Montraine sailed into the house like a barque in a strong wind.

"I received your note, Michael. I am glad to see that you have come to your senses after all this time," she said, removing her bonnet with one hand and gesturing for her daughters to similarly divest themselves of their outer garments. One by one they did so, layering Smytheton's arms so heavily that the poor man looked to be dropping from the weight.

"Where is this new grandchild of mine?"

"Sleeping, I believe," Margaret said.

"She shall awake," the countess declared peremptorily. "It is not every day that she meets her grandmother for the very first time."

The countess turned, raised her voice. "Smytheton!"

Smytheton appeared, arms free once more.

"Send for the nurserymaid. I would see my grandchild. A girl, you say?" She turned to Margaret with a frown.

"Never mind, Smytheton," Michael interrupted. "I will get Veronica." He left them and quickly mounted the stairs. An occurrence that must not happen often, Margaret thought, the sight of the Dowager Countess of Montraine silent, with a particular look of surprise on her face.

Ada sidled up to Margaret as they walked into the morning room. "Jane would have given him a son," she whispered.

Margaret only stared at her.

"They are friends," Elizabeth explained.

"You see, all the attention will be given to a baby. No one will notice that I'm getting married."

"Hush, Charlotte!" Ada and Elizabeth said at once. The two sisters looked at each other in surprise. Margaret wondered if it was the first occasion in which they felt some accord. The blessed silence was not, however, to last.

"I am sorry, Charlotte," Ada said. "We should not have been so cruel. Even Horace said that anger is a brief lunacy."

Charlotte threw up her hands, turned to Elizabeth. "Stop her! She's quoting again."

Elizabeth frowned at her sister. "What do you expect me to do, Charlotte? It could be worse; it could be Wollstonecraft."

"But it's not. It's all those old Latin men!"

Michael entered the morning room with Veronica and placed his daughter in his mother's arms. The countess stood gazing down at the newest member of the Hawthorne family, a look of tenderness on her face.

"It's been a very long time since I held an infant, little one," she said. "But I haven't forgotten how."

The countess looked up, her eyes sparkling with tears. "She looks very much like me, doesn't she?"

Margaret nodded, more in an effort to spare the countess's feelings than in agreement. In truth, she thought Veronica looked like her father. Her eyes were the same shade of sapphire and there were tufts of black hair on her head.

"Just wait until I tell Helen Kittridge about you, Veronica," the countess said. "Her daughter has yet to wed, and I already have a granddaughter."

The rest of the countess's conversation was in a language only Veronica could understand. The three aunts gathered around their new niece, and for once, none spoke over the others. Veronica, accustomed from birth to adulation, grew bored with the cooing after a time and began to fuss. Michael took her from his mother, only to transfer her to Margaret's arms.

"There are some things," he said smiling, "that even I cannot do."

"You cannot mean that you suckle the child?" the countess asked sharply. "That will never do."

Margaret walked calmly from the room. Her

mother-in-law followed her, stood at the base of the staircase staring up after her.

"Say good-bye to your grandmother, Veronica," Margaret said, glancing down at the countess. "It will be the last time you see her."

"You cannot mean that," the countess huffed, frowning up at her.

"I'm afraid she does," Michael said, smiling up at Margaret. "My wife refuses to be cowed by the nobility." His grin warmed her. "*Any* of the nobility."

"I cannot be dictated to in this fashion," the countess said, turning to Michael. He only smiled, leaned against the door frame, and watched his wife.

Margaret began slowly to mount the stairs again.

"Shall I have no say at all?"

Margaret raised one eyebrow at her mother-in-law.

"I welcome your opinions," Margaret said, glancing down. "Not your dictates."

For the next moment, not a word was spoken between the two women. A battle of wills silently yet fervently waged. Finally, a nod was the only concession from the countess.

"Your nose isn't too large," she said surprisingly, studying Margaret. "And your ears do not protrude, for all that you come from peasant stock. Plus, you've given me quite a lovely granddaughter. I shall launch you into society myself. We need a new modiste for you, a decent lady's maid to style your hair. Do you dance?" she asked abruptly.

Michael cleared his throat. His mother glanced at him, frowned, then sighed in surrender.

"Very well, Michael. But with all those economies you insist upon, I can barely afford to outfit myself. Besides, you cannot live as hermits the rest of your life. Both of you have outraged the *ton*."

"Why, because we're happy?" He smiled at his mother and she shook her head at him. But Margaret suspected that the gesture was one less of censure than of capitulation.

Margaret turned and slowly began to descend the steps.

"There is dear Charlotte's wedding, don't forget," the countess said. "You mustn't be miserly with funds on that occasion."

"It will be a subdued affair, I trust? Something elegant and reserved for family only? Something *modest*?" he asked, accentuating the word.

"Ada's wedding will most definitely be small, Michael. Her intended does not like large gatherings," Elizabeth said. "A very surprising alliance, Ada, to marry a duke." She smiled at her sister.

"He's a very learned man," Ada said, her pale cheeks taking on a pink hue.

"And wealthy," the countess said, glancing at Michael. "Very, very wealthy."

Margaret smiled at Michael's silence. The Foreign Office had recently paid him quite generously for his mathematical engine. In fact, they were negotiating a large development fund for him to refine and expand its abilities.

His first act after the mathematical engine was accepted by the government was to enlarge the third floor. Then, he had surprisingly and whimsically commissioned a work of art. Her smile grew as she thought of it.

"He is quite a student of Egypt," Ada said, speaking of her fiancé.

"Not again, Ada," her mother said, waving her hand in the air. "I do not want to hear one more word about those nasty mummies."

"Ada's fiancé says that partaking of ground mummy aids in the digestion," Elizabeth whispered in an aside to Margaret.

She felt vaguely ill but managed a smile. When the nursemaid appeared, Margaret gently surrendered Veronica to her care.

"Smytheton!"

The butler appeared again, seemingly unperturbed by the countess's shriek.

"I want you," Aphra announced. Such a decree had the effect of raising Michael's eyebrows.

Smytheton, however, seemed to understand perfectly. "I regret, my lady," Smytheton said, bowing, "that I am currently employed."

"We shall trade." The countess turned and directed a stern look at her son. "You'll take that ancient Peterson and I'll have your man here. He, at least, can walk upright."

"I'm perfectly satisfied with Smytheton," Michael said. "One might even say that I've grown quite fond of him."

The countess slitted her eyes and looked from Smytheton to Michael. "Have you no wish to serve me, Smytheton?"

A delicate question requiring a very politic response.

Smytheton smiled. "Indeed, my lady. But I have been taught that loyalty is of paramount importance. I would not be demonstrating my loyalty should I change employers at this time. Therefore, my worth would be diminished before I ever began to serve you."

The dowager countess knew full well that she had been declined, but in the most delicate fashion. "Chocolate," she said to Smytheton, who looked mildly discomfited at her response.

"If you are going to nurse that child," she said, turning to Margaret, "you must have chocolate at least three times a day. Have I your word on it, Smytheton?"

The poor man could only nod in reply.

She turned to Michael. "Do change your shirt, dear boy. You look positively unkempt."

The countess proffered her cheek to Margaret. She glanced at Michael helplessly. He only grinned and shrugged. Finally, she placed a quick peck on her mother-in-law's cheek.

With that, Aphra glided from the room, her arm upraised. The girls, not unlike three little ducklings, followed in her wake.

The silence echoed.

Margaret sent a horrified glance in Michael's direction.

"You have a look on your face," he said, amused, "that I know I've worn myself on many occasions."

"Will it always be like that?" Margaret felt as if a gale had whirled her end over end.

"You were the one who insisted upon a reconciliation," Michael reminded her.

He walked to the door of the morning room, locked it, then returned to her side and reached for her. She looped her arms around his neck, lost all thoughts in his kiss.

"What would you have done if you had met me before you were a widow?" he asked a moment later.

"No doubt hurt a man who did not deserve it," she admitted.

"And if we had seen each other before that?"

"Then I would have ruined myself for you. Is that what you want to hear?" she teased. "I would have, you know. And you, Michael? What would you have done if you had met me earlier?"

"Been as I am now," he confessed. "Illogical at times. Decidedly emotional. Incredibly happy."

He pulled back and smiled at her. Slowly and deliberately he withdrew a length of red ribbon from his waistcoat, dangled it in front of her.

"Isn't red the color of ecstasy?"

"Here? In the morning room?"

"Where else?" he said, tilting his head back and studying the ceiling.

The artist had finished the work the day before, and the odor of drying oil paint still lingered in the air. Like the library ceiling, the panorama was of a dawn sky, with tendrils of pink and blue and yellow heralding a new day. But the cherubs embracing in the corner were not diminutive nor plump. Instead, they bore a remarkable resemblance to the Earl of Montraine and his countess.

Smytheton looked toward the morning room, heard the laughter, and shook his head. His stern face, however, was altered by a fleeting, and fond, smile.

Afterword

The history of cryptography dates back 4,000 years. It was fascinating to discover that of all the codes that have been created in that time, only a handful still remain in use. The others have been discarded because they were either too cumbersome to use or they had been deciphered.

The idea for Michael's mathematical engine, the forerunner of the modern computer, came into existence about this time, as did the idea of two sets of disks that would create a nearly unbreakable code. In fact, Thomas Jefferson invented a similar wheel cipher in the eighteenth century.

Black Chambers operated throughout Europe in the eighteenth and nineteenth centuries. Most of them, however, were dissolved by 1860.

There has always been some speculation about whether or not the British aided Napoleon in escaping from Elba. Their purposes in doing so might have been as the Duke of Tarrant articulated.

In March 1815, Talleyrand informed Louis XVIII of Napoleon's escape. His accusations were against the English, who were instrumental, he believed, in allowing Napoleon to leave Elba. Talleyrand thought that the ruse was accomplished for one of two reasons: to justify treating Napoleon more severely when he was recaptured; or, as he told the King, the English might simply have wished to send Napoleon to America in order to limit his influence.

From the bestselling author of *THE DANGEROUS LORD* and *THE PIRATE LORD*, comes a love story of thrilling power and passion . . .

A DANGEROUS LOVE

by

Sabrina Jeffries

A November Avon Romantic Treasure

Lady Rosalind and her sisters are outraged when they learn their father has invited their distant cousin to choose one of them as a bride.

Griff Knighton has no intentions of getting married "only" for his inheritance, so he disguises himself as his man of affairs . . .

Only to discover that an "affair" with Rosalind is a very tempting proposition indeed.

TRE 1000

Avon Romantic Treasures

Unforgettable, enthralling love stories,
sparkling with passion and adventure
from Romance's bestselling authors

HAPPILY EVER AFTER	*by Tanya Anne Crosby* 0-380-78574-9/$5.99 US/$7.99 Can
THE WEDDING BARGAIN	*by Victoria Alexander* 0-380-80629-0/$5.99 US/$7.99 Can
THE DUKE AND I	*by Julia Quinn* 0-380-80082-9/$5.99 US/$7.99 Can
MY TRUE LOVE	*by Karen Ranney* 0-380-80591-X/$5.99 US/$7.99 Can
THE DANGEROUS LORD	*by Sabrina Jeffries* 0-380-80927-3/$5.99 US/$7.99 Can
THE MAIDEN BRIDE	*by Linda Needham* 0-380-79636-8/$5.99 US/$7.99 Can
A TASTE OF SIN	*by Connie Mason* 0-380-80801-3/$5.99 US/$7.99 Can
THE MOST WANTED BACHELOR	*by Susan K. Law* 0-380-80497-2/$5.99 US/$7.99 Can
LION HEART	*by Tanya Anne Crosby* 0-380-78575-7/$5.99 US/$7.99 Can
THE HUSBAND LIST	*by Victoria Alexander* 0-380-80631-2/$5.99 US/$7.99 Can